1

DEDICATION

TO ALL THE GOOD GIRLS WHO PRETEND TO BE BAD

PROLOGUE

"Why are you both sad?" a little girl in pink fluffy frock asks twins whose clothes are dirty and mud covered.

The teenage boys reply her smiling sweetly, "Because we are dirty, no one wants to play with us".

The innocent little girl frowns at his response, holds their hands, and pulls them into the park.

"Here let's play volleyball", she tells beaming widely as she tosses her ball to one of the twins and stands with other.

As the twins smile at her and the elder nods his head to start the game she interrupts.

"Oh! No! We are only three, so you would be alone", she frowns kicking the ground with a sad pout.

"Idea!" she beams as she gestures the boy in her front to throw the ball and she waits till the elder twin knocks it to the younger then she runs to the younger twin, letting him knock the ball to the elder.

Seeing her struggle both brothers stop the game and give her confused and worried look.

She huffs and breathes, her cheeks turned pink due to her struggle and gestures them to keep playing.

"Doll, you will be tired if you play with us like this", the elder tells worried.

"He is right, you can't play with both teams at the same time", younger twin tells glancing at his brother.

3

"No, I can and I will play with both of you", the little girl declares with a huge tired grin on her face making their heart swoon.

But she never knew that she will regret saying these words to them when she grows up into a beautiful woman.

ICE CREAM

AUTHOR'S POV

Marco and Mario were excited. Excited that their mother gave them few Euros, so that they could be able to buy Ice cream which they wanted to eat so badly. They have seen kids eating it with their parents near park usually and whenever they asked, their mother said that it is not good for their health and they can't eat it because if they get sick, they have to eat medicines. Which Marco don't like at all.

Being thirteen years, the twins knew that their financial status is not as good as it used to be once and they never complained their mother by demanding for more.

"Marco, after eating ice cream let's play in the park with others, it's always us, am bored", whines Mario making Marco nod his head just as excited as his brother was.

"Come on, Madre wants us home after an hour, let's hurry up", Mario tells pulling his brother towards the ice cream stall in front of the park.

"Two Ice creams please", Marco requests happily giving the seller two Euros.

The seller looks at him then the cash he placed on the counter judgementally.

"Did you steal this money from somewhere?" the seller asks suspiciously seeing their dirty clothes, which weren't washed for days.

"No, we did not steal sir, our mother gave us this", Mario tells smiling at the seller proudly.

The seller rolls his eyes at them as he asks them again, "Which flavour?"

Twins looks confused and glances at each other before questioning the seller.

"What do you mean by flavour?" the seller huffs annoyed and looks behind the twins as he sees a long line forming, he gets angry on them.

"Here, you both beggars don't even know flavour and came to buy ice creams", the seller scoffs as he gives them dirty looks before shoving a single cup with two scoops of vanilla ice cream.

"But...but sir we asked for two", innocent Mario asks the seller as Marco kept his head down offended because the seller called them beggars.

They never begged in their life for anything. They slept with empty stomach but never complained. Just because they are poor people can't call them beggars, Marco thought while looking at his worn-out shoes from which his toes are peeking.

"That's what you get in two fucking Euros now fuck off you piece of shit", the seller yells at them making the twins flinch.

"It's okay brother, we can share", Marco whispers to his brother pulling him far from the line.

They both were walking in the park to find an empty bench to eat their ice cream peacefully. Marco kicks the stones in his way walking with his head down as he complains to his brother.

"I didn't like how he spoke", he tells making Mario smile at him sadly.

"Don't feel bad Marco, didn't you see how long was the line, he was busy so he got mad", the elder twin calms his brother down.

As he was walking while seeing Marco, he didn't see a girl in his way and ran into her making ice cream fall all over her frock.

"Oh my god!", the girl's eyes widened in horror seeing the ice cream fall on her cream frock.

Twins were as horrified as her, not because their ice cream fell but because the frock seemed costly that they can't even imagine it's price. If the girl asks for compensation, they will not be able to pay it back.

"I'm sorry, I didn't see", Mario tells quickly.

"We are sorry, we can clean it for you", Marco tells panicked.

The girl who is one or two years younger than the twins are glares at them and calls for her elder brother.

"Look, Elijah, what these two idiots did", she complains to her brother.

Elijah who is taller and more built up than twins look deadly mad and shoves Mario back making him hit the ground.

"Mario!" Marco gasps as he tries to lift his brother from the ground.

"We said sorry", Marco screams at Elijah who kicks him in stomach making him cry in pain.

"Do you even know how costly that dress was?" Elijah scoffs as he kicks Mario who tried to cover his younger brother.

"Please we said sorry", Mario cries as he groans in pain.

"How would you even know you piece of shit", Elijah laughs at them spitting at them before taking his sister's hand.

"Come on Anna, let's go from here", Elijah tells dragging a smirking Anna from there who mumbles "Filthy beggars", enough loud for twins to hear and leave from their so that they could play with their friends.

"Marco, get up brother", Mario tells pulling him so that he can stand on his legs.

"Why does every one call us beggars?" Marco cries holding Mario tightly.

"Don't cry Marco, it was my fault though", Mario tells softly wiping his own tears after wiping his brother's.

"Why did you step in between when you know you would get hurt?" Mario scolds his brother.

"Nothing hurts me more than seeing you get hurt", Marco tells looking down making Mario smile.

Mario locks his twin's head in his arm playfully walking towards the empty bench making him laugh.

FRIEND

AUTHOR'S POV

Park is filled with kids' laughter and parent's chatter. Every kid in the park is with his or her parents or with either of them. Old people are holding their hands and walking on the grass looking at each other with love in their eyes, which only grew with time.

Twins sitting on the bench in a corner under the tree protected from the Italy's summer sun kept admiring the families around.

"I wish we had our padre still with us", tells Marco looking down at the ground which is covered in green grass. A little habit of Marco, he never looks into eyes when he is admitting something, which is deep in his heart.

"I know Marco, Madre would be happy, she didn't have to fake she is happy in front of us", tells Mario.

"Why we don't have which others don't value brother", Marco asks his elder twin looking at kids throwing half-eaten ice cream in the Dustbin.

Marco and Mario lick their dry lips as their mouth waters at the sight of untasted sweetness. They both sigh without saying a word and divert their eyes to the kids playing with the football.

"Let's play with them", Mario beams at his brother dragging him to the group of kids to divert his little brother's mind from thinking about everything and feel bad.

"Slow down", Marco chuckles following him.

"Hey! Can we play with you?" Mario asks politely to the group of boys.

They look from a rich family; their shoes are new and clothes smell so good from a distance itself. Their hair is well groomed and they look beautiful in their crisp ironed clothes.

"Look at yourself", one kid laughs at Mario and Marco mockingly.

"I don't think we will be comfortable to play with dirty kids like you", another snicker making Marco and Mario put their heads down in shame.

Marco's eyes were blurred with tears forming in them. He never asked to be born in a middle-class family, though he was happy. They used to get to wear new clothes on every special occasion, on their birthday, Christmas... but after their father's death, everything in their life was ruined. Their mother being not well educated had to work in others home as a maid but after some unknown reasons she was fired and had to work as a waitress in a small restaurant, which paid enough to earn a single meal a day for three of them. However, their mother never stopped them from sending school. Both brothers were smart. They worked day and night studying hard as they know it was only their way out from their poverty. Even though they were bullied and beaten up in school they never skipped a day and their hard work paid off when they saw their mother's proud smile when she saw their report cards with A plus grades on it.

They never had friends, as they were jealous of them and always found a way to make Marco and Mario hurt.

"We just want to play with you all", Marco mumbles softly.

The boys look at them disgustingly and roll their eyes on them.

"Come on guys, let's go from here, these two made this place dirty by their presence", said one of them as they leave that place giving dirty looks at twins making Marco burst in tears.

Mario was good in hiding his feelings where Marco never hid them. Mario thought it was his responsibility to stay strong for his brother and never let weakness take over him, which would only hurt his younger brother.

There were days when Mario saved his lunch money so that he could buy new bag for Marco who was bullied for using old pink bag given by a woman at who's their mother used to work. The woman was generous that she used to donate few old clothes and things, which were treasure for their family. Marco was smart enough to notice that his brother was hungry but still saving money for him and shared his lunch with Mario happily. Sharing became their thing

This time Mario couldn't hold his tears and he let them flow silently rubbing his brother's back.

After crying their eyes out silently both brothers removed any evidence of tears as they wanted to go back to their mother who is waiting for them in their house. At least they have their mother on whose lap they could sleep, who would sing the songs to make them feel good, who would run her soft hands in their hair taking all the unwanted thoughts out from their head.

While going out of the park, which they thought they didn't belong there, they were stopped by a little girl who was wearing pink fluffy frock.

She stopped them holding their both hands, which was united as twins always walked holding each other's hand when they felt down. That made them think they are not alone, at least they have each other's back.

"Why are you both sad?" the girl questions them with confusion written all over her face.

Her skin was pale white. She looked foreigner. Her jet-black hair tied into two tiny pig tails with matching pink rubber bands, her shoes were white sneakers, which looked new, her pink pouty lips and dark brown eyes, were eye catching. If other kids in park looked rich, she looked like a princess to twins. They kept watching her in awe when they hear her giggle then tug their hands they come out of their thoughts and blush immensely.

No one gave them a soft look let along hold their hand and this girl giggled at them, not like mocking laughs of kids they heard. It was innocent as twins were.

"Why do you both look sad?" she asked again this time softly.

"Because we are dirty and no one wants to play with us", tells Marco while snorting at his own fate.

Twin never lied; it was what their mother forbidden it in their home. Though they didn't lie, they didn't tell the bad things their classmates do to them, instead of saying truth, they simply said it was fine and they are tired.

The innocent little girl frowns at his response, holds their hands, and pulls them into the park.

"Here let's play volleyball", she tells beaming widely as she tosses her ball to one of the twins and stands with other. It was the first time someone offered to play with them; they were shocked that why the girl who looks like a doll wants to play with them when their clothes are dirty.

Eventually shaking off their thoughts the twins smile at her and Mario nods his head to start the game she interrupts.

"Oh! No! We are only three, so you would be alone", she frowns kicking the ground with a sad pout looking at Marco.

"Idea!" she beams as she gestures Marco who is standing in front of her and Mario to throw the ball and she waits till the elder twin knocks it to the younger then she runs to the younger twin, letting him knock the ball to the elder.

Seeing her struggle both brothers stop the game and give her confused and worried look.

She huffs and breathes heavily, her cheeks turned pink due to her struggle though she gestures them to keep playing.

"Doll, you will be tired if you play with us like this", the Mario tells worried.

"He is right, doll, you can't play with both teams the same time", younger twin tells glancing between her and his brother.

"No, I can and I will play with both of you", the little girl declares with a huge tired grin on her face making their heart swoon.

No one joined twin to play with them but here she is putting effort to play with both of them, which is new to twins. The way she grinned at them made them smile widely.

Mario started walking away from her making her frown.

"What are you doing?" the little girl asks confused.

Mario only grins at her and stand at a spot, which made them look as if they are standing in the corners of a triangle.

Soon Marco understands what his brother is doing and he grins wide.

"See now you can play with both of us and you won't be needed to run", Mario tells passing the ball to the girl as she catches it stumbling cutely.

"Now pass that ball to me", Marco tells smiling widely, the girl does as she was asked.

"Now catch the ball again", Marco sings making the girl chuckle and catch the ball.

"It's my turn", Mario adds with a smile.

"What are your names?" the girl asks with a smile on her lips as they continue playing.

"My name is Mario and he is Marco my twin", tells Mario happily.

"Why are you playing with us? Don't we look dirty?" Marco asks the girl smiling sadly as he stopped playing with the ball.

The girl frowns and walks towards him and asks him to bend to her height, which he gladly does.

14

"Don't cry Marco", the girl tells wiping his tears from his eyes, which he himself doesn't know were flowing.

"Yes why did you play with us?" Mario asks the same question.

"You both are not dirty". The girl tells frowning.

"Who ever told you that, they are dirty", she adds nodding her head at end as if she is trying to prove a point.

"But…" Mario was cut off when she speaks again.

"Your clothes aren't clean but that doesn't make you dirty", she tells smiling widely at them.

"You speak like our mother, how old are you", Mario asks chuckling cutely at her statement.

"My daddy also tells I speak like his mother", the girl gloats proudly before adding; "I am six and half years".

Before they could exchange any more conversation, someone approached the little girl calling for her.

"Princess, where were you? Your father is searching for you", a woman in her mid thirties tells smiling at her.

Oh, she is a real princess, thought twins seeing a woman who is in her professional caretaker suit, which once their mother used to wear when she worked in homes of rich people.

"I was playing with my new friends Mrs Grayson", the girl tells politely smiling widely.

The woman now watches two teenage boys who look similar as if they are brothers. Their hair is brown locks with their blue eyes they look beautiful but their clothes are dirty but that didn't stop her for being good to the twins.

Twins couldn't believe their ears that she introduced them as her friends but they were so horrified that the woman would scold them for playing with her with their dirty clothes. They began to take a step back looking at ground sadly but Mrs Grayson stops them with her warm words.

"Hello I am Mrs Grayson, what are your names?" the woman asks with motherly voice.

Twins were so shocked to reply, their jaws almost hitting the floor making the girl giggle.

"He is Marco and he is Mario", she tells making them smile at her sweetly.

"It's nice to meet you both, sorry I have to take your friend back with me", the woman tells softly.

Both didn't want to let her go but they know it's time for good-bye; they simply nodded their heads in unison.

The little girl pecks twins cheeks biding her goodbye making their eyes widen in surprise. No one except their mother kissed them. Twins were so happy that they almost forgot to ask the kind girl, her name.

When she was in her car and waving her hand to them smiling widely Marco asks her name.

"Doll, you didn't tell us your name?"

"My name is Oddy", the girl shouts so that they could hear her.

As the car starts to move, she peeks her head out and shouts at them again.

"Marco, Mario, ask your mother to read red shoes and seven dwarfs story book for you".

Twins smile at her widely and replies back "Okay", happily in unison.

Now they couldn't wait to run back to their home and tell their mother about new friend and ask her to read the story she recommended.

Little did they know what painful destiny holds their future.

BROKEN

"I am so happy", Marco exclaims smiling cutely at his twin.

"I know brother, I am happy too", Mario tells ruffling his brother's hair making him giggle.

"It feels like dream, don't you think Mario, we made our first friend! ", tells Marco kicking pebbles on his way to their home.

"It feels like dream", Mario tells looking at sky.

No one ever played with them nor behaved well, Oddy was the first one who played and treated them with respect and love in a friendly way, and she gave warmth, which they only received from their mother.

"I can't wait to tell Madre, let's run", Marco declares running towards their home holding Mario's hand.

Mario giggles and run behind him thinking how they would tell their mother and she will be happy for them. she would happily read them the story Oddy suggested.

As twins were running towards their home, they found a group of people gathered at a place. They frowned and saw each other's face questioning internally. As Mario nodded his head, Marco walked towards the group of people.

"What happened here?" asked Marco as Mario stayed beside him with a visible frown on his face. Something felt off for twins but they couldn't point out what it is.

The people gathered gave twins pitiful looks making them frown more.

"What happened?" asked Mario to an elder woman who was giving them sad look.

"What will happen to these kids?"

"Poor kids they lost their father when they were five and now their mother".

These were the murmurings twins heard from the group making their heart drop in their stomach.

"Mario…" Marco pleads his brother.

He don't know for what he is pleading and why but Mario understood.

Mario held his brother's hand tightly in his own and pushed the people away making way for themselves.

What they saw was they couldn't imagine in their whole life even in their worst dream. Their mother in a pink dress was laying on the road, there was strawberries around which probably fell out from the bag she was carrying and there were two more paper bags but twins don't know what is in them.

Their main attention was on their mother who is bleeding to death. She isn't dead, not yet, that's what the twins believed.

A loud scream erupted from Mario. As Marco stood their silently with his eyes on his mother's blood stained body.

Mario rushed towards Alesia's body and cradled her head in his laps. His loud cries were echoing on the street, where Marco was stood broken and without a moment. Not even a single tear slipped out of Marco's eye.

"Madre... please wake up... Madre", Mario cries shaking her head with his small hands.

"Madre... please... wake up, why are you sleeping on the road like this?" he chokes as blood oozes on his palm from her head.

There is blood, a lot of blood, that people were afraid to take her to hospital and didn't call ambulance because they would be dead just like her if they go against him.

"Ma... Madre, we have... so much to tell you", cries Mario putting his head on Alesia's chest crying his eyes out.

"We... w... We made a friend, she I... Is beautiful... just like you... she told us to ask you to read... red shoes and seven dwarfs s... sto...story", Mario cries stuttering badly.

This was the first time Mario is crying like this, he always hid his tears from Marco, from his mother but not today, the little innocent soul who used to think about other's before himself is broken to the extent that he couldn't be healed. He needed to cry his eyes out, let all the tears he kept hidden in his chest to be able to breathe again and he did. Sadly, there wasn't a single hand that came forward to wipe his tears.

"Mar... Marco.... Brother.... Please ask Madre... to wake up, she... she always listens to y... You", Mario chokes getting up leaving his mother gently back on the road shaking Marco with his blood stained hands placing on Marco's shoulders.

"She left us Mario, don't cry, no one is there for us now, it's just you and me", Marco tells making Mario choke on his tears badly.

"Brother...please..." Mario speaks but Marco cut him off immediately.

"Ca... can anyone help us to bury o... our mother", he asks in a pleading tone blinking his eyes to get rid of any tears forming in his eyes.

No one replied him; in fact, everyone started to back away. Leaving those twins and their mother's dead body on the street, with no intention to help those shattered innocent souls.

Mario stilled, he moved his eyes to every corner possible to search for someone who could help them, people either ignored their cries completely without glancing their way or few gave them pitiful look then shook their head denying humanity to them.

Mario kept crying and sobbing until his eyes turned puffy and red. Where as Marco stood few steps away without blinking a single tear.

Hours passed but no one helped them. They were broken wanted to be embraced by single person but no one had enough humanity to help them, they couldn't leave their mother like that on the streets for hungry dogs, which were howling in the darkness of night.

Evening to midnight passed they didn't get a second of sleep. How could they when they were habituated to sleep in their mother's warmth because lack of comfortable blankets in their home.

A group of dogs started to walk towards them, twin got horrified and stepped back. Nevertheless, when dogs started running towards them they know that those dogs wanted to dig their teeth in their mother's body.

21

Seeing them coming Marco and Mario covered Alesia's body with their own. The hungry howls made their bones shiver in fear along the coldness of night.

Still crying Mario said to his brother.

"Marco run from here, they will hurt you", but Marco wasn't the one who is going to leave his brother and his mother alone in danger. He shook his head vigorously holding tight on his only family.

"I don't want to die now, Marco, I promised you but I didn't fulfil them", Mario cries hugging his mother and wrapping a hand around his brother.

"If you run, you will be able to fulfil them", Mario tried to explain his brother but Marco was stubborn he wasn't the one who would leave his family behind.

As they heard multiple howls, their hearts dropped.

"Mario… I will be happy to die tonight with you but I won't be able to live without you after mom leaving", Marco chokes but didn't cry.

Both kids closed their eyes with a smile on their lips ready to accept their fate but it didn't reach them. Five loud bangs echoed making then flinch and open their eyes in fear. Those five dogs running to them are now laying dead few feet away from them.

When they lift there, eyes confused seeing dogs' dead they saw a woman standing there with two guns in her hands. She is wearing a black pencil skirt with white shirt. Her eyes covered with shades she is wearing.

She helped them, but why?

When no one showed them mercy and denied help then why this woman helped them?

They were glad someone helped them but were confused why?

Twins knew there must be any reason behind it, because they understood people don't help unless they need something from them.

Only one word escaped from their mouths in unison "Why?"

The woman lowered her guns and tucked then behind. Smirking at twins, she answered, "Such brave boys shouldn't die this easily, *not at least now*".

PROMISE

Two little kids tip toe their grandfather's office to scare him but the older man was smart enough to recognize who made entry in his office as he kept his gaze on the computer working.

He decided to let them have fun knowing if he stop them now they would keep doing it in repeat till he had to get tired of it and pretend he was scared and shocked.

The twins grinned at each other in victory as they thought they successfully thought they made it inside the office without their grandfather's attention.

"One, two, three", they both whispered in unison and jumped at the old man with a loud and cute "Bow".

The old man gasped and held his hand on his chest faking to be afraid of the two little monsters of his elder daughter.

"Oh mon dieu, you guys scared me", he complains in his gruff voice trying to sound it softer for the children.

"Yeahhhh, we scared you, we scared you", twins sang jumping up and down in happiness and the older man admired their every feature.

The guards at his office door were always surprised thinking how could a cruel man as Andre Francois who is French mafia boss could be this calm around his grandchildren.

Andre chuckles at them shaking his head and asks them "Where is your mother?"

As he spoke those words, his elder daughter aurora came into the room tiredly and plopped herself on the couch making her dad laugh.

"Is here dad, am alive", she tells making him laugh more.

"I see you guys are troubling my daughter a lot", Andre tells narrowing his eyes on the twins who looks guilty.

"Yes dad, they didn't let me rest whole flight asking when we will reach for every minute and their father was however busy in his mafia stuff", aurora tells whining tiredly.

"By the way where is Dimitri?" Andre asks his daughter.

"Meeting with his new clients, told he would be back by the time party starts", she replies tiredly.

There was a knock on the door, which made Andre get back to his cold self.

"Master, princess Odette isn't waking up, she dismissed and threatened to kill if anyone disturbs her sleep", the maid said with her head down.

Andre sighed heavily, without his wife it was hard for him to raise his two daughters, one of them was easy to handle and the other was a brat.

Aurora was always the girly one who behaved as a high class French lady and wore dresses as a princess of French mafia would, for making allies with Russian mafia Andre married her off to the Russian mafia boss and now she has two sons with him.

She fit well in the Russian family who hide their women as a prised possession. All she had to do was stay at home, pleasure her husband, bear his kids, handle disputes between women of mafia families and attend parties as a trophy beside her husband.

However, Odette was rebel, her first choice of studying feminism made Andre mad for the first time, the other day she got some piercings on her lower lip and ears are studded with multiple piercings. What got him hyper was the tattoo she got engraved on her wrist, waist and neck.

Literally who wouldn't be mad who has a daughter who wears leather jacket, short shorts and skirts with kinky stockings and all when she was born in a mafia family who was supposed to carry the dignity.

"I'm losing my head", Andre groans tiredly tilting his head back.

"Do you want me to take care of her?" aurora offers looking at her old father in sympathy.

"Please, also take her for shopping, buy her some clothes in which she looks presentable for her engagement, you know how Italian men wants their women to be", he tells sighing to which aurora nods her head pressing her lips together.

"Don't worry dad I will take care of it", she assures him kissing his cheek softly then leaves the room with her twins following her behind.

"Aunt Oddy wake up", a little boy jumped on Odette making her groan.

"Please wake up we are bored", another kid wined as he made himself comfortable on her legs.

"What the hell, go to your mama", she groans pushing them away and covering her eyes with her arm on them.

"Time to wake up, it's your engagement tonight and we have so many things to do", Odette's elder sister, aurora spoke in chirpy voice as she pulled the blinds away and let sunshine peek into Oddy's room making her groan.

"I don't want to do anything today, so please get the hell out of my room with your twins", Oddy groans covering her face with the pillow.

"Paul, Peter, go and play in the garden, I will tell someone to send you muffins in few minutes", aurora tells smiling at her twins to which they clap their hands excitedly then ran away from their without a word.

"Oddy, you need to get up, we have so many errands to run before your engagement party starts", Arora tells pulling the blanket off her sister making her kick her legs in air trying to attack aurora.

"Are you mad?" Arora gasp madly.

"Yes I am mad, because I don't know why am getting forced to get engaged to an Italian mafia boss when am just seventeen!" Odette growls angrily throwing the pillow away and getting up from bed.

"I don't even know his name nor I have seen him", she screams at her elder sister.

Odette was mad because every time she tried to adjust into her family environment, they enlarged their expectations, which she had to fulfil, but one day she just snapped turning off her ok dad card and became a bratty bitch. However, inside she is still the one who cares for every worker in her mansion, every animal who gets hurt, even the plants in her garden, which she grew with so much love and care.

Tears started slipping from Odette's eyes and she hugs her sister tightly.

"I'm sorry, rora, I didn't mean to speak to you like that", she apologies quickly sobbing on her sister's shoulder.

Aurora bites her cheek to stop crying and tries to be strong for her sister but deep down she knows what her little sister is going through. But they have no other option instead of listening to their father.

"I know...Oddy", aurora tells sniffing embracing her sister tightly in her protective hold.

"Oddy... trust me... if you fight this it will hurt a lot, just accept this baby, I know he will love you and treat you as a queen", she assures her sister with her own experience.

"You know I can't do this", Oddy cries shaking her head.

"Shhh stop crying, last time when I met you, you made your four bodyguards cry which was more like you", aurora tells chuckling sadly.

"They deserved it, they weren't letting me go inside to meet you", she complains wiping her tears as she snorts.

"I'm afraid..." Odette tells looking at her sister whose face is tear stained.

"Why? Because you don't know him?" Aurora sighs sadly.

"Trust me Oddy, I didn't knew Dimitri before I got engaged to him, but when we did, he became close and took care of me and loved me", aurora tells making Oddy shake her head.

"Dimitri was a kind man that doesn't mean this Italian guy would be the same, consider you got lucky", Oddy tells her sister rolling her eyes.

"He would be happy to hear this". Aurora tells making her chuckle.

"I'm not afraid because of it", Oddy tells sadly biting her lower lip tugging the ring of her lip, which is at the corner of the lower lip to the right side.

"You know how Russian and Italian mafia hates each other's guts, am afraid they will not let us meet anymore", Odette tells sadly.

"Don't worry, I will talk to Dimitri about this", aurora assures her sister sadly knowing well that Dimitri would never let her close to Italian mafia not even when his sister in law is married to the mafia boss.

He is here just because she is his sister in law and Andre requested his presence, as he is his elder son in law. Nevertheless, when she gets married she is nothing more than wife of his enemy.

"Now let's go and have some girls time", aurora tells pulling her sister up with her and push her into her washroom making Oddy chuckle.

Odette strip her nightdress and stands under the shower letting warm water fall on her tired body. Last night she wasn't able to sleep. Who would when their dad tells she has to marry an Italian mafia boss who is just a stranger to her.

She fists her hand angrily pulling her pain to her rage. She clenches her teeth and seethe.

"All these happened because of you, I will never forgive you, you aren't taking a wife but your own destruction home", she growls fisting her hair madly. "I promise".

BADASS

"What do you think about this?" Odette asks her sister showing her a pair of stockings.

Aurora grins at her then winks "if you want to surprise your fiancé... go for it", she tells playfully making Odette roll her eyes on her, scoffing.

"You know I never wear anything to please men", Odette tells air quoting most obvious thing.

"Oh come on, now don't become the feminist bitch", aurora whines shoving a red gown in Odette's hand.

Odette glares at her then the dress for a few minutes but aurora held a still face not backing up, Odette sighs heavily then points at other dresses.

"Red?".

"Seriously?".

"come on choose other", Odette tells frowning.

"Men like women better in red, specifically mafia men", aurora tells folding her hands on her chest.

"Ha! I will make sure the man who is getting engaged to me sees all red-*danger*", Odette tells scoffing and getting inside the trial room to try on the dress.

She removes her jacket and top along her shorts, keeping the stockings on she pull the red dress up chosen by her sister.

When she tries to pull the zip on, she wasn't able to reach it. She groans annoyed with the dress, she always though wearing clothes like this is a struggle though she used to wear frocks when she was a kid but that was back when she was a kid now she feels comfortable in denim shorts or skirts, when in cold days she wears jeans and army pants with shirts, t-shirts or crop top layering it with a jacket or hoodie.

"Rora.... I swear I already hate this dress", Odette shouts so that her sister could hear her.

"Now fucking get inside and help me pull the zip up", Odette orders sighing as she places her hands on the mirror and lower her head tiredly.

"Rora!" she shouts again.

"Get in and help me", she snarls angrily.

First of all she didn't wanted to come for shopping and now her sister pulled her out of home forcefully promising a movie night out as a normal sisters not mafia princess or queen. Then she shoved a red dress and now she isn't answering her.

"Rora, get your ass in now!" Odette yells again.

The door of the changing room opens as Odette sighs thinking its aurora.

"Hurry up, so that I can show you this dress and get out of it as soon as possible", Odette tells looking down not raising her eyes from the floor.

The cold fingers touches her skin trailing the opening of the dress, which is below her waist, those fingers grab the zipper of the dress and pull them up sensually making Odette release a relieved sigh.

Her eyes rise up looking herself in the mirror then behind her. She gasps turning her back to the mirror with wide eyes seeing the person in front of her standing proudly without any shame checking her out.

"Who the hell are you and what you are doing here?" she shouts at the person angrily making him smirk.

"You were in need of help and no one was out, how can I leave such a pretty lady by herself struggling with the zip", he tells in his rough voice making goose bumps rise on Odette's skin.

Seeing her react to his voice he smirk internally trailing his finger on her bare arm then looks into her dark brown eyes.

His blue eyes piercing her soul as his eyes rake her body poking his tongue in his cheek then he curses under his breathe looking at the stockings she is wearing.

"Fuck! This is too killer", he tells and Odette rolls her eyes.

"Oh you didn't see the heels down there, they are definitely a better killer", she mocks scoffing at him with a glare.

The stranger just kept his amused face and looked at the clothes she hung; he nodded his head understandingly then said, "Badass much".

Odette shook her head then said "A little too much that you should want to leave this place soon".

He chuckled amused with her encounter. Shoving his hands in his jeans pockets, he looks at her admiring her features. The way she is all mad with her furrowed eyebrows and an angry pout, her nose is slightly red and puffed cheeks wanting him to kiss her breathlessly.

"If you have taken enough entertainment for today, I request you to leave me fucking alone", Odette rasps glaring at the man.

His hand came in contact with her ass as he pulled her front with his other hand smacked her ass making her release a breathy 'owe' he chuckled darkly and looking into her eyes straight then said "I don't like when women curse".

This made Odette flare in anger as she raised her eyebrow amused then smiled seductively biting her lower lip clutching her lip piercing between her teeth.

His eyes fell on her lips admiring them and controlling his sinful desires of what he wanted to do to them, when he was so immersed Odette twisted him as now his back is presses on the mirror and she is pushing her whole body on him making him curse under his breathe.

"Fuck, feisty little thing you are", he growls in excitement.

This made Odette smirk and wrapped her hand around his neck. No matter how long heels she is wearing she is just near his shoulder without her heels she will be only up to his chest but this little Odette can bring any man to his knees with her beauty.

"Do you think women shouldn't curse?" she asks seductively.

He nods his head biting his lip "Yes, not unless am fucking her senses out of her head", he tells in his raspy voice.

"Uh- hmm", Odette hums against his skin bringing her face close to his.

"Do you think women shouldn't smoke?" she asks again to which he breathes out "No".

"What do you think about day drinking?" she asks coming close to his face.

"No baby", he rasps closing the distance between them but Odette pushes him against the mirror making him groan impatiently.

"Do you think am beautiful?" she asks after chuckling.

"Yes", he breathes out expecting a kiss from her but he didn't expect what was coming his way.

Odette raised her knee and hit him in his groin making him yelp in pain as his hands quickly went to hold his most prised possession. He breathes heavily in anger for being played like this by a girl.

"You fucking bitch", he growls angrily glaring at Odette.

"Good luck with that, hope it functions as it used to before", Odette mocks smirking at him and leaves the changing room with the red dress on her swaying her hips gracefully.

The man glared at her head, if looks could kill then she would be dead meat by now. When Odette thought she is done with him and wouldn't see him again in her life she was so wrong.

The blue-eyed man's phone rang brining him out of his thoughts deciding to punish and teach a lesson to her.

"Hello brother", he tells answering the phone.

"No, am on my way, how can I miss my little brother's engagement", he chuckles teasingly.

After a little chat, he hangs up the call walking towards his car.

"Who ever you are miss badass too much bitch... no one could save you from me... no one", he rasps angrily punching the steering of his car in fuming rage.

MONSTER

"Tell me... water or fire?", asked Marco sitting in his comfortable chair swirling from left to right with a wicked smirk on his face.

"Boss am so sorry boss, please forgive me... I have a family", James choked out coughing blood.

It was a time when James used to see people getting tortured but now he is in their place, miserable and badly beaten to death and afraid of most cunning game his boss plays.

Marco releases a dark chuckle sending shivers to James spine. His eyes are bulged due to the cuts Marco mercilessly drew with a knife; his nails were pulled out along with one ear chopped. James face is all stained with his blood and salty tears making him wince and scream in pain but Marco wasn't the one who would forgive people who crossed him. James body was stabbed with small knife in several places and two screwdrivers drives in his two feet to the ground as no animal would be treated as human is far away.

"You should have thought about the consequences when you double crossed me". Marco tells tsking.

"Please sir forgive me, I will never go to cops again, I will leave this place and never show you my face please forgive me", James cries harder making Marco chuckle.

After coming down from his laughter fit seeing James all bloody and helpless, satisfied an inner demon of Marco. He likes to see people covered in blood and pain begging in front of him.

That's what he became after these many years—a *monster*.

"Choose….fire or water, if I choose you know how painful will be your death", Marco growls impatiently.

"W… Water", James mumbles with tears streaming down as he looks down in defeat. No one can escape this monster now when he went against him and informed about the illegal deal of weapons he is having to the cops. Somehow, he found out, obviously with the power Marco holds.

He closed his eyes expecting a bullet to hit him in the head and imagining his wife and daughter's face in his last minute of life.

However, to his horror Marco chuckled darkly making him snap his eyes open in fear. There wasn't hope because he knows how his boss was.

"You thought your death will be this easy?" Marco growls landing a punch on his face breaking his jaw bone as James screams in pain.

"Chop this bastards every part, piece by piece and throw him in Mediterranean Sea", Marco orders his guards who were looking down the whole time in fear that their boss's anger would burn them if they did anything out of line.

"Yes boss", his right hand who was enjoying the view of torturing James smirked and answered behalf of everyone in the room.

It was not disgusting to them or like they were afraid they were just silent because they fear their boss so much.

Marco nodded his head without a next word he walked out of the dungeon to his mansion which is few meters away from his dungeon where he torcher his enemies.

As soon as he reached his mansion, he went straight into his room, which is painted in all black and grey furniture with black bed sheets on his king sized bed. He went straight into the washroom and stripped down throwing his blood covered clothes in a corner and turned the shower on.

His whole chest is covered in tattoos along with his hands till his wrist and his fingers, making him look intimidating and dangerous. His body well built and slightly tanned which is adding a good contrast to his tattoos making him look too sinister to desire.

As warm water washed off the blood he applied body wash and got rid of anything else covered his Greek god like body along with his brown silky hair. After a quick shower, he dried himself and put on a white shirt with black dress pants with matching coat leaving few shirt buttons open giving a teasing glance of his tattoos.

As he was almost ready, wearing his Rolex limited addition watch and Gucci perfume as he was wearing his shoes he heard a knock on his door.

He knows who is behind the door, only two people could dare to disturb him when he was in his bedroom resting or in his office working. As the other person was out taking care of the arrangements of something important in Paris.

"Come in, ma", Marco said looking one last time himself in the mirror after wearing the belt on his trouser.

A women in her early fifties walk inside wearing blue knee length dress with cream heals and cream clutch gracefully.

She smiles genuinely seeing Marco all dressed up as she requested. "You look handsome as always", she tells smiling softly at him.

"Thanks ma, you don't look bad yourself", Marco tells winking at elder woman making her chuckle.

The atmosphere of the room fell silent as no one spoke a word. The woman sighs heavily in relief when she reads the text she received.

"Everything is arranged", she tells smirking at Marco in victory.

"Good, I knew Mario would finish the task", Marco adds proudly.

"He did…," she tells smiling proudly.

"You know saving you boys on that day was the best thing I did in my life… I may never take your mother's place but you both are like my own children", she tells smiling sadly.

Marco hugs her comforting and speaks "You know whatever we are today… it's because of you ma", Marco tells breaking the hug.

"Don't give me all the credits I just supported you guys and everything you both are now… it's because of your own hard work", she tells politely.

Marco nods his head with a genuine smile on his lips which very few people gets to see.

"Today is the day… where we will get close to our revenge", she tells sighing with wicked expression on her face.

"Yes ma… I swear to God, I will never forgive those people who killed my parents", Marco tells with hatred as his fists clenched and eyes turned red due to anger.

"Rumours tell she is really beautiful", she tells narrowing her eyes at Marco testing him.

"I don't mind how beautiful she is ma... I will make sure she sees hell when she steps her foot in our home", Marco adds with hatred.

A satisfied smile planted on her lips hearing his answer. She made sure the Italian mafia boss never gets attached to any women for her beauty so she brought every miss universe to miss world to Marco and Mario's bed. She also made sure the Italian mafia doesn't fall because disputes between brothers for any women so she made sure they have a habit of sharing women as if they are some toys. Both brothers corrupted many women together but now she was worried because it's the first time she is getting a single brother married to the French mafia boss daughter and her being beautiful, as an angel dropped from heaven rumours didn't help her.

She sighed in relief internally understanding the only thing Marco and Mario thinks about is destroying their enemy by inflicting pain to his lovely daughter.

Least did she know she is bringing their world, their love, their life to them unknowingly.

DESTINY

The hall of Odette's mansion was decorated with white lilies, curtains were cream colour and the dance floor was shining as a new marble, which would allow seeing ones reflection in it. The waiters running from here to there with a tray in their hand. This had expensive champagne glasses and cocktails what not.

The guests are already arrived and waiting to see Odette who was kept hidden for her whole life. It would be a lie if one tells that they aren't excited to see her and her future husband who is none other that most dangerous Italian mafia boss who have made alley with French mafia for their upper hand in country.

Whereas Marco was calling his brother sitting in his limo along with his right hand and his ma. He kept calling his elder twin to which he didn't lift any of his calls.

"Should we track his number?", asked Bianca Ferrari.

"I don't think it's needed ma, he said he will take care of the trouble but am just worried he didn't updated me", Marco tells frowning.

No matter how cruel and merciless both brothers are but they care for each other immensely and their loved ones which happened to be Bianca alone.

They would never even think twice before shoving all bullets in their right hand man, Draco Lombardi.

As soon as Marco expressed his worry, his phone rang immediately. He answered the call without a second late and spoke.

"Where the hell are you bro, you are supposed to be with me now", Marco said.

"I'm caught up with these fuckers, it might take more time, I guess I will be late to your engagement", Mario tells tiredly.

Marco sighs heavily, he knows he sent his brother for an important meeting and if it is taking time, Mario would probably kill them if they piss him off then return. It doesn't matter; Mario is good in handing such men so Marco didn't ask him to come back soon.

"Okay, take care", Marco, said to which Mario said "Okay", then hung up the call.

~~~

"Princess, put this on", said an older maid to Odette who just rolled her eyes.

"I don't want that thing on my thigh, get lost from here before I decide to kill you", Odette growled in anger making the old lady flinch.

"Odette!", a manly angry voice echoed from behind her making her flinch.

Her father never shouts at her but this is one of the times he cannot bear these tantrums. There are guests in their mansion who are waiting to see youngest French mafia princess and witness her engagement but here she is behaving as a kid.

"Is this a way to talk to the elders who are helping you? "Odette's father scold her angrily.

She glares him back and rolls her eyes, "isn't it amusing coming from you, who kill people", she scoffs making Andre clench his jaw in anger.

"Dad... I will take care of this, you go and watch guests, Italians might be on their way", Aurora tells sighing, as she look cold glare of Odette and her father's angry face, which looks like he will burst in any second as a volcano.

"Fill this Brat's head with some senses Aurora, tell her to behave well and keep her mouth shut", Andre tells angrily as he turns his feet around and leave the room shutting the door loudly.

Aurora sighs heavily looking at her sister.

"Oddy... please, don't create any scene... please, your engagement with him will bound two countries, it's good for everyone", Aurora explains to her sister who keeps her eyes on the mirror looking at herself.

"Why?" it was the only word escaped from Odette's mouth in a broken voice.

"Why? Rora? Why it is we? To sacrifice ourselves for the other people's well beings?" she asks looking at Aurora with tears in her eyes.

The maid nods her head as Aurora gestured her to leave, she hands the thigh chain to Aurora before leaving the room, giving privacy for two sisters.

"We are born in mafia family, it wasn't our choice oddy... it wasn't yours nor mine", aurora tells in her softest voice.

"But we are destined... the power our men hold is dangerous, we need to keep them sane, keep them on the right path, take care of the women of the people who work under them", she tells as she knee in front of her sister.

"We are not weak oddy... we are powerful". "We watch our men getting injured and fight death everyday". "Sometimes we might think that this work they are doing is not fair but do you think if *there isn't a lion in a forest, who would save animals from hyenas?*", she asks as she ties the thigh piece on her sister, securing it properly.

She let's the dress fall, getting up on her feet she cups her sister's cheek.

"Marrying will not stop your freedom oddy; I hope he will be the man who respects your wishes and choices... *I do believe he will be a better man... at least for you*, you just have to stay strong and give a chance trusting your fate", she tells pressing a kiss on Odette's forehead and a lone tear escapes Odette's eyes.

Aurora gently wipes the tears and smile at her motherly.

"Mom would have been proud looking at how strong you are". She tells smiling sadly.

"I'm Afraid", Odette tells sobbing in her sister's arms making her cry too.

"I was too…" Aurora tells sighing as she bites her cheek to control her cries.

"You are just seventeen, I know dad will give you time till you turn eighteen, I hope you get time to meet him and understand each other before marriage", Aurora tells in her broken voice.

"What if he doesn't agree? "Odette asks biting her lip referring to her future husband as she wipes her own tears sniffing.

"I will ask Dimitri to blast his ass with a bomb", Aurora tells determined making her little sister chuckle.

"Come on, let's get you ready, everyone are waiting to see this little princess", Aurora tells fixing Odette's makeup and hair one last time.

When she was about to get out from the room along Odette a maid knocks the door making sisters frown.

"What?" Aurora asks looking at the maid who looks worried and afraid.

"Princess Aurora, master asked princess Odette's presence in his office, the Italian mafia boss is here", she tells making Odette hold her sister's hand tightly.

"Everything will be fine oddy". Aurora tells assuring her sister.

"I will be outside if you need me just call", she tells pressing a kiss on Odette's forehead.

She nods her head weakly as she drags her feet along her sister towards her destiny, which will ruin her, as she never imagined in her darkest nightmares.

ENGAGED

Marco was sitting on the chair in Andre's office as Bianca and his right hand is sitting on the couch.

The couch was placed right in front of the door facing it with a centre table. A bottle of most expensive champagne was placed in an ice bucket on the centre table with few glasses.

Bianca was looking at the interior of the office judgmentally. It wasn't her taste even so she wouldn't praise it because her hate for French mafia is limitless.

"My daughter is getting ready, she will be here in few minutes", Andre tells after sending a maid to bring his daughter to his office.

"It's okay, she might be nervous and shy, girls tend to be so in front of my Marco", Bianca tells smiling but that wasn't a friendly one.

Marco just smirked at Andre's speechless expression secretly. Of course Andre knows that men in mafia have affairs and one night stands but when they gets married it's written with blood that their loyalty lies with their own wife.

Just like woman's loyalty lies with her husband. However, telling about other women in front of Andre... he didn't like it.

Without telling anything in counter back, he kept his mouth shut. It is safe for them to not talk anything against Italian mafia when French mafia is without an heir – male child. Intending to protect it, he decided to marry off one of his daughter to Russia mafia and other to Italian. This would be enough examples showing that how much desperate Andre is to keep his empire safe.

There was a knock on the door as Andre gave them a smile. "Come in", he announced sitting calmly but his inner peace is struck in hurricane imagining the things his daughter would do or say.

To say least he was terrified to his bones but it takes years of practice to keep a chill face in the moment of crisis in mafia and he mastered the art.

"Meet my daughter... Odette Francois", he announce proudly as Odette enters the room.

Her eyes were not on the floor nor her walk was nervous, she carried herself gracefully. She entered swaying her hips in her red dress with a thigh length slit revealing her milky skin with a thigh chain made up of diamonds, which was customised beautifully.

Her toes were painted black as her finger nails, adding contrast to her look. Besides Odette always likes to paint her nails black and it looks good on her fair pale skin.

Her tattoos were revealing, as she didn't listen to her father. Didn't hide them under the concealer. Eyes with dramatic wing eyeliner with a red lipstick she is looking as a seductress in a good way. If Bianca heard about Odette being really beautiful then the word and praises didn't do any justice to her beauty. Her long black hair was tied in a tight ponytail giving her a strong look.

She in simple words looked like a goddess. Draco's mouth hung open looking at Odette's beauty but one glare from Bianca made him snap his eyes down in his limits.

Odette didn't broke eye contact with Bianca since the second she stepped in the room. Her aura spoke power to Bianca, which somehow looked challenging to her. She was the first women who didn't felt intimidated in presence of Bianca, which made her clench her jaw.

This took Odette's attention and she smirked at the woman.

"Hello, nice to meet you", Odette spoke in her angelic voice. This made Marco turn his head and look at the ethereal beauty standing behind him.

He swirled the chair and laid his eyes on Odette looking at her as if he is admiring her every inch of skin with his fingers.

The intense gaze on herself made Odette turn her head towards Marco and the second she made eye contact with him her breathe hitched.

She gulped but composed herself immediately. How could this be possible, she saw almost same man as Marco in mall today? His brown locks are just as the stranger's whom she rewarded for helping her and those captivating blue eyes... held something so deep and intense making her stare into them without blinking.

As if she is trying to unfold the story behind every single thing those eyes were laid on.

"Marco de Luca", Marco tells smirking at her as he gets up from the chair and walks towards Odette. His height is also same as the stranger she met at the mall.

Odette gulped as he held her palm in his huge hand and gave a kiss on back of her hand making goose bumps rise on her skin.

His smirk grew looking at it but soon he turned it into a smile and spoke.

"You are beautiful", his compliment made odette blush.

"Thank you, you aren't bad yourself", Odette spoke softly as she looked at her father to which he nodded his head with a smile encouraging her to carry on her behaviour.

"I am Bianca Ferrari", Bianca stated getting up from the couch.

"This is Draco Lombardi, Marco's right hand man", she tells gesturing to Draco who is standing on his feet as a solider with his chest puffed out.

Odette smiled at the woman then the man, nodded her head acknowledging them, and spoke. "It's nice to meet you all", she said softly.

"You are a pretty woman, I could be at peace knowing your children will be as pretty as you", Bianca said smiling viciously.

This made Odette snap. She clenched her fists behind her back still with a innocent smile on her lips she spoke, "Born in mafia family I just wish my children to be strong, beauty however lies in ones heart". Odette's comments made Bianca chuckle awkwardly.

She wanted to make Odette feel awkward but what she intended for *her*, she tasted it.

"Beautiful thoughts as a beautiful face".

Marco commented smirking.

He already liked her; she was different from other girls he has met. Being born in royalty, she had tattoos especially with the curses and her lip piercing is drinking him crazy already. Her strong and powerful aura was speaking heights which he wanted to discover.

"I think we should come straight to the point", Bianca tells cutting Marco's hungry gaze from Odette.

This girl stepped in her life just few minutes ago and she became a threat to her power, which Bianca couldn't digest.

"Sure", Andre tells smiling as he gestures towards the file placed on his table.

Bianca takes the file and read it with concentration since she doesn't want to miss any point.

When she felt everything is right she smiled at Andre then Marco and handed Marco the file.

Marco signs the file without even glancing at it making Bianca smirk. That's how much power she has on Marco and Mario. She thought she shouldn't be afraid of mere teenager as she scoffed internally.

"Here", Andre hands file to Odette. She reads the file with concentration as she bites her lower lip focusing on the context and treaty between French and Italian mafia.

51

She frowns at some points, which didn't go un noticed by Marco. Even though he admired how she looked hot as she read the file without even trusting her own father made him hard.

He likes women, but specially women with brains and Odette is definitely a beauty with brain.

A smirk plastered on his face.

"Is there anything wrong... princess?" he asks in his deep voice making Odette shiver.

"A child will bind the treaty?" she asks frowning.

Marco nods his head and speaks. "Yes... a de Luca and Francois's child will bound this treaty, without this, contract will end", he tells smirking.

Odette gulps as she looks at her father; he glares at her secretly to which she almost rolls her eyes. Clenching her teeth, she picks the pen and signs the papers.

Least did she know with a single sign, *she sold her soul to the devil.*

Marco smirks in victory as Bianca smiles at him.

"Give me the rings", Bianca tells as Draco hands her two velvet boxes, which are red in colour.

She takes out a beautiful huge rock size diamond ring, which is not something Odette haven't seen before. Then hand it to Marco who slides it on Odette's ring finger, kiss her hand once again making her suck huge amount of air.

Bianca then hands another ring to Odette, which she slides it on Marco's ring finger.

"Congratulations", she tells Andre smiling widely.

"Congratulations to you too Mrs Ferrari", Andre tells smiling widely.

Soon they congratulate the couple, popped the champagne, and served the drinks celebrating the engagement of two mafias, which once were enemies and now a family.

DESTINY

After singing, the papers and celebrating their engagement with a glass of champagne both Marco and Odette were brought in the main hall where guests are waiting for their arrival.

The lights were dimmed and a spot light landed on both Marco and Odette now connected their arms gracefully.

Andre and Bianca stood on the stairs little low from Marco and Odette and announced to the crowd.

"This is my son, Marco de Luca", said Bianca proudly.

"The Italian mafia boss", she announced with her head held high.

"This is my daughter, Odette Francois, princess of French mafia", Andre announced proudly.

There were many gasps and awes in the hall as women looked at Odette with jealousy for having such amazing body and beautiful features which are a die for and of course, Marco wasn't the ignored man, women would fall on their knees right then and there for him.

Men were looking at Odette with desire and lust, which didn't went un noticed by Marco.

He gently placed his large hand on Odette's ass bringing her closer to him making her release a shivering gasp.

"But now she is *my queen*", he announced smashing his lips on Odette's making her eyes widen.

Andre was happy that Marco addressed her as his queen and according to the engagement, treaty it was fine Marco could do anything with his daughter even though she is just seventeen. These things never mattered in the mafia families.

Bianca clenched her fists in anger but kept her face unfazed with the little heated moment happening there which made guests rooted with applause along with gasps and awe at the sweet couple.

Least did they know they could be anything but sweet. Slowly gazed his tongue on Odette's lower lip asking her for entrance but without experience she didn't know what to do, she was just frozen not responding to Marco's kiss which made him growl internally in annoyance.

He bit Odette's lower lip as he squeezed her pulp ass making her gasp as she opened her mouth he took advantage of it and thrust his tongue in her mouth devouring her sweet taste.

She tasted divine like no one else did and Marco knows if he did not stop here it will not stop until he take her virginity right away.

He broke the kiss leaving Odette all breathing heavily with a flushed face. As much as Marco know about Odette, she is a brat who likes to rebel. That's what those tattoos and her lip piercing speaking. Not to mention how badly he wanted to tug on the lip ring but he knows it would overwhelm her and he didn't want to put that show in front of hungry eyes of men who wanted to be in his position.

A hot cute kiss was enough to announce that she was his and other could poke their eyes out if they don't want to accept it.

Marco thought that Odette didn't kiss him back intentionally which made him angry but he thought he would deal with it later when he is alone with her.

He smiled softly at Odette just to show people and brushed her stray hair behind her ear making her blush. Too real for people to understand that it's fake.

"I want to announce that from today we formed a greater alliance with Italian mafia as we did with Russian mafia seven years ago", Andre announces making the crowd cheer and clap.

"I request you to enjoy tonight's party in celebration of my daughter's engagement with the strongest and powerful man, Marco de Luca and the announcement of our blood bond treaty". Andre tells raising the toast.

Everyone follows him, raise a toast for the newly engaged couple, and take a sip of the drink served.

"Let's welcome our newly engaged couple on the dance floor to begin tonight's party", Andre tells clapping his hands which everyone follows cheering.

The dim lights and a sensual music along with the stop light on Marco and Odette, they both looked like beauty and the beast. Dancing on the music with Odette close to him. This felt surreal to both Odette and Marco. There is something for them, which is weaving two souls into one, might be the music, the ambience or each other's presence but soon Odette found herself enjoying dance with Marco.

Her hands snaked around his neck as he held her hips swaying them, with their legs being tangled in a graceful way before getting detangled. Soon everyone joined the dance floor with their dates.

The whole dance Marco was smiling at her, which was rare, he never smiled at women except Bianca and she can clearly see that the little red riding hood who also has a smart mouth caged the big bad wolf.

Before it gets out of her hand she has to do something, her head has many ideas of what she could do, and the best among her evil plans was to bring Mario in between them.

"Hello, Mario, where are you my son, your brother is engaged and you are missing the party, hurry up". She said in her soft tone which she use for twins.

"I'm few minutes away ma, I will be there soon", Mario said before hanging up the call.

A smirk plastered on Bianca's lips as she eyed Odette and Marco who are now dancing on *sway with me* song.

Odette kept her eyes locked with Marco's blue eyes, his beautiful smile that she liked, as she never thought she could.

His eyes were only on her, making her feel butterflies in her stomach.

"Why didn't you kiss me back?" Marco whisper asked her close to her lips lifting her up.

He twirled her gently as her back is pressed against Marco's hard length formed in his pants because of her.

Odette gulped thickly understanding what it is as she blushed turning as red as beetroot.

"I... I didn't know how to kiss... that was... my first kiss", Odette stuttered badly making Marco smirk.

"Nice tattoo you got here", he murdered in her ear making goose bumps on her skin. "You liked it?" she asks breathlessly.

"Yes, sois belle a ta facon", he reads the quote on her neck making her smile.

"Be beautiful in your own way", she translates it smiling.

"I know...", he tells her making her smile widely as she turns around wrapping her hands and lock them behind his neck.

"Uh – hum", she hums.

"What else do you know?" she asks raising her eyebrow and smirk at him.

He grins at her making her heart skip a beat.

He smacks her ass making her gasp in surprise. Odette glares at him angrily making him smirk. She smacks his chest and he raise his eye brows amused.

"Though French sounds sexy coming from your mouth... I won't give you right to spank me", she tells seriously narrowing her eyes on him.

"Intenso?" she asks warningly.

This made Marco's cock twitch in his pants as he smirked looked at her lips, which he wanted to devour them right away. First time in his life, he found himself nodding to a woman after so many years.

"Good boy", Odette coos stopping the dance and pinches his cheeks and he groan internally.

She sways her hips and leaves the main hall to her room to use washroom. Their cute interaction brought a smile on Aurora's face. For a reason she trusted Odette with Marco that he would treat her sister right, she just hoped she wouldn't be proved wrong for trusting him. When Marco tried to follow her, Aurora stopped him in his track.

"Following my little sister?" she asks smirking.

Marco raised his eyebrows surprised; he didn't expect queen of Russian mafia would be standing in his way even though he knows that she is his fiancee's sister.

"Mrs Aurora Dimitri Anrep, its pleasure to meet you", Marco tells kissing the back of Aurora's hand.

"Pleasure to meet you too, my husband would be happy to meet you", Aurora, tells smiling.

"Ah yes, I didn't find him", he tells looking around for him.

"He is running late, will be here soon", she tells looking at Bianca.

Aurora frowns as she looks at her, she looks as if she is planning something in her head which made her to find out more about this woman, she mentally made a note to ask everything about Bianca from Dimitri which he will gladly do for Odette.

"She went to her room, third from the right", Aurora tells taking a step back making way for him.

"Thank you", Marco tells nodding his head and let his feet drag him to where his heart desire. Looking at Marco following Odette made Bianca's blood boil, she knows no woman can come between twins for them their brotherhood is important and it will be forever till their deaths, hoping Mario will do what is needed to put Odette in her place she prayed internally.

But little did she know where Odette actually belongs.

HE KNOWS

The bedroom door of Odette's was not locked, which made Marco smirk and step inside the room with his hands stuffed in his pockets.

He expected her room to be pink or girly shades of walls and furniture but to his surprise, it was all black and white just as his and Mario's room.

Marco's room was black while Mario's was grey. However, one single blanket caught his attention. It was not same as the room or similar to it, it was in pink colour.

Why this is standing out in the room? Is it her own or someone's? He shrugged it off as soon as the bathroom door opened.

There stood odette shocked seeing him standing in the middle of her room with his hands burrowed in his crisp black trousers, he looks majestic in his black coat. It would be a lie if she tells she does not feel attracted to him.

"Already in love with me?". Odette mocks him coming back from her shock and a smirk made its way on Marco's lips.

"Well... isn't it illegal to fall in love with seventeen years, seven months and eight days old?". Marco asks raising his eyebrows amused making Odette's jaw hit the floor.

But she smirked hiding her shock and spoke, "Oh, isn't it amusing Italian mafia boss considering illegal or legal things?".

Odette's comment earned a chuckle from him.

"Trust me princess, this is the first time, I want something so badly but am controlling myself so bad to not do the illegal thing which I want to do to you right now against the fucking wall of your room", he growls making Odette's stomach do flip flops and somersaults.

Instead of replying to his sinful words, she changed the topic, "Ho... How... how do you know my exact age? "Odette's voice doesn't hide surprise in it as her eyes.

Marco chuckles softly as he steps towards Odette, "trust me, I know every single detail about you princess", he tells pushing few strands of hair behind her ear making her suck huge amount of air.

"About the food you like to the places you want to visit, your hobbies to your studies...about your every single tattoo on your

61

skin to your belly and nipple piercings", Marco groans in Odette's ear making her clench her thighs tightly.

This felt weird and new to her, never in her life she was this close to a man and the voice he owns is not a joke, its sending shivers to her bones.

She exhales a shaky breathe making macro inhale her sweet fragrance. First time in his life he want to take his time in devouring the goddess in front of him instead fuck her right there roughly as he always does.

"It... It's creepy that you know everything about me", Odette whispers making him take a step a back.

She sighs in relief but there is something in her, which is disappointed that he created distance in between them.

"It's not creepy when you are princess of a powerful mafia", he tells making her roll her eyes.

"Don't", he warns her in his dark voice.

His pupils dilated in lust making a dark black circle clearly visible in his blue icy marbles, which made her soul shiver.

"Don't what?". Odette talk back smirking. As Marco clenches his teeth trying to push back his animalistic side, rip her clothes off, and take her right there.

"Lemme guess, you want to punish me? Right? Mr de Luca", Odette smirks whispering it sensually.

Though she does not have any experience in any kind of sexual activities but she knows what happens between a man and women behind the closed doors.

"Fuck!". Marco growls cursing under his breath and pins Odette on the wall making her gasp.

As Odette is pressed between his hard chest and wall taking deep breathes Marco attacks her neck kissing and biting her pale white skin making her hiss and moan in both pleasure and pain.

However, Odette didn't let the sinful pleasure get to her head as she fisted his brown locks yanking it back.

Peeling him off her skin. There are definitely dark purple Hickeys formed on her neck but those are her least concern.

She took her knife out from the strap she has on her thigh under her dress and put it on Marco's neck smirking.

Marco was impressed with her little stunt, he smirked back not getting fazed by the sudden attack, if he wanted he could slit her throat with the same knife in a second as his skills and strength is much more than Odette.

"No touching until am eighteen... Bello", she whispered against his lips making him smirk.

Winking at him seductively, she swayed her hips and went out from her room before patting his cheek playfully.

"Fucking tease she is..."Marco growled licking his lips trying to feel her taste on them and sighed closing his eyes. He groans throwing his head back and lighting his cigarette, bringing it to his lips he takes a whiff and blow the smoke out thinking about how he is going to tame the little vixen in her.

~~~

"Meet Marco's twin brother", Bianca introduced Mario to Andre with her fake smiling.

"Oh! It's nice to meet you am Andre Francois", Andre greets shaking Mario's hand.

"I'm Mario de Luca", Mario tells smiling at the elder man.

He was least bit interested in talking to Andre, moreover he wants to kill him right there but they need his support as he has biggest weapon making industry in England.

"Where are Odette and Marco? "Andre asks frowning searching for them in the crowd.

Bianca laughs placing her hand in front of her mouth and tells, "Your daughter has captivated my son with her beauty... I saw him following her to her room, probably to have some alone time with his future wife". Andre sighed praying internally that his little bad wold doesn't stab the man who followed her thinking she is little red riding Hood.

"It's okay I will meet them later", Mario tells smiling at Andre looking at his devastated face.

"Oh, no, it's... it's just, she is a trouble maker, and I just hope she doesn't offend Marco", Andre tells sighing. "Don't worry its okay, she is after all princess and soon queen of Italian mafia", Bianca tells chuckling.

"She has every right to be spoiled". She tells smiling.

Before anyone could speak Mario's phone rang making him sigh.

"Don't worry, go on", Bianca tells encouraging him to take the call.

Mario smiled at her and pecked her cheek before bidding his good bye to Andre.

"Work comes first", Andre comments waving his hand off which Mario nodded his head smiling as he left the hall.

"Have you found about her? "Mario asks in his cold voice earning a answer from the other line.

"Yes boss, she studies feminism in PSL University in France", the man answered making Mario smirk.

"Good, anymore details?", he asks to which the man on other line speaks, "No boss, no one was ready to give out her information as if she is someone important, if you want me to find out more details about her I have to find a detective", he tells making Mario sigh.

"No, its okay, I will pay her visit tomorrow", Mario, tells coldly.

"Boss we also have a problem", the man tells stuttering making Mario clench his jaw.

"What now? "Mario growls angrily.

"The products which were coming from US were caught by the Italian cops at eastern coast", he tells making Mario curse under his breathe.

"Sho… Should we inform boss Marco?" he asks stuttering.

"No, I will come there, no need to tell him now, I will speak to him tomorrow", Mario spat walking towards his car.

"I am coming to Italy", Mario said before hanging up the call.

"Leaving for work", Mario typed text to Bianca as he settled in car and drove off without waiting for reply.

Hoping he will come back France to deal with the little girl not knowing she is now his own brother's finance.

KINDNESS

Finally, after engagement party ended odette went to bed tiredly. Laying on her soft bed with her pink blanket in her arms, she sighed smelling it as a smile formed on her lips.

"Mama… this still smells like you", Odette breathed out exhaling heavily.

"I miss you mama", she breathe out again as a lone tear escaped her doe eyes.

"I am engaged to Marco, the Italian mafia boss", she spoke again as if she is talking to her therapist or writing her day in a journal.

66

This gave her peace and Odette did this quiet after her mother's death, which Aurora suggested her to do.

Aurora couldn't see her little sister struggling for her mother's warmth in such young age and said her mother isn't gone completely, she is there, still around her, watches her, but from above the sky as she became a star.

Odette got better after doing this and it became a habit to talk seeing the sky before sleeping.

Odette's phone beeped making her sigh. Thinking it should be phone company's message she ignored it but it beeped again making her sigh as she got up from her bed and reached for her phone on the night table.

"Good night, princess, will meet you soon".

-your Bello ;)

A faint smile formed on her lips as she shook her head in disbelief, Marco got her number and started texting too! Great!

"Bad night to you".

She replied chuckling to herself and locked the phone after muting it so that she could sleep peacefully as it was already too late.

~

"I don't have time to eat, am already late, I have important exam today", Odette spoke frantically panicking.

"Princess, please eat something or master will scold us", the maid requested her making her sigh.

"Mrs Smith, please tell him I ate, he wouldn't care", Odette said rolling her eyes as she packed her bag and ran out of her room.

"Hurry up, I am already late", she said to the driver who drives her to the college regularly.

"Okay princess", the driver replied politely but kept a safe speed as her safety matters most.

She sighed as she leaned back and closed her eyes for one second then open them as the car came to halt.

"What the fuck?" Odette gasped looking at the road seeing huge traffic in front of her.

The driver spoke to someone who informed that there was an accident happened and the traffic is jammed and it will take time to clear.

Which he informed to Odette making her groan.

"Why the hell it's happening today!" she whines as she fist her hair.

"I will go by walk, I don't have time", she said as she glanced at her watch then got out of the car making driver horrified.

"Princess, you can't go without guards, it's dangerous", the driver cried making her roll her eyes.

"Nothing will happen", she said without taking another glance at him she ran off into the cars, which are jammed, on the road.

Running between the gaps of the car in her leather shorts along with mesh stockings and black oversized shirt with funky silver chains and rings in black leather boots she looked a bad baby girl which any man would desire to make her his own sugar baby.

In between her running, she didn't notice someone who had his eyes on her since the day he met is looking at her alluring figure running in between the cars.

Struck between the traffic he groaned and got off his own car leaving it to driver and followed odette secretly.

As soon as odette reached her college, she took deep breathes and placed her palms against her knees. Bending and taking huge amount of oxygen she laughed.

"Well it was a good exercise", she told to herself as she caught her breathe and calmed herself down.

When she was about to step in the college suddenly heavy rain started pouring down as the sky turned dark and clouds thundered against each other.

As the campus was too far inside, she rushed towards the bus stop of the college, which is right beside the gate. "God! Why are you angry at me?", she yelled at the sky glaring as the person who followed her chuckled looking at her in amusement though he was drenched in rain.

"I have a exam today, I barely slept last night, didn't eat my breakfast, ran all the way to college and not you now who couldn't control your mood swings and let it rain?!", she yelled again cutely looking at dark sky which thundered as if it's replying to her.

"Oh shut up! Don't act as you are on your periods", she scolded rolling her eyes making the man keeping his eyes on her laugh badly.

She sighed and sat on the bench and pouted swaying her legs off. Her eyes fell on the two puppies that are drenched in rain and were shivering.

Her heart clenched at the sight as she saw those two cute brown puppies trembling in rain and no one was around to help them.

She ran off into the street without thinking twice about her decision, held those two puppies in her arms securely, close to her chest, and ran back to the bus stop.

"Oh no... You both are wet and cold", she said sadly as she opened her backpack and took out her jacket from it.

She started drying their fur with her expensive jacket with so much care making the man admire her from afar thinking how could one be this caring one day and other day a bitch. At least to him she was a bitch he thought.

Two puppies wined as she dried them off and put the jacket around them keeping them safe from the cold and she looked around for help.

The man who was staring at her hid behind the wall as fast as possible so that she did not see him standing there.

"There is no one around, how should I ask for help now?" she asked those two puppies as if they could reply.

They blinked at her dumbfounded, as she was deep in thought and suddenly exclaimed happily clapping her hands.

"The fuck! I have a fucking phone", she exclaimed slapping her forehead and tried to find it in her pockets but wasn't able to find it there.

She rummaged her bag but it wasn't there too. She slapped her forehead again and shook her head sadly at puppies.

"Sorry, I think I forgot it at home or in the car, here you can eat some biscuits", she said sadly then took two biscuits from her bag and fed those puppies happily.

They devoured them as if they were starving for years making her chuckle.

"I have more don't worry", Odette cooed at them and fed them few more.

"What should I call you?" she asked them making them bark at her cutely as they licked her fingers making her giggle.

"Hmmm… yes!" Odette exclaims in joy as she picks a light brown puppy with a black mark on its leg.

"Your name is Nike, I like Nike shoes a lot, that's why", she reasoned making the man chuckle at her.

The puppy barked happily, as he licked all over her face making her giggle.

Odette placed Nike down gentle and then picked another same light brown puppy, which didn't have any mark on.

"Your name will be Gucci, as I love there jackets", she reasoned making it bark in happiness and he licked her cheek making her laugh.

"You both wait here, I will get in side the campus and call my driver so that I could take you home", she said gently as she rushed into the campus getting drenched in rain.

When she was gone, the man who was watching everything came towards the puppies and lifted then up in his hands.

"So you are Nike and Gucci, nice meeting you", he cooed and a car stopped in front of him.

"Let's go to your new home with me, your mummy will be home soon", he cooed making them relax.

He got in the car and ordered to take them to his home – Italy.

"Remove the Red Cross from her and if anyone hurt her or think so, I will fucking kill them, keep an eye on her, I want her safe", he warned the driver sternly which made him shiver in fear and nod his head saying "Okay boss".

The man whose heart melted seeing her kindness doesn't know what it was until someone showed them eleven years ago.

Odette reminded him of her and her kindness, which ignited a feeling to find that little girl.

This time he will not let her go away.

"Hello, Am Mario de Luca, I want you to find someone, will send you details", the man said in his cold voice.

Little did he know he already met the person whom he and his brother were dying to see again.

HALF TRUTH

"Where they went?" Odette frowned searching for the puppies everywhere around her university but couldn't find them.

Her eyes teared up when she understood that they went away and she probably wouldn't see them again.

"I'm sorry, Odette, they are nowhere", her friend Charlotte said in pity. She knows Odette has a fear of people walking away from her since her mother died and her father drowned himself in his business.

Then she started seeing him rarely at home and very rarely in a good mood. Then her favourite caretaker had to go because her own family needed her as she couldn't leave her own daughter in an unknown country all by herself.

Odette was left alone completely when Aurora married to Dimitri and shifted to Russia to stay with him, too far from her.

"It's okay Charlotte, people or animals they all leave one day, not now then some other day", she said gulping down her sob and walked into her university in her wet clothes.

After changing into fresh pair of clothes, which were, Charlotte's as she was a cheerleader of her university and had to have spare clothes in her locker, which she could wear when she needed let Odette borrow her dress. This was a white knee length floral frock with pink flowers and green leaves printed on the organza fabric.

Odette felt weird in such dress, she never put such clothes on. Sighing she combed her black hair with her hands which were semi wet now and good to go to class. Walking as she sat on her desk and her professor gave her exam sheet, which she wrote unmindful and bothered about the two puppies, which she thought to take them with her to her home, but Odette doesn't know they were at her home, which she doesn't know yet.

~~~

"You are leaving?" Odette asked her sister who was packing her bags.

Aurora sighed as she saw odette standing at her door with twins holding her both hands who also had a pout on their faces.

74

"Mama we want to stay with aunt oddy, we don't want to come", twins whined holding Odette's hands tightly which made Odette's eyes water.

"I'm sorry babies, your dad needs us, we have to go, bring your toys which you threw around or we could but new ones there", Aurora said stealing glances with her twins without eye contacting Odette.

Odette understood what her sister is doing, she gently slipped her hands from twins without looking at Aurora she left the room with a broken heart.

"Good byes are always hard but for me they are harder", she said to herself looking at her own reflection in the mirror.

Her nose turned red and eyes are fluffy and turned red. Because of staying in rain for long, she is definitely feeling cold and her body is shivering.

Sighing to herself, she took off her frock she borrowed from Charlotte and went under her duvet after turning heater on. It has been one hour she fell asleep without eating her lunch. Her temperature is high than before and Odette started mumbling something in her sleep which no one can understand.

"Princess", a maid knocked on her door but she didn't answer, she wasn't in a condition to answer her.

"Princess", she knocked again but again silence was what she heard.

In fact, the entire mansion was in deadly silence as there was no one except few maids working here and there but that too without making a noise

The maid panicked because she knows something is wrong, it always happened when Aurora left and today was the same day as those times.

She did what she was asked to do. She didn't call Andre this time but to the person who warned her to call him if anything... *anything* happens to Odette.

"Sir, princess Odette didn't eat anything since morning she locked herself in her room and isn't answering, am afraid", the maid said to Marco in panicked voice.

Marco's eyebrows furrowed thinking what could have happened to Odette. She was perfectly fine yesterday but today. Suddenly?

Is this because she is taking their engagement stressful way?

No matter how many times Bianca said she was just a part of their revenge and told to not catch feelings for odette Marco couldn't help when he heard Odette is in trouble, which he doesn't know how and why?

"Try to make her open the door am coming in few minutes", that's what he said as he was close to France for some business meeting along his brother. He just need few minutes to drive to Odette.

"Where are you going brother? "Mario asked confused as he never saw macro this stressed.

"I'm going to Francois mansion, its emergency", macro said hurriedly getting up from middle of the important deal.

76

"But... The deal isn't settled yet!". Mario reasoned asking macro to stay for few minutes.

"Cancel the meeting or you take care of it, I don't mind", he said rudely rushing out from the conference hall.

Mario was beyond shocked to respond, he never thought his brother would speak to him in this tone. He knows to not speak further, which will piss macro off more than he already is, so he stayed silent.

Marco was already in the car on his way to Odette; Mario took his phone out from his pocket and texted Bianca.

"You are right... that chic started playing with my brother, we should do it soon or else we might lose him to that bitch".

"Told you... I want you to take her to bed, before wedding". Was Bianca's reply.

Being a woman herself how cruel she is to ask someone to do this to another woman who is nothing but all innocent.

"Will be on it, send me her details". Mario sent the text to Bianca with a smirk on his face.

Glancing at his phone, he was waiting for his brother's fiancee details but his smirk fell off his face as well as his phone hitting the floor and his heart clenched at the sight.

The same long dark jet-black hair, same pink pulp lips with piercing, same eyes, which held emotions, which no one could read until she opens her heart to them, she was none other than the girl he met today and wanted nothing to do with her than ravish and worship her in his bed.

He took a deep breathe clenching his jaw hard, "this isn't true", he said to himself not ready to accept the fact that she was his brother's fiancee.

This surprise and shock is nothing compared to the one, which is waiting for the brothers in future when they find out the little girl they were searching for is none other than Odette Francois herself, their enemy's daughter.

FEELINGS

"Princess?!"Marco knocked the door worried as he didn't hear Odette answering him.

"Since when she is in?" he growled at the maid who was already shivering in fear.

"It...It's been more than one hour". The maid answered stuttering badly.

This made macro's blood boil in anger, how could they not do their damn job properly.

"Next time she locks herself up.... Inform me right away!" he growled at the maid angrily as he stepped close to the door to break it.

After smacking his upper arm to the wooden plank of the door few times, the door flung open with a thud making Marco sigh but the sight in front of him wasn't a good one. There Odette was lying down near her desk where her pink blanket was placed on the chair and she held it in her right hand tightly while she was laying unconscious there half-naked just in her black set of lingerie.

"Odette!" he gasped, his eyes widened as he hurried towards her and lift her unconscious petite body in his arms and laid her carefully on the bed covering her up with duvet. Though the maid was a woman, he doesn't want anyone to see what is his.

Her body was burning as fire, which made his stomach churn. Marco never cared for a woman far away for a teenager like Odette. He never felt this possessiveness and urge to protect someone too. It's overwhelming feeling for his cold heart, which far away he knows he could get used to it.

"Call the fucking doctor!" he yelled at the maid who was just standing at the door dumbfounded.

"Y... Yes", she mumbled before running off from there to the main hall and picked the landline phone of the home and called the family doctor.

Marco kept rubbing Odette's legs and hands occasionally as he jerked her few times to wake her up but she didn't. Her heartbeat was normal but her body temperature wasn't which was clear that she is unconscious and have high fever.

"Hang on there baby, you will be fine", Marco said against her forehead pecking her head lovingly.

"S... Sir, the doctor is here", the maid informed standing at the door with a female doctor behind her.

"Hurry check her up, she is passed out since God knows when", he snapped at the doctor who stepped in Odette's room.

"It's okay, she has a fever she will be fine by tomorrow morning, I will give her an injection and medicines she have to take tonight and morning", doctor said after checking Odette.

"Won't it hurt?" Marco asked making doctor's eyes wide.

The doctor is family doctor of Francois mafia. She has been working for them and her parents to theirs from long time and in these many years, she never heard a mafia boss asking *will injection hurt*. She was at the party last night so she knows who Marco is but she never expected this kind of question from a cold man like him.

"No... No, it will but just little", she said unable to process words with amusement in her eyes.

She took the syringe out from her suitcase, filled medicine in it, and rubbed the damp cotton on Odette's arm, which was held by Marco protectively.

"Please make it less hurtful", he said making doctor's hand shake in fear. She understood if Odette hissed a little he wouldn't think twice before he empty his gun in her head. The sight was shocking but amusing to the maid, which happened to gather few other head maids outside of Odette's room to get a look of worried mafia boss for his fiancee. They were all in awe when Marco hissed as if he felt the pain when the needle pierced Odette's skin and closed his eyes unable to see it.

If this word passed out from the Francois mansion people will start laughing hearing the cruel ruthless mafia boss who chop people in multiple pieces to keep his sanity is hissing with his closed eyes in fear of seeing a damn syringe pierce his fiancee's delicate arm.

Thankfully, Odette didn't move or showed any kind of discomfort to which the doctor was more than happy.

"Done", she sighed in relief, picked her things up after writing few medicines on a paper and handed it to the maid who stood with five other maids at the door with smile on their faces.

"Buy these medicines she will be fine", doctor said running out from the mansion for her dear life.

Marco kept caressing odette's hair with his tattooed fingers making the sight look ethereal as if a big monster is playing with a delicate doll gently in fear that he might break it.

The maids didn't made a moment which made Marco frown as he lift his eyes from Odette to the maids giving them a deadly glare they all stumbled back and ran from there panicked as if he might kill them for seeing him admire their princess.

"Si... Sir, these are medicines and I... I brought soup as you... you asked", the maid who called Marco here in the first place stuttered as she said she completed the work he gave her.

He took the tray from her and put it on the bedside table beside Odette. Then he gently lifts her up cooing sweet nothings in her ear.

"Wake up baby, let's feed you something", Marco said as he gently held Odette up, as she was half-asleep.

"I don't want to", she whined sleepily but Marco wasn't the one who would let her defy him.

"I know you don't want to but you need to eat something", he said in his raspy voice gently and brought a spoonful of soup to her lips pressing it so that she opens her mouth letting her stomach fill with the warm soup.

He gently blew air on the spoonful of soup before feeding Odette making sure it doesn't burn her tongue.

"Enough... am full", Odette whines sleepily which made Marco sigh and drop the spoon in the bowl. He then took tablets from the tray and made her swallow them with a glass of water. Odette did everything he asked for in her sleepy state not conscious about in whose arms she was and who was feeding her.

"Good girl", Marco cooed pecking Odette's forehead and tucked her back in the bed.

When he called the maid to take the empty tray back, who was waiting at the door seeing him do everything so carefully and lovingly she couldn't help but comment something, which Marco wasn't ready to hear – yet.

"You love her so much... Thank you for taking care of her", she blurted out making Marco clench his jaw.

His hands fisted as he glanced at the maid who silently took the tray away. His eyes raked on Odette's innocent face, which is flushed, and looking beyond cute which could destroy him and his existence in a blink, which made a new fear arise in his heart. Which he thought, was didn't exist until today.

The fear of falling in love with her was most terrifying to him than the cruel Intentions he had to do to her to make Andre suffer.

He knows he can't let his feelings ruin the only thing, which kept him alive for these eleven years after losing his everything – his mother.

He turned his back on Odette letting her sleep peacefully tearing his not so peaceful heart away from her and walked out of the mansion with a thunderstorm of his newly erupting feelings in his chest.

WHO

Odette stretched yawning as she opened her tired eyes due to the sunlight peeking into her room as she forgot to drag the blinds down last night.

"Last night?" she mumbled rubbing her eyes cutely and sighed.

"Oh, aurora and the two little monkeys left me alone", she said sighing getting up from the bed.

Her bones felt sore and she felt tired walking towards the washroom. Looking at herself, she sighed. There are dark circles under her eyes, her lips are chapped, and she smells fever in her mouth.

Disgusted she picks up her toothbrush and brushes her teeth and use mouth wash then clean up herself by washing her face with cold water.

Jumping in the warm shower after taking off her undergarments, she placed her hands on the glass wall of the shower area and sighed in content.

"A long shower when we don't feel good does feel fucking good", she tell herself scrubbing off foam on her body then rinse it humming to some classic music as she wraps herself in a towel and get out of her washroom.

A maid stood at her bedroom door with a tray in her hand and smiled widely at Odette.

Odette gave her confused half smile, as she doesn't know the reason behind the wide smile of the maid standing in front of her door.

"Good morning, princess, sir said you should take your breakfast now with the medicines and asked you to take rest today, your exams got postponed to next week, so that you could write them when you are healthy ", the maid said in her joyful voice making Odette frown.

"How many times should I have to tell dad that he doesn't need to interfere in my studies? I want to study as normal students, I was fucking home schooled my whole life and now he is bribing my lecturers to postpone the exams!?", Odette groan in disbelief shaking her head tiredly she dashed out from her room to her father's office knowing well that he would be there at this early hours as always.

"Dad!" Odette yells pushing the door open making it hit against the wall behind with a loud thud and Andre sighed.

"Here we go", Andre, mumbles as he lifts his eyes from his laptop to Odette but he wasn't looking at her in anger or annoyed he was looking at her with worried eyes.

"You just got better and started trashing my office already?", Andre scolds coming close to Odette placing his hand on her forehead he checks her temperature which was normal but she had to take medicines as prescribed because if she don't her fever will get back.

"Why did you postpone my exams?" Odette glared at her father slapping his hand away making him frown.

"What!? Who said I did?" he asked her dumbfounded.

"Don't act now, then who did?" Odette exclaimed angrily throwing her hands in air. "I swear to God, dad, I just started my college, I wanted everything to be as every normal student has, then why did you..." The maid who brought her breakfast this morning cut off Odette.

"Sorry to interrupt princess, but master wasn't the one who postponed your exams it was Marco De Luca sir", maid said with a beam of happiness on her face.

"What?!", both Andre and Odette asked in shock looking at each other then back at the maid.

"I wanted to tell everything to you but Marco sir warned me to not tell, but since am loyal to you, princess Odette as I pledged my Loyalty I will speak only truth to you", the maid said with fear and happiness which were confusing together.

"Last evening when princess aurora left as usual without saying goodbye..." the maid said and gulped thickly.

"Princess Odette locked herself in her room and she was not opening the door as you were busy Marco sir asked me to contact him if it comes to princess Odette's safety and... and I called him and... When... he came he had to break the door to get into princess's room, she was passed out near her desk, he took care of her, called doctor, he even fed her soup and medicines, do you know what he was so worried when doctor said she had to give you injection because he thought it would hurt you, he was about to kill the doctor if she did hurt but thankfully she ran away all good", the maid said everything in a single breathe making both Andre and Odette look at each other with wide eyes and totally dumbfounded.

Andre had no words to speak, first he was little afraid about how Marco would treat his daughter but now he can rest in peace as he heard what he has done for her. Which being a mafia man showing weakness was a big deal, it wouldn't be at least for the act, as no mafia boss would like to be addressed as weak but he – Marco went vulnerable for Odette, a smile formed on Andre's lips as he shook his head to not let tears of his happiness fall but Odette was so confused and slowly after thinking a lot she remember what had happened last night.

She remembered how she went to take her pink blanket and went blank, she also remembers how sweetly Marco spoke to her and took care of her, and fed her...she remembered everything.

A tear escaped her eyes because after all the good things he did, she woke up alone in her room. She was alone and this time the feelings she felt over powdered her sanity. She can't believe who took such care of her could leave her alone.

Angrily she went out from her room to her bedroom and put appropriate clothes to wear outside.

Taking a blue jeans and white shirt, she didn't think to layer it up with any jacket and rushed out of her home with just phone in her hand.

Dialling Marco's number, she got into the car, which was ready with a driver for her.

"Hello?".

Marco's raspy voice echoed on the other line as he lift the call.

"Where the hell are you?" Odette rasped angrily clutching the phone tightly in her hand.

Marco frowned not understanding why she is all angry on him, what was his fault? Oh! Because he decided for her that her exams will be postponed? He thought, as she doesn't like men decide her life that's so what her feminism classes teach her.

"I am busy, am in a meeting", Marco said in his bored tone. No matter how happy he was hearing her sweet voice and she unleashing her anger on him as if she owns him was making her damn cute for his own good.

"Tell me where the fuck you are?!" she rasped again rolling her eyes.

"You can't come here, am busy, I will talk to you later", he said hanging up the call because he was in an important meeting with Chinese dealers who wanted to import drugs from him

Too stubborn to listen to him Odette did what a sane person who was raised in a mafia would do.

She called a number of the worker in her mafia and ordered him to do something for her. Which she doesn't know, how much of a huge trouble it will bring her.

"Suivrecenuméro", she said to the person on the other line.

(Track this number)

"Bien sur, princess", he answered her and sent the address of Marco's location to her phone.

(Of course, princess)

A smirk played on Odette's lips as she asked driver to take her to that address too oblivious of coming danger.

KRYPTONITE

"Mr Chan, I believe we have already discussed about this deal, I will let you trade my drugs when you send me women you have trafficked without their will", Marco tells calmly as he studies the face of the Chinese man who is around his forties.

Though being in the mafia Marco and Mario always helped the women who doesn't want to be in a place which wasn't for them. They don't like to take women without their consent and that was the only humanity they think was left in them because they know how some women wants to live with dignity even though they might die of hunger – because they have seen their mother go through it, she was always a strong headed woman. Never kneed in front of a man and always kept her chastity and worked as a maid in multiple homes but never choose the other way.

"I have already said that we don't have women from Italy, Chinese men doesn't find them cute to fuck", Chan lied plainly snorting making Marco clench his teeth in anger.

If Marco doesn't like one thing that is lie... not even Mario likes to be lied.

"I am sure we have information of our women missing who are locked up in your brothels and strip clubs", Marco growls angrily.

Mr Chan scoffs looking at his two men who are standing behind him as he was sitting on a chair of the conference hall opposite to Marco and his own two men and other two guarding the door.

"If you are pressing this, I will look around but I guarantee no one was brought forcefully", Mr Chan tells raising his hands in air.

He was a cunning and smart man who would do anything to get what he wants, he wasn't that fool to get on Marco's bad side when his company was the only which provides drugs in extreme quantity in a single shipment and safe too, because his brother Mario is in FBI.

"I hope you keep your word, Mr Chan, you know how much I hate being lied and played if it isn't my favourite game", Marco declares warning him to keep his things together or he would love to rip them apart and enjoy his torture session with him.

Mr Chan gulps thickly hiding his nervousness but smiles upwards pushing his uneasy thoughts down his head.

"Then we should...." Mr Chan was cut off when a guard appeared on the door hastily and he was definitely afraid of something or someone.

Mr Chan saw intently as Marco's eyes widened at something the guard murmured in his ear and he jolted up on his feet and rushed out side the conference hall leaving Mr Chan and his men confused and curious.

Marco never gives any emotions away especially not worry; it's not even a word in his dictionary. However, today they saw worry along with another emotion which would be their lethal weapon.

They saw fear, for the first time in Marco's eyes. First time Marco failed to hide his emotions at his work, that too letting them flow in front of his enemy who is wearing a friendly skin.

Marco rushed towards his office where he supposed the person came to meet him is there. There are many branches of de Luca industries in France especially now when they formed a treaty with Odette's father they will open more offices here in future.

Marco was beyond angry that he would kill the person who was in his office right now if that wasn't someone who don't hold his heart in her palms.

Opening the door he saw Odette sitting on the couch calmly. But when his eyes fell on her, his anger disappeared, as he noticed those black doe eyes were at the verge of tearing up.

She looks troubled, a lot but she was so good in hiding her emotions just as Marco.

His eyes softened at her sight taking her ethereal form in, she looked healthy than before which made his heart rest in ease but her presence here wasn't a good idea as he knows the men around him wants nothing more than a reaction from him, so that he gives away his weakness which wasn't anything till then but now it is, now standing right in front of him, seeing him with her longing teary eyes with a red nose and pouty lips and flushed cheeks – she became his weakness.

"Odette Francois!" Marco rasped as he took a step towards her. It was clear of him using her full name that he was angry at her but to his surprise Odette took multiple steps towards him and delivered a tight slap across his face hardly.

Marco didn't even flinch but she hissed due to the sting rose in her palm due to the contact with his hard chiselled jaw.

He clenched his teeth in anger as his jaw shook in immense rage. He didn't expect this, but what was coming next was more unexpected than the slap she delivered him.

"Why did you leave me alone", Odette cried breaking down in front of him and fat tears rolled down her eyes.

"Why…why did you leave me alone huh?" she cried more punching him on his chest making him clench his fists.

This time, not in rage. But to let her take everything out on him without interfering.

Somewhere he knows she needed it from the person himself hiding his emotions he knows everyone needs that someone to take their emotions out, it might be rage, hurt, tears or anything else.

The longer it stays in, the lonelier the person gets. That's what he is and he don't want Odette to be like him.

Still in the cold eyes of hers, he saw a bubbly girl who wanted to fly and he was going to crumble the damn cage to let her free if it means killing anyone and everyone in the process.

"You are a bad man", Odette sobbed fisting his black shirt in her delicate palms and finally hugged him, she found peace.

Her head was resting on his chest where his heart beats, where she belonged.

Marco sighed as he slowly wrapped his hands around her petite body and embraced her broken self with one and only intention of fixing her.

"Its okay, am here", he said softly, his voice huskier than usual with the bubbling feeling inside his chest, which he didn't notice that he too had to let them out to someone but for him that someone was the person who is none other than his enemy's daughter.

"You are here… but you weren't with me, when I woke up, you were there… but you left me, when you knew I would want to see you there for me", Odette mumbled against his hard chest with her ragged voice.

Marco chuckled softly pressing his lips on her head making her break the hug but she still held him and he held her in his arms.

"You would have liked seeing me there?" he asked making her look down not meeting his gaze.

He gently pushed her head up holding her chin with his two fingers and demanded.

His blue eyes amused but grateful for what? For the feelings she started to build for him, those genuine feelings which he have seen in only one person's eyes who was a stranger to him then but became his first friend.

He furrowed his eyebrows to get rid of those thoughts. It wasn't time for that.

"I would have loved to, I hate people running away from me", Odette murmurs but quiet loud for him to hear.

"I would never run away from you princess", Marco's words surprised himself. It was true somehow, he doesn't want to run away from her but from his own feelings, which are undoubtedly a trouble for the plan he approached.

"Promise me", Odette asks taking her pinkie finger and puckering her lower lip cutely.

Before he could make any sense of what she asked from him his hand flew towards her own and he gently locked his pinkie with hers promising her something which he himself doesn't know if he is capable of.

"I promise", that's it as soon as she heard those two words she slammed her lips to his taking him by surprise and kissed him softly making his eyes wide but soon he let his body calm against her and gave in the kiss enjoying the little life he felt in these eleven years of life. Too oblivious that he have given someone the only way of his destruction, the kryptonite – Odette Francois.

SPECIAL

Marco held Odette close to himself as he took lead and started kissing her deeply. He let all his emotions in even though his words couldn't explain.

Odette was out of breathe already and panting hard which made him to break the kiss with one last peck on her lips.

While their foreheads were attached together, he stares in her eyes with his blue cold ones, which seemed lustful but warm because those eyes were mirrors of his heart, which Odette could read easily.

"You need to stop doing that or else I won't be able to control myself from taking you right now and then, princess", Marco rasps in his thick Italian accent making her insides clench.

"Then don't control", Odette whispered in his arms. Marco groaned as a hungry wild animal and threw his head back before pinning Odette to the nearby wall making her gasp in surprise.

"No! I won't!" he grumbles helplessly as he watched deep in her soul through her doe eyes.

Suddenly those eyes seemed.....disappointed? Sad? Nevertheless, that look wasn't a good thing for Marco's sanity.

"I mean, I want to fuck you so hard, princess.....but I won't touch you until we get married", he admits making her frown.

"Why? I want you to touch me", Odette tells with a frown and a cute pout forming on her full pink lips while her cheeks are flushed due to the kiss which they both shared which meant something more than the one they shared in front of everyone.

"Is it because am not eighteen?" she asks sadly but Marco's expressions weren't giving her the answers but just a smile which could mean anything.

Is he smiling because he thinks am being needy? Or he is thinking I have given myself to him easily? Why? She kept thinking in her head, which gave her expression off that she is definitely thinking hard.

Marco brought his fingers towards her temple, gently erased her frown with his thumb and finger, and flicked it playfully making her yelp a small ouch!

"What the fuck?!" Odette tells rubbing her forehead scowling at Marco completely pissed off.

Marco chuckles shaking his head and suddenly becomes all-serious then speaks.

"I won't touch you before marriage, I really suggest we don't meet till our marriage, princess", he tells seriously shoving his hands in his pockets of the trousers.

"But...", when Odette was going to ask he immediately cut her off softly cupping her face in his palms and said.

"Because... I had such relationship with other women before and I don't want to have same with you... because you aren't like them, you are special, you are my woman and I will touch you when you officially become Mrs De Luca from Miss Francois", he tells softly making her heart thud loud in her chest.

Did he just say he had relationships with other women before? Did he also said am not like them? Did he say am special? Did he said am his woman? Hell he did said! Odette thought dumbfounded in her head, clearly not expecting him to speak so openly about it.

She blushed hard when she let his words sink, how this man can be so respective towards her and gave her such place in his life when it's been nearly forty-eight or less than those hours of their meeting.

"Do you understand?" he asks softly to which Odette nods her head shyly.

"Words!" he asks sternly, which made her answer him immediately.

"Yes! Yes I understood", she tells and Marco smiles tucking her hair behind.

"Are you feeling well now?" he asks checking her temperature with his palm.

"I am fine thank you… for taking care of me", she tells smiling at him gratefully.

"It was my pleasure", he sighs in content after conforming himself that she is fine and smile at her.

It's been long since Marco smiled and now he couldn't even hide his smile around Odette.

She can also feel that something between them is changed after last night and she like whatever it is.

"Hey!" Odette exclaims remembering something slapping him on his chest.

"Ouch!" Marco gasps rubbing his chest playfully faking hurt when clearly they both know he didn't even felt the sting as much as an ant bite.

Odette rolls her eyes and snaps at Marco folding her hands on her chest.

"Why did you made my exams postponed and how?" she asks glaring at him which made him smirk at the thought of how he convinced or one could say *threatened* the principal do as what he said.

Marco wouldn't lie, when it isn't necessary.

"I just threatened him that I will kill him if he didn't postpone your exams", he tells shrugging his shoulders as if it was a normal thing. Though it was very normal thing for him.

"You did not", Odette gasps her eyes widened hearing his careless words.

"It was my first year studying in college... I mean not home schooled, like really going out to college as normal people does and I wanted everything to be normal! Why the hell did you ruin it?" she scolds him throwing her hands in air pacing front and back in his office angrily.

"You mafia men are same, you won't let women to breathe as she wants, you will choke her then put them on ventilation, why can't you guys be normal for one goddamn time and let us decide what we want?!", she tells madly.

Marco looks at her in admiration as he takes a cigarette box out from his pocket, taking one out and push it against Odette's lips so that she hold it in between her lips but she didn't.

Her eyes widened as soon as she saw Marco offering her cigarette. Is she dreaming? Is this a joke? What is it? Has he lost his mind? She thought lamely looking as a fish with her open mouth. Marco chuckles as he orders her.

"Close your mouth", he tells snapping her out of her shock and she does as he ordered.

He lights the lighter and lit the cigarette and Odette takes a huff and smiles at the taste as she breathes the smoke out.

"It tastes like strawberry, what is this?" she asks surprised at the taste making Marco grin.

"One of the products of our company princess, strawberry flavour", he tells making her smile widely.

Her eyes lighten up as the way he mentioned his business as our, though she never expected or thought he would consider her more than his personal fuck toy or a breeding womb he proved her wrong.

She takes another puff smiling and tells chuckling, "This thing is good; you should probably send some to my home".

Marco lifts his hand up checking time on his watch then grins at her and says, "Already delivered, they might be in your room now, four different flavours – strawberry, mint, chocolate and orange".

Looking at her shocked face with a cigarette in between her fingers, she looks adorable to him.

"Are those not enough? Should I send more flavours?" he asks faking worry but he knows Odette didn't even expect to get a single cigarette from him because he knows mafia men wouldn't let their women on buzz.

"Pinch me please", she tells making Marco grin. Instead of pinching, he pecks her forehead making her sigh.

"This means it's a dream", she tells shaking her head off and Marco looks at her in amusement.

He raises his single eyebrow and asks her cockily, "Do you mean you dreamt about me kissing you?"

Odette's eyes widened again realizing what she said.

"N.no... No", she tells but her shutter gave the truth away making Marco grin wide.

"Don't worry am pleased to know", he tells smirking.

"How do you feel now? It doesn't have nicotine...Did this calm your nerves?" he asks her raising his eyebrows. "What?" she asks shocked. "This doesn't have nicotine?" she asks again making him smile.

"Yes, these are pure herbs with dried fruit so it is not toxic, the herbs used are to calm your mind but doesn't make adrenaline rush in your body", he tells smartly making her jaw hit the floor.

"Th…. These are amazing", she tells genuinely making him smile satisfied. "Why we don't have these in market?" she asks complaining. Marco simply shrugs and tells, "Because I got them made especially for you". Now again it's time for Odette to choke on surprise.

SHARE HER

Marco was tired, with his busy schedule, which he had to finish before the dead line, and dealing with Chinese dealers wasn't easy thing when he was losing his temper repeatedly because of their cunning nature.

Marco would have dug bullets into their heads if he was ready for the war but he wouldn't let his people suffer for his own temper. Though being the dangerous man of Italy, he also provides food for people who couldn't survive out without his help. He runs many bars, which is means of earning for thousands of people.

He makes sure no child gets involve in his dirty business because he knows what it feels like to be in the dark world in such a young age coming from there. He made sure every girl child is treated equally and given opportunity to live her life just as a boy child gets.

There is no doubt people respect him, many politicians wanted him to join politics for their own benefits and Marco wasn't the man who would stand in front of crowd and give them a promising speech.

Finding their own benefit in this deal Marco sent Mario into legal field but as an FBI agent who would gather any information from insides, which will clearly make their cheque clear and neat.

It wasn't hard for Mario to find about the little girl he met when he was thirteen. They remember how she looks, how she spoke, how she smiled. Her every inch of the skin is imprinted in the minds of both brothers.

Which they both don't want to deny. They do have feelings for her, as a promise for eternity, they wanted to share her. Her love for them and their love is only for her.

When Marco entered his room it was dead dark, the silence of the night was deafening, but Marco was used to this. Removing his shirt, he tossed it out on the couch not looking around in his room.

Odette's chuckling giggling was only thing his head was kept playing repeatedly which brought a faint smile on macro's lips.

Seeing him smile made Mario happy but dead angry too. Why? Because he was breaking a promise, for his attraction towards a girl who is nothing but a pawn for revenge.

"It seems you enjoyed your little date", Mario's cold voice hit Marco's ears making him frown.

"What do you mean?" Marco asked turning his head from where he heard the voice.

Marco turned the bedside lamp on and off while he kept fidgeting with his phone in his hand leaning on the headboard of the bed while his legs are crossed over bed.

"I mean what I say Marco... Did you find her that beautiful that you are forgetting your main motive of marrying her? "Mario asks coldly and a shudder ran down through the entire self of Marco.

Marco's frown never left his face while he kept watching his brother playing with the switch of the lamp.

"Or...did you forget the promise we made years ago......of finding our doll, and bringing her in our lives and making her queen of the throne?". Mario asked through his clenched teeth as his hand yanked the lamp and threw it breaking it into pieces.

Marco's heart clenched at the mention of their doll and how he easily let another girl inside his head who wasn't their doll. His hands fisted at his side while his features turned deadly.

He knows he couldn't love anyone except the little girl who came in their lives when they had nothing yet he let his heart play with his head. But it wasn't Marco's fault he thought inside his head. Odette was carrying aura of their doll, the little girl that she hid behind those dark doe eyes, which only Marco saw, but only when she let him see in his office today.

Marco's jaw clenched so hard that it started shaking in anger, not only towards himself but towards Odette too. There is no doubt Mario sensed the little girl's presence in Odette too but that was a reminder for him to find their doll whose time has come to return to them, where she belonged.

"You started loving her? Don't you Marco?". Mario taunted his brother trying to bring out the demon in him.

But when it happens, it's not his demon but he himself becomes a demon which Mario wanted his brother to be.

"I.DON'T.LOVE.HER", Marco seethed in immense anger.

"Is that so?", Mario mocks him smirking as he approached him.

"Tell me looking into my eyes, brother", Mario added as he stood right in front of Marco looking into his blue eyes shimmering with immense anger.

"I don't love her brother", Marco said looking dead in the eyes of his twin without blinking with his clenched teeth.

"Prove me", Mario demanded making Marco scowl at him.

It was hard for him to push his feelings for Odette aside and...proving –What that supposed to mean? Is this even possible?

He kept thinking not diverting his eyes from Mario's.

"How would I do that?" Marco asked crocking his head to the side waiting for his brother's answer.

A devious smirk plastered on Mario's lips as he spilled those words easily making Marco's heartburn with unfamiliar sensation.

"Share her with me", Mario stated holding his head high.

"After your marriage with her, she will be just another slut of us... Nothing more nothing less", Mario carried on making Marco's chest heave with unfamiliar tension.

Taking a deep breath Marco closed his eyes remembering the only face which was his calmness – his mother's face.

The bright smile on her lips and happiness in her blue eyes when she gave them few Euros to buy ice cream was the last time he saw those azure eyes. However, the very beautiful memory turned into a nightmare when he saw his mother in a pool of her own blood. Her bright eyes weren't bright anymore, they were soul less and that sent shiver to his spine and he snapped his eyes open exhaling a heavy breathe.

Getting himself together, he looked in his twin's eyes and said, "I'm ready to share her with you".

Mario's smirk didn't fade away but it only got wider taking another step towards his brother he stated playing the last card of his game.

"Promise me, I will be the one taking her virginity".

AISLE

~After Odette's Eighteenth Birthday~

Finally the day has came where the beauty will be tied with the beast forever – but in Odette's case she doesn't know that she is going to be struck with two beasts for her whole life. Odette never expected to grow a soft spot for Marco when she heard she has to marry an Italian mafia boss.

But all these months she was thinking just about him. Her life turned boring without him. In addition, the void she is feeling today was not so calming to her already nervous nerves.

"Will you stop pacing here and there... you will ruin your gown". Aurora tells sighing looking at her sister who is worried about something.

"I can't, I am nervous and I can't wait here anymore, I need to talk to him rora", Odette says in a pleading tone making Aurora sigh deeply.

"Outside there are many men related to the mafia, you going out at this time is not a good idea Oddy – not after that attack on you", Aurora said and Odette remained still at the mention of the attack, which happened few months ago.

Without wanting to think about that again, she closed her eyes tightly as she kept breathing in and out.

"Is Mrs Grayson here?" Odette asks in distress.

"I'm afraid she won't be able to come today Oddy, the weather in Rome is not good to take a flight", Aurora tells. Odette's dark doe eyes watered at the memory of Mrs Grayson taking care of her when she was kid. She attending her wedding was important deal for her but sadly, she can't.

Sighing heavily she plops herself on the couch in the dressing room.

Her white fluffy wedding gown was not a joke with seven meters of tail she was looking ethereal. Her dark black hair was tied up in a beautiful bun decorated with flowers and beautiful pins making her look nothing less than a flower goddess.

Her bold eyes and nude pink lips were complimenting her pale skin tone making her look as a fairy fallen from heaven.

Obviously being Odette she didn't wear any heals under her dress in fact she wore a pair of white sneakers. And her reason to switch to sneakers was she could run away if she needed but little did she know her heart won't let her run away from marco.

"But I have to talk to Marco, rora, he was all caring and sweet then he kind of ignored me these whole ass months, even yesterday he didn't call me to wish me my birthday", Odette tells throwing her hands up dramatically.

"I mean the man who took care of me when I was sick, didn't even call me when I got into a dangerous war, those bastards would have kidnapped me if I didn't run from there as soon as I got chance", Odette tells as her eyes gets teary.

"I'm so sorry, Oddy, you had to go through that, trust me Dimitri is on it, he said those people were from China and had some rivalry with Marco, Dimitri will find more details and give them what they deserve", Aurora said softly wiping Odette's doe eyes making her sigh.

"I just … want to know Marco is ready for marriage", Odette whispers hugging her sister close.

"You can talk and sort things out after the wedding, okay?" Aurora smiled encouragingly.

"I guess", Odette shrugged taking a deep breath.

"Mam…, Mr Francois is here", a maid said knocking the door.

"Now put the smile on, don't let our dad think you are sad when you are clearly excited to meet your husband", Aurora teased winking at Odette and she turned thirty shades of red when she understood what her sister was implying.

"Shut up and go", Odette smacked Aurora on her ass making her gasps and rub it while she playfully glared at her little sister.

Soon the room turned less tense as Andre stepped inside with a huge smile on his lips.

"Look at my little princess, how beautiful she is", Andre said admiring her daughter smiling happily as she had natural blush of a bride on her face.

"Thank you dad, you don't look bad either", Odette, said hugging her father tightly.

As soon as his little daughter was in his arms, he sighed heavily and pecked her head with love. When Odette felt something wet on her shoulder, she lifts her head up and her heart sank seeing tears in her father's eyes.

"Dad! Why are you crying?!" Odette said shaking her head.

"You were so eager to kick me out of home, hey! now don't get senti, I will keep coming home even you kick me out right near the gate", Odette said playfully after breaking the hug with her hands resting on her hips.

Andre laughed wiping his tears looking at his daughter lovingly.

"I wish your mother was here", he mentioned and Odette's heart clenched hearing her father's weak voice.

He loved her mother so much that even after her death he neither dated anyone nor had flings. He was a loyal husband. But he happened to drown himself into work to feel less void of his wife.

"I'm sorry, Oddy", Andre said out of nowhere making her frown.

Shaking her head, she immediately stopped her father from saying anything.

"Don't".

"Don't tell that, please, you didn't do anything wrong and I know whatever you did was for my own good", Odette said smiling.

"I never thought that I would tell this but… thank you for bringing Marco in my life, he is really a nice person and I think we can get along… Ahem at least until he doesn't threaten my principal", she adds making Andre and Aurora laugh.

"Come on sweetheart, your beautiful future is waiting for you", Andre said giving his daughter his arm and walked her down the aisle.

Marco choose everything perfect, there is no doubt he will do anything less for his own marriage when it has to be showed off to whole world the treaty between the French and Italian mafia, telling that they are one.

There was choppers around full of media wanting to take Arial view of most eligible bachelor getting married to the great Francois's business's little princess.

The garden around the church was decorated with white fresh Lilies and the tables were set for the buffet with variety of food from all over the world along with a beautiful dance floor setup for after wedding party.

"This was the same church your mother and I got married in", Andre said admiring the beauty of the ancient place where the memories of his own wedding with the love of his life played in his head.

"I bet you cried as a baby", Odette said smirking through the veil teasing her father playfully.

Andre chuckled and countered back saying, "Not when I was getting married but yes after getting married, I cried… but I bet Marco will cry more, after all my daughter is not a little red riding Hood but a little bad wolf", he said chuckling.

"Oh… I guarantee he will", Odette said chuckling along her father.

The heavy doors of the church were opened and the slow hum of the music made Goosebumps rise on Odette's skin.

She didn't lift her head to look around, instead put her head down imagining her mother with her. Standing there and smiling widely at her beautiful little daughter, whom she always used to read the story of a prince Charming who will steal her heart.

Little she didn't tell her that few beauties end up being with beast but the fate choose Odette not only one beast but two, and the little girl knows nothing about their cruel Intentions of ruining her.

Tainting her.

Breaking her.

Until it gets too hard for her to breathe, but little did those monsters know that their souls are in Odette's heart. If it stopped beating… they will stop breathing.

I DO

"You remember this marriage is just a game, you marry that girl, use her, get her signatures and drop her on her ass for her father to collect", those vicious words rolled out of Bianca's mouth without a hint of humanity or respect for another woman, her own kind.

"Yes, ma, I remember", Marco declares sighing heavily.

"Why do you people always reminding me about what I should do, I am a fucking don of Italian mafia", Marco growled getting mad by Bianca and his brother reminding him again and again of Odette's place in his life as if he is a kid who should be reminded to not talk to strangers or accept food from them.

"Because I can't risk the only chance to get back at Andre, remember good and better Marco...Odette is daughter of Andre who is not only mine but your enemy too", Bianca seethed as her eyes narrowed with a glare and warning she is well used to give them off to twins since she took them in her home.

"I know my boy will never disappoint me", Bianca said looking at macro's clenched fists smirking internally as she knows her words were getting in his head.

She never had to manipulate Marco to do something. It was natural for him. He took his pain off by inflicting the pain in others, he enjoyed instinctive hunt, he doesn't think with his head when he see red; he only does what he was trained for – to kill people without a remorse.

So does Mario but Mario need to be manipulated, specially because he was well controlled than Marco. Mario had a naturally merging into room quality without being noticed which made her offer FIB seat for Mario and don chair for Marco.

The work those two brothers does is always together. But Bianca held the strings of them as if they are her puppets. Never in her life had she seen marco feel something beside anger and depression, he was in awe and was falling in love with Odette. She knew it better than anyone did. That is why she made mario to approach marco and confront him about his changing behaviour. Little she didn't know was they promised their hearts and loyalty to a girl who they don't know is Odette herself. No doubt Mario felt her inside her too that's why he was determined to find their doll.

"And...", Bianca carries away speaking adding those sinful words which no woman would be able to utter nor support such act.

"I heard you promised Mario her virginity", she said fixing his tie one last time. Her those words stirred Marco to an extent that he shoved Bianca away as if her presence was disgusting him. In fact it was.

"I did that because I wanted to prove that I don't love her", Marco told dragging every word making sure she put those words in her head crystal clear.

"With whom we sleep, whom we share is none of your business, we are in this together because our enemy is same", Marco growled angrily. His blue cold eyes darkened making Bianca gulp in horror.

Though Marco was her pawn, she wouldn't dare to pull strings making herself the target of his wrath.

"I was... Just..." her words were halted when the door sprung open revealing a stressed Mario.

Both Bianca and Marco fixed themselves and a single nod from Marco was enough for Bianca to understand his order for her to leave them alone.

After they made sure Bianca is no more there to eavesdrop on their conversation Marco spoke.

"Did you find her?"

"She wasn't from Italy, her caretaker Mrs Grayson too", Mario said in his stressed tone sighing.

"For fucks sake we don't know even her full name except Oddy and that caretaker's surname, their details aren't mentioned which obviously states that they used private jet", Mario tells as he pour himself a drink and gulp it down in one go.

"Then how are we supposed to find her?". Marco asked through his clenched teeth.

"It's only possible when we find that caretaker... that too if she is alive", Mario said in his gravel voice. Those words were sounding heavier when they know there aren't many chances to see their doll again.

However, little did they know she was right in front of their eyes dolled up for one of them and walking through the aisle towards them.

~

"Please take care of my daughter", Andre said giving Odette's little hand in macro's huge and rough one in which her hand fit perfectly as if it's made just for him.

"I will", macro promised though he knows he was going to just hurt her.

Pulling Odette upon stage gracefully, macro let her hand go now standing facing her. The priest of Chartres Cathedral started reciting rituals for the wedding of the decade happening again in that place. "Do you have your own vows for the wedding?" the priest asked them with a smile on his face.

Marco simply denied while Odette whispered a no politely.

"Then we will go with traditional vows", priest conformed and they both nodded their heads.

"Mr Marco De Luca, do you take Odette Francois to be your lawfully wedded wife and promise to be true to her in good times and in bad, in sickness and in health. And will love her and honour her all the days of your life?" the priest asked as his voice echoing in between the walls of the church.

"I do", Marco, said clenching his jaw not showing a single doubt to anyone present in the hall.

Bianca and Mario exchanged a victory smiles secretly before the priest started asking the same question to Odette.

114

"Do you, Odette Francois, take Marco De Luca to be your lawfully wedded husband and promise to be true to him in good times and in bad, in sickness and in health? And will love him and honour him all the days of your life?"

"I do", Odette, announced with a huge smile on her lips

"I announce you officially husband and wife, now you may kiss the bride", the priest declared making Odette's heart thunder against her chest.

Marco took a step towards her and took her veil off revealing her beautiful face. Reminding himself it is just a show for revenge nothing more he pushed his unfamiliar feelings away, he brought his lips towards Odette's.

Feeling his breathe she closed her eyes before sucking huge amount of air in anticipation. Marco's hands rested on her waist pulling her close towards him while he let himself devour her soft lips.

But something felt weird to Odette. This kiss wasn't like the previous kisses she shared with him. Those were warm and sweet while this one felt cold and bitter just as his current feelings for hers.

This kiss was supposed to feel special, like the kiss, which cured Snow White from the poison of the Apple, like the kiss, which broke the curse of the sleeping beauty, the kiss that turned frog into the prince, but this kiss was no magical.

A frown painted on Odette's beautiful features her eyes reflecting the confusion, which she couldn't understand. The kiss was short and soulless which stirred many questions in her head but then she saw the similar blue eyes behind Marco, who was smirking at her devilishly making a chill run down her spine.

But she didn't realize the 'I DO' she declared wasn't for the holy vows of the sacred wedding but for a forbidden sinful relation she signed with the devils who are determined to break her to the extent she can't be fixed not even by God himself.

HIS TWIN

The sun set beautifully painting the bright sky now in darkness, there isn't a single star or moon visible in the sky. That is how Odette and Marco's marriage is and so does his vows.

To the contrast for the climate, the church is decorated with beautiful lighting as if it's a Disney fairy tale wedding. It would be if the kiss felt real.

Odette is dancing with Marco, which is a mandatory tradition of mafia families; the first dance was always by newly wedded couple.

"I missed you", Odette whisper tells Marco so only he could hear her.

Twirling her with his one hand, another folded behind he brought her back close to his chest.

"Can I know why?" he whispered huskily in her ear sending shivers to her soul.

Goosebumps rose on Odette's skin which is usual thing that happens whenever he whispers something in her ear and he wouldn't admit it but he likes it.

"You were my fiance why wouldn't I miss you", she asks turning around placing her little palms on his broad shoulder blades and pout her plump nude pink lips at him making his heart skip its beat.

"How about I make it up for the time? Huh?" Marco suggested bringing a forced smile on his lips.

"Really? Then yes", Odette beams at him smiling brightly. Swaying her from one foot to another he admired how tiny his wife feel in his arms. Her curves are worth killing. She naturally smells as jasmine, which any man would like to be high on its fragrance.

"So... We are going to Italy tonight?" Odette asks Hesitantly.

She knows Mrs Grayson is coming and don't want to leave without meeting her, well she also don't know if Marco would be okay to let her meet her old nanny.

"It's already late, baby, we will stay at our honeymoon suit then leave tomorrow morning after breakfast", Marco said giving her a small smile to assure her as she looked worried.

"Oh ok", Odette said disappointed then forced a smile enjoying her first dance with her husband.

Looking into his blue eyes, she could not help but remember those similar eyes, which terrified her.

"Marco…" Odette started thinking if she should tell him about that man but bit her lip thinking it is not right time to ask.

"Yes, baby", Marco, asked nudging her to speak whatever she wanted to.

"T…Tha…that ma….."Bianca cut her off.

"Marco, Odette… Come on, my friends are here and I want to show you off", Bianca stated dragging them from dance floor towards her group of friends.

Marco spoke to them for few minutes before taking his leave, leaving Odette alone with Bianca and her cunning friends.

"Odette…" a woman snickered.

"Isn't it a weird name for princess of French mafia and now queen of Italian mafia?" one of Bianca's friends commented making Odette clench her jaw in anger.

Her mother was the one who named both sisters with love. Odette doesn't like anyone comment about her, especially about her name.

"Either way…… my name suits me, am princess so does Odette from the swan Princess is, Odette name actually originated from French and German languages which means wealthy", Odette tells shrugging her shoulders.

"I think I don't need to drop my bank receipts to show how wealthy I am", Odette said smirking at the woman.

"You…" the woman was cut off when Mario interrupted them smiling.

"Hello beautiful ladies if you don't mind, can I borrow the bride for a dance?" he asked smiling at them.

"Oh Mario, of course son, you don't have to request, it's your right", the woman smirked stating.

"Isn't it, Bianca? of course they are habituated to share women", the cunning woman said laughing a humourless laugh making Odette's blood run cold.

~~~

"Who are you?" Odette asked through her gritted teeth glaring at Mario while he was dancing with her on the dance floor on a slow hum of seventy's music.

"That's disappointing, princess, that you don't even know your husband's elder twin", Mario tells making her narrow her eyes at him frowning.

"What were those ladies saying before?" Odette asked again with her heart in her throat beating rapidly.

She is not dumb to get what they were saying but she wanted to confirm if they were saying truth or just some fabricated lies to get back on her.

"Oh just how strong our brotherhood is, we share women as we used to share toys", Mario tells without any filter.

Odette couldn't think straight for a second, her head screaming her to stop dancing with him and run but his hold on her is painful and strong making her whimper.

"L... Leave me", Odette bites disgusted with his touch on her waist.

"Oh relax princess, I didn't start anything... yet", Mario tells grinning at her cruelly.

"Leave me", Odette grit out twisting her hands from his steel like grip. However, his tight hold on her was so strong that she could feel her skin burning.

"Leave me...Mario", she grit again making Mario chuckle at her mockingly.

"I will tell about you to Marco", she stated glaring at him still trying to free herself.

"Oh and what he will do? Fight his own brother? His own blood?". Mario mocks her smirking at her failed tries to free herself.

If only she wasn't in between whole people she would have kicked him in the groin and freed herself but after finding out that he is her husband's twin brother she doesn't wanted to create a scene.

"I guess you have forgotten the price I gave you in trial room for putting your filthy hands on me Mario? Didn't you?" Odette tells struggling but her struggle wasn't noticed by anyone because of the dim mood lighting which made the dance floor almost dark.

Mario tsks and shakes his head and brings his face close to Odette's ear and whispers, " I didn't forget, princess and I would like to show you that it's working as good as it's used to before", his comment made her lose all her control.

"Leave me or else....." Odette's threat was cut off by a husky voice which she was so familiar with.

"Take your hands off my wife brother", Marco growled angrily but only they could here over the blazing music.

Mario scowled clearly not liking how Marco spoke to him in rude tone just for a girl, that too for the second time in their lives.

"I was just…." Marco abruptly stopped Mario without giving him a chance to speak.

"Baby, it's late, let's go to our suite so you can rest", Marco said smiling warmly at Odette as he snaked his hand around her thin waist making Mario clench his jaw in anger.

"Ok", Odette breathed out in relief seeing her husband rescuing her and taking her to their suite with his hand around her protectively.

Before sitting in the car odette took one last glance at Mario who was glaring at her in hatred and she gulps visibly.

"You never said you had a twin", Odette stated sighing heavily as she kept looking outside the car window as the driver is driving them to their honeymoon suite which Mario booked specially because he wanted to take her tonight.

"If I didn't tell…then that shouldn't have been important", Marco said looking at her fingers which are fidgeting with the engagement ring.

"I have met him before our engagement, he was dick to me so I kneed him in his dick", Odette tells looking at macro to see his reaction.

But he kept his face unaffected but his eyes were dripping amusement for his wife.

"I bet he deserved", Marco states curving his lips slightly up making her chuckle.

"He did but... but he also said something tonight, which... I don't..." Odette stopped in between without saying as she struggled to ask and she bit her lower lip gripping her lip ring between her teeth and chewed on it nervously.

"You can tell me anything baby I am all ears", Marco stated intertwining his hand with hers.

Odette gazed at their joined hands and gulped hard before speaking.

"He said that you both share women as you used to share toys", she tells with her heart on the verge of collapsing.

"I... I want to know from you that... .. That.... Is it true?" she asks her voice coming hoarse with the tension building in her throat.

His face was stoic not giving away any displeasure for asking him that question but when she met his eyes she knows but she didn't wanted to see the truth in them, she closed her eyes tightly not brave enough to hear the disgusting habit of her husband sharing woman with his twin.

But to her horror, Marco stated the truth, which was hard to see, and it felt horrible to hear.

"Yes, it's true, we share women".

Those words escaped easily which she never expected to hear from her husband.

MY WOMAN

MARCO'S POV

I look at my beautiful wife trying hard not to cry in front of me, but the day she asked me, to not leave her again; she gave me key to her eyes, which reflect truth.

She is hurt, angry, this is better. She shouldn't be broken – like me.

First time I saw life was in her eyes after these eleven years and I will not be the person to take that life away from her.

I will do anything in my best to keep her safe. My enmity is with her father and I will make sure that man begs for my mercy and beg me to kill him as soon as possible.

I see her doe dark brown eyes shimmer with tears in the darkness of the car. For a long moment no one spoke another word I just kept looking into her eyes wanting to hear her lash at me.

"Those girls we shared weren't my wife Oddy", I said and before I could stop the name Oddy it rolled out of my tongue surprising me.

Oddy... The little girl who held my hand when people were disgusted to stand beside me, the girl who let me play with her when everyone insulted, the girl who called herself as my friend, the girl who wiped my tears...... I see her in my wife, in Odette.

Is it possible that our doll is Odette?

No it can't be. Odette was raised behind the closed door and the enmity between Italian and French mafia was so bad those days that they would have killed each other right then and there.

Shaking off those thoughts, I look at my wife again. She is confused, "Wha... What do you mean macro?" she asked pleading for the truth, which would not hurt her.

I almost wanted to laugh because there is no such truth, which wouldn't hurt. It hurts and that's why I like to hear truth.

Whether in business or in my personal life. I hate lies and I torture liars enjoying blood-curling screams they choke.

"I mean what I said Oddy", I tell her seriously pressing my words to show her how truthful I am.

"You are *my wife*... *Mine* and I will be damned if I share you with anyone, hell not even with my brother with whom I shared every woman I slept with", I tell looking into her teary eyes.

"Y... you will choose me over your brother?" Odette asked with her lip quivering as she hugged herself tightly trying to find comfort.

"I will choose you first, but I guess you know blood is always thicker than water, baby, specially in mafia, I just hope you don't get yourself in trouble from which I can't save you", I tell her looking into her eyes giving a slight warning beforehand.

This wedding might be our path to revenge but I will make sure Odette doesn't get hurt in any way, after we get what we want I will let her free. Away from me, away from the danger around me.

I can't risk her life again; I wanted to run to her to see if she was hurt when that bastard Chan tried to grow balls to go behind *my woman*. I didn't give him death painless but worst.

~**Flashback**~

"How did you find about where and when she was leaving?" I ask him stalking him around as he was whimpering pathetically as a dog struck in storm.

"Please... Please Marco, let me go, I swear I will never return back to your lands", Chan begs choking on blood making me smirk evilly.

"Tsk, tsk, tsk, tsk, how shameful of you Chan, the Chinese mafia boss, the drug dealer, women trafficker, illegal weapon industry owner...and what not! You are begging me to free you just after thirty minutes of fun my boys had with you?" I chuckle throwing my head behind.

His hands are tied up to the ceiling with the help of extended rods and ropes specially for torturing my enemies and he became my worst enemy from my alley by going after *my woman, my Odette.*

125

"I didn't started my game yet Chan, you know how mad I get if I don't get to play my game", I tell mocking him enjoying his every cry of agony.

"Please I beg you, I will send all the women we have taken from Italy for our sex clubs, please leave me", Chan begged his eyes are disgustingly bruised and jaw broken with a bleeding nose, he doesn't look any better than a bleeding pig.

"Hmmm, quiet and impressive offer but don't you think I can take anything to everything when I kill you?", I ask him raising my eyebrows.

"Please I beg you", the man who was honoured with mafia throne kept begging and pleading for his life making me enjoy his execution more than anything.

"Tsk, tsk, tsk, *there is no mercy when you play with the devil*, Chan, not when *I am my own demon*", I state taking a last look of his bloody face.

"What was the game?" I hum as if I forgot.

Draco chuckled as he raised his eyebrows knowing very well am taking my time playing with the man who tried to hurt my woman. *Mine.*

"I guess its fire or water boss", he tells smiling cunningly at Chan making his eyes widen as big as saucers.

"Hmmm, but it's kind of easy death for people who tried to go behind my back to get my woman, Draco", I state humming a mindless tune while stalking chan.

"Get me a bucket", I order and one of my guards rushed out to get one.

"Hang this bastard upside down", I order one and he oblige as I asked for.

They tied Chan's legs together and hanged him to the same rod and he started struggling trying to free himself but it isn't possible. If he freed himself successfully I would like to hunt him as an animal and I know I will enjoy every second of it.

"What are you doing?"

"Please leave me".

"I swear I will never think about going your back".

"Please forgive me".

The pathetic cries of him was fucking music to my ears and I can feel adrenaline pumping in my blood due to the excitement thinking the new way of killing am going to start with him.

"Pocket knife", I order and Draco throws it towards me and I catch it gracefully without even turning around.

I kick the bucket as it stays right below Chan's head and I smile at him evilly looking into his eyes.

I stab the knife right into his throat and blood splatters all over my face but I didn't flinch. He chokes and coughs with the small knife still in his throat as blood runs out from him as if someone opened the tap.

I let the bucket fill with his blood holding his head aright. He is still alive, it will take only few more minutes for him to leave his body painfully but I am not going to give him that time.

I gestured with my hand, understanding what I am asking one of my boys lowered the rope and Chan's head was dunked in his own blood.

Whimpering and choking in his own blood gasping for air he struggled for two minutes before dying, as he deserved.

"Whoever tries to go behind my woman, make sure they die in their own blood then burn them before throwing their ashes in Mediterranean", I stated before leaving the dungeon knowing very well that Draco will make sure do whatever I said with Chan's body.

No one dares to touch my woman, my woman.

~**present**~

My woman?!

Why the fuck did I even think that?!

No, she isn't emotionally but professionally. She is now Odette Marco de Luca – because she is carrying my name it's my responsibility to protect her then I will leave her to let her live her own life but all my reasons of pushing her away vanished when her soft rose petals like lips smashed on my own taking my soul little by little through the magical kiss – just as in those fairy tales my mom used to read for me when I was a kid.

HIS DOLL

AUTHOR'S POV

Odette started kissing macro pouring all her emotions she was feeling – happy, grateful, relief and specially love!

Was she supposed to fall in love with a monster who didn't show his real side yet?

Debatable because he is the same monster who is saving her from the dangers around her which are creeping up on her lively life.

"Oddy", macro murmured in between the kiss groaning at her sweet taste pulling her on his laps.

He couldn't control himself when he lost all his senses in that magical kiss which Odette wanted it to be her wedding kiss.

"Marco…" Odette moaned closing her eyes tightly when macro started rocking her on his hard girth with his hands on her plump ass possessively.

Both were eager to devour each other and were glad to have a car partition between them and driver because no matter what macro wasn't the one who would let his woman seen or heard by another man who isn't him.

"*Shhh, only I could hear your sweet moans, baby*", macro growled animalistically and nibbled her lower lip making her whimper.

"I like this Alpha Marco", Odette giggled teasingly making Marco chuckle and tug her hair, yank it behind making her whimper but making sure she doesn't get hurt and feel pleasure.

"This alpha Marco is *daddy* to you", Marco growled in her ear huskily pressing his lips on her throat and Odette gulped audible as goosebumps formed on her skin making him smirk against it.

"You like it baby?" he asked looking into her doe eyes filled with lust and another emotion he couldn't describe it was unfamiliar to him, at least since a long time.

Odette bit her lower lip as her eyes searched for those blue iris, which are dilated in lust as much as she is desiring.

They both want one thing; Odette wanted Marco as much as Marco wanted her. Now there are no boundaries in between them as they are married and Odette is above eighteen, which means she can give her consent.

Marco wasn't the person who goes following legal rules but he also wasn't the man who fucked any girl under eighteen, even when they gave him their consent.

Without able to form any words without fear of moaning Odette simply nodded her head making Marco smirk. He is a dominant who will set rules on his bed for Odette and she is obviously a brat who would like to break them and Marco would be more than thrilled to punish the little brat and take her roughly as he wanted until her legs give up and she wouldn't be able to walk for weeks.

As soon as car stopped in front of the enormous hotel Marco opened the door and carried his bride in his strong arms. Odette was clinging on his steel like shoulders wrapping her arms around his neck while looking into his blue eyes.

"You have no idea what I wanted to do to you baby", Marco said grinning at her making her core clench in unfamiliar need.

Noticing the little thing she did in his arms he smirked and said, "Don't worry I intend to take care of your problem tonight, without punishing you for not answering me in words", he said making Odette's deer like eyes widen.

Opening the suite door with one hand, he carried Odette to their bedroom as if she weights nothing.

The bedroom was decorated with blood red roses with white crisp sheets on the bed with scented candles lit adding a romantic touch for everything.

Odette eyes widened in awe as she saw the beautiful room she ever saw in her life. The glass windows were till the ceiling from the floor giving a beautiful view of the France city lit with lights twinkling as if stars in the sky.

"This is beautiful", Odette gasped in awe making Marco smile at her. "Not more than you baby", he cooed before throwing her on the bed roughly making her yelp.

"Oh my god", Odette gasped giggling but Marco took off his black coat and tie throwing them God knows where and took his shoes off standing on the floor bare feet.

Smirking at his wife, he unbuttoned few buttons of his shirt and sleeves and rolled them making him look sexier than before.

His tattoos on display for his wife's eyes as she stared at them appreciating the beauty on his Greek god like tanned skin. His abs and muscles painfully traced by the white shirt clinging on his perfectly sculpted body as if he is from heaven – *no from hell, he is lust himself while his aura is temptation* and Odette was getting dripping wet just seeing her husband who was looking at her as if she was his prey and he is a hungry lion.

Marco climbed on the bed and Odette's heart was beating wildly as he was trailing kisses all over her leg after taking off her shoes smirking. He knew she wouldn't have wore any heels under her gown and he enjoyed every second of it, she looked tiny and cute yet sexy as fuck in that wedding gown which he tore roughly making her gasp.

"Oh my god", Odette gasped in horror but Marco quickly shut her up kissing her lips passionately yet roughly taking his time tasting every inch of her mouth with his tongue inside her and Odette tried to kiss him back with same intensity. But he was a fucking alpha he would never allow Odette try to dominate him nor go slow and soft with her.

Odette moaned into kiss making Marco groan hungrily as his hands roamed all over her soft body before he broke the kiss and attacked her neck leaving multiple hickeys on her pale skin which he would never allow her to cover.

"M*ine*", he growled as he tore her white lace bra and latched on her perky pink pebbles sucking, biting and nibbling on them while he kept pinching and flicking the other one with his rough hand in between his long tattooed finger.

Odette moaned out loud whimpering under him with immense need as she tried to get some friction down there, chuckling he did same with her other pebble blowing his breathe on the sensitive nub and rubbing his hard erection on her core above her irritatingly wet panties.

"Fuck!" Marco growled as he tore the barrier away in between him and her pink glistening pussy as he crawled below in between her legs. Odette was panting hard as her breathing turned rigid and heavy and she could feel her throat getting dry because of her moans due to his sinful attack on her lips, neck and perfect round globes.

Kissing his way on her thighs making her legs shiver in anticipation while he moved a bit further to her core.

"You are dripping wet for me baby", Marco growled huskily seeing his wife's arousal which was caused by him.

"Marco..." Odette whimpered making Marco smirk. He stopped and sat on his heels looking at his wife's flushed face, which was looking more beautiful under the candle light. She was biting her lower lip mercilessly as her eyes are hooded with lust and need.

Smirking at her, he traced his finger from her pierced boobs to her belly button tugging her jewellery playfully; he slapped his hand on her pussy making her yelp and moan before he growled.

"It's daddy", he said looking at her now closed legs and ordered with authority.

"Spread those pretty legs for daddy as a good girl you are".

Odette need not to be told twice while his dominant aura stirred all her senses and she obliged as her husband ordered pleasing him.

Marco released a satisfied hum while he kissed her thighs biting playfully and slowly teasingly licked her slick slit and growled tasting her arousal.

"FUCK! SO SWEET!" he growled in delight and attacked her lower lips licking and kissing them making her scream for him.

He thrust his tongue in her tight little cunt and Odette gripped sheets tightly trashing due to the immense pleasure she was feeling first time in her life.

Her untouched part was now being licked, bitten, groped, eaten and tongue fucked by her husband.

He pushed her on the bed with his hand on her lower stomach as he continued his pleasurably painful torture in between her legs.

Soon Marco felt her tightening around his tongue, he growled sending vibrations to her core, and she screamed releasing herself all over her husband's mouth.

134

Marco licked and ate every drop of her sweetness moaning against her sore core. When he pulled himself away from her wiping his mouth before licking his lips trying to memorize her honey like sweetness on his tongue.

Odette's was already passed out because of her life's first ever orgasm. The corner of her eyes was glistening with tears, which Marco knows those aren't because of pain, but the pleasure, which he introduced to her.

Smiling softly while he draped the duvet on her naked body pressing a kiss on her forehead he murmured.

"Good night my doll".

WHAT IF

MARIO'S POV

From the day I let my eyes fall on her, that girl grabbed all my attention, the way she seduced me to distract from her attack on my dick made me fucking hard and mad that I wanted to slap her and fuck her at the same time.

And I swear I would have done that the very next time I saw her for that I followed her. To my surprise, she wasn't that bitch she was with me. Instead, she was kind. The way she saved two little puppies reminded me about our doll.

And then it hit me that we almost forgot her, we were going to bring her into our lives when we are done with our revenge until

135

then we had to keep her safe and safe means by not searching for her because once we find her we will never leave her, not until one of us is alive.

I was beyond mad when I found my brother was growing interest in our enemy's daughter. People might think that Odette haven't done anything, hell I know Marco thinks same but what would growing feelings towards Odette will bring? – Weakness.

Yes, weakness, once Marco realize that he fell in love with Odette he wouldn't be able to hurt her. We hurting Andre for revenge will eventually hurt Odette and I know better than anything no one in this world would be able to love killer of their parents.

She will hate Marco and so in love Marco wouldn't want to be hated by his love so he will do what it needs to keep her happy – instead of our revenge, she will become his priority and all the hard work we did all these years to build our name in mafia families, keeping our record clean so that we didn't get caught without taking our revenge was fucking hard then the humiliation, the pain, the hate we have experienced in our childhood was hardest. No child deserved it, but then our little innocent doll came in our lives, showing us how it feels to be liked by someone else who isn't our mom.

The girl who considered us as her friends…… she deserves world, I will make sure to give her and somehow I think it's time to bring her into our lives. I have to find her as soon as possible to bring Marco out of that bitch, Odette's grasps.

~~~

Driving to the hotel suite I booked and decorated specially for Odette to take her first time was still in my head. That shit was something romantic I never did in my life but I never fucked a virgin before neither did Marco so it's fair for us to give her that when we are going to take something from her brutally.

Thinking about fucking that tight virgin cunt got me on fucking hard on. I can't wait another minute to thrust my length into her.

"Hello ma", I answer the call via Bluetooth.

"Are you going to take her tonight?" Bianca asked and I can see a smirk on her face without even seeing her.

"Hmm, Marco promised me her virginity, knowing the looks he was giving her whole day, am sure he wants to fuck her today", I tell chuckling.

"I don't want to be late if he is that eager", I add as I drive towards the suite.

"From what I have seen he was also looking out for her from you", she stated with her voice coming hoarse as if she is drunk.

"Oh that was just to show off, we can't risk her going to Andre knowing our true intentions", I said shrugging my shoulders.

First, I was angry then I thought what he did was best; we would have risk everything and all the plan would go in vain when we didn't even got her signatures on the papers.

"Are those papers ready?" I ask her wanting to make sure everything is ready before we take her to Rome. Yes, we aren't taking her to our real home in Italy.

"Yes, papers are ready, better you fuck some senses into her along your dicks so that she doesn't make much fuss in signing them", she said and I can hear hate in her voice.

"Don't worry I will make sure", I said throwing my car keys to the valet of the hotel walking towards the lift to go to the top floor I booked.

"Good, don't let her meet anyone tomorrow, you will bring her to Rome by helicopter from the roof of the same building", she ordered and hung up the call before I reply. Sighing to myself a wicked smile played on my lips.

Every step I was taking to the suite was exciting to me to the extent making my cock twitch in my pants. As soon as I opened the door of the suite, I heard moan.

Fucking moan?!

Did Marco started fucking her?

He promised me her virginity, no, he wouldn't fuck her.

But the moans and screams were telling something else. Pouring myself a drink, I sat on the couch letting him have his time if and only if he doesn't put his dick in her.

The door opened revealing a strained Marco but that smile on his lips caught my attention. As soon as he saw me, it vanished.

I don't like it.

"I see you did a good job making her ready to take me", I said smirking but my eyes were on his hands.

He always clenches his hands tightly if he was angry and his jaw twitch when he lies. I know my brother that well that I could understand his mood without his words and that's why I know Odette is getting into his head.

"She passed out and I don't want you to go near her", he said his hands fisted.

'Clearly brother, you are angry because I wanted to fuck that girl, you already let her get into your head', I think internally nodding my head.

Looking into his eyes, I demanded, "then when you will fulfil your promise?" To be honest I expected him to deny but he surprised me.

His jaw clenched as he tightened his fists and his knuckles turned white.

"We should wait until we take her out of France, we don't know if her family wants to meet her tomorrow for saying goodbye, she isn't dumb that she will fear us and not try to alert Andre, we can't risk everything now, not when the bird is in our cage", he said looking straight into my eyes.

For a reason I know my brother isn't lying and am glad that he choose his revenge over the little crush on the girl.

"I got news from Stefan, Mrs Grayson is in Rome", I announced with a smile on my lips.

"I ordered him to search where she is living so that we could find our doll soon", I said pouring another glass of whiskey for my brother.

"Here", I handed him the drink while his expression was of relief and happiness. I could see the smile he wanted to bite off but not now, not when it is related to our doll.

"You could smile, you know our doll would love to see you smile often", I tell him chugging my drink as he held his glass.

"What do you think, how does she now looks like?" Marco asked taking a sip of his drink then looked into my eyes.

I frowned then closed my eyes to see the little girl still playing in my imagination. Her dark black hair tied into pigtails, her dark brown eyes, pink pouty lips, her cute wide smile, her pale skin...... everything so ethereal and similar........ Similar to Odette.

I snapped my eyes open immediately and exhaled heavily. No, it can't be, she can't be our doll. There are familiarities but that couldn't be possible.

"You saw her right?" to my agony Marco asked with half smile on his lips adding to my already distress state.

"I... I..." I couldn't deny because I saw her.

I saw Odette.

"I know, I saw her too and that's why I want you to find our doll as soon as possible, so that we could send Odette away from our lives", He said before chugging the whole glass of whiskey in one go and slammed it on the counter of the bar.

"What if our doll is Odette?" I asked stopping him from going away.

He is still facing the door with his back towards me. His muscles clenched uncomfortably before he released a sigh.

"Knowing what we are going to do to Odette and her father I know she would hate me, our doll would hate me and I love our doll so much that if she doesn't love me I will die", saying those words without turning back he left shutting the door with a loud thud.

My eyes darkened at the thought of our doll hating us. No, she couldn't hate us, not when we love her with our everything.

Fisting the empty glass in my hand so hard I didn't realize it shattered and the broken pieces poked my palm while the blood dripped on the white marble floor.

"If our doll hates me there is no doubt that I will kill her, Marco, that's how much I love her, that I couldn't imagine her living without one of us", I growled slamming my hand on the counter and left the suite after locking the door behind me.

A SINGLE TEAR

ODETTE'S POV

If someone have said me few months ago I will be waking naked in my honeymoon suite after having my life's first and mind blowing orgasm given by my husband I would have laughed on them. No, I would have punched them into a pulp.

But now here I am rubbing my puffy eyes as I yawn and stretch walking up to the most beautiful view of the France. Looking at the blue sky glowing with the bright sun beaming at me with white fluffy clouds decorating it in most beautiful way nature can provide.

A huge smile plastered on my face as I realized am still naked with only white comforter on my body and the side of my bed was cold and empty.

Anyone would have felt bad waking up alone but I was grateful because I could collect my thoughts and not flash my red face as soon as macro woke up.

Biting my lip, I couldn't help but remember the night with my husband. How he kissed me, how he said am not the one he could share. That wasn't romantic but animalistic.

Low-key I felt bad that he didn't tell he loves me and he wouldn't think of sharing me, but when one says that they wouldn't share something with anyone that means that they love them right?

I know he loves me or else he wouldn't have taken care of me leaving his important meeting and I could see in his eyes he loves me, it might take some time for us to accept and express but it will happen one day eventually and I am sure about it.

Shaking my head as I chuckle at the thoughts and walk into the en suite to take a shower.

After a warm shower I dry myself wearing blue jeans with white shirt above my grey lace set and didn't mind wearing a jacket today, it's pretty sunny and not cold outside.

As I come out of the washroom with my semi dry hair I never thought, I would see this man today, not at least the very morning.

Mario looked at me from head to toe and wolf whistles making my jaw clench and I fist my hands walking towards him angrily.

He is sitting on the edge of the bed with a smug expression making my blood boil more that it does when I see this piece of shit.

There is no doubt he is as handsome as macro, their blue eyes are similar yet unfamiliar. I could read macro's easily but mario's… it's like he drew a curtain on them to hide his true self from me.

"What the hell are you doing here?" I seethe at him with my nostrils flaring in anger. That wasn't a sexy thing but I don't want to look sexy in front of him, I wouldn't mind picking my nose in front of him if that would keep him away from me.

I laughed internally at my crazy thoughts. God! This man is getting on my nerves.

"You are glowing", he comments taking me off guard.

I expected a dirty comment from him but he didn't… and when am thinking this, he proved me wrong.

"I guess my brother did a great work last night", he said with that stupid smirk on his face.

"That's none of your fucking business you asshole", I glare at him wishing I had Aladdin's magical lamp so I could ask for three favours.

One I wish Mario disappears.

Two I wish Mario vanishes.

Three I wish Mario fade away.

Ughhh God!!!!! Give me fucking patience!!! For fucks sake!!!

"No matter how much I like your dirty mouth I would like it shut around my cock". He tells smirking at me.

This bastard is getting off by getting on my nerves.

Do not give him what he is asking for Odette... I kept telling myself as I closed my eyes and took a deep breath in and out twice to gain my non-existing patience.

"Why the hell are you here?" I demand opening my eyes. As I fold my hands on my chest trying to look intimidating.

That bastard made himself more comfortable hearing me and that stupid smirk got wider.

"I like this", he said nodding his head on my folded arms and I narrow my eyes on him glaring.

"You know you don't look intimidating by folding your hands...... in fact you look a good obedient student who is ready to take professor's cock whenever and wherever he demands", he states biting his lower lip.

"I'm not into role play but I would like to if it's..."

144

I didn't let him speak further. He was wearing off my every level of patience.

"GET OUT!" I yell at him.

"GET THE FUCK OUT YOU ASSHOLE", I scream at him pointing my finger towards the door in case he forgot from where he came in.

He stood on his feet dragging himself lazily towards me. Not wanting to step back but I did when he was coming close in my personal space.

I was backed off on the washroom door and he placed his both palms on each side of my body making it impossible to move without touching him.

I didn't even realize I was shaking in anger until he pointed it out.

"You are shaking princess... Calm down".

Even I wanted to kick him in the balls as I did first time I met him, I couldn't move.

"Just breathe in and breathe out", he said again, his face so close to mine, his breathe fanning my right cheek as his blue eyes scan my own dark brown as if he knew those since years.

"Just breathe", he whispered again and I caught a faint smell of whiskey and peppermint. He smells so different from macro.

What the fuck am thinking, I shouldn't compare my husband to this asshole.

But surprisingly I found myself breathing in and out as he asked. I swear to God I saw a genuine smile on his lips where he always wears a smug cocky look or that stupid smirk.

"Good girl", he cooed and I held my breathe right in my lungs with my thighs clenched.

I shouldn't feel like this, not like this when am fucking married to his twin.

Oh Jesus!! Forgive me!!! I cry internally as I look into his blue azure eyes, which held secrets. Secrets I wanted to explore but too afraid to fall in the web of lies.

"I just wanted to ask a single question and you will answer me in a yes or no, no more question", he said and I found myself nodding.

"Good, have you ever happened to visit Italy?" he asked and this time I saw an emotion different from anger or disgust towards me.

Its anticipation, eagerness and hope.

But why?

I shook my head as no.

I don't remember going to Italy, never in my life.

"No?" he asked again and I whispered a low "No".

His eyes darkened as he clenched his jaw so hard that I could hear his teeth grit. I gulped visibly but this time in fear.

Why the fuck I am afraid of him?

"No, I never went to Italy, never in my life", I stated confidently.

Because that's what the truth is, I don't remember going anywhere out from my home.

He didn't spoke but simply nodded his head walking back from me and suddenly I felt cold.

His eyes speaking a promise, promise of destruction, I want to fold myself into a ball and cry. Those eyes are dangerous and sinister. Marco never saw me with that amount of hate or anger. Not even one percent of it.

Mario slammed the door hard after getting out from the room and I released the breathe I was holding in. I fell on my knees holding my chest and a single tear escaped my eye.

"What's wrong with me?" I questioned myself wiping the tear away.

Getting myself together, I didn't think twice to call my sister. Thankfully, she answered my call in first ring and her motherly voice gave me the comfort I would seek from my mother if she was alive.

"Rora, will you please meet me at the suite am staying, I want to talk to you", saying that I hung up the call knowing my sister would run bare feet for me if I needed something.

Right now, I needed the warmth and comfort, which my mother failed to provide me by accepting death.

FORBIDDEN QUESTION

AUTHOR'S POV

"Oddy, they are not letting me in", Aurora said on the call to Odette who was sitting with Marco on the breakfast table eating her pancakes while Marco was eating eggs and bacon with some salad.

"Marco, the hotel receptionist aren't letting my sister in", Odette asked Marco while holding her phone in her right hand while she was poking strawberry with a fork with her left hand.

"Obviously they wouldn't, it's our honeymoon suite baby, I asked for privacy", Marco said making Odette blush.

Aurora cleared her throat indicating that she was still on line while she was suppressing her own smile.

"Ahem, can you ask them to let my sister in? I want to talk to her before we leave", Odette requested giving puppy eyes to Marco.

"I will inform them to let your sister in", Marco said taking his phone from his suit pocket and called the Receptionists letting them know to that they can send Aurora in.

As soon as aurora said, she was in front of the door odette sprung off her seat giving a small peck on Marco's cheek as a thank you and ran towards the door to welcome her sister.

~~~

"I should tell that Marco choose best place for your wedding night", Aurora said looking outside of their bedroom's balcony admiring the view.

Odette blushed again, which was not her type at all. However, Aurora caught her little sister blushing and wanted to tease her more.

"Did you call me here to tell how your night with your husband was?" Aurora teased making Odette's eyes as wide as saucers.

While Marco was listening to their talk secretly standing behind the door he just shook his head thinking odette called her sister for girly talk and rolled his eyes leaving them alone so that he could check if Draco has everything settled for their departure to Rome.

Odette shook her head in disbelief at her sister's comment and went towards the bedroom door to check if Marco or Mario was there because she wanted to talk something important with her sister.

Sighing as she saw no one nearby, she locked the door and turned and glared at her sister playfully making Aurora chuckle.

Soon Odette's face turned into frown as she thought about what Mario asked but wasn't able to gather dare to ask the lingering question on her tongue to her sister.

"Rora... I wanted to ask something important" Odette said in gravel voice now Aurora felt the thickening atmosphere around them too.

"What is it Oddy?" Aurora asked softly so Odette could feel comfortable to talk about the problem she is in.

"I... did... I..." Odette stuttered badly and groaned yanking her hair furiously.

"Oddy, relax and talk to me, I know you are worried and missing Mrs Grayson but I promise I will find a way to ask dad to convince Marco about her meeting you at your place", Aurora assured her sister trying to ease her worry.

"It's not... I mean I want to meet Mrs Grayson and I will ask Marco to let her in but... but I want to ask something else", Odette said gulping hardly.

The questions which were forbidden to ask was now going to be asked by Odette and the way Mario saw her with disgust and anger while his eyes also screamed hurt and pain she couldn't stop thinking about him and the question he asked again and again.

If anyone could answer that question, it should be Aurora or Mrs Grayson because Andre wasn't going to talk anything about the past.

Taking a deep breath Odette saw in her sister's eyes begging for answers and truth without uttering a single word. Knowing her sister too well Aurora understood and nodded her head assuring her to give answers.

"Have I ever been to Italy before?" Odette asked making Aurora's heart drop in her stomach. Her eyes widened and her jaw dropped open thinking of the worst possibility Odette remembered her past.

If Odette not remembering her past was painful then she remembering that horrible past would be worse than anything that she would want to take her own life.

Odette frowned watching Aurora's expression, which gave her answer as clear as fresh water. Because as much as Aurora can read her sister so does Odette.

150

Odette frowned looking at Aurora who was battling with herself if she should ask her if she remember anything or have any dream about her past but she couldn't when a knock on the door interrupted them.

Scowling Odette went to open the door and found a worker in her maid dress standing in front of her door. She bowed politely without even looking at Odette she said what she was told to do.

"Mrs De Luca, Master Marco is waiting for you in the hallway", hearing her Odette clenched her teeth while Aurora sighed in relief that she wouldn't have to answer Odette's questions.

Nevertheless, Odette wasn't the one who would let go this easily. "Tell him to wait for few minutes I need to freshen up then I will join him", Odette lied smoothly before dismissing the maid.

"Rora, tell me, I need to know if I have been to Italy", Odette pleaded making Aurora sigh in relief.

"But... why Oddy? Is anything wrong? Why suddenly this question?" Aurora asked smiling at her sister trying to act as if she asked nothing serious.

"Nothing I just wanted to know", Odette said not wanting to mention about Mario asking her the same question.

Hearing this Aurora sighed mentally and thought, this means she just wanted to know, if she knew anything else Odette wouldn't lie to me.

"No Oddy, you know how was our dad, he never sent us out from the mansion", Aurora lied without stuttering. That is what she and whole family kept telling Odette from that horrible day happened in Francois family. When they didn't lose one but two special members of their family.

Aurora hastily went towards the door to check no one is listening before she said the important thing she found about Bianca. Sighing no one was around she turned and hugged her sister tightly.

"Odette I wanted to tell you something, it's really important and I couldn't tell you before because it took time for Dimitri to find it out", Aurora said making Odette frown.

What could make her sister this worried? Odette thought and broke the hug to see in her sister's eyes.

"What is it?", Odette asked and the expression on Aurora was screaming danger.

Odette gulped hardly waiting for her sister to speak. Still looking around Aurora held Odette's hands before telling her.

"Stay away from Bianca, that woman is bad news, I found out that she wasn't the wife of previous Italian boss, Elijah De Luca, they didn't marry nor she gave him divorce as she claims, Marco and Mario aren't her own children, they were adopted from streets", Aurora said making Odette gasp.

Odette's heart was in her throat hearing that. "No way, it's clear from the way they love her..." Odette tried to deny the fact that Bianca is not their real mother.

"Yes, if they love her like that, there must be some hidden secrets in the family which you have to stay alert and away from them, Bianca doesn't like people take her power, as you wished to have a normal life, stay so, go to college and don't get involved in their mafia business for your own good, until Dimitri brings me more information about her, we can't talk about this in phone, I will find a way because of Russian and Italian mafia enmity", Aurora said hastily.

"I don't understand anything", Odette said sighing heavily shaking her head.

When Aurora tried to speak, further they were interrupted by a masculine voice making their blood turn cold.

"What do you don't understand, Odette De Luca?" Mario asked through his clenched teeth. His every word held threat making both sisters' gulp in horror.

NEW HOME

AUTHOR'S POV

Aurora was the first one to speak, gulping the lump forming in her throat she cleared it before speaking, wishing that he didn't hear anything so that her lie could get them out clean.

"Odette's favourite blanket was missing when we were packing her things but today I found it in our dad's office, but she tells she didn't take it there, so we don't understand how it ended up there", she lied smoothly.

Staying with Dimitri and men in her mafia family she feel less intimidating of men like them, where as Odette is always a trouble and rebel against them by lying and going against their rules so honestly Aurora was surprised her sister didn't come up faster with a lie.

Mario diverted his gaze from Aurora to Odette and asked, "So you have packed everything right? We should keep moving, Marco is waiting for you", Mario said coldly.

Nodding her head to him, Odette hugged her sister one last time and of course it was devastating to say good-bye to her family and she ended up crying a lot.

Mario rolled his eyes thinking she was being dramatic and waited for her to finish it so that they could leave as soon as possible.

"Please take care of yourself, I love you", Aurora whispered in her little sister's ear making her choke on her own sob.

"Shhh, it's okay, you can do this", she murmured again lovingly.

Odette nodded her head while breaking the hug and wiped her tears not wanting to show any weakness in front of Mario more than she already did.

"Love you", Odette said before leaving.

The helicopter was waiting on the terrace and it was already started. Marco who was waiting for Odette smiled at her as soon as he saw her coming along with Mario.

He didn't miss the glares they were giving each other but as soon as her eyes fell on her husband, she smiled widely running towards him as a little girl.

"Come on let's go", Marco said as he snaked his arm around her waist and another tucked in the trouser pocket gracefully. The man is ethereal. His blue eyes were shimmering in sunlight as if they are crystals, his dark brown hair messy yet perfect in its own twisted way making him look breath taking.

Odette bit her lip before glancing around the city, this was the place she was born, she is leaving it behind but with a promise that she will come back one day. She smiled at Marco before nodding her head indicating that she is ready.

As Marco settled her and secured the seat belt, he did his own.

"Mario isn't coming with us?" Odette asked in a loud voice so that Marco could hear her.

He put headsets on her after putting one on himself and gestured the mic through which they could talk properly without any problem.

THEIR DOLL BY SKILLED SMILE

Odette smiled and asked, "Isn't Mario coming with us?", again and this time Marco half smiled before answering.

"No, baby, he is coming by road with ma and Draco, we are going by helicopter because I wanted to show you our properties", Marco said making Odette smile widely in excitement.

"Oh my god! Really?" Odette gasped while Marco chuckled at her poking her nose and nodded his head towards the view they were flying on.

Odette was seeing the Rome in awe with her twinkling eyes, every building and every landscape made her coo and appreciate how beautiful and pretty the city is.

"Is this Rome?" Odette asked with wide eyes.

"Yes, we live in Rome, baby", Marco said giving a faint smile.

"Oh my god! I have seen this city in movies and I love it, I never thought you live here", Odette commented looking at Marco with those doe happy eyes.

"We live here", Marco added and Odette felt those butterflies in her stomach again.

Holding her hand, he nodded his towards a certain huge building before saying.

"That's sapienza, you will be studying there as I promised", Marco says making Odette gasp.

"Thank you so much", Odette tells gratefully pecking his cheek making him smile.

"Marco, I wanted to ask something, can I call my nanny to meet me here? She missed the wedding because flights were cancelled because of bad weather", Odette tells giving Marco puppy eyes.

Marco smirk at her tracing his thumb on her lips and Odette parts them eventually sucking a deep breath, this made Marco's smirk wider as he leans forward with his lips close to Odette's.

"I guess you have figured out how to convince me using your those doe eyes", Marco rasped against Odette's lips making her whimper.

She closed her eyes immediately ashamed of how she reacted to the closeness and turned red in embarrassment.

Marco simply smirked at her reaction before pressing his lips on the corner of her own petals.

"I will consider everything you ask for princess, you don't need to give me those eyes for making me do what you want", he said making Odette open her eyes.

She was mesmerized in his azure eyes, when he growled huskily.

"Solo un fottutoassaggio del tuo e sonogià in ginocchio per te", Marco's this confession made Odette blush furiously as she widened her eyes gesturing to the pilot.

(Just one fucking taste of yours and am already on my knees for you)

"Don't worry, he doesn't know Italian", Marco stated assuring her with an amused look on his face.

Odette sighed smacking Marco's chest making a throaty chuckle erupt from his chest, which warmed her whole heart.

~~~

"This is your and master Marco's room", a maid showed the room making Odette sigh.

She smiled at the maid and nodded her head as her eyes trailed from one corner to another. The room was black in colour with grey furniture with a hint of white. It's simple and plain, a classic bedroom not total boyish.

She frowned when she did not see any pictures hanging on the wall, as they should be in any normal room.

"Why there are no pictures here....uhm?" Odette asked.

"My name is Sofia, Mrs De Luca", the old woman answered Odette's unspoken question smiling at her warmly.

"And I don't know about the question you asked", Sofia tells then adds, "I'm sorry".

"No it's fine, miss Sofia, how about you give me complete tour now, am not tired", Odette beamed at Sofia making her smile widely.

Sofia wasn't habituated to see smiles from her owners and here Odette was speaking to her with respect and smiling at her, which made her comfortable around her.

Mrs De Luca is sweet even though she is a princess, she is not like Bianca at all, and I hope she brings happiness in Marco's life as he deserves, thought Sofia before shaking her head off and beamed "let's go".

The house was three-storey building, every room had spacious balcony, as the colours were natural of the interior not like Marco's bedroom. Sofia said there is dungeon underground and said Marco would be see there usually. This wasn't surprising at all for Odette because she was herself coming from a dangerous mafia family.

"This place is beautiful", Odette spoke in awe looking at the giant pool in middle of the terrace.

"Master Mario has designed this place by himself", Sofia said gesturing a hand to the whole place.

"Hmm, impressive, since how long are you working here Miss Sofia", Odette asked making the old woman frown as she counted the years on her hands.

"May be... Twenty years? Yes, I am working since twenty years in de Luca family", the maid said making Odette frown.

She is working here since twenty years so she might have known something about Marco and Mario but will she tell me when I ask it? Odette shook her head thinking it would be a dumb move knowing she just arrived here and of course, in mafia families the loyalty lies with the owner.

Odette is not her owner.

"What are these two rooms?" Odette asked as she reached a corner in the second floor while they were walking down.

Those two doors were huge and different from each other and not to mention those two rooms where exactly on opposite side to each other.

The English style carving on the door made it look so elegant and delicate yet strong because of the golden colour of the doors.

Sofia was about to speak but it was too late Odette put her hand on the doorknob to open it but a hand yanked her hand hardly from the door making Sofia and Odette gasp.

"What... the... fuck... are... you... doing... here?", Mario fumed at her with his eyes dark and red, his jaw clenched and shaking in anger still holding her hand in a painful grip making Odette hiss.

"Leave me", she demanded struggling.

Mario pushed her away making her land on her ass as she yelped in pain glaring at Mario. Sofia held her head low whole time not making an eye contact with Mario as she always does.

"This is the first and last time am warning you, Odette, stay the fuck away from these two rooms, it's none of your business what is behind them", with that Mario walked away without giving a single glance at Odette.

QUEEN

ODETTE'S POV

I suck a huge amount of breathe to hold myself back from crying because of the insult Mario caused me in front of Sofia. I am supposed to be member of this family; this house was supposed to be my home and am not even allowed to go behind few doors?

"I'm so sorry, I should have said you before Mrs. De Luca, am so sorry", Sofia tells guilty as she looks at me with pity.

The admiration and respect she had for me was now replaced with pity.

Pity…

I don't like people to pity on me; this makes me feel weak and I am not weak.

Trying to lift me up she holds me tighter. Though I didn't want to take her help but I feel my ankle sore. It seems it was twisted when Mario yanked me harshly away from the door.

Why the hell he had to hate me?

Shaking of those thoughts, I try to pretend that his hate doesn't affect me but in reality, it burns as a bee sting.

"Are you okay Mrs De Luca?" the maid asks and I nod my head before speaking.

"I'm fine, thank you for helping me to my room, I will take rest", I tell her lying the first part.

"Please let me know if you need something", she tells softly before looking at my leg.

I clear my throat and nod my head shutting the door behind my back. Searching drawers to find any painkiller I stumble across the room.

Almost all the drawers are locked and there weren't any keys. My luggage is yet to be unpacked and this made me frown a little. I remember when my sister said she didn't even need to unpack her bag because her cupboard was already filled with all type of clothes from comfortable to classy and from sports bras to lace sets, not to mention all were her size.

It's okay Oddy, you don't need him buying things for you, you are a fucking French mafia princess, you just need to make space, space in sense of universe space because there is no way your clothes are going to fit in his single walk in closet while it took a huge room for me to put my clothes at my dad's home.

Dad's home!? He did say it would be always mine. Mine... my home.

Finally, I found a painkiller spray in the washroom and I sprayed it on my ankle hissing. It felt cold on my skin and started turning numb soon which gave me relief.

Unable to keep my eyes open I decided to arrange my clothes in the closet later and lay on the bed. Pulling comforter up I slip in the deep ambers of the day light closing my eyes welcoming the darkness.

I don't remember how long I have slept but I was woken up with a loud banging on the door.

Why Mario is banging on the door if he wants to get in don't he know the pass code nor have a key with him? Glancing at the watch I realized it's ten p.m. already.

Fuck! I have slept throughout the day. I hurriedly walk towards the door and surprisingly my leg didn't sting that much. The spray did work really well.

"What the hell are you doing in my son's room?" Bianca snarled at me as soon as I opened the door strolling towards me and raised her hand up to slap me.

In her fucking dreams.

I grab her wrist before it smacks my cheek, twist her hand, push her on the wall beside, and press right side of her face into the wall hardly with one hand as I lock her both hands behind her back in my single palm.

She struggles as she tries to get out of my hold but I chuckle at her amused.

"Leave me", she snarled realizing she wasn't going to slip from my grip as stinky and slippery fish she is.

Disgusting old piece of shit.

"Tsk tsk tsk, before raising your old fucking hand on me you should have given some work to your experienced brain, my father doesn't calls me little bad wolf for granted", I muse at her smirking as I push her head further in the wall.

I swear if I push more harder it will leave her imprint in the wall but at this rate it will surely imprint the makeup she has on her fucking old wrinkled face.

"You might be princess there Odette but I am the queen here", she warns me as if am here to take her shit. I really didn't like her the first day we met and after knowing she isn't real mother of my husband I don't give a flying fuck about this oldie, specially after my sister warned me to stay away from her.

The little riding Hood is supposed to hide and run while in our case it's this old bitch.

"You know my son will kill you if he finds out that you are mishandling his mother", she warns again making me chuckle.

"Uhh hmm...By the way Mrs Ferrari, why the hell you keep chanting my son my son... is it to remind yourself that..." I tell with a chuckle, get close to her ear, and whisper the last part.

"You aren't their real mother?". She gasps and struggle in my hold again and tired of pinning her on the wall I leave her free and she didn't take a second to turn her face towards me with her shock written on it.

I raise an eyebrow smirking at her, assuming her question and she didn't disappoint me. "How do you know?" she asks concluding that am nowhere near to eat her lies as everyone kept feeding on them. Folding my hands on my chest, I examine my nude french polished perfect nails before answering.

"A little birdie flew from Rome to France and whispered in my ear", I tell in a mocking tone scoffing a laugh at her to fuel up her anger.

I enjoy it.

I am *goddess for angels* and *fucking Satan for demons* and for Bianca…Hmm debatable, she is not qualified to be a demon as she was sticking her face in my bedroom wall. She is hellhound. Yeah, hell bitch.

"You are going to regret it, mark my words", she glared looking at me as if she is stabbing in my head with a nail hammer multiple times.

She turn her heels storming out of the room but my voice halt her steps just when she steps out of the door.

"Oh yes, Mrs Ferrari, last time I checked, my husband Marco de Luca was the king of Italian mafia and being his wife, I am the queen of this empire not you, so sober up, I think you are still little tipsy from last night having too many drinks with your bitch mates", I comment before shoving my shoulder in hers as I make my way towards the kitchen.

Ugh, this bitch ate away my energy. I need something to eat.

AUTHOR'S POV

"Queen?!" Bianca chuckles as soon as Odette left from there.

Her green eyes darkened as she glares at disappearing figure of Odette who is too oblivious to the surroundings she is in.

"You are just another slut those brothers will share, nothing more and nothing less, I just need to ask them to hurry up the plan and I would not wait a second to show you, your real place... soon", Bianca mutters and there is a promise in her tone.

She would go to any extent to take revenge on Andre and what would be more fun than hurting his most loved child after she killed one with her own hands eleven years ago.

WAIT

MARCO'S POV

I couldn't control myself when I am with her, so it's better this way, till I get her signatures better stay out of my own home. Damn!

I should not feel anything for her specially when I sworn my love and heart to our doll.

Loosening my tie, I sigh turning my laptop off, before pouring a drink for myself. I decided I would go spend tonight at one of de luca's penthouse. As I was about to take a sip a furious Mario barged into my room without knocking.

He is the only one who is alive even though he barge into my room which is a miracle because I kill people who knock on my door when am busy.

"How dare she is!!! Do you even know what she was doing?" Mario growled at me and am not even surprised seeing his furious state because I know the reason behind is Odette.

Wincing due to throbbing headache, I rub my temple and ask him tired.

"What she did now?" hearing me question as if nothing happened he chuckled.

"My head is fucking blasting Mario, spill and fuck off or deal with her in your own way", I tell him tired of how he keeps coming to me to complain about her as if they both are kindergarten kids and am a fucking teacher in a pencil skirt.

"She was trying to go into the golden door!" he exclaimed angrily and my jaw locked.

I froze as I felt anger pump in my blood. I let her live in my home and she is already invading the property as if it's her. Specially she even dared to step in the golden corner of the mansion. I am sure that our maids have warned her but she likes to be a brat.

My anger was taking worst out of me and I just want to shoot all the bullets of my gun into her smart skull. How dare she is to step in the corner where we literally worship the land. The two rooms specially made for our doll, where no one were allowed to peek, not even Bianca. That was our holy place but nothing was holy we would do there except our love for her but that too is fucking twisted up to call it holy. I mean who would share their lover with his brother and here we couldn't imagine keeping her selfishly for our own self.

As much as I need her, I want *her* needing my brother just as I need her and I swear on my life Mario feels the same way too.

But right now I regret letting her invade the place we choose for our doll and crossing that limit I know she will regret it too..... Soon.

"Marco!!!" another angry voice snapped me out of my thoughts of how to hurt Odette de Luca.

The door sprung open and a pissed off Bianca was standing in front of us. Mario was looking at her with the same expression as me.

She was wearing a black knee length dress and one strap of the dress was ripped off. There were deep nail marks and dried blood on it. This made me fucking mad.

No one dares to touch the woman who gave us reason to live and she did. I don't even need her to tell who was behind this, as I know crystal clear it was Odette.

"She was sleeping in your room, on *your bed*", she emphasis each word fuelling my anger.

"When I questioned her, dare I say she threw her fists at me", Bianca tells through her gritted teeth.

My knuckles were white with how tight my hold was on the whiskey glass and Mario growled in anger feeling the same way as me.

"Did you take her in your bedroom?" Mario asked narrowing his eyes on me.

I didn't blink away, I kept hold of his sight as I answered truth.

"I didn't", I declared and there is no way my voice was soft, it's hoarse because of how mad I am. But that wasn't enough for the two most important people in my life to believe me. So I had to explain myself and I swear this will be the last time am doing it. Am over with her and am more than mad she tried to invade the place we decorated for our doll.

"I asked a maid to show her to her room, the room which you choose for her", I add looking staring into Bianca's green eyes.

Bianca scoffed a chuckle wrapping her hands around herself for any warmth and Mario was the first one to offer her his jacket which she gladly accepted giving him a soft smile before turning towards me.

"She was in your room", she states as if it's a deadly sin and I swear to God, *it is*.

"I will take care of it", I tell her in my cold voice that made her snort rolling her eyes and I clenched my jaw so hard and was almost snapped the glass in my palm.

"Take care?!, that's what you have been kept doing all these time Marco, you kept talking care of her", she snapped at me angrily and am not complaining about it.

I did care about Odette, her eyes reminds me of those same eyes of the person who wiped my tears with her little hands and there is no way those two persons are same.

Mario is finding our doll and I hope he gets succeed as soon as possible because I can't wait to have her in my arms, specially when my own heart is defying me for the first time in my life. I want it to behave and beat only for our doll.

"I don't care about her", I stated looking into their eyes.

"Then why didn't you let Mario take her?" she questioned taking a step towards me and I locked my eyes with his.

"Because we were in *her* territory", I stated without even stuttering.

It's a single truth while the other was I was worried for her and if I said that aloud I would prove their own point.

"That means I can have her tonight?" Mario asked raising his eyebrow.

"Yes!!!" I yelled at him throwing the glass on the wall and let it break into pieces just as my head is pounding.

Pulling my hair in my palms I sighed plopping myself on the couch. Bianca placed her hand on my shoulder rubbing it motherly.

I never felt my Madre's touch in hers but she is the only woman who touches me similar as my Madre and I closed my eyes sighing.

"She is growing her wings Marco, I want you both put her to good use, treat her as you both treat any other woman, make her your slut and show her, her real place", she tells softly as if there is no poisonous words slipping out of her mouth.

"But first I want you make her sign the weapon factory papers", she adds and I open my eyes looking at her. She has that smirk on her face when she took us from the street that night.

"I will be on it", I answer her clearly as my voice calm and I bite my inner cheek stopping myself letting the memories of that night invade my head again.

Not now, not this moment.

She smiled at me before turning her head towards my brother and smirked while telling.

"Meanwhile Mario will take good care of her".

Her words brought a smirk on his face and I need not imagine what is running in his cunning head, I know him better and I know what he is thinking clearly.

My phone rang bringing us all out of our trace and I sighed taking it out of my pocket.

"It's Andre", I stated before answering the call and put it on speaker.

"Hello, son", he said as soon as I lift the call and I pushed all my strength in my body to my hand to not throw the phone hearing my enemy address me as his son.

"Hello, Andre", I stated not bothering to use the language he used.

"Sorry to call you this moment but I am going to visit Rome next month, there was a problem in the legal documents of weapon factory, since Odette turned eighteen I was busy with the wedding and didn't check them, today my lawyer went to get them registered and found the fault, I need to take her signatures again but I am going to New York today for an important work, hope that's okay", he said and I can't even hide my anger now.

171

Bianca nodded her head gesturing me to keep my cool and Mario punched the wall in anger.

"It's fine, you can visit whenever you want", I stated coldly after clearing my throat.

"Thank you so much you don't know how relieved I am, please take care of my daughter", he said sighing heavily.

Before I answer a lie, he spoke again.

"I trust you, you will take care of her", then without a word I hung up the call.

"I guess we have to wait for a month to show her, her real place, but I can tell Mario could have some fun with her", Bianca stated smirking at him and I kept staring at my phone blankly.

WHO HURT YOU

AUTHOR'S POV

Next day Odette woke up from her deep sleep when she heard someone knock on her door. Groaning to herself, she yawned placing her palm on her lips and stumbled to the door.

As soon as opened the door she found Sofia standing there with a tray of breakfast, which was covered with a plate.

"Good morning Mrs de Luca, Master asked me to make sure you are fed", Sofia beamed smiling at Odette.

Rubbing her eyes as a cute little child, she frowned looking at plate then Sofia.

"Where is Marco?" she asked her voice coming out ragged and she clears her throat.

Frowning Sofia answered. "Sorry Mrs de Luca but Master Marco didn't come home and neither informed about his well abouts".

"He didn't come home and already ordering me around!" Odette huffs scoffing as she folds her hands on her chest.

Sofia frowns then smiles shaking her head, "No, Mrs De Luca, it was Master Mario who sent breakfast for you".

Hearing Mario's name from Sofia, Odette clenched her jaw as her heart clenched in ache remembering how he treated her yesterday.

"Place the food in the kitchen, am not hungry, I will just hit the gym", Odette said turning around smacking the door rudely on Sofia's face.

Mario who was standing right beside Sofia leaning on the wall so that Odette doesn't catch him hearing her smirked at her reaction.

"What should I do now master?" Sofia asked not knowing if she knock the door again and persuade Odette to eat something or leave her behind.

"You heard her", Mario stated coldly and Sofia didn't need him to repeat, she hastily went to the kitchen and got herself busy with her daily errands.

~~~

After brushing her teeth, Odette scrolled through her phone while she was going to gym.

Putting some good workout music, she plugged her ear pods and didn't pay much attention to Mario who was already working out there. Whereas Mario's eyes were locked on Odette. She was wearing a sports bra with a matching pair of shorts. Her dark black hair tied up in a ponytail, which Mario wanted to wrap around his hand. Her hair was bouncing on her ass making Mario's cock twitch in his shorts. She went straight towards the treadmill and ran for thirty minutes then opened the cap of the water bottle and took a sip too oblivious to the pair of blue eyes drinking her up from head to toe.

Taking a deep breath she lifted a dumbbell and bent her back and lift it then dropped, she did this for quiet few times. Her plump ass wasn't any help for the hard girth throbbing in Mario's gym shorts. All he wanted to do was thrust into it after yanking her shorts down.

Noticing her back isn't straight as it should be Mario silently walked towards Odette and placed his hand on her back and within next second the dumbbell in her hand smacked right on Mario's head with a thud and he fell down unconscious.

Odette's eyes widened and she gasped seeing Mario, lying on the floor unconscious. His dark brown hair was sprawled on his forehead. She knew she hit that on his forehead, hoping she didn't draw blood out of his head she gently pushed his hair away as she sat on her heels. She didn't want to hurt him but the damage was done.

"Thank god!" she muttered seeing it didn't leave a scratch or else he would have definitely sued her for destroying his handsome face.

Falling on her knees, she took his head on her lap and slapped across his face twice softly.

"Oh my god! Mario! Mario! Wake up!" she kept telling while shaking his body.

Odette grabbed the water bottle beside her which she was drinking from and opened the cap and emptied the whole bottle on his face. Mario coughed and jolt opened his eyes breathing heavily, as he choked on the cold water.

"Barvoragazzo", Odette stated patting his back fuelling up his anger.

(Good boy)

"Puttana! You want to kill me or something!?", he growled making Odette laugh throwing her head back but coming down from her laughing fit she rubbed his back which made mario more mad and he smacked her hand away and Odette pouted trying to look offended.

"Don't touch me!" Mario growled getting up on his feet and winced at the throbbing pain in his head.

"But...", Odette was cut off when Mario took a step and slid and fell his ass down due to the slippery mat because of the water Odette threw on him.

This time Odette laughed so hard that tears slid out of her eyes, which made her eyes blurry.

"Checazzo!". Mario cursed under his breath wincing at the pain.

(What the fuck)

Odette held her stomach tight her cheeks and nose turned red due to laughing so hard, she got up on her feet and gave a hand to Mario smirking at him as she bit her lip harshly trying to control her laughter. But her whole body was shaking, making Mario clench his jaw and he turned red due to embarrassment.

"Get up old man", Odette taunted looking into his blue eyes, which was darkened dangerous making her gulp.

"Old man?" Mario snarled at her making Odette's heart drop in her stomach.

Odette was mesmerised in his eyes, which didn't made her realize Mario's next move.

He yanked her extended hand so hard that she yelped and fell on his hard body and hissed. Mario flipped her now he was on top of her as she was below him with her legs spread wide and his hard erection wasn't concealed at all making Odette's eyes widened.

Mario just smirked at her reaction of him between her legs and sensually closed the gap between them and let his lips trail the pulse of her neck, which was throbbing under her skin.

Goosebumps pricked her skin feeling his soft lips along with his rough trimmed beard making every inch of her skin burn as hot lava.

She started struggling under him trying to free herself but she didn't realize that would only create more friction between her clothed core and his hard member until he groaned and bit her neck leaving a mark on it.

"Fuck!" Mario muttered bringing his one hand towards her hip bone and held it on place so that she couldn't move and torture him more.

He held her neck in his other hand and gazed in her dark brown eyes getting lost in depths of her unsaid secrets. For the first time he was able to read those eyes as Marco did and this time he didn't question his brother's weakness towards her. Because he felt that too.

Odette's pulse was beating hard against his thumb and liking the way it felt he pressed more making her gulp hardly.

She neither pushed him away nor gave him permission to move further but he did. He brought his lips so close to hers that her cold lip ring was touching his own lips making blood rush to his groin.

Both were breathing heavily, mesmerised with the forbidden pull towards each other but no word was spoken for good few minutes until Odette closed her eyes.

She felt Mario's lips move when he questioned her.

"Tell me... Odette and don't dare about thinking you can lie to me", he stated making her eyes snap open.

His azure eyes were sad and broken which she badly wanted to collect the memory behind that pain and burn it with her own hands.

"Are you into witchcraft? Huh?" Mario asked making Odette frown.

His question made her wonder what's going in his head and her thoughts were running around only him and him, forgetting that this is forbidden, she shouldn't be thinking about fixing a man who isn't her husband, specially when he is her husband's own blood, his twin.

"Why do I feel like this? That I want to slap you and fuck you at the same time", as soon as Mario uttered those words a gasp escaped Odette's pouty lips.

Her heart was almost in her throat throbbing against his palm. "What are you doing to me?" He questioned again.

"What are you doing to us?" he asked again and his voice soft and pleading against her quivering lips.

"Tell me you have a voodoo doll under your bed, tell me you are doing black magic on us", he uttered making her scowl.

"Why do you hate me Mario?" she asked and her voice was surprisingly calmer than she expected because of the storm roaring in her heart. Mario gulped visibly as he shifted his eyes from her pink lips to her dark brown doe eyes, his Adams apple bobbed making Odette gulp. Water was dripping from his dark brown locks on her face but that didn't bother her.

"These eyes… are exactly like hers", he stated looking into her eyes making her head run around all the words he was speaking.

Someone hurt him? She thought looking into his broken eyes.

"Who is she Mario? Did she hurt you?" Odette pleaded cupping his face in her little palm.

Mario closed his eyes tightly feeling her warm touch and found himself leaning into her touch as an abandoned puppy needing some assurance of safety.

He snapped his eyes open realizing what he was doing and got off her immediately, without turning back to look her he walked away without speaking a word leaving Odette all alone.

Odette sighed heavily looking at his disappearing figure and muttered.

"Oh my Mario, who hurt you so bad that you couldn't even tell me".

Little did she know that the person about who she was talking about is herself and she didn't hurt him. Even if she wanted to, she couldn't. For her when they could burn the world, she could walk on fires for them and it will take some time for her to accept the fact she is denying.

THANK FUCK

MARCO'S POV

The slow hum of the music is blasting in the red room and I am man spreading on the red leather couch.

Mario is in the bar having his drink to pick up on what we are going to do tonight. It's been so long we had threesome and the thought of fucking the same chic is getting me hard.

But not as hard as I get just with a single look from Odette.

"Come to me", I ordered her spreading my legs wide on the couch and resting my hands ideally.

The black shirt am wearing is half way opened with matching trousers and Mario is wearing his FBI uniform as he came right from his work. The girl wearing nothing but just a black lace set and garter started walking towards me. Moreover, for some reasons I can only see *her*.

Odette.

She looks damn sexy in black.

"Crawl towards him", Mario warned her for me and shivering due to the blast of air conditioning she dropped on her knees and started crawling towards me.

As soon as she stopped in between my legs, I saw into her eyes, which were afraid.

I don't like it.

I don't like odette fear me like this. But again this wasn't odette.

Domination is pleasurable when a submissive is willing to break, trusting us that we will fix them, hold them when it happen but she is afraid.

To loosen up I gave her a weak smile.

"Is this your first time?" I asked looking at her, she bit her lip nodding her head conforming my doubt.

Threesome is new for her.

"Take off my belt and suck me off", I ordered bringing my single hand on her blonde hair and don't ask how badly I wanted this to be *her* dark black hair...

I see Mario walking towards us slowly taking his shirt off. It's all time game that he takes them first as he is gentle than me but don't get me wrong, the key word speaks itself – than me. But he do fuck hard.

He slowly slid his hand between her huge tits, which are perked up, and rubbing against the lace material as she stumbled with my belt and freed my throbbing cock.

When her lips met my member, all I could imagine was her lips on it. The way her pouty lips would feel around my cock, her doe dark brown eyes, which would turn teary, and that fucking lip piercing!!

The girl on her knees licked all the way along making me groan and sucked my balls. Leaving them with a pop, she licked the tip of my hard angry red cock and took it in her mouth just as I wanted.

Moving her mouth time-to-time while she licked the pre cum leaking as she moaned and groaned on my cock was bringing me to the edge with the thoughts of Odette doing it.

Mario slid his hand between her pussy and chuckled mocking her and spanked her ass making her gasp on my cock. "This slut is

181

already dripping wet for us brother", he stated cockily delivering another smack and she groaned.

She likes it.

And there is nothing more pleasurable for a Dom than his sub who likes pain.

The only thought of whipping, spanking and clamping got me off immediately. Groaning I use her head as I want to making sure she could breathe and increased my pace and got myself off emptying every drop in her mouth.

Swallowing as a good little slut she is, she turned towards Mario who was standing with ropes and handcuffs.

"Now what do you say when we give you our come?" he asks raising an eyebrow reminding her she forgot to thank me.

"Thank you daddy", the blonde moans as she rubs her needy pussy on her heel.

"Get up", Mario growled and she complied without complaining.

"Strip", I order and she looks between my brother and me and gulped hardly before taking off the skimpy material from her body.

Naked.

Vulnerable.

Needy.

Just as we want.

"Lay on the bed", I order and she does as she was told as a good girl.

With her face towards the ceiling, she bit her lip in anticipation and I could clearly see in the dim light how her chest is rising and falling down.

Mario got on the bed, handcuffed her wrists, and locked it with bedpost. Spreading her legs wide he tied her two legs similarly.

A good view of *her* glistening pussy was in my view. I licked my lower lip looking intensely at *her* while Mario started playing with *her* in his own way.

This bastard likes to take control of the orgasm. He will bring any woman to edge and leave her unfinished to start over repeatedly until they beg him to fuck their brains off.

Neither of us has gone down to any woman. Well it has changed because I have gone down on Odette on our wedding night and fuck! If I wasn't addicted to her sweet tight cunt then fuck me!

I am addicted to her, her moans, her scream, and the way she calls *daddy...*

"What you are supposed to tell when you are wide spread on our bed?" Mario inquired when he was looking at our toy collection to choose what he should push in her slippery and needy cunt.

The woman started struggling to rub her thighs so that she could create any friction she needed but it's impossible with the way she is tied down on the bed.

Helpless.

Wide.

On our mercy.

"We are being merciful because it's your first time with both of us... that means you can't take our mercy for granted and act as if you don't know how we like a woman on our bed", I fumed at her lack of answering to us.

"So.... Sorry sir", she mewled but it was too late.

Mario pushed a bullet vibrator into her pussy just as she want and with the way, she is struggling and screaming I know it is on highest speed.

Looking at how my brother is playing with the cunt while the toy fucked with her head along with her pussy he placed another toy on her clit and she trashed screaming.

She is close.

In addition, the sick bastard stopped the vibrator with a shit-eating smirk on his face and I chuckled.

Following me, he chuckled while tsking.

"You should have behaved well sweetheart, we would have let you come", he taunted while he smacked hard on her red pussy.

"Please sir", she begged again.

It's good that she didn't whine or else he would have taken another round teasing her and leaving her unfinished.

Stripping down he rolled a condom on his member, pumping it with his one hand he removed the vibrator from her cunt and dig his fingers in, rolling them inside for two minutes.

Then he leaned on her and placed a kiss on her neck before whispering something in her ear, which made her smile.

And just like that, he slid his whole length in her. Without giving her time to adjust, he fucked her brain out of her skull.

I stroked my member looking at them biting my lip, as my cock was hard and throbbing.

After good few minutes she reached her high and came on his cock and he didn't took time to remove bondage from bed, her handcuffs was on as he flipped her over. Gripping her hips as he dug his fingers in her ass and fucked her hard from behind and she screamed as she came all over again and this time Mario growled as he reached his own high and smacked her ass as he emptied everything in condom.

Leaving her on the bed limp, he walked towards the dustbin to throw the used condom and in the meanwhile, I stripped off my clothes and rolled a condom on my hard throbbing cock. Taking a whip from the toys, I walked towards her smacking it against the floor as the sound echoed, she shivered.

Her blonde hair sticking to her sweaty body as she started rubbing her needy cunt again on her heels. I wacked her ass with the whip and she screamed at the contact as the leather left a red mark on her already red ass because of Mario's torture.

"You were a bad girl, now count ten", I stated and started whipping her ass and she screamed and counted as she was asked.

Seven.

Eight.

Nine.

Ten.

I threw the whip away and didn't mind to grab a lubricant, as her ass is already stretched good and perfect. When I ran my fingers on her pussy as I rubbed my cock on her ass hole kneeing behind her she wiggled her ass back wanting more and she was dripping wet.

I chuckled darkly as I rubbed my length from her ass to her cunt teasing her as she screamed my name.

My name. My name.

How dare she call me with my name!!!

Marco! Marco!

You fucking bastard!!!!

I snapped my eyes open as I felt someone kick me so hard that I fell off from the bed.

Mario was sitting on the bed covering himself with duvet even though he is fully dressed.

I rubbed my eyes and frowned looking at his annoyed face as he scoffed and glared at me. "What?" I asked him groaning annoyed that he woke me up in an unpleasant way.

"You fucking bastard!" he snarled at me getting out of bed and folded his hands on his chest offended. "I like to share women with you but that doesn't mean I will share my asshole with you, you sick fuck!!!", he went on making me scoff.

"Yuk", I made a gagging sound as I lift my sore ass from the floor and stood on my feet glaring at him." I am not interested in your asshole, you asshole", I retorted rolling my eyes.

"Yeah!? And here you were few minutes ago dry humping me in your sleep! Thank god I wasn't drunk to not notice!!! You would have taken my virginity! You bastard!" he growled making me scoff.

"I didn't do that", I declared even though I don't remember doing it.

It's better this way.

I couldn't imagine humping my brother, Yuk; the only thought would make me puke blood from my stomach.

"You!!!! Fuck!!! Am not even talking about this! Next time remind me to not sleep beside you!" he snapped and walked out of the door closing it with a loud thud making me wince.

"What the actual fuck happened!" I growled pulling my hair.

"I had a fucking wet dream as a teenage boy", I remember this part too well that it felt real.

But I don't remember the part I was humping him and I would do anything… *anything* in my life to keep it that way.

I look down at my hard cock and sigh.

Well now, I have to take care of it in shower.

STAY WITH ME

MARIO'S POV

Cringing to myself at the horrible memory, I walked into the mansion. It was fifteen days since I returned here, Odette was alone surrounded with maids who were taking care of everything she needed.

Of course not answering the questions she asked. Marco and I kept up to date about what she was doing and where she was going. She is definitely pissed off and the way she knocked my head with a fucking dumbbell wasn't a good memory to come back home when she is all mad.

Well this is better than staying with horny Marco and get my ass fucked in sleep. I can't believe he fucking did that!

As soon as I entered the home the loud music which was blasting made me wince.

"What the hell?!" I grumbled walking towards the direction from where the music was playing.

"Master Mario!" the maid exclaimed while she came towards me running and two others followed her with the same expression.

"Sofia, what the hell is going on?" I snarled looking at her deadly.

She gulped hardly as she stated. "I'm so sorry, master mario, I was just coming down to call you, Mrs. de Luca...." the older maid trailed off making me grit my teeth.

"What the hell is going on? What she did?" I asked again taking a breathe to calm my nerves.

"Mrs de Luca... she... She..." the maid kept stuttering making me hiss as I rubbed my temple.

"I will look at that myself", I stated storming towards the pool.

As I kept walking, the sound of music turned louder than it was. Fuck! My ears would bleed any second if I stayed more.

Opening the door angrily I stormed inside but my eyes widened looking at the view in front of my eyes.

The pool was full of girls there was a DJ, not to mention it was a girl too, all were wearing bikini, and some in the pool were top less. With glasses of drinks which I know Odette have grabbed from our bar.

She was there with few girls dancing beside the pool while everyone enjoyed their own company. Few girls were making out themselves and right now, I don't know what to feel. To be angry or to laugh. To be mad that she brought a bunch of teenage girls into my pool or to be thankful that she didn't bring guys.

Odette's body was wet and her white two-piece swimsuit was sticking to her body as if it was a second skin. Her nipples were hard and not an ass that could stand nears hers. The view of curvy and round perfect ass that I could do anything to dip my cock in it.

189

Her thin waist and boobs would alone get any man fucking out with multiple orgasms. That's how perfectly sculpted she was, a goddess — a fucking sex goddess. Then a brown skinned brunette walked towards her and wrapped her hands around odette and started kissing her lips which odette smiled and kissed her back. Odette's hand was resting on the brunette's ass while she squeezed her ass and started massaging her perfect tits and jealously ran through my veins burning my sanity.

I brought my attention back to the chaos around me, took my gun out from my jeans, and shot it straight into the speakers and everyone flinched and screamed hearing gunshot but Odette was calm as she turned back and I was giving my deadliest glare that could burn her soul and she smirked - fucking smirked.

"Oh Mario! I thought you got a memory loss after the stunt in the gym, since you weren't home for how many days?", she asked mockingly as she placed her left palm on her hip and tapping the right of her head faking to think.

"OUT!" I snarled and it didn't took much time that everyone ran out of the mansion as head less chickens.

Odette swayed her hips tsking as she walked towards the bar to grab a drink but I didn't let her reach the bottle, instead I yanked her hand and threw her on my shoulder and smacked her ass so hard that she screamed and trashed on my broad shoulder.

"You asshole! You fucking piece of shi....." I didn't let her finish.

Smack!

"Oh god!" Odette screamed again making me smirk.

I was beyond angry and I fucking don't know why.

"If you speak another word before I ask you, your ass will be so sore that you wouldn't be able to sit on it for weeks", I growled as I walked towards my room.

My fucking room!!!!

It was too late I realized I was taking her to my room not even when I threw her on the bed and her tiny body bounced on it and she yelped at the impact.

Glaring at me, she twisted her mouth hatefully making me release a throaty chuckle deep from my chest.

"What the fuck you think you are doing Mario?!" she scolded me as if she has a right to talk to me like this after she made out with a chick under my fucking roof.

"What was that?" I ask her with my dark voice which I know make people piss in their pants and accept their crimes when am investigating.

"What – what was that?", she scoffs folding her hands on her chest as she sat comfortably on my bed with her wet body and the tiny wet bikini covering very little body leaving nothing much for imagination.

Suddenly I have an urge to get her naked, taste that wet pussy, bath in her slickness and devour her as a fucking animal I am.

But not now, not like this.

"You know damn well what am asking about Odette de Luca". I ask her again looking into her dark brown eyes which are gazing at me in hate but there is also a lacking expression which I was able to understand.

"What I was supposed to do? The man who married me didn't come home since the day I stepped in this damn home, you should be fucking kidding me when he didn't even call me!", she screamed frustration running straight out of her words and body language.

"You should have known this, you are born into a mafia family yourself," I tell her coldly looking in to her angry eyes.

"Okay I was born into the mafia family but I didn't ask for it!", she screamed at me getting up from my bed.

"I didn't ask to get married this early and wait as a fucking perfect obedient wife for her husband to return from God knows where he is!" she screamed again and this time I saw a tear slipping out from her eyes.

All I ever wanted was to see her in pain and cry but it hurts, it fucking hurts seeing tears in her eyes and for feeling this, I want to rip my own heart from my chest.

"I was all alone in this huge ass house and maids who tell nothing but Mrs de Luca your breakfast is ready, your lunch is ready, your dinner is ready", she choked as she spoke while she wrapped her hands around herself.

"No one from college wanted to talk to me because....because", she choked again and this time she cried hard.

Falling on her knees, she hugged herself bringing her knees to her chest and cradled herself.

"Because you are a de Luca", I finished her sentence and my voice surprisingly heavy and ragged.

I know this feeling very well, being ignored by people, as they know what we are. Something's never change and so does this.

We were always bullied that we badly used to pray that we get ignored. But now the situation is same but reasons are different.

People know what de Luca's are. Merciless hunters but we hunt humans not animals. The ways of Marco's painful torture before he took someone's life is a wide spread rumour. Rumours at least that's what some people think because lack of proofs but they wouldn't dare to doubt what they hear specially with the dark aura surrounding us.

"I miss him, I really miss him but what is eating my head is that I missed you too", she said and I felt a pang in my chest.

She missed me? After me being dick to her, she missed me?

I couldn't bring any words to comfort her, not when my own head is messed up.

"I'm here now, Marco… well Marco will take some time to come home, he has important business to deal", I tell her looking at her timid figure admiring the way she is curled up into a ball.

"I need to talk to him, I need to make sure he is okay, he is my husband for God's sake", she cried and I couldn't help as a faint smile formed on my lips.

She really likes Marco.

"I will make a call to him, freshen up so that you could eat something", I promised and she raised her lashes at me flattering them to get rid of fat tears on them.

And I swear to God I would do anything to get same look of her *this* face when she is under me, in my bed crying with pleasure, withering beneath me.

"Do you promise?" she asked bringing her pinkie finger forward and I gave a pointed look narrowing my eyes at her finger and then her face.

Fuck! I couldn't resist!

Bringing my finger and intertwining it with her own I gave her a smile, which made her grin as a cat and she got up on her legs by her own. I didn't mind to help her not when her body is practically almost naked.

"I will go get ready", she said running out of the room and fuck me right there! Fucking kill me! The way her ass wiggled and it took every inch of patience in me to not grab her and throw her on my bed and smack those beautiful pulp ass cheeks until they turned red.

"This girl will be end of me", I growled pulling my hair and walked into the kitchen.

"Go and get the pool all cleaned up", I order and Sofia with other two maids ran straight out of the kitchen with a single "Yes master".

Grabbing a pan from the cabinet, I placed it on the stove as I emptied a pre mix pancake ingredients and battered it up with

194

adding some milk and poured it on the non-stick pan and placed the lid on it so it is cooked well.

Once bubbles formed on them I flipped them, did same making good amount of pancakes for both of us, and chopped few strawberries in the meantime while the water boiled and made two cups of Americano adding ice cubes and fried some bacon and eggs.

Placing everything on the plates, I took them to the dining table and Odette was out from her room in time wearing a black leather shorts and white sheer shirt with a black lace bra underneath it.

Her wet hair sprawled on her face as she tied them in a messy bun and her face bare without make up made my cock twitch in my jeans painfully.

Gulping hardly I cleared my throat as I gestured her towards the plates and she gasped and awed as she sat on one of the chair and to maintain a good distance to not bend her over the table and pound her I sat far from her across her seat.

"You really lost your memory don't you?" she asks narrowing her eyes at me and I can sense the teasing playful tone from her voice, which isn't doing justice to my throbbing girth.

"Shut up and eat", I scoff rolling my eyes fighting hard against my own smile and she grins biting her lip chewing her lip piercing before leaving it free and devoured the food on the table mouth fully without shying away as the other women does when they eat with us.

She is something else!

"Oh my god! These are fucking tasty", she moaned and I had to fist my palms so hard under my table taking a deep breath.

But when she took a sip of the Americano, she choked and wiped her mouth as if she drank a bitter poison.

"What?" I shrugged looking at her amused.

"I don't drink this shit", she said wiping her mouth with back of her palm and dipped her finger in Nutella and sucked on it innocently and yes! Fuck me!!!!

"This is better", she said and suddenly started itching her skin and her breathing turned heavy.

"Hey", I called her calming my nerves but she was turning red.

Frowning I got up from my seat and walked towards her worriedly.

"Hey Odette", I called shaking her as she was trying to take huge amount of air and choking as if something is blocking it.

My heart started beating so hard that all I could hear was her gasping and it's thundering in my ear.

"What's wrong, Odette?" I said rubbing her back as she looked me with teary eyes.

"V… va... Vanilla", she choked and then it hit me.

"Are you allergic to vanilla?" I ask with my heart in my throat and she gave a weak nod.

"Shit!" I said as I took her in my arms and walked out of the mansion hurriedly.

"Drive to the hospital", I ordered as soon as I sat in the car with Odette in my arms. Driver did as he was ordered and I felt Odette turning cold and sweaty in my arms.

"Odette, hang on baby", I said and I couldn't hear my own words, as the only fear eating me alive was what if something happens to her.

I couldn't let something happen to her, no! I couldn't!

She was choking and gasping as she was closing her eyes making my heart drop in my stomach.

No!

No no fucking no!

"Odette! Baby!" I kept calling as I hugged her close to my chest.

Letting her know that I won't let something bad happens to her.

"Stay with me", I said and my voice choked at the end and I didn't realize a tear slipped my eyes until it fell on her closed eyelid.

"Please stay with me", I begged.

I forgot everything else, my revenge, hate and grudge against anyone and everyone.

All I want right at this moment is Odette safe in my arms. I would fucking kill myself if something happens to her.

SAFE

AUTHOR'S POV

"Marco", Mario said through call, as soon as doctors took Odette into emergency unit trying to get her allergic reaction in control saying her life is in danger and couldn't promise anything.

His voice choked as if he was crying, indeed he cried. For the first time after those eleven years, Mario cried again and this time it was for unknown reason.

He couldn't stop his heart from feeling her pain and as soon as he realized he couldn't help, tears flowed which screamed sorry.

Sorry...

"What's wrong Mario?" Marco who was in the meeting spoke with heavy weight on his heart. He could feel it, in his brother's voice. Something is wrong – something is terribly wrong.

"Odette", Mario choked and Marco stood from his seat abruptly making others in the meeting flinch.

"What happened Mario?" Marco asked deadly. Like he asks those people who tries to backstab him or tries to cross him.

Mario gulped hardly and told everything happened this morning. How Odette invited a group of lesbians from a Face book group and let them party in their pool and when Mario reached there everything she said and how she broke down, specially how other students didn't talk to her because she was de Luca and the pancakes he made had vanilla in them and how her life is in danger now.

"Couldn't you check before feeding her damn vanilla?! You should have known well as you were the one I said to make sure the wedding cake doesn't contain vanilla!" Marco seethed as soon as he punched Mario across his face.

He arrived as fast as he could drive, leaving his meeting. He was beyond angry but what he is feeling now is fear than anger. Which made him lose his mind and he punched his own brother for the first time in their life.

Mario stumbled back as Marco's fist bumped on his jaw and his lips bled a little and he tasted the similar metallic taste in his mouth. Wiping the blood with back of his hand, he simply stared Marco with guilty feeling and teary eyes, which were reflecting same as Marco's.

"Tell me you didn't do this knowing how fucking dangerous it could be for her?!". Marco demanded fisting his brother's collar in his hands.

"Tell me!" he yelled on his face as a single tear slid his eye.

"I swear to God, brother, I didn't know", Mario stated the truth, as he looked straight into his brother's eyes.

Clenching his jaw Marco freed Mario's collar pushing him behind but Mario embraced himself as he slid down along the wall of the hospital lobby.

"Sir, we need AB negative blood immediately, patient's condition is critical, she coughed a lot of blood and our hospital blood bank doesn't have AB negative blood", a nurse came out of the emergency unit and said making twins heart shatter as their hope that Odette will be okay soon which they kept telling in their heads holding their heart in their palms.

"Our, our blood group is AB negative", Marco stated immediately as soon as he heard the news. If it wouldn't have their blood same as hers and hospital couldn't provide what she needed they both would have lit fire to the damn hospital with all their doctors and employees in it.

"Thank god, please hurry up, we don't have time", the nurse stated but Mario held Marco's hand pleading.

"Please, let me do this", Mario stared looking into Marco's worried eyes with his own broken ones.

Without uttering a word, Marco nodded his head and the nurse took Mario inside the emergency unit, drew his blood, and arranged it for Odette.

Few hours ago, he was thirsty for his enemy's blood and now he was giving his own blood, which will run in her veins. He was not only becoming a part of her, in her blood, in her veins but in her heart – making his own way without realizing.

Just as she became their part since the day, she held their joined hands. Placed her own tiny palm on their little ones eleven years ago and destiny promised to keep them that way.

It's now or then, sooner or later, these three souls will realize that they were meant to be together.

And she was their doll, which held their souls in her. Just as the old myth, which stated a pirate's soul was held in a parrot but *this* wasn't a myth. It was truth.

As true as she belonged to them just as they belonged to her.

Marco was pacing outside the operation theatre worriedly, praying silently that Odette's health gets better. As Mario was gazing at Odette with so much love and sorrow in his eyes which he doesn't know.

The thick red blood flowed from Mario's veins through thin transparent pipes and entered Odette, which saved some time for doctors to treat her.

Her heartbeat was stable and doctor gave a weak smile to Mario telling everything will be okay.

Even doctors and nurses couldn't believe that most dangerous brothers who were spoken about their dangerous ways to kill people are crying for a girl not to mention for a single girl.

They know better to not ask anything if they value their life. Silently they prayed for Odette's life as their depends on hers now.

"How is she?" Marco asked as Mario stepped outside pulling the sleeve of his shirt down.

"Doctors said she is stable and they have time to work on her, I swear to god, Marco, I really didn't know she is allergic to vanilla, I would have been careful", Mario explained painfully.

Marco sighed as he placed his hand on Mario's shoulder and hugged him wrapping his arms around Mario and patted his back as he spoke.

"It's okay, thank you for bringing her in time to the hospital, am sorry for punching you", Marco apologized feeling sorry for losing his temper on his brother.

"It's okay, I would have killed myself if I didn't make it up in time", Mario said meaning every word.

"Mr de Luca!" the doctor called coming out of the room as he took off his glasses and mask. Smiling at the worried twins, he gave them the news they were waiting to hear.

"The patient is out of danger and stable, she will get conscious in an hour".

Both brothers smiled widely and hugged each other once again their happiness didn't had any boundary as they spoke to the doctor.

"Thank you so much doctor", they said in unison making doctor's eyes widened.

They never heard de Luca brothers thanking or saying sorry to anyone and here they were thanking him for the first time in his life as he worked with them since the years they started getting injured practicing fights to now when they gets injured on any mission.

Gulping thickly doctor nodded as he spoke stuttering, "It... It wa... Was my job, Mr de Luca".

Thanking to God he got some more time to live the doctor happily left them as they asked Odette to be sent home as they couldn't risk her safety in hospital though the amount of security they have with their own guards.

Doctors were more than happy to let them go and do as they asked and sent their best help with them so that she could take care of Odette if something unexpected happened.

BAD DREAM

ODETTE'S POV

I couldn't figure out who was speaking but their words were muffled as if I was under water. My whole body felt numb as I tried to move them but I couldn't. What happened to me?

Breathing softly I sighed as I opened my eyes and snapped them shut with the amount of light beaming in my room.

Who the fuck brought a fucking sun in my room?!

"Mama, please shut the blinds, I want to sleep more", I groaned and my throat burned as I spoke.

"Mama...", I groaned again but I didn't get an answer.

"Ivette... please, will you shut the blinds", I pleaded as I stretched my right arm to reach my twin sister who always sleep beside me.

Our parents offered us different rooms when we turned five old but we were so close that we didn't want to stay away from each other, we were literally each other's shadows. So our parents got us two single beds in our room. My side was painted pink with all unicorns and rainbows with fluffy white throw blankets with pink tassels.

My side of the room was a complete pretty princess type but not Ivette's. Her style was rock star. She had a guitar hung behind her grey bed on black painted wall. Which our mother gave her saying that it was her childhood best friend's.

We still didn't meet her; she said her name was Alesia. She said we can meet her soon, next year if possible. She also said she lives in Italy and it's a secret we should not tell daddy and promised she will take us all to meet her and her family, am so excited to go there, out of our home for the first time with Ivette and Aurora.

"Odette, Ivette, my beautiful princesses, please listen to mama and don't come out of this room, hide under the bed and don't come out until your daddy comes here", I suddenly see my mom's face. She was injured on her forehead and she was bleeding.

I remember how this happened. I remember it very well.

"Bye Mrs Grayson", Ivette and I sang as soon as our mama started driving us to her friend's home.

Aurora was with daddy. She said she wants to buy souvenirs from the trip as we were leaving tomorrow from Italy to our home.

"Are you excited to meet aunt Alesia's twins?", our mama asked looking at us from rear mirror.

I glanced at Ivette grinning and we both clapped our hands.

"Yes we are, mama, I also made two friends in the park, you know, they are also twins", I exclaimed excitedly happy to share that I made friends for the first time in my life.

A car dashed into the trunk of our car and we jerked screaming.

"Mama", both Ivette and I cried hugging each other tightly.

"Oh my god", mama said as she straitened herself and then we saw blood streaming down from her forehead.

"Please, promise me, you both will not come out of this place until daddy calls you out", our mama pleaded giving each of us few kisses on our face as tears streamed down from our eyes.

We were afraid, so afraid.

"You know right what happens when you break promise?" our mother asked and we both nodded sobbing silently.

"Yes, we will lose our pinkie finger", I mumbled wiping my tears away though they kept falling stubbornly.

"Yes, princess and now be good girls and wait for daddy", mama said and she went out of the room turning lights off giving us one last smile and it terrified us to our bones.

"Ivette... don't go, we will lose our pinkie", I begged holding my sister's hand tightly.

"Oddy, please, it's not true, I will come back soon", my twin sister said yanking my hand away.

She was wrong, she was so wrong.

She not only lost her pinkie finger but all her fingers then her hands and then her head. I was under the bed when I saw a woman wearing red heels walk into the room and first chopped my twins sister's fingers then hands and her head and I didn't scream, I didn't cry, I was just looking at my own face, my identical twin, laying on the white marble floor in her own blood in pieces.

"IVETTE!!!!!" A blood chilling scream escaped my mouth as I snapped my eyes open.

My hands were connected to IV's and machines, which I don't know.

"Baby", Marco was the one who hugged me tightly as I sobbed.

I wrapped my arms around him forgetting that he left me alone since the day I came here.

"Mar... Marco... I... saw... I saw a horrible dream", I cried in his arms as he embraced me tightly.

"Shhh, it's okay, you are okay", he stated firmly rubbing my back.

"You are okay sweetheart", he said again and again as I forced myself to take deep breathes.

"Shhh, everything is fine now, am here", he said again and this time I sighed into his chest holding him tightly as I gulped thickly.

My throat burned in need of water and thankfully Marco picked glass of water from bedside table and brought it to my lips and I gulped everything down in few seconds and realized I was thirstier.

"I want some more water", I spoke and my own voice seemed foreign to me.

"Just a minute, I will fetch some water and food for you, I will be back", Marco said pressing a kiss on my forehead.

I weakly nodded my head as he wiped my tears.

"Please come fast", I said and he left through the door giving me a weak smile just as my mother gave me in my dream.

I placed my hand on my pounding heart as I sighed heavily.

"Thank god it was a dream", I spoke to myself closing my eyes for a second and opened them as I heard the door clicked open.

"I'm sorry Odette, I swear I didn't knew you were severely allergic to vanilla", Mario said and I swear I saw it in his eyes that he was sorry.

"Its fine, am fine", I assured smiling at him weakly with my chapped lips, which I assume might bleed if I smiled wide.

In few steps, he was standing right in front of me and embraced me in a tight hug as he cried.

This must be a dream, am I seeing Mario cry?! The biggest asshole of the world?!

"Please don't scare me like that again", he said with his thick clogged voice.

"Please don't leave me again", he pleaded with his face buried in my neck and I can feel his warm tears on my cold skin.

"I won't", I promised wrapping my own hands around him.

"I won't leave you", I spoke meaning every word.

The dream I had messed up my head, it felt so real and for a second I believed it was truth.

I shrugged those thoughts as I broke the hug and smiled at Mario wiping his tears.

"Now, as you tried to kill me, you need to make it up", I tell him grinning as I shove my palms in front of him.

His smile widened and I swear his smile is just as beautiful as Marco's and my heart fluttered as I saw genuine happy expression on his beautiful features for the first time.

"What I have for you will not fit in these little palms of yours, spread your arms a little wide", he said grinning and I looked at him dumbfounded.

"What do you mean?" I asked but I found myself doing just as he said.

"You will see", he stated as he blew whistle, curving his finger in his mouth and I saw Nike and Gucci running towards us with their little legs.

My eyes widened as I saw them and Mario with my jaw dropped on the floor while he kept his grin folding his hands on his chest.

"You asshole, you fucking stole them from me that day!?" I scolded as I smacked him hard on his head.

WE WERE

MARIO'S POV

"Hey, I saved them, I didn't steal them!" I fight back knowing very well that I actually stole them from her.

These boys didn't take much time in recognising her and jumped on her licking all over her face and she giggled.

One day... she was passed out for one day and just woke up, the home is already bright with her smiles and giggles, and that little complains.

She is something else.

I grin looking at her as Marco walks in with a tray of food, which I suppose is soup and garlic bread. Doctor suggested giving her light food.

I fucking don't know how this little thing got into my heart and head. I guess it's true; she is the little witch who wrapped us around her fingers and I am more than sure we should start finding our doll soon or else we wouldn't want to find her.

Suddenly my aura changed and Marco was the first one to sense it. Frowning he gave me a nod and I cleared my throat gaining Odette's attention.

"I have some work to do now, you can keep Nike and Gucci with you so that you don't feel alone anymore in our home", I stated giving a small smile to her as she grinned widely.

"Thank you, Mario", she stated then smiled softly at Marco.

"I brought tomato soup for you", Marco said placing it on the bed and I took one last glance at both of them and strolled out of the room with multiple unfamiliar emotions in my heart.

At least am happy that she is alive, I almost killed her and am sorry for it.

I will make sure I will tell Bianca that we will keep Odette out of business; she will leave safely after signing those papers – out of our lives.

I need her out of our lives before we do something we regret.

Thinking how I will convince Bianca agree to me on not hurting Odette I hop in my car as I burn engine to life my phone rang and as soon as I saw Stefan's Id I smiled unable to hold.

"Boss, I found Mrs Grayson in Rome, our detectives tells she landed few days ago here and I heard her talking to someone about Oddy on phone, she said Oddy shouldn't know anything about what happened in Italy and she also said something about Ive..., I couldn't hear detail as it was rush in cafe", he stated and I didn't knew how to feel.

I was happy, beyond happy that I have finally found Mrs Grayson, the kind lady who didn't scold us for playing with our doll though we were covered in dirt and mud.

"Boss..." Stefan sighed heavily as he spoke again and this made my heart rise and fall in terrible anger and I fisted my phone so hard turning my knuckles white.

"Mrs Grayson also met with someone... precisely, our biggest enemy in Italy, your cousin *Elijah Donovan*".

Elijah...Elijah... the same Elijah who beat the shit out of me and my brother for ruining his little sister's frock in an accident when we were kids.

"It's okay, I guess it's time to pay our old enemy a visit, get ready a team for me, we are raiding Donovan's company and warehouses and also keep an eye on Mrs Grayson, don't let that woman leave Rome", I stated and hung up the call and ran my hands in my hair before fisting it tightly as I groaned tiredly.

I will take care of Elijah and his business with Mrs Grayson and then I will tell Marco about we are getting close to our doll, after that we could talk about Odette with Bianca and I know she won't try anything with Odette after the shit she gave her to eat – at least without telling anyone among us.

211

With that thought, I drove away.

AUTHOR'S POV

"Give me a reason why should I agree to you and finish this bowl of soup?" Odette asked narrowing her eyes at Marco making him sigh.

He dropped the spoon in bowl gently as he looked in her dark brown eyes darkly.

"You are being disobedient to me Odette and I swear to God I will be more than happy to throw you across my knees and spank that little ass of yours then make you sit on your sore ass and feed you everything", Marco threatened her looking at her with a smirk that said he will indeed enjoy it.

Odette folded her hands on her chest giving distasteful look to Marco as she glared.

"So now you became my daddy and want to spank me?! Where the hell you were these many days?!" Odette snapped pushing the bowl away.

Marco saved it not letting the contains fall and placed it on bedside table.

"I'm asking you to eat for your own good Odette, don't be a brat now", Marco stated looking into her eyes and a warning in his tone.

"For my own good?!" Odette scoffed rolling her eyes making Marco clench his jaw hardly.

His patience was thinning and Odette was playing with fire not fearing the consequences of her words.

"Did you worry for my good when you didn't come back to your wife who was fucking waiting for you? I was freaking worried all this time! You didn't even call me! And the college! You dumb ass said that am your wife to everyone and plastered my face on every damn banner as I was most wanted criminal!" Odette lashed out on him scoffing loudly.

"Everyone was afraid of me! As if I kill people for pleasure like you!" she screamed standing up from the bed.

In one long stride, Marco was in Odette's face, pushed her on bed, and hovered her angrily.

"I left you alone because I had work to do, I have business to take care of", he seethed his breathe fanning on her lips as she glared at him. Her chest rising and falling touching his rock hard chest making her breathe heavily because of the closeness.

"You shouldn't worry about me, I don't deserve it", he stated making Odette frown.

His eyes radiated anger but his voice was sad almost he was sorry that he was telling something else which he didn't want to.

"About the college, you need not worry, we bought the college, those students will be all friendly to you if they want to study or stay alive", he said and this time his voice was serious.

"What the fuck you are saying, you freaking bought the university?!" Odette snapped in her own shock when she saw a faint smile which quickly vanished.

"On lease, until you finish your college", Marco stated looking into her eyes.

"You are unbelievable! I just wanted to study as normal people for fucks sake and you all have to ruin that for me", she grumbled angrily glaring at Marco.

"Do you know how worried I was for you?" he asked now softly with his lips close to Odette's.

His eyes softened as she sulked and tried to push him away.

"Leave me!" Odette scolded trashing under him and Marco growled as he pressed his lips to hers.

He kissed her breathlessly pouring all his emotions into the kiss. His sorry for not being there for her, for putting her life in danger and thinking about using her and hurt her, then throw her away as if she was nothing to them. However, in reality she was something – more than something, which their heart knows but their stubborn heads are not ready to accept.

Odette gasped as he bit her lower lip sensually and he took that as a chance and slid his tongue in her then kissed her as if it's keeping him alive.

Not thinking about anything Odette kissed him back telling him through the kiss how she has missed him.

Breaking the kiss he pressed his forehead to hers as she shut her eyes tightly, her face flushed due to the intense kiss. Without opening her eyes she asked, "You were worried for me?"

"We were", Marco, stated and she doesn't need to ask about whom he was mentioning.

Mario was worried for her too and she has seen it in his eyes, felt them there more than from his words. He showed her his vulnerable side and gave a genuine apology by showing his true tears to her.

"You are my husband, I worry about you too", Odette said shrugging Mario's thoughts.

"Uhhm, you were asking if I was your daddy few minutes ago and now declaring me as your husband." Marco asked raising his eyebrow smirking.

"Though you screaming daddy when you came last time on my mouth still fucking make it waters but it felt good when you claim me as your husband", Marco said smirking.

Odette blushed in bright shade of red hearing his comment and she cleared her throat before looking at half finished bowl trying to change the topic.

"There is no more space in my tummy, macro", she said giving him puppy eyes.

"Those eyes won't help you this time Odette, you should eat something, you denied to eat bread along soup so you have to finish the whole bowl", Marco said sternly sounding as a dad who is scolding his child for not finishing dinner and ate desserts.

"I swear I will puke, I promise, I will eat something after three hours", she promised giving him puppy eyes.

Marco sighed heavily narrowing his eyes on her and got off her taking the tray in his hands.

"Fine, but two hours", he declared and Odette whined and one look from Marco was enough to make her shut.

Holding the doorknob, he said without turning back, "And one more thing Odette, I don't kill for pleasure, I find pleasure in killing, it's different".

With that, he shut the door leaving odette alone with her disturbing thoughts.

EYES ON HIM

AUTHOR'S POV

"We will count three, with that we will barge into the warehouse", Mario tells to his team via Bluetooth.

"One.two.three, go go!" he tells as he jumps through the window breaking the glass with his elbow smashing it into pieces.

The glass shattered all over, the place and he jumped on the broken pieces and ran towards few men who were chilling with all the drugs and guns sprawled on the tables.

"What the hell!" a man noticed six group of agents storming towards them and took his gun out of his jeans and pull the trigger aiming on Mario who was rushing towards them as a hungry lion on hunt in his FBI uniform.

216

"We want them alive", Mario yelled making sure his team don't shoot them fatally.

"Yes sir", answered his team and the bullet aimed for Mario didn't get him but instead hit the wall behind him.

"Run and inform boss", one said afraid because he was caught by most dangerous officer who doesn't let go people easily when his hands fall on them.

The group of men in the warehouse was mostly teenagers who wanted money to do drugs and were high and not good in weapon use so they were of no match with Mario and his well-trained team.

They ran away throwing gun in their hands hurriedly but Mario chased the one who tried to shoot him and held him in headlock then shoved him on the ground locking his hands behind in handcuffs.

His team did same, as they all gathered those eight people at one place. Mario and his team started searching for illegal things running in the warehouse in the name of liquor production.

Drugs, guns, bombs and what not! They gathered everything along with huge amount of Euros and dollars and put them on the table.

Sighing to himself Mario took off his bulletproof jacket and threw it on the table while he ordered his team

"Angela, Merkel", you both get the car and put these in to the trunk.

"Remaining get these little shits into the van and make sure to take their phones from them", Mario stated looking with a cocky smirk on his face while he looked at the boy who tried to shoot him.

There is definitely something worst coming for him for even trying to pull the trigger. He is not among the one who forgives for their mistake and the mistake of the young boy was thinking he could hit Mario de Luca.

When his team was doing their job, Mario simply followed behind them with his gun tugged in his trousers.

His mind wasn't in a place, especially thinking what could be related to their doll and Elijah whom they despise with their everything. They kept him still alive because he was one of the richest alcohol production company's owners and have a good name in their world.

Not to mention the girl who hated them for ruining her dress was on their bed treated as a slut but she still came back to have them. They obviously showed her place yet she dreams about marrying them one day.

"Mario!" Angela screamed as she saw someone aiming gun at Mario who was in his own thoughts.

Running towards him, she pulled him off way but she was late and the bullet shot pierced Mario's arm and he winced at the pain.

"Fuck!" he muttered and searched for the shooter and saw him trying to hit once again.

This time he missed Mario, bullet went straight through Angela's stomach, and she coughed blood as she yelped.

"Shit!" Mario cursed under his breath holding Angela close to him, took his gun out and shot the shooter straight in his head and he fell dead.

"Hurry! Take her to the hospital!" Mario ordered and Merkel hurriedly came towards Angela with wide eyes.

"Shit! Why you have to do this!" he scolded picking her up in his arms.

He always had feelings for her but she was blind in her own love for Mario and didn't see it.

"Mario… Please stay with me", she pleaded holding his arm as he tried to walk away.

Mario looked at her coldly and stated, "thank you for saving me from that bullet but you didn't have to Angela, you should leave now", Mario stated yanking his hand from Angela's and Merkel visibly frowned not because of Mario's cold behaviour towards Angela but Angela's another try to hold on Mario who shows no interest in her.

A lone tear escaped Angela's eyes as she thought internally. "I might have lost Marco to that bitch, but I won't lose Mario too".

With that thought, she let Merkel carry her to the hospital.

Mario was angry and devastated, not wanting to go hospital to get his bleeding wound treated he just tore his shirt off and threw it in the back seat of his car and drew away to his home.

Half-naked and covered in blood he walked inside the mansion just to hear chuckling of Odette and Marco's laugh.

It caught his interest and he walked towards the owner of those voices.

Marco was swimming in the pool and Odette was trying to not let him pull her into pool. It was easy for Marco if he intend to drag her inside; it's just a matter of time.

But Marco was enjoying playing with her and a faint smile spread on Mario's face seeing true happiness in his brother's eyes.

"Oh my god! Marco! Get the fuck off from my legs", Odette scolded trying to pull herself out of Marco's grasps still sitting on the edge of the pool with her legs hanging in the pool.

"Trust me sweetheart, I love it when you curse but I prefer to hear it when my tongue is buried deep inside your cunt", macro stated in his husky voice and Odette's body slumped against his tight hold. Her breathe hitched when he slowly parted her legs and pushed her skirt up making her arch her back automatically as if she was compiling an order given by his eyes.

Marco smirked looking at her and her submissive response to his touch. Liking the way her body left goose bumps where his cold fingers trailed on her skin.

Her stocking were wet now along with her panties due to macro's sweet pleasurable torture.

"Are you wet baby?" Marco asked knowingly with a smirk on his face making Odette blush hard.

She closed her eyes so hard that all she could see was darkness and feel macro's face in between her legs.

"Marco... please", she begged as she felt macro's lips on her soft velvety inner thighs and her body jolted as he slapped hard against her pussy.

Odette gasped and snapped her eyes open and glared at macro but he just smirked raising his eyebrow reminding her, what she should call him when his tongue, fingers or cock buried in between her legs.

"D... Daddy....Please", Odette begged and both twins cock's twitched in their pants hearing her beg for the pleasure she wanted.

"Good girl", macro praised as he slipped her panties to side and pressed his thumb on her clit and started assaulting her mercilessly.

Odette threw her head back feeling her high building up and suddenly her eyes fell on Mario who was looking at her with lust in his eyes. His right side of the body is hid behind the wall so she couldn't see blood dripping from his wound. Any sane person would have jumped back and covered themselves but the pleasurable torture macro was giving her turned her insane and she didn't stop macro from continuing.

"Ahhh", Odette moaned biting her lower lip but her eyes were fixed on Mario.

"Does it feel good?" macro asked increasing his pace and she nodded her head profusely.

Lack of her answers in words macro slapped her pussy hard, she yelped, and screamed daddy and her orgasm hit her hard making macro smirk widely.

"You come when you feel pain?", he asked more than telling himself that she just came as he slapped her pussy hard.

It was such a turn on for him and Odette blushed brightly looking at macro then mario.

Marco knows Mario was standing behind him as he could see his reflection in the mirror and he didn't mind Odette kept her eyes on his brother instead of her husband who was making her come on his fingers.

Wanting to see how far she would go macro yanked her hoodie off her body and Odette didn't fight to cover herself. Her round tits in grey lace Bralette were on full display for their hungry eyes, specially her perky pink pebbles begging for attention.

Marco trailed his two tattooed fingers on which she came, from her pierced belly button to in between the valley of her tits to her neck.

Odette gulped hard as Marco brought his fingers to her lips and ordered.

"Suck".

Odette held Marco's gaze and closed her eyes as she sucked his fingers clean. Her eyes opened as she released with a pop, snapped them towards Mario, and gulped hard knowing his gaze was on her the whole time and for a fact that turned her on more.

"Good girl", macro praised her again and ran his hand in his wet dark brown hair looking at Odette with his blue piercing eyes.

"Go and get dressed, you will get sick", he ordered and Odette stood on her shaky legs, grabbed the robe and draped it on her body.

When she turned, she didn't find Mario on the door and she was a little bit disappointed for not finding him there.

As she walked towards the entrance of the door, her eyes widened when she saw a pool of blood where Mario was standing.

"Oh my god!", Odette muttered as she ran towards Mario's room without thinking for another second why she was feeling like this for another man who was her husband's twin.

KISS ME PLEASE

MARIO'S POV

I was jealous, jealous of my own brother. The way he touched her, the way her body reacted to his touch, the way she moaned, screamed and yelped. Her flushed face when she came, yet the way she blushed on his comments.

Everything was a fucking turn on!

I couldn't help myself from seeing her as macro unwrapped the little eye candy.

He knew I was there, he knows she kept her eyes on me when he was assaulting her clit. I just know he didn't fuck her with his fingers, not yet.

That would be mine.

Her tight little cunt will be mine to take first.

Few hours ago, all I wanted was to leave her for good but there is a voice in my head asking me to hold her tight, to never let her go and now I feel it in my heart too.

When the fuck it started caring for someone else whom I don't consider my family?! But also, I never cried for someone whom I don't consider my family!

I did for her. I was vulnerable for her! She has me wrapped around her little fingers since my eyes fell on her.

Little vixen!

I want to bound her hands to my bed and fuck her so hard that she learns a lesson for making me feel things, which are foreign for me.

I even forgot the stinging pain in my arm as the wound turned numb but my cock was twitching and begging for attention.

Attention just from her.

Will she let me touch her as she let macro touch her?

It's debatable, I guess.

But the looks in her eyes when my brother's hand was on her pussy was begging for mine too.

I just know it.

Pushing my jealously back of my head, I open the bathroom door and walk inside to find a first aid kit so that I could treat my injury myself.

"Fuck!", I hissed as I tried to move my hand but it hurt like a bitch and I shut my eyes taking a deep breath to gather some will power to press the fucking antiseptic on injury and clean it.

"Mario!" I hear the voice of the little vixen at my bathroom door and halt my steps keeping my eyes on the mirror.

"What the hell happened to you?" she wailed as she ran towards me in her little bath robe that barely covers anything.

"Just a little injury, I will be fine", I said coldly holding myself for not spanking her little ass for teasing the hell of my cock.

"Idiot! Your injury is deep, it needs to get stitched", Odette scolded examining my arm with her tiny soft fingers and I sucked a breathe.

"I said I will be fine, get out!" I snap at her angrily.

"Get out my ass! Am not leaving you here like this, in this condition", she snapped back scoffing as she took some cotton from the first aid kit, pouring antiseptic she cleaned my wound and analysed it with a frown on her face.

"It was from the bullet", she stated not looking into my eyes.

Taking the needle and material to stitch my wound up she put them aside to grab regional anaesthesia.

"That won't be needed", I comment looking at her plump lips. She bit her lower lip concentrating on her work, hearing me she raised her eyebrow challenging me to speak further without speaking a work.

"Fine!" I sigh and let her do whatever she thinks is needed.

Giving me the injection to my right arm, she waited for few minutes to let the medicine show effect.

Those few minutes were deadly silent with just our breathes and I could practically hear her heart thumping along mine.

"Tell me if it hurts", she said as she pinched my arm and the poked her finger in my muscle.

I bit back my smile and nodded my head gesturing her to move on.

"How did you get hurt?" she asked stitching my injury with utmost care and I was mesmerised in her looks.

Her post orgasm glow is radiating on her pale fair skin and her eyes glistening with satisfaction, which my brother provided. Yet a frown on her face and the torture she is putting on her lips is breath taking.

Because the frown on her face was for me, because she was feeling my pain, as I felt hers when she was ill.

Her dark black hair sprawled on her face and she pushed it behind with her elbow and failed miserably making me chuckle softly.

"Wanna give a hand", she said smiling and I swear to God it was most beautiful thing I have ever seen.

"Sure", I tell pushing her stubborn hair back tucking them behind her ear and let my fingers linger on her skin as much as time possible.

"If you forgot I asked something", she said without looking in my eyes and I can swear to God that she have rolled her eyes.

"Just as you said, with bullet", I said and she gave me a killer look narrowing her eyes on me.

"Fine, someone shot me and I shot him in the head", I said rolling my eyes and I saw her wince.

Sighing to herself, she didn't spoke much working on my injury. Cutting the suture delicately with the scissors and wrapped it up in a clean bandage, she gave me a smile making my heart jump in excitement.

"How do you know this?" I ask her wanting to gain few more minutes with her selfishly for just myself.

She turned the tap on, washed her hands looking at me through the mirror and shrugged her shoulders.

"Training to be a good wife of a mafia boss", she said and pressed her lips together.

"I saw my mom doing this to my dad in childhood, though I didn't get much time to spend with her... I knew my mom was a doctor as I heard from my dad and others, I wanted her this part to be with me, so I learnt this, remaining – I just didn't gave a fuck", she said and her words were pained as she spoke about her mother.

I wonder what happened to her.

"What happened to her?" I ask out of curiosity to know more about her.

Sighing to herself, she turned her head towards me as she spoke.

"What usually happens to a mafia wife, she was killed by my dad's enemies and the sad part is that I don't know much about it and my dad refuse to talk about it", she says as she closed her eyes tightly.

"Shut up, shut up", she scolds herself mumbling something under her breathe and opens her eyes which were red as she was trying her best to not cry.

My heart felt the pain she was pushing away and I mindlessly wrapped my arms around her waist pulling her close in my chest.

As my breathe was fanning against her neck she sucked a huge amount of breathe and exhaled and I saw goose bumps trailing on her skin.

"We all were hurt and sometimes its better we don't remember the pain, if the wound is invisible", I tell her and a lone tear escapes her eyes and I felt a pang in my chest.

"Wound... is still visible, Mario, my mom's isn't here", she tells looking into my eyes through the mirror.

"She is in a better place, place where there are rainbow slides, flying unicorns and chocolate fountains", I tell her and a beautiful smile breaks on her face.

"Fairy tale much, Mr Mario de Luca?" she teases and I smile at her unable to hide it.

"What can I say, I was a dreamer and our mom used to read so many fairy tales for us, so that was my imagination about heaven – if it really exist", I tell her smiling softly.

"I hope so too", she tells and smiles at me and this time her dark brown eyes light up.

"Do you feel this?" I ask her and she turns around to look into my eyes.

"What?" she asks and I close the distance between us backing her up against the sink.

"This", I tell placing her tiny palm against my heart and I swear to God I don't know what possessed me.

She saw into my eyes then to our hands where they are placed and exhaled heavily. Biting her lip guilty, she snapped her eyes towards mine and whispered.

"It's wrong, I shouldn't feel like this", she admits and I was a sick bastard, I was happy to hear that she feels this too.

"Kiss me", I beg her, my voice broke in the end wanting her lips on mine, badly.

Lifting her up and placing her ass on the platform beside sink, I caged her in between my legs not giving her chance to run.

She closed her eyes tightly backed against the mirror and shook her head denying me the kiss I asked.

"I can't", she said and I was not letting her leave this place without taking a kiss from her.

"Please, Odette, kiss me, please", I begged and my breathe was fanning her cheek desperately with my hand on her jaw and neck.

She shook her head again.

"I can't kiss you Mario, am your brother's wife, this is wrong", she explained and I could hear her telling the same thing to her stupid heart which wants me just as I want her.

"Kiss me, please", I pleaded and I felt her whimper against my hold.

"I... I can't kiss you Mario", she said pushing me away with her hands on my chest.

My heart clenched in pain hearing her denial repeatedly then she spoke.

"B... But I will kiss you", her words rushed straight to my heart filing it will immense happiness and pleasure I couldn't express.

"There", she said and turned my head holding my chin in her fingers and I did as she asked.

There were our shadows on the wall of the washroom and the lights behind is illuminated enough to make the shadows darker.

Then she brought her shadow close to mine and let our lips meet without actually kissing me.

She let our shadows linger together with lips locked and I bit back my smile about her cute gesture. "There you go", she said leaving my chin and I backed away from her giving her space to get down.

230

She jumped down adjusting her robe and ran away from the bathroom and I swear to God, I heard her giggles across the room all the way and chuckled to myself.

KEY TO PAST

AUTHOR'S POV

Mario was sitting in his cabin working on his laptop about all the illegal stuff they were able to successfully get from Elijah's warehouse.

"It's time to call him", Mario said picking up the phone, which rang, in his office.

"Yes, sir", Angela said then hung up the call.

When she kept trying to call Elijah the number was not reachable, yes, he had to run from Rome thinking the cops will come to arrest him, when Mario took order from seniors after showing the proof and culprits he caught in Elijah's warehouse, the higher officials demanded Elijah behind bars. When Mario knocked on his door, he was out of the town.

"Hello, Mr. Donovan, we are calling from FBI, we found some illegal things in your company along that one of your employees shot us, I assume you knew about that, we want you in our office as soon as possible, we will make sure you won't get any more problems if you listen to us and get back to Rome, we can talk and deal with this", with that Angela hung up the voice mail.

Angela walked into Mario's cabin and Mario raised his eyebrow at her disconsolate.

"Should I remind you to knock the door Angela?" Mario's authorative voice boomed in his office while Angela shrugged it off and walked towards him.

She made sure to unbutton few buttons of her shirt so that her boobs are on full display to Mario. She seductively walked towards him swaying her hips and he just sighed with a frown on his face while he massaged his temples.

"Sir, you are stressed, why don't you allow me to take care of you?" she asked as she bit her lip and dropped on her knees in front of Mario.

"I guess you healed really quick in fifteen days of time?". Mario asked raising his eyebrows at her then took her in from head to toe.

Nothing makes him hard as Odette does, macro and mario are spending good time at home and it actually felt real. Nothing sexual happened after that day and Odette was enjoying her college time good and in fact made some good friends too. Of course, twins made sure no boy get close to their girl.

"I was always ready to take you sir, no matter how my condition is", Angela retorted and Mario rolled his eyes internally.

"Get up!" he ordered and Angela got on her feet excited that Mario will do something to her.

"I know you will say yes to me, sir, it's been long we had sex, how many days? More than a month?" she asked as she walked towards Mario and sat comfortably on his lap.

Mario clenched his jaw so hard and put his hands on Angela's hips. Angela started grinding herself on Mario with a satisfied smirk on his face but Mario kept his cold gaze on her, groped her hips, and put them in place so that she does not rock against his member.

"When did we last time had sex?" Mario questioned raising his single eye brow with a cold expression on his face.

"Quiet a few weeks..." Angela replied twisting her lip as she was thinking.

Mario smirked and asked again, "When did we last have sex, Angela?", and this time his voice was blood chilling cold and Angela was no fool to get that he is mad.

"It.... It's..." she started stuttering badly and tried to get up from his lap but Mario stopped her from getting off him.

"It was never Angela", he said digging his nails in her face and she winced and tried to free herself from his grasp.

"What we did with you was just a fuck, we fucked you hard, just as a whore you are", he said through his gritted teeth.

"Please", Angela Whimpered trying to make Mario let her go but he held her tight leaving a bruise on the places where he held her.

"Yes, just like this, you begged for our cocks and we gave you what you wanted, now that doesn't mean we will give you whenever you want", he said through his gritted teeth.

"Mario, please", she cried and a lone tear escaped her eyes as she saw in his cold blue ones.

"Don't you dare to think am oblivious to your intentions Angela, I keep my eyes on every fucking corner of this building and you... Searching about Odette and keeping tabs on her where she goes, what she does won't bring you anything but pain and a painful death", he warned and pushed her off his lap and she fell on her ass sobbing hard.

Mario stood on his feet fixing his uniform and walked towards the door as soon as his hand fell on the knob Angela dared to speak.

Through her ragged voice she asked, "Is it because she is virgin? She is pretty but she is merely a woman, she is a fucking teenager, she won't be handling two of you, not to mention she won't be able to satisfy your darkest desires like I did!"

Mario's jaw clenched as he stormed towards Angela, grabbed her hair in his fist, pulled her up on her knees, and pushed the gun in her mouth as he growled.

"Stay in your limits or I won't think twice to empty my gun in your needy mouth", saying that he pushed her and stormed out of his office leaving Angela all alone with her cunning thoughts.

"Just once, just once I get my hands on you Odette, you will regret the day you were born", she tells to herself and fists her hands so hard turning her knuckles white. Buttoning up her uniform shirt, she stormed out of Mario's cabin to her own.

~~~

"I was away for few fucking weeks and you both grew soft spot for her?!" Bianca screamed at twins.

They were standing in macro's office in underground dungeon where they torture people.

"It's not like what you are thinking", macro said raising his arms in defence earning a scoff from Bianca.

"Don't tell me you didn't hit your twin for that bitch!" she yelled totally pissed off of their behaviour towards Odette.

She was their enemy's Daughter; they should torture her not save her.

"You didn't let her die, you Mario, you gave your blood to save her! And what not! All these things I am hearing now from the maids!". she exclaimed throwing the glass of her wine on the floor.

"It's not as you are thinking, ma, we had to save her because she didn't sign those factory papers yet", Mario retorted sighing.

"Is it?". Bianca scoffed folding her hands on her chest.

"You should know better boys, that girl's dad was one who killed your mother, your father, my husband... I gave you my husband's throne to help me take revenge as well as yours too, if you don't want to do justice to your dead parents by killed their murderer, so be it, am going to do this my way from today", with that Bianca picked her purse from the table and stormed towards the door to her car. A wide smirk spread on her face as soon as she hopped in the car.

Calling someone she said, "Our work is done, I made sure Odette hear everything we spoke in dungeon, now she will be coming to you, you know what to do with her, don't you?". Bianca asked to the person in the phone.

"Of course I know Mrs Ferrari, after all am her favourite nanny and her Godmother, I will take care of her, just as I did that day", the person replied on the phone cunningly and Bianca chuckled evilly thinking she have won this game.

Little did she know she was sending odette to the key of her past where she will find a huge part of it, which was related to macro and mario.

BEHIND THE DOORS

AUTHOR'S POV

Odette's whole body turned numb as she stayed in the same place she was standing since bianca came into home.

She knew if she is here it might be something and that curiosity brought Odette towards the dungeon and she couldn't tell if she regrets coming here or don't.

"We fucked up man", Mario exclaimed flipping the table up and it fell down with a thud.

"We should have known, she was our enemy's daughter, nothing more, just because her eyes are like our doll, we can't forget the main fact that her father was the one who ruined our lives", macro stated through his gritted teeth.

"Now what we are going to do?" Mario asked his little twin making him sigh heavily.

"Nothing we didn't plan, we will get her signatures first then we will let her go, we don't need to hurt her, remaining is Andre's fate how he is going to die in our hands", macro stated and his voice felt foreign to Odette shattering her heart into pieces.

"Did you find our doll? How far you are?", macro asked with a frown on his face and he looked tired, tired of everything he is doing, all he wanted to do was start a new life with their doll far away from here, at least far away from his cruel mundane jobs which would definitely make their doll sick to her stomach.

"Mrs Grayson is here, she also met with Elijah talking about something which Stefan predicts that something is related to our doll", Mario said sighing heavily as he pulled his hair in agony.

"I just want our doll in our arms brother, am tired of doing this shit everyday", Mario admitted truthfully just as macro's heart was saying.

"Make sure you get someone clean our doll's room and our red room too, I promise, we are close to her, if Mrs. Grayson is here, I know our doll is here too, somewhere close to us", Marco said without realizing that his wife was literally standing outside and hearing their conversation.

With broken heart, Odette rushed towards her room not wanting to hear anything more. Her heart shattered into innumerable pieces hearing her marriage with macro was nothing but revenge for him, that her father was killer of their parents and knowing herself that how it feels if one doesn't have a parent she could imagine the pain of macro and mario for not having both of them.

Aurora said something is wrong with them but she didn't tell Bianca's husband was killed by Andre too and if he really killed, the question is – why?

Odette closed the bathroom door and started sobbing under the running shower letting all the pain her heart felt release under the shower through her eyes.

She waited till the water turn cold and when she felt her body shivering and giving up she turned the shower off and walked off after taking her wet clothes off her body and put on a fresh pair of blue jeans and black shirt.

Their doll, they were waiting for their doll when they not only played with her feelings but physically too.

The way macro's hands felt on her body disgusted her to her core and the way she let Mario watch her as if she was some other normal girl they sleep with whom they share made her feel like to puke all over the floor.

Gulping the bile rising in her throat she sighed heavily and didn't even care to dry her wet black silky hair. Leaving them free she walked towards those doors where Mario didn't let her walk in.

This should be the rooms they were talking about! She thought to herself and turned around to make sure no one is around to catch her sneaking into the golden door rooms.

Her hands trembled as her lips quivered wanting to release another sob but she bit her lip hard making it bleed and didn't wince.

The pain her heart was enduring was worse than the little one she caused on herself.

Opening the door, she sighed heavily as she saw darkness. The windows were shut and the lights of the room were all gone.

"Where the hell is light", Odette mumbled under her breathe as she placed her hand on the wall beside the door trying to search for switch light.

When her fingers collided with it, she turned them on and her eyes shut close due to sudden brightness in the room.

Everything was pink and white, from the big round bed and the closet to the amazing pink colour wall decorated with rainbows and unicorns with dream catchers hanging on every corner of the room, not to mention the flooring was covered in fluffy white fur carpet and a fire place with lot of books beside in the bookshelf with a loveseat comfortable enough for three.

Big neon lights behind the bed stating doll and Odette's heart felt a pang in her chest looking around.

This room was a dream room for any girl but for Odette it felt nauseating, it felt suffocating. She couldn't stand a single second there as soon as she saw a huge walk in closet and every dress to underwear sets hanging in the closet with lots of jewellery to heels and bags she ran out of the room gasping for air and forgot to turn off the lighting.

Stepping into the other golden door she searched for the light and successful turned it on.

But the room didn't brighten up as the other but a red dim light was spread in every corner of the room making the room feel intimidating.

There was a huge bed with bed posts, not to mention the room has a bar in the corner a black leather couch right in front of the black wood bed which was covered in red silk bed sheets. The tiles of the room were all black and she could see her own reflection in them clearly even under the dim lighting.

There was a huge mirror above the bed and the sex toys, which she hasn't even seen in her whole life.

This made her puke, she ran outside of the room putting her hand over her mouth and shutting the door behind her, she ran to the closet washroom and emptied her stomach as she sobbed hard.

Cleaning herself up she saw her reflection in the mirror, she was wrecked and not to mention the realization of what the room was made her stomach sick.

The man whom she trusted and gave her heart was waiting for another girl whom he was going to share her with his brother.

She was nothing but a pawn they used for revenge and all this realization took her to the only place she could get answers from.

Not from her father, not from her sister but from the person she consider her Godmother.

"Mrs Grayson, where are you? I want to meet you, it's urgent, please", Odette choked and Mrs Grayson gasped as if she was worried for innocent Odette.

"Fine, I will be there in one hour", Odette agreed to meet Mrs Grayson at the address she said.

Little did Odette know this one meeting would turn her life up and down in totally unexpected way.

BLACK CANVAS

ODETTE'S POV

I didn't even mind to get a jacket, it's cold outside but not as much as in my heart. I feel so cold that I might break from inside.

Even if macro and mario didn't do as bianca said for which I am thankful but again I am broken.

Why?

Because I loved them, I loved them both and they both won my trust just to break it.

They broke my trust they broke my heart.

I tried really hard to not close my eyes, even blink them because I can see everything is blurred just like the façade they both kept in front of my eye so that I couldn't find their true intentions.

I am afraid that if I let my tears flow, I will let my pain flow through them and might forgive them. That's how am madly in love with them – both of them.

The stinging pain in my heart isn't going away no matter how hard I try to erase the thoughts of their hurtful words echoing in my head.

I pressed the accelerator into full speed, driving the car through the darkness all I could think about the questions in my head and answers, which only Mrs Grayson could give.

I was driving recklessly and suddenly I heard a loud horn and my eyes widened. I turned my car so that it could get out of the way of the truck coming behind, I spin the steering wheel with so much

242

force that almost my car was in air due to the speed I was driving it.

The truck collided with the trunk of my car and I felt the most powerful pain in my head. It started pounding so hard that I screamed.

I screamed for mama.

"Mama!" I cried and suddenly I was beside my twin sister who looks exactly like me. The same black hair, same dark brown eyes, same lips but her hair is shorter than mine is and more pretty.

Though she was exactly like me, she was prettier than I was and I could never envy.

I smiled at my sister, "it's okay, we will be fine Ivette", I said as I hugged her tightly.

I wasn't in the driver's seat again. I was behind and I saw my mom in driver's seat just as she was in my dream.

Dream?!

That wasn't a dream, it was reality, that happened when my mother died – no got killed. Along with my little twin.

"Oddy, Ive, hold on to each other tight, we need to go to safe house", our mother said ignoring her blood and pain with worry only for us, only for our safety.

She started driving the car in the full speed and Ive and I held on to each other tight as our life depends on each other.

We heard loud bangs behind us and screamed again.

"Oh god! Please pick up the phone, please pick up the phone!" our mother cried as she kept driving. "Babies can you please get down from the seat and hide beneath the seat", she requested and we complied with our shaking bodies.

"Good girls baby, am calling Mrs Grayson, she will bring daddy here soon", our mother said and we nodded our heads with tears staining our clothes.

As soon as we reached the safe house our mother got down of the car, opened the door, picked both of us in her arms and started running inside the safe house.

"Mama, am so afraid", I cried and held on her tightly.

"I'm afraid too mama, please I want to go to daddy", Ive cried as our mother brought us all the way up in the most secured room of the mansion.

"I swear baby, daddy will come, we will be safe, you just have to stay here until daddy calls you out, don't come", our mother pleaded as she pushed us under the bed to hide.

"Mama it's dark here, am afraid", I cried and my mother pressed a kiss to my sister then me on our foreheads before speaking.

"This is black canvas, sweetie, paint them in your imagination as you wish, be wild with it", my mother stated with a smile.

Pressing another kiss to our forehead and multiple kisses on our tear stained faces she left us in the dark room.

I did just as she said painting the dark canvas in my imagination and to my surprise; I painted those two pair of bright blue eyes, which saw me with hope, love and fascination.

244

Adornment and care, my first friends I made in my whole life. Their dark brown hair sprawled on their forehead.

But now I know really well, who they were.

Marco and Mario and the doll they are searching for is none other than me.

With that, I took a deep breath and wiped my tears, instead of going to Mrs Grayson, I picked up my phone and called my father.

"Dad….." I said waiting for him to answer.

"Yes, my little bad wolf, how are you? Is macro taking good care of you?" my father asked hopefully.

I pressed a smile on my lips as I nodded my head though he couldn't see it.

"Yes, dad, I just want you to send the factory papers in fax I will sign them, macro and I are planning for our honeymoon and we won't be able to stay here till you return back", I lie remorselessly.

"Oh that's great I guess, I was missing you so wanted to meet you, I think its okay, I will send those papers in fax", my father tells cheerfully but I hear the disappointment of not able to meet me in his voice.

"Thank you dad, am missing you too, don't worry I will come back to you, *very soon*", I said and this time I didn't lie.

~~~

"Macro, can you please come back to home, I need to discuss important thing with you".

As soon as I reached home, I called macro. I need to sign those papers and give him so that I could get the hell out of here, away from them.

I successful received fax through dad and got them from macro's home office and I didn't think twice about going into his office. It was restricted area but now I restrict them from my life and playing with it.

"I'm on my way, Odette, is something wrong? "Macro asked and I can feel it in his voice he wants this to end.

"Yeah, everything is fine am just waiting", I said and hung up the call.

Marco came into the home calling my name and I stood on my feet feeling weak.

"Marco, here, take these papers", I said handing them to him and a visible frown painted on his forehead as he took them from my hands.

"What is this?" he asked and took a look and his frown deepened.

"This was what you wanted from me right?" I ask him but didn't wait for his answer.

"I made sure to put you as the sole owner of Francois weapons industry, it's yours now", I tell with my heavy heart and push my tears away not wanting to cry in front of him.

"Why?" he asked and his voice held the dominance and power, which made my knees buckle.

"I don't know if my father was the one who killed your parents, but I know my father wouldn't kill any innocent person, I have seen him my whole life, he was man of values, I don't believe he killed your parents Marco, but am so sorry for your loss, I just want to go away from you, from everything and I want my father safe", I tell and my voice broke in the end.

Marco stormed towards me in few strides and I gasped and walked back. Cornering me on the wall, he wrapped his palm around my neck in a chokehold and I gasped for air.

He pressed my neck so hard that I couldn't breathe.

Pushing him with my whole strength, I tried to escape his hold but he was like a man possessed by a demon.

Marco's eyes turned red and his iris darkened in anger.

His jaw was tightly clenched, as he looked straight into my eyes.

I can't believe these were the same eyes who saw me as if am an angle walking on the earth, I can't believe with the hands am struggling to get his hold off me once wiped his tears.

I can't believe this Marco was the same Marco who ran behind my car to ask my name.

"You dare to eavesdrop in our conversation?", he seethed and I closed my eyes accepting his wrath unable to fight back.

His hand loosened around my throat, I slumped against the wall on my ass and brought my knees close to my chest and cried hard as I took huge amount of breathe.

Coughing and choking on my own breathe I tried to regain my senses and then a maid walked in.

"Master Marco, the golden doors were unlocked and the lights were on too", the maid said with her head hung low.

My body shivered not because of the weather but due to the tone Marco spoke to me in the first time.

"You dare to step in those rooms when Mario clearly warned you?!"

Little did he knew that room were supposed to be mine, but I won't tell this, not now not in my whole life.

They shouldn't know that I am *their doll*.

THEIR WRATH

AUTHOR'S POV

"WHY?!", Marco yelled at Odette making her flinch and she sobbed hard witnessing his anger for the first time.

Mario was a dick to her but Marco was always the soft lover boy in whose arms she found love, care and affection.

Marco walked towards her and fisted his hands so hard that they turned white and Odette was glaring at him with as much as hatred he has in his eyes.

Diverting her gaze from his black polished shoes, she looked straight into his blue eyes before she spat.

"Why Marco, you didn't like me finding about your slut?" she said every word with venom in her tone.

"That room where you will share another woman with your brother for your own sick pleasures and what not? I think, I should agree with the way you guys address her", she said with a smirk on her face pouring gasoline on macro's already burning fire.

"What do you call her again?" Odette said pretending as if she was thinking before wiping her tears.

"Oh yes, doll, right, a very good way to address another sex toy of yours and your brother", Odette snapped totally losing her senses in anger and hatred and spoke bad about his doll.

Marco's jaw clenched so hard that one could hear his teeth grinding.

"You dare to speak about our doll like that again….", Marco warned one last time but Odette chuckles mockingly as she tsked.

"Again… What macro?" she taunted pushing all the limits of Marco.

"Did it hurt to call your slut a slut?" she mocked and in one shift motion Marco's hand collided with Odette's cheek that she tasted her own blood and her cheek turned red.

A lone tear escaped her eye as she fell on the floor due to the hard impact on her cheek and she spit the blood and glared at Marco as if she could kill him right now and then.

"You bitch! Don't call our doll a slut, or else you will regret the day you have ever started speaking, I will chop your tongue in so many pieces and shove it down your throat and watch you choke and die pathetically", Marco seethed and a bone shattering smirk plastered on Marco's face and Odette couldn't even recognise the Marco she knows in the same man standing in front of her.

She pressed his all buttons and brought him to the insane level, which he shows only to the worst enemies when he plays his favourite game with them.

Yanking Odette's hair back he brought her on her feet and her heart thundered against her chest in immense fear that she was considering flight or fight.

Obviously, she couldn't fight a man like Marco but she could escape from there and find some help.

Odette's eyes widened as she saw Marco looking at her from head to toe as if he was debating with himself in which way he was going to kill her.

"Leave me", Odette spat glaring at him as she struggled trying to free her hair from his iron like hold.

"Leave me", she cried feeling helpless but Marco chuckled evilly and Odette's heart almost came out of her throat because of the way she was feeling – sick, sick to her bones.

"I am being kind with you sweetheart, letting you select the way you want to die", Marco stated in his cold tone and the evil smirk on his face and his darkened eyes made him look like an evil villain of any story.

Odette stilled in his arm and he took this chance to leave her hair thinking she wouldn't try anything now.

Pushing her stray hair behind her ear, he leaned and whispered in her ear.

"Choose from fire, water or *blood*".

Odette gulped hard as her eyes widened and fear crawled up in her head through her toes and she did what she thought would get her out of this place. She kneed him hard in his groin and Marco groaned painfully, He cupped his precious part of his manhood and fell on his knees giving Odette a distasteful murderous look.

"This Christmas sing jingle bells holding your broken balls you fuck face", Odette screamed as she ran away from the mansion for her dear life.

Little did she know she was running from one monster to another.

ODETTE'S POV

I was terrified but that word wouldn't be able to justify the fear I felt. I never felt fear like this in my whole life and to escape it I started to run away as a mad woman.

My dad could save me from him, he was always my superhero, he will save me now too.

With that hope, I didn't mind I was running bare feet. I just needed to go to police station and ask them to bring my father here.

It is easy. You could do this Odette.

I motivated myself and took deep breathes as I ran without looking back if macro is following me or not.

My legs started trembling with every step I took, there was no one around me in midnight hours and I doubt they would have helped me if they knew from whom I am running away.

I saw a police station on my way to college. It should be there. If I could make it in time before Marco finds me, I will be alive, back to my home.

My lungs felt heavy as my throat and mouth turned dry that I couldn't even swallow my own saliva because there wasn't anything.

My whole body was covered in cold sweat even in the chilly weather. The rough texture of the road was piercing my feet and I could feel wetness under them, for a matter of fact I know it's blood and I didn't took a single glance at them with only determination to run away from Rome.

Thankfully, I found a police station and breathed a sigh and my eyes teared up again. I didn't cry in the way and now I couldn't stop.

I ran into the station and heads of the officers turned towards me judging me from the way I might be looking. I know I look like a mess and I would have snapped at them for giving me this look but now I don't have any energy to fight, I just want to cry in my dad's arms.

As I used to when I was a little girl.

"Please help me", I begged at the very first table I was able to reach.

It was a female officer and her eyes were wide as saucers seeing me. Obviously, they know I am Mrs de Luca and I just hope they don't bug about me to Marco.

"Mrs de Luca?!", she gasped and saw behind me and afraid that macro might have followed me I snapped my head back to see no one just my blood stains on the white marble of the station in my foot prints.

Sighing in relief, I turned my head back to the lady officer and begged folding my hands.

"Please, call my father, I don't have my phone with me", I said and my eyes teared up.

"Please this way, our head officer is in his cabin", she said gesturing me towards a glass office and I smiled softly at her in gratefulness.

She pressed her lips together, led me the way and opened the door of the cabin before closing it behind me.

The chair was turned back and I couldn't see the person who was sitting the other side of the desk but I was grateful that I reached to a safe place away from macro.

"The wind carried a message, said the princess is missing from the castle", the voice echoed in the room and my smile dropped immediately and my blood turned cold.

I don't need the person to turn towards me to recognize who it was. However he did.

There was Mario, who was sitting in the chair and smirked at me, which resembled just as macro's.

When those dangerous azure eyes, which I used to fascinate, met with mine, my heart dropped in my stomach.

"Let's go to home princess, oops, my bad, its hell for you now".

That's how I ran from one monster to get caught by another.

DEAL WITH DEVILS

AUTHOR'S POV

"Leave me you fucking bastard", Odette screamed trashing around on Mario's shoulder.

His uniform was on so his badge was hurting her stomach badly but she was so stubborn to accept her defeat.

"I swear to God Odette, you are for hell of a ride, you saw our good side now you will see our worst, you shouldn't have spoken about our doll like that", Mario growled throwing her in the car.

Odette yelped and then took this chance to escape but Mario pushed her back and locked the door properly making sure she doesn't escape.

"You people never showed your good side to me you assholes, you covered your bad side with lies, you people deceived me and that isn't what showing good side looks like you shitface", Odette screamed at him banging her hands on the window.

"Be careful with what you speak sweetheart", Mario warned as he drove the car towards their mansion – which odette once supposedly called it her home now it's nothing but a dangerous hell hole.

Mario stopped the car in front of him, went towards the backside, opened the door and dragged Odette holding her hair so hard that she felt the stinging pain in her roots and sobbed.

"Leave me you fucker!" Odette cursed and trashed but Mario didn't show any mercy and dragged her into dungeon.

With his each step, Odette's heart was pounding so hard against her chest and all she could do was concentrate on her breathing.

Mario opened the door of dungeon and threw her on the ground so hard that her head hit the floor as it would leave a bruised but didn't bleed thankfully.

She yelped and cried, with her quivering lips she pushed herself up just to see a pair of black shoes shining in front of her eyes. She embraced herself and sat with her palms resting on the floor and met those cold blue eyes whose owner was sitting on the black leather chair in front of her and his expression was beyond anger.

"I believe you enjoyed your little run on Rome's midnight roads", macro's cold voice sent shivers straight through her bones.

"How about we start talking about your mistakes?", Mario announced walking towards another chair resting beside macro's.

"She eavesdropped our conversation with Bianca, she went past golden doors, she asked to let our enemy free, asked to keep him alive after the things he put us through", macro said calmly without any expression on his face.

"Not to mention she called *our doll* a slut", Mario added through his gritted teeth.

"I hate you, I fucking loath you", Odette spat glaring at macro.

"So am I a villain in your story now, princess?", macro chuckled darkly while Mario just smirked evilly.

"If she already knew everything, why don't you enlighten her about your marriage, macro?", Mario stated with a smirk on his face and Odette's heart thundered in her chest so loud that she could hear it in her ears.

"Ah, yes, our marriage", macro said and threw his head back and chuckled wickedly.

"Our marriage wasn't even real sweetheart, it was fake, fake papers and fake vows", macro said looking straight into Odette's teary eyes.

Odette felt numb unable to speak anything. She held her heart as if it was bleeding; her pain was devastating and unbearable.

"Everything was a lie?". Odette breathed out looking at those two pair of cold eyes.

"Of course", Mario snickered as if she just cracked a joke.

Odette simply nodded her head brokenly, sighed heavily, and closed her eyes as she wiped her running stubborn tears.

"You do hate me so much right?", she asked opening her eyes.

"Isn't it a mutual feeling, princess?", macro countered and she nodded her head again.

"Leave me, let me go back to my father", she pleaded biting her lip hard.

"What do we get if we let our enemy's lovely daughter out of our hands this easily?", Mario asked looking at tear stained face of Odette.

"You have weapon factory all for yourself", she said gulping hard but macro and mario looked at each other smirking.

"We would have taken that from you even if you didn't offer", macro stated cunningly.

"You have nothing you could give us now, Odette Francois", macro's statement broke her heart beyond repair.

Not because he made her feel helpless but because he called her Odette Francois not Odette de Luca.

There was pin drop silence in dungeon as no one spoke another word.

After which felt eternity Odette looked into those blue eyes and stated.

"Myself".

"I have myself, I will give you my body and you will let me free and not cause my father any harm", Odette said staring into those eyes coldly.

A sinister smirk formed on those brothers lips as Mario spoke.

"What makes you think we cannot snatch that from you?"

Mario's sentence made her whole body tremble. Her heart was already broken now this discussion was bringing her nowhere but to the devils and she has only one way to escape them by offering her body. Allowing them to break her completely but she was determined that she will not allow them to break her soul.

"Satisfaction", Odette blurted out as she gulped hard looking at floor.

"What gives you more satisfaction than your enemy's daughter gave herself to you, to both of you willingly knowing that you were going to break her?", she spoke then met those eyes again.

Marco and Mario looked at each other silently as if they are considering her offer and talking to each other in their heads.

They both snapped her eyes towards Odette and she gulped hard waiting for their answer.

"Strip", macro ordered and odette's heart dropped in her stomach. However, without debating with herself, she weekly stood on her legs and kept her gaze on twins as she slowly started unbuttoning her black shirt.

They both were looking at her with so much lust and hunger but Odette couldn't find a single ounce of love in their eyes, which they showed her in past few days. Dropping her shirt on floor, she spoke.

"I loved you", Odette's confession made them freeze. Macro was surprised to hear but he kept his cold facade on not letting her see his emotional side. Odette laughed maniacally as she diverted her gaze from macro to mario then spoke again.

"I must be insane, because I loved you too", her words were cold just as her eyes, which were showing no emotions in them.

"But not anymore, this Odette Francois will never give her heart to monsters like you", she said as she took off her jeans.

Standing in her only undergarments, she promised herself and smiled at them.

"This will be the first and last time you will ever touch Odette Francois".

THEIR DOLL

AUTHOR'S POV

Marco and Mario smirked at her in a sinister way as they both stood on their feet. The room was dark with only a single light hanging from the floor making the room look more dangerous than it was before.

Odette gulped hard as they started walking towards her as predators and she was little deer stuck in the woods.

"Strip", Mario ordered and Odette's hands started shaking severely as she reached for the claps of her bra. In a few seconds, she freed her blossoms from her grey lace bra.

Closing her eyes tightly she breathed heavily and with shaky hands she slipped off her panties and saw in those azure eyes with her own dark brown ones.

Mario walked towards the ropes and took one wrapping it around his hand as macro walked towards the setup where they hang people to torture them.

Pulling the equipment down he turned around and walked towards Odette who wrapped her hands around her naked self-shivering.

Mario walked towards her, wrapped the rope below her blossoms, and tied it behind her back giving her blossoms a hard squeeze and pinched her erect pebbles in between his fingers painfully making Odette whimper and bit her neck softly making her body react to his touch in various ways.

Odette was disgusted with his touch but the more he played with her body she felt more disgusted by herself for reacting to his sinful touch.

A deep moan escaped her lips when Mario bit a particular spot on her neck and that made Mario smirk against her skin and macro chuckled mockingly.

Marco slid his hands on her petite body sensually and grabbed the rope and tied it around her taking it from her breasts as her two soft globes are pressed together in a painful hold but that excited her and she found herself getting more wet than before and she bit her cheek so hard tasting her own blood to lessen the need between her legs.

Slowly kissing his way around Odette's neck leaving multiple hickeys Mario bonded her neck then brought the rope between her legs and tied it back on her hips leaving a spine like structure behind her back and her body tied yet free for their hunger eyes and hands to feel.

Odette gulped hard when Marco took off his shirt and unbuckled his belt and freed his member which is standing proudly and

Odette's eyes widened seeing most monstrous thing she have ever seen in her life.

A skull tattoo on his happy tail just below his perfectly sculptured abs caught her attention and she found herself staring right at his cock.

Marco wrapped his tattooed hand around his thick cock and pumped it sensually looking straight at Odette.

Mario pushed her on her knees and ordered.

"Crawl to him and suck his cock as a good little slut you are".

Odette turned red in shame but complied Mario's order. With her shaking hands, she crawled towards macro and kneed in front of him. His cock was straight in front of her as he was standing proudly with his trousers laying on his ankles.

Gulping hard Odette raised her eyes to meet those blue ones and her insides clenched so hard that she wanted to burry herself in shame somewhere.

Slowly with shaking hand she wrapped her palm around his thick member and exhaled heavily as she felt it hard yet velvety in her grip.

She brought it to her plump lips, opened her mouth, took head of his glorious cock in her mouth and sucked it as it was a candy.

Marco threw his head back at the feel of her warm wet mouth and Odette worked her way on sucking his cock and taking it in her mouth as far as she could while she worked her hand on remaining length pumping it bringing him to edge.

Unable to resist himself Mario stripped off completely, walked towards them, pumped his cock, brought it close to odette's mouth and ordered.

"Suck".

Odette shifted her eyes from macro to mario and when she looked at his length she gulped hard because it was not any lesser glorious than macro's.

Still holding macro's cock in her hand, she held mario's cock, took it in her mouth, sucked, licked her way all over his length and kept pumping it.

She repeatedly took Marco's then Mario's cock in her mouth sucked them and left it with a pop doing it repeatedly.

Marco suddenly fisted her hair in his hand and deep throated her pushing his length as far as she could take making her gag on his cock and fresh tears escaped her doe eyes.

Mario pressed his fingers on her wet folds making odette flinch and gasp at his sudden touch and chuckled darkly when he found her wet and taunted.

"She is enjoying sucking our cocks as a hungry slut".

Marco grunted and chuckled making her shut her eyes in shame when Mario ordered.

"Play with your needy cunt and come, while you suck our cocks dry".

Odette didn't listen, this made marco clench his jaw, he fucked her mouth faster and she gagged more as more tears streamed out of her eyes.

She was whimpering around his cock and Marco groaned and spat.

"Do as he said".

She blinked her teary eyes as she brought her hand towards her pussy and played with her clit when both brothers took their turns to fuck her mouth as they pleased making her gag. The room was filled with their grunts and groans along with mewled moans and gasps and gagging sound of Odette with wet sounds of sex.

Breathing through her nose as she took them in one by one Marco was the first one to release himself in her mouth and she struggled taking it in when some of his come slipped out of her mouth.

"Swallow", Marco, ordered and she did as he said.

Mario pumped himself and released himself all over her face and chest, she shut her eyes feeling dirty and used but soon she reached her high becoming more ashamed of herself as she moaned and came all over her fingers.

Marco and Mario tsked as they brushed her dark black hair sprawled on her face and tucked them behind her ear as marco stated.

"Do you think it's over princess?".

"Then you are so, so wrong sweetheart", Mario mocked and they chuckled darkly making goosebumps rise on her skin.

"We will fuck you so hard that you would never forget tonight in your whole life", Mario rasped digging his nails in her flushed cheeks making her whimper.

Odette turned her eyes around but Marco tsked understanding her unspoken thoughts and made her clear.

"Do you think we will take you to bed to fuck you? No sweetheart we will fuck you here hanging you in air with this bondage and fuck your two tight holes at same time", he said tugging her up on her feet pulling the rope tied on her body.

Marco's those words made her eyes widened and she silently teared up in fear.

"Do you think you can take it?", macro taunted with a smirk on his face making her blood turn cold.

"Don't scare away our little slut brother, we will take this slow", Mario assured but the look on his face wasn't matching his words making odette gulp hard.

She felt black dots in her vision as she tried to look into their eyes but before collapsing into the darkness, she whispered loud enough for them to hear.

"I guess you haven't asked your mother to read the story red shoes and seven dwarfs, even if you did, you might have not learnt the moral of the story, your clothes were dirty then and now your hearts are more dirtier than anything".

With that, she collapsed and twins embraced her in their arms with wide eyes and their hearts shattered when they realized that *she is their doll.*

FORGIVE US

AUTHOR'S POV

"What are we going to do now?" Mario sighed his voice deep and hoarse as if he is trying so hard not to cry.

A lone tear escaped from macro's eye as he lovingly pushes odette's hair away from her face.

After she collapsed in their arms, they took off rope from her and winced at the marks formed on her body because of tight bondage. Mario gently picked her in his arms and they brought her in their doll's – now Odette's room which they made sure maids have cleaned it up neatly.

Marco brought warm water in a bowl and wiped her body with wet towel and odette winced at the stinging feeling and every time she hissed in pain twins teared up silently blew on her bruises. After cleaning her up, they cleaned her feet, applied ointment on her bruises, and tucked her in fluffy pink bed.

"She knew that she was our doll", Marco whispered enough loud for Mario to hear.

"Why do you think she didn't tell this before?", Mario asked his brother frowning.

"Isn't it clear, she heard us talking about our doll and she knows we hate Andre because he killed our parents and she is his daughter, precisely our enemy", Marco said looking at unconscious figure of Odette. "We were really dumbasses as she says", Mario countered making Marco chuckle humourlessly. "She is changed, completely changed", macro said still brushing her hair with so much love.

"She said she loved us brother and we fucked up in our own messed up way", Mario exhaled and a lone tear from his eye fell on Odette's foot.

"We will win her again, we will", macro said with so much hope and pressing a kiss on her feet mario closed his eyes laying beside her legs over the duvet he fell asleep for the first time with so much guilt as well as contentment without taking a sleeping pill.

Marco held her hand tight as if she would run away and closed his eyes feeling the same way as Mario he embraced the peaceful darkness for the first time in contentment.

~~~

Odette winced and opened her eyes slowly moaning as she stretched her body that was hurting so badly, her throat and jaw was sore and she rubbed her jaw with her palm frowning with her eyes closed.

As soon as she realized what happened last night she snapped out of her sleepy state and found herself in pink bedroom.

Marco was wearing all black suit and shirt with matching trousers, sitting on the edge of the bed near her legs and beside him was sitting Mario, who was wearing a white t-shirt with blue jeans.

Odette glared at their smiling faces, which she remember how cruelly they were smirking last night.

"So after all you took me to bed?", Odette snapped covering her body with duvet.

"Did you finish what you started yesterday?", Odette scoffed rolling her eyes.

"However it doesn't matter, because the deal is over, one night and out of your lives", Odette declared and covered her body with duvet and tried to get on her feet.

As soon as she put her legs down she winced and scowled at the immense pain she felt in them but Mario was the first one to rush towards her with a worried expression and held her in his arms not letting her fall.

Marco released a sigh finding her safe and smiled at his brother who was smiling softly at their doll.

"Its okay doll, I caught you", Mario stated but Odette punched in his ribs trying to free herself.

In the struggle, she let the duvet covering her drop on the floor, she gasped and Mario froze at the closeness of her naked body.

The light marks on her skin started to disappear, which was a good sign but both of them diverted their eyes from her naked body to her glossy eyes, which were looking at them disgusted.

"Fuck off, you shit face fuckers, you have already seen it", she yelled at them and stormed out of her room naked still struggling on her sore feet.

"Doll please, please we beg you forgive us", Marco pleaded walking behind her.

She fisted her hands so tight and walked into her share room with Marco, stumbled around for her clothes, and put on a white pair of undergarments and black jeans with blue shirt.

"Forgive? my ass, don't call me doll or else I won't mind kicking you in your balls again and this time I will make sure I apply more force", Odette scoffed and tied her hair in a loose bun.

"She kicked you too in the balls?" Mario asked grinning at Marco thinking he wasn't alone who received the special treatment.

"What did she tell you? She said me to check if it's working properly as it used to before and thank god it did", Mario said looking at his twin without even paying attention to odette who was standing in the same room.

Marco rubbed his neck shaking his head but Mario punched him on his shoulder forcing to spill the beans.

Odette rolled her eyes and she scoffed loudly gaining their attention and spoke.

"I said him to sing jingle bells this Christmas holding his broken balls and I won't mind joining you in the club too if you don't get off my way", Odette announced and Mario threw his head back and laughed so loud holding his stomach and said in between his laughter.

"This was funny", Mario said placing his hand on Odette's shoulder and she slapped it away and pushed him.

Mario stopped his laughter and panicked as she walked past him.

"Please, doll, forgive us give us another chance", macro pleaded behind her and she rolled her eye.

"Where are you going?" Marco asked and there was a horror in his voice thinking what Odette was doing.

"Going to my home you bastards because someone said this place is hell for me and they weren't wrong", Odette retorted looking at Mario with immense anger and turned her back walking towards the door.

"Fuck! Am sorry, doll", Mario begged running behind her as a little kid pleading his parents for a particular Christmas toy.

"I hate you, I hate you both", Odette choked and cried trying to open the door.

"Damn, this thing isn't opening", she growled and punched but was of no use.

"Please doll, please, we are really sorry, this door won't open unless we are leaving to the honeymoon you said to your dad", Marco added and this caught Odette's attention.

"Last time I checked we weren't married", Odette scoffed punching the code to open the door but everything she punched showed access denied.

Turning behind she saw with wide eyes, twins were on their knees and tears in their eyes as they folded their hands as if they were praying in a church.

"We fucked up, we agree but we can't live without you doll, we have been waiting for you our whole damn lives and we fucked up when we finally found you, this is killing us enough, we know you loved us and we broke your heart but please give us another chance", Mario pleaded and his voice broke at the end.

Odette turned her back on them unable to see, as the pain in her heart was unbearable for the little soul, which was left in her after the disgusting night. She closed her eyes tightly trying to not breakdown in front of her sinners and then a gun slid to her feet making her open her glossy eyes and a visible frown plastered on her beautiful face. "If you want to walk out of that door, you have to kill us", Marco declared with seriousness in his voice which made Odette's whole body shiver.

She froze for a few minutes, picked up the gun and turned towards twin and there wasn't fear in their eyes, if there is something it's just love and guilt which she can see through their blue eyes into their souls clearly.

"I wouldn't mind killing you, especially if you are behind my father's life", Odette rasped through her gritted teeth with gun clenched in her small palm.

"We are not, not anymore", Marco said and this made Odette's heart pound hard against her chest.

"Even if my father was the one who killed your parents?", Odette asked and her voice was so weak as she was thinking the possibility of andre killing macro and mario's parents.

"We grew up without our parents, we know what it feels like, we don't want you to go through the same pain, doll, not by our own hands", Marco said truthfully.

Odette was beyond shocked hearing them and the gun from hands fell on the floor with a thud.

"Why?" the only word escaped from her mouth.

"Because for you, my doll, we can kill our friends and forgive our enemies", Mario stated looking straight into her dark brown doe eyes and the next second she found herself crying out loud as if she was broke beyond repair and indeed they broke her beyond repair and they only had the power to mend her broken pieces.

They did, hugging her tightly in their arms that their warmth spread through her body then to her heart embedding her broken pieces but this wasn't the day she was going to forgive them, not yet.

"I hate you both", she cried and punched then and they let her take her anger on them with tears in their eyes but a smile on their faces that she was going to forgive them not now but one day and they can't wait for that day to come fast in their lives.

RED

ODETTE'S POV

It has been five days since we three are locked in this mansion. Marco and Mario didn't go for work and tagged behind my ass as Nike and Gucci and this was getting on my nerves.

They are grinning and smiling as two idiots and I couldn't breathe a sigh around them because they would run to me and carry me to bed telling I need to rest because am tired or ask if they need to call doctor if I have any breathing problem.

I mean... What the actual fucking fuck?!

No matter how hard they tried, I gave them my best silent treatment and expressed my anger towards them. I was not staying in the puking pink room but in Marco's and he is not stepping inside his own room. Of course it's mine now and he is not allowed anywhere near me.

"Doll, what do you want to eat?", macro asked strolling towards me shirtless and in a blue jeans which was hanging low on his hips giving a perfect view of his abs and pecs, not to mention the perfectly trimmed hair on his chest. His arms are fully painted in tattoos, which were looking beyond ethereal on his tanned skin.

God! These Italian men have tempting body to not resist. When he finds me staring, a smirk plastered on his face and I twist my lips to meet his azure eyes and glared at him.

Rolling my eyes, I walked into the kitchen without looking at Mario who was chopping fruits for smoothie. "You need anything doll? You could have ordered and we would have brought it right away", Mario tells giving me a soft smile while he turned on the mixer.

I glare at him before taking a milk carton out from the refrigerator and pour myself a glass of milk and grab a banana from the fruit basket and sit on the couch after turning the TV on then search for a interesting show to watch but end up choosing the vampire diaries – come on who can resist the charms of TVD men!

Both Marco and Mario comes to me holding plates of yummy smelling food and glass of smoothie. Marco sat on my left side and Mario sat on my right but they didn't pass me plate as they used to do.

Instead, those fuckers started moaning at the taste of their food and side glanced me with the stupid killer smiles on their faces.

I tried to ignore them and took a sip of my milk keeping my eyes on the screen where Klaus leaves a drawing of Caroline and horse, I gushed an aww as I peeled the banana and took a mouthful of bite.

"You liked that drawing?", Mario asked looking at me fondly as he poked his pancakes with fork. I eyed his breakfast and my mouth watered immediately; I remember how tasty he cooks. While Marco doesn't know cooking but he does makes an amazing coffee.

They two were feeding me even if I didn't spoke but today they didn't even offer me food and made my favourite breakfast and swallowing it down while moaning beside me.

Narrowing my eyes at him, I twisted my mouth, chewed my banana and forced my eyes back on TV. "I just asked, I thought if you liked that drawing you would love yours too, Marco is a good artist", Mario said shrugging his shoulders and I snapped my eyes at Marco to confirm it.

He smiled at me softly, my eyes immediately lit up with amazement and his smile grew wider than before.

Stupid Oddy, you are freaking angry for fucks sake! I reminded myself, got up from my seat, and took a step towards my room. The smell of tasty pancakes and its flavour from yesterday was still in my system, which made my each step away painful making me groan internally.

Fuck it!

I ran back to the couch and saw their frowned sad faces which I know for a fact that they were sad because of no words from me.

Seeing me, return their faces suddenly lightened up and I snatched the plate of Mario as well as stole his smoothie and ran towards my room without turning back and I heard those heartfelt laughter behind me, which made me smile.

~~~

Should I go and see what they are doing? I thought internally as I rolled on the bed with a romance novel in my hand.

Mario said Marco draws and I wanted to see how he draws! Am just curious.

Debating with myself I groan into my pillow, come on I don't have anything to do, nowhere to go!

So I tiptoe and walk out of the room slowly so that those cunning handsome brothers don't catch me.

I don't even know in which room he paints so I decide to go on a adventure. First, I find Marco out in the pool and Mario playing catch with Nike and Gucci.

Grinning to myself thinking my path is clear I ran off to the direction where Sofia didn't show me. If it has to be somewhere, it should be there.

Finally reaching the door, I debate with myself, look around for any camera and sigh when I don't find any I giggle opening the door and walk inside the dark room.

Trying to find the lights, I stumble on something. A scream escapes my mouth and I find my hands and face wet immediately.

"What the fuck! What the hell is this?!", I groan at the pungent smell and then realize it must be paint.

"Fuck you, brain, fuck you!", I scold my brain for being curious and bring me here.

When I try to get up my hand slips and I drop straight into the paint again.

"Who the fuck puts paint out like this?!" I groan and next second my eyes snap closed because of the bright light in the room.

"You literally got caught red handed doll", a husky voice filled with amusement sings behind me and I don't need to turn to look who was the owner of that deep voice.

I look down at the tray, which is filled with red paint, then clench my jaw as I try another time to get out of this mess but for my clumsy ass, I had to embarrass myself and fall into the same shit again. This time I hear Marco chuckle loudly and this is the first time I heard him laugh this loud and heat rushed to my cheeks and my lower stomach. One due to embarrassment and two because of his effect on me.

"Let me help you, doll", Marco, said as he lift me up from the red paint and I blushed hard seeing him only in towel.

Thank god for this red paint.

I must be looking like a joker with it but I wouldn't make joke of myself blushing in front of him.

Then my eyes flew on the large painting, which is size of a wall of the room, and my mouth hangs open wide for all the flies and mosquitoes of the world to pass, hell! All the aeroplanes could pass using my tongue as a runway too.

There was my painting completely in red paint, hair, eyebrows, nose, lips every fucking detail is in different shades of red except eyes.

He painted them as they are dark brown but they were prettier than real in this painting.

"This is amazing", I spoke for the first time in a week.

Astonishing is even a down rated word to express his art.

"When you have a beautiful muse your paintings turns amazing", Marco countered and walked somewhere and got tissues and wiped my face holding it delicately.

I looked into his eyes, which are smiling, how could these eyes be that dark that could shatter one's soul and brighten one's life?

"Thankfully this paint will get off your skin if you wash it with warm water", he tells cleaning up my face as much as he could and I stare into his eyes letting myself explore his soul through them.

Then my eyes travel all around the room and I frown looking at all the black and grey paintings, which were dark in their own way.

Except a single painting, which was, exactly as my eyes and dark black hair sprawled in air without other features detailed?

I walk towards it, run my fingers on it and sigh.

"This was my first painting", Marco said standing right behind me and I silently gasp thinking how did he mastered the art this good in his first time.

"Why did you paint me in red?", I ask him turning back looking into his eyes.

"The only colour I see here is dark and dull colours then why red? It doesn't seem your aesthetics", I tell and a smile spread on his face as he turned to look at the masterpiece he created.

"What does red colour imply for doll?", he asked still looking at the painting.

I frown then walk and stood behind him and said, "Love?".

"Love?", he asks back now looking into my eyes with his neck crooked and he smiles.

I fold my hands on my chest as I wait for him to speak and he does as he walks towards me and I suddenly feel small in front of his six four height in my own five four.

I gulp as he push my sticky hair behind my ear then he speaks.

"Love doesn't describe my love for you doll", he tells looking straight into my eyes and I hold my breath in and my heart starts thumping hard against my chest.

I search his eyes for answer but his lips spill.

"Blood, that's what implies my love for you, doll, as long as I have a single drop of blood in my body, I will keep loving you".

As soon as those words escaped from his mouth he bends towards me with his lips so close to mine and I found myself leaning into his touch and I almost let him kiss me but a sudden sound of Nike and Gucci snapped me out of my messed up state and I pushed him back and ran towards my room holding my heart in my palms and my heart beat in my throat.

FAMILY

AUTHOR'S POV

"Mama... it's dark here, please don't leave us", Odette said in her sleepy state hugging herself.

"Ivette", she cried as she was sweating terribly even in the blast of air conditioner.

Again, she was seeing her past in her dream, which made her restless in her sleep. Hugging her pink duvet, she teared up in her sleep.

"IVETTE!", a scream escaped her mouth as she snapped her eyes open and found herself out of that terrifying dream.

"Oh my god", Odette gasped thanking that it was another nightmare but she couldn't neglect how real it felt.

She frowned as she rubbed her dry throat trying to swallow to make it ease but she winced. Turning beside to pour herself a glass of water, she found the mug empty.

Sighing to herself, she stood on her legs and walked out of the room in her Pikachu print tank top and booty shorts.

As soon as she opened the door her eyes widened in surprise to see Marco and Mario sleeping while they leaned on the wall of each side of her door.

The weather was cold and they were shivering in their sleeps, this melted her heart as a sad smile spread on her lips. She went inside her room, grabbed extra duvets, walked back to them and covered their bodies in a duvet each. Running her hands in their hair with so much warmth and love in her touch she exhaled.

"You hurt me but I can't hate you, I can never hate you", she said as a lone tear escape her eye, which fell on Marco's nose as she pecked his forehead.

She pressed a kiss on Mario's cheek and smiled how cute he looks in his sleep.

They both look ethereal with their dark brown hair sprawled on their foreheads.

Sighing to herself, she walked towards the kitchen to drink some water and when she filled the mug. Marco and Mario stormed in the kitchen panicked.

"Doll", they both sighed in unison, embraced Odette in a hug and sighed into her neck.

"We thought you went away", Marco whispered softly still clinging on her.

"We were afraid", Mario admitted and Odette frowned and hugged them back as she spoke.

"I just came to drink some water but why were you sleeping near my door? In this weather?", Odette asked softly.

Breaking the hug, they both gave each other side-glances then looked back at her as they spoke.

"You were screaming in your sleep, so we thought we should stay if you needed something", Marco said looking guilty.

"We are so sorry, it's because of us", Mario spoke not looking into her eyes as Odette frowned.

"You are sleeping out of my door from how many days? Whole damn week?", she rasped in disbelief as she crossed her hands on her chest.

"We are so sorry, please forgive us", they both pleaded making her sigh.

"I... I... just... It's, it's not about you", she said pinching her temple.

"Not about us?", Mario asked his expression frowned and macro's face resembled just as his brother's.

"I... That night, when I gave you those papers, I went to meet Mrs Grayson, I got myself in an accident, that's when I remember that day I played with you in the park", Odette said sighing heavily.

"What do you mean you remembered it that day?", Mario asked with his expression looking devastated.

"You asked me if I ever came to Italy before we came here", Odette reminds Mario about when he asked this question; he nods his head clearly understanding it.

"I didn't lie that day, I really don't remember I was in Italy before a week ago", she tells exhaling loudly.

"I don't remember anything, *anything* and I am getting these nightmares which feels like real, I even got the dream about me playing in the park but that turned into a horrible nightmare that I saw someone chopping my non existing twin sister!", Odette cried out as her voice broke along with all her walls she built for them.

Marco embraced her soon and ran his fingers in back of her head massaging her scalp as he spoke.

"Shhh relax, do you think anyone might know about this, about your condition that you didn't remember anything?", he asks and Odette cries in his chest as she nods her head weakly.

"Aurora, she was startled when I asked her if I ever visited Italy, when I asked her when she came to hotel, actually it was the reason why I called her", Odette tells breathing heavily as macro tried his best to calm her down.

Mario nodded his head telling silently that macro should talk about this with her so that they find what happened to Odette in the first place.

"Its okay doll, we will find out what it is", macro coos as he pressed a kiss on her forehead.

"I will go to Russia and talk to your sister", macro announced as he broke the hug.

"But... Aren't you enemies.....", Odette was cut off when macro spoke.

"We made it clear doll, for you we will forgive our enemies", macro said with an assuring smile on his lips.

Odette beamed wiping her tears as she nodded her head and whispered a thank you and took few steps out of the kitchen to only come back and give each of them a hug and walked away from them to her bedroom leaving them smiling as idiots.

~~~

The door of odette's room opened and she closed her eyes tight hearing footsteps walking towards her. She was wide-awake even it was 3am in the morning as she wasn't able to sleep because of the nightmare and the assuring words macro said.

If he was ready to go out of his comfort to step his foot in Russia it was a huge thing for her, not to mention how easily they forgave Andre for their parents death left odette wondering if she could do same for them? No and that was sending shivers to her spine thinking the undefined boundaries of their love for her.

Soon the person who walked inside slid inside the duvet, wrapped his arm around her waist and pulled her into his chest and odette sighed feeling the warmth.

"Where is macro?", Odette asked knowing well that the person behind her was Mario.

"He went to Russia to fix a meeting with Dimitri and Aurora, in fact he asked for Andre's help that it would be less awkward", Mario chuckled and vibrations emitted from his chest spread under her skin leaving goose bumps.

"How can you forgive the killer of your parents? If it was me I wouldn't have done that", Odette said biting her lip as a tear escaped her eye.

"Growing up without our parents...", Mario said and exhaled heavily in the crook of Odette's neck as he spoke.

"We realized that family is everything... and you was our family from the very second you held our dirty hands, without you we don't have a family and no reason to live doll", he whispered truthfully in his raspy voice.

Odette closed her eyes tightly as she turned now facing Mario, with tears glistening in her eyes without speaking a word she gazed into his blue eyes, which were shining brightly in the moonlight, his ethereal features enhanced in the moonlight making odette gulp as she ran her hand in his silky brown hair.

"You were not dirty", Odette whispered the same words she told when she met them for the first time. Smiling softly she added, "Who ever told you that, they were dirty". Mario beamed at her words remembering the little girl who didn't judge them for their looks. His heartbeat skipped when Odette placed her soft palm on his cheek and pressed her lips to his own capturing them in a passionate kiss, which he saved only for his doll – for her.

ACCEPTING US

MARIO'S POV

As soon as her lips met mine, all I could think about keep devouring them and I did.

Wrapping my hand around her waist I pulled her close to me if that's even possible, gripped her hair I let my lips dance on hers on their own accord.

Her cold lip piercing on my lips felt so fucking good that I bit on it between my teeth pulling it a little then leaving it just to wrap my lips on hers repeatedly.

Odette moaned into my mouth as I squeezed her plump ass and my cock twitched in my pants at the sweet little moan she slipped.

I want to hear more.

Just like that, I flipped her and hovered, kissing her hard, passionately, soft and slow and then as if my life depends on it.

Pushing my tongue between her mouth she let it explore as I wished and it was fucking addiction, which I don't want to get rid off at cost of my fucking life.

She tastes sweet and sugary which made me wonder how does she tastes down there and with that I broke the kiss and her closed eyes snapped open looking into my own lustful eyes with need.

Odette answered my unasked question with a nod of her head and a smile on her lips as I whispered.

"I never kissed anyone like this". Odette's eyes widened as a blush crept on her face as she bit her lip to hide her smile making my cock jump in excitement.

"Why?", she asked innocently flattering those beautiful eyes making me groan internally.

"Because... I always wanted to kiss you and only you even macro, we never kissed anyone except you", I breathe out with my lips close to hers.

"But you both slept with others", she complained and a smile paints my face as I look at her pouty lips.

"Are you jealous, doll?" I ask her raising my eyebrows and to my surprise she said, "Yes, I am".

I thought she will deny her true feelings for me but her truthfulness set my stomach on fire. Is this the feeling what people calls as butterflies in stomach? - Then they are wrong! So fucking wrong! Because this feeling is like a fire in a forest, hungry to devour the beauty with its insatiable wildness and indeed that's how exactly I feel about devouring the beauty underneath me but right now I want to worship her so I do.

I kiss her lips softly, sensually letting the feeling sprawl into every atom of our bodies as I quench my thirst greedily, she let me take every inch of her, kissing me back with the same passion and need as I do.

I whisper against her lips in between our kiss letting the words settle in between us before I go any further, "You don't need to be jealous, because we were and will be always yours and you will be ours, our doll, not because we like to play with you as we played with others but to decorate you with so much love and respect as you stand right between us, not behind but in front of us, because we will always follow you, with our minds and our heart to heaven and hell, only for you".

Then she kissed me hard as I felt her tearing up under me I embraced every tear of her letting it sink into me, promising myself that these will be the last tears she is going to shed.

I slowly kiss her tears away then peel off her clothes leaving her naked in front of me. I bring my lips back to hers before giving a assuring kiss as my palms start playing with her round blossoms twisting and pinching the perky pebble in between my fingers. She curves her body dancing to the music am creating in her with so fucking good chores of her moans and gasps as I wrap my tongue on her needy cunt without wasting any time while I came down kissing my way through her stomach. She arched more into me spreading her legs to take her – all of her. And one taste and I am in fucking heaven!

I lick the slick slit of her lower lips devouring them with so much hunger that left me wondering if I had proper meal since the day I found she is our doll.

"You remember I said how heaven might be?", I rasp on her pink flushed dripping cunt letting my hot breathe fan on it as she moans and gasps nodding her head unable to speak.

"That was wrong, this is how heaven feels like, my fucking mouth buried deep in your cunt", I rasp as she moans and without letting her speak any, further so greedy to hear her moans I fuck her cunt with my tongue deep into the tiny cave, which swallowed me greedily.

She tastes fucking sweet, just like honey.

In my own sanity I held her thighs tighter as I worked on her cunt with my tongue pulling a orgasm from her for my own pleasure and she screamed, trashed under me moaning my name as she gasped for breathe she came, once and all letting herself free from the denial, accepting me as hers – accepting us and a silent promise to be ours.

She screamed my name "Mario!!!!!", and I swallowed her moan into my mouth, kissing her like a hungry caveman as I slid my finger into her tight little swollen cunt and fingered her mercilessly dragging another orgasm.

She moaned and gasped into my mouth digging her nails into my shoulders through my shirt, I feel them leave their beautiful marks, which I would cherish in my lone time smiling like an idiot.

I am fucked up. She fucked me up.

"I'm going to…..", she cried biting down on my shoulder and I embrace the pain proudly as I suck on her sweet spot leaving my marks all over her milky pale skin.

I feel her clench around my finger and I rasp in her neck.

"Fuck! Come on my finger, doll, just like that, let it go".

And she did screaming my name as she released herself with so much force that I felt her push my finger out and I slowed the pace down letting her enjoy the euphoric feeling and when I lift my face from the crook of her neck, she is already asleep. Her face flushed and sweat was glistening on her forehead, which was at peace and her lips swollen because of me - made me smile widely as I press a kiss on her forehead and whisper, "I love you".

Not wanting to leave her, alone I slip under the blanket and wrap my hand around her waist and she snuggled into my chest as she groggily whispered, "I love you too, Mario".

Just when I thought my day couldn't get any better she mumbled softly, "I love you too, macro".

With a wide smile I typed on my phone, "Doll is asleep, she said she loves you, stay safe".

Without waiting for a text, back I know he would be grinning widely on the seventh sky and no one couldn't drag him to type a return text, I lock my phone placing it on the side table and slip in the depths of night hoping to wake up beside my sunshine the next morning.

VICTIM OR CRIMINAL

MARCO'S POV

A huge grin plastered on my face as I saw text from Mario. He said he will take care of Odette and I was more than happy to leave them both so they could bond and the text from him speaks volumes.

As soon as I saw Andre's gaze on me with a smile on his wrinkled face, I couldn't help but clench my jaw and smile back, he is father of our doll before our enemy.

I kept reminding myself as I walked further into the mansion.

"It's so nice to meet you macro, it's a surprise, Odette said you were leaving to honeymoon", he said shaking his hand with mine.

"Yes, actually, I am here to talk about Odette, I wish to keep this private", I add glancing around though I don't find maids at this hour but we can't afford to let the information about our woman which might be God knows what slip in the ears of people waiting to spill it out for money.

"Of course", Andre said and I could see a visible frown on his face as he walked us to his office.

Sitting on the couch he poured a glass of whiskey for himself and me with a heavy sigh he sat back holding his back tiredly.

He is getting old.

"My body isn't as it used to be before, sorry", he said settling back leaning on the couch and I smile shaking my head at him.

"Its fine, I can understand", I tell assuring him and take a sip of my whiskey as I lick my lips at the taste he speaks.

"So, I hope Odette is being nice, I swear to God, I know she is brat but trust me give her some time, she always wanted a normal life and was mad because I wasn't able to give it to her and with you she is continuously in spotlight for being the wife of the most successful man of Italy", he tells and my chest swells with pride hearing him.

Of course I was counted in most successful man as well as my brother but hearing it from our enemy, of course our ex enemy is a sweet to eat.

"I am lucky enough to have a woman like odette on my side", I tell him truthfully as a wide smile spread on his face he leans back now calming himself.

"Then what is it about you wanted to talk at this hour macro?", Andre asked smiling in relief which soon faded as the question escaped from my lips.

"About Odette's past".

Andre's face turned pale as he gawked at me in shock as he frowned shaking his head.

"Her past should be locked behind, it was never my favourite thing to talk about macro and I want to keep it that way", Andre said as he got on his feet turning his back on me and poured another glass of whiskey for himself.

I leaned back on the couch and said, "No one likes the past, Andre, specially those who was victim or a criminal, who were you among these two?". I ask him clenching my jaw in anger.

He frowned looking bewildered and shook his head as he drowned another glass of whiskey.

"Sometimes we don't need to be victim or criminal of someone to have a dark past macro, just as Odette, she was neither victim nor criminal, just a witness and I think she is lucky enough to not remember that and live her life in present and future, I would give my anything to have that blessing", Andre said walking back towards me now with a whiskey bottle in his hand.

I look at him frowning, this man doesn't looks like he is lying and if he is saying it's better for odette to not remember anything then that must be something horrible she witnessed and sadly I couldn't stop what is happening with her right now. One way I am happy that she remembered us, having the most memorable - best memory with us but that led her to the darkness, which should have stayed in dark, not shadowing on her bright future.

"Sadly.... She says she is remembering something, something in which she was in a car with her twin, Ivette and her mother, the accident, going to safe house, hiding under the bed and.....", I pause looking at Andre's reaction which was none less than the expression of a actress who have seen a ghost in horror movie.

He turned pale and the sweat glistened on his forehead as he gulped visibly and asked ".....and someone chopping off Ivette", he said and he fell on the couch as the glass from his hand slipped on the floor breaking into pieces.

"This shouldn't have to be like this, Odette didn't deserve this, no one deserves this", he cried out as tears streamed down his wrinkled face and he didn't even bother to wipe them off.

"Who killed your wife and Odette's twin? Who was their killer?", I ask him in my softened voice but it comes out hoarse in anticipation. "My lovely daughter, Ivette, she was killed brutally, without showing mercy to the little girl, that woman chopped her into pieces while she was still alive, while she was screaming and begging for mercy, she didn't show", he cried brokenly sobbing at the horrible memory of his daughter's death.

My heart felt a pang in my chest thinking what could have gone on this man's heart, losing his blood, who was just a little girl and that too this brutally, if it was me in his place I would have gone insane and kill the person again and again till he or she begged to be killed completely.

To be honest I would never let a shadow, which seemed danger stroll behind my daughter.

"Who?", I ask him holding my breath.

"Arianna Ferrari, your Godmother's cousin, I killed her, just like she killed my daughter, I chopped her into pieces little by little before digging my nails into her heart and squeezed life out of it, out of her", he said through his gritted teeth with a wicked smile on his face.

There was a moment of silence in between us when I decided to ask, "What happened to Odette's mother?".

He looked into my eyes with his own dark brown ones just as Odette's as he said darkly, "She is dead, at least to me, she is good as dead".

This made me frown, what does this mean? She is alive.

But without being asked he answered it by himself, "She is alive, happy, far from our lives, with love of her life, leaving us behind in our dark times – she decided to live her life normally, after death of Ivette she couldn't step into my world, she left me", he stated looking dead in my eyes.

"She is alive?", I ask him stupidly even after hearing him tell that but it was hard to digest that the person we thought was dead is alive and happy when their loved ones are left behind in their lives mourning their death.

Odette couldn't take this, she didn't deserve this, not to be grown without a parent thinking she was dead and crying herself to sleep. If not anything, she deserved the truth.

"If you knew Bianca is related to the woman you killed how could you let Odette marry me?", I ask him sceptically.

He smiled genuinely as he looked into my confused eyes as he spoke.

"Do you know who your father is?"

His question bubbled anger inside me as I clenched my jaw in anger, fisting my hand I weakly nodded my head.

"Elijah de Ricci". I answered him; my voice was heavy with the tension building up in my throat.

"My best friend, Elijah de Ricci, who left his throne for the woman he loved, your mother, Alexia – Odette's mother, Julia's best friend", he tells making me frown.

My heart started racing so fast that I couldn't understand if it's in anger or anticipation which is growing inside my chest with every second of silence in between us.

How dare he mention my parents as his best friends? But specially, branding my father as a mafia when he was a business man.

"When Ivette and Odette was born we decided to convert our friendship into more stronger bond – family, we decided we will let Mario marry Ivette and Odette was always yours since she was born, after death of your parents, this was the only wish of them I could fulfil", he tells with a sad smile on his lips which made my blood boil.

"You are lying", I grit out with so much hatred that he was taken aback.

"You are fucking lying", I scream and unknowingly I clench my palm around the glass so hard that it shattered in my palm and the glass pieces pierced my skin making blood flow through them painfully but that wasn't a pain near to the immense pain we felt growing up without parents.

"If they were your friends then why did you kill them?", I growled standing up and he followed my movements with confused expression on his face.

"First you killed our father when we were just five then you killed our mother when we were eleven", I screamed again storming towards him but restrained myself from not laying a finger on him.

297

I can't, I promised her, I promised our doll.

"What are you talking macro, your mother and father died in a car accident at the same time", he said and for a reason I know he isn't lying but if he isn't lying then our whole life would be a lie!

"We did their burial ritual with respect, with our own hands, we buried them behind the church you married Odette, you both were missing since the accident and then when I found you, Bianca took you in and brought you to the ball when you were eighteen", he tells. Then I understood we were all played hard that now we don't even know who is victim or criminal in each other's lives.

A WALK IN THE PAST

~19 years ago~

AUTHOR'S POV

"Are you ready sweetheart, we are getting late", Andre asked walking into Julia and his shared bedroom.

Julia sighed heavily as she shook her head and said, "I'm just afraid, how would I be able to see my children in other woman's womb?! This is insane Andre", she complains throwing her hands in air as Andre walks towards her.

"Sweetheart, your condition is not good for having a baby by yourself, after Aurora you barely survived because of blood loss and I can't take chance with your life, I love you so much to lose you in my life", Andre said hugging his wife lovingly.

"Who is the surrogate? I want to know all about her", Julia demanded looking into her husband's eyes.

"The file is already in my office – both actually, one the hospital sent and the other I did myself, the lady is in her early 20's and want to be surrogate for money, she doesn't have criminal background nor any health issues, she doesn't even drink", Andre said assuring Julia about the surrogate they hired.

"What is her name?" she asked looking into her husband's eyes and he answered smiling.

"Arianna Ferrari".

~~~

"Ahhh, mommy, fuck me harder", Arianna screamed as the woman fucked her from behind with a strap on.

Pinching her nipples from behind she pounded hard into her pussy making her come all over it again and again before taking it out and this time Arianna took the lead.

She spread the wet folds of the woman lying underneath her and licked, sucked and spit on it before doing same and smudged her come all over the other woman's pussy before tasting it on her.

"I like to taste my come on your pussy", Arianna whispers sensually in her ear and she moans aloud.

Teasing her already, attentive nipples Arianna sucks them on as a baby while she pinches the other then repeat same on the other tit.

"Ahh, fuck me already", the woman cried out pushing her hips up making Arianna chuckle.

She took her time teasing the perky pebbles, rubbed her tits over the woman's laying underneath her and kissed her lips passionately before telling against her lips.

"I love you", and started rubbing the strap on her pussy as she slowly slid it into her pussy and fucked her hard as she begged. Filling the room with sinful moans and groans of two women who are madly in love with each other.

~~~

"Tomorrow is your appointment?" she asked as Arianna nodded her head.

"Yes, they are rich, I will get huge amount from them for this pregnancy as they want twins", Arianna said glancing at the laptop she was filling the details. "That's great, you know how much I like to fuck you with your bump, and your pregnant belly just turns me on so fucking much! Not to mention those leaking tits…. Yum!!!", the woman with Arianna comments making her eyes widen and a blush spread on her face making her look cuter than before.

"Shut up Bianca and get the hell out or else your brother will start doubting you again", Arianna tells pushing Bianca out playfully.

Bianca chuckles as she pecks her lips one last time stealing a kiss with her hands locked in the brunette hair of Arianna making her moan into her mouth she leaves to her home with a huge grin on her face.

~*After Odette and Ivette's birth*~

"There was a princess, who was lost in the woods and a bad wolf was following her behind silently to eat her", Alesia reads the story sitting in her rocking chair as five years old macro and mario are laying in their beds covering themselves in the duvet with their eyes wide.

"What happened then mama?", macro asks tensed as mario nods his head agreeing to his twin.

"Then she started crying as she heard the voice of the bad wolf laughing evilly", Alesia tells adding special effects to the story with deepening her tone.

"I am afraid mom", Mario said hiding himself deeper into the duvet as his eyes were fixed on his mother.

"My little champs, you don't need to fear, when daddy is here", Elijah said as he walked into the room.

"Daddy!", both macro and Mario jumped in joy and ran towards Elijah who was walking towards them after a tiresome day at his new company.

Elijah's Heartfull laugh echoed in their home as well as twins giggle making alesia's eyes teary but she didn't let them flow fearing the happiness will fall out of their lives just as her tears from her eyes.

"Daddy, today we both played football, mama said we are playing good just like you", macro tells proudly grinning at his father.

Elijah saw those blue eyes of their mother which he fell for her at first sight from then he kept falling for them again and again.

Now seeing those beautiful eyes of hers in his children was a blessing for him.

"Daddy bought ice cream for you all", Elijah sings and Alesia frown shaking her head as both macro and mario screams in joy.

"Later, it's your bedtime now babies, you can't eat ice cream before going to bed or else monsters will eat your teeth", Alesia explain to her twins smiling as she send a cute glare at Elijah.

"But mama.....", both brothers whine but Elijah press a kiss on their foreheads and tells, "it's okay, tomorrow we can eat ice creams and chocolates because uncle Andy invited us to meet his cute daughters".

"Arianna gave birth?!" Alesia gasped and a huge grin spread on her lips making Elijah's heart pound hard against his chest.

"Yes, she did, before you pull your *my bestie didn't tell me!* She did, just now when I entered the home, your phone was on the tea table as you were busy reading fairy tales for our boys", Elijah tells rolling his eyes.

"You dare roll your eyes on my fairy tales!?", Alesia gasps offended resting her hands on her hips glaring at Elijah.

"Oh! Come on! I mean who reads fairy tales for boys?!", Elijah tells rolling his eyes again.

"How dare you! Fairy tales have princes as well as princesses, girls read because they are princess and boys read because they are prince!", Alesia tells folding her hands on her chest.

"My sons are not less than any princes", Alesia tells looking at her kids who are smiling widely.

"Yes, daddy, we are princes", Macro and Mario sings grinning at their mother nodding their head politely and bows to her as princes does to the queen.

Indeed, they were her little princes and she was their queen.

Elijah's eyes soften at his kids as he smiles and tells, "Of course you are", then tuck them in the bed before kissing his kids and Alesia does same before they leave their sleepy kids and go to their room.

Elijah's eyes rake all over her body and his eyes linger on her full boobs which were looking more bigger than before, he licks his lips smirking at her then tell, "You are looking more sexier each and every day".

Alesia blush brightly as she bites her lip lowering her gaze. Elijah walks towards her lifting her chin up with fingers as he brush his lips on hers. "I love you baby", he tells making Alesia beam.

"I know, I love you too, we four of them love you too", alesia's confession made him frown but soon his eyes widened as she placed his hand on her tiny bump as she said.

"Hello, daddy".

"Really!?", Elijah smiled widely feeling her stomach and when she smiled and nodded her head profusely he fell on his knees and kissed her stomach with so much love as a his eyes glistened with tears.

No one will believe if someone said the great Italian don Elijah de Luca, falls on his knees for a woman and here he is kneeing in front of her who isn't just a woman for him, she is a goddess, an angel who came into his dark world just to drag him into her light, so does he did, held her hand tightly and walked out of his dark life into goodness, leaving his throne to his capo, second in command and started living a life—real life with his three pieces of heart in seclusion not letting anyone know existence of these people in his life to keep any harm a mile away from them and now his world is welcoming another life in his life which he would love and cherish, take care of this tiny soul as he took care of Alesia, his wife and their twins Macro and Mario.

~~~

"Mama, are we going to meet two princesses of Uncle Andy?" twins asks gazing at their mother.

"Yes babies, we are", Alesia tells beaming happily as she tuck them in their car seats.

"Will those princesses marry us? Because we are princes", Mario asks pouting cutely making Elijah chuckle from behind.

"Of course they will", he tells ruffling their hair as they both smile widely.

"My princess will be beautiful", mario tells to macro who pouts his lips offended. "My princess will be beautiful too", macro tells folding his hands on his chest.

Their parents saw the cute banter of their kids and smiled softly shaking their head as Alesia said.

"They both are beautiful, they are identical twins, which mean they look alike", she tells smiling at her sons whose eyes were widened.

"Did Uncle Andy dropped them in magical pot?! So they doubled?!", macro asks gasping making Elijah and Alesia laugh throwing their heads back.

Alesia wipes her tears while she press a kiss on macro's head she tells, "Ask this to your uncle Andy".

"Uncle Andy is grumpy, I won't ask him, I will ask aunt juli", macro tells making them shake their heads.

"Okay ask your jolly juli aunt leave my grumpy man alone", Elijah jokes kissing their heads one last time not knowing that this will indeed be the last time he was kissing his kids.

Alesia frowns looking back and forth between the two cars in front of her, Elijah always made them to travel in other car instead of the car he was in, making sure his family was safe.

But today Alesia doesn't want to leave her husband alone, so she walked towards his car and Elijah frowned.

"Baby…" he spoke but Alesia cut him off hastily telling, "take this as what your baby is making me do, she doesn't want to leave daddy alone".

Then she sat inside the car in the backseat leaving the door open for Elijah to get inside.

Elijah just shook his head in disbelief and smiled to himself getting into the car beside his wife.

"Good morning Mrs de Luca", Elijah's assistant greeted Alesia and she smiled politely at the young lady and said, "good morning".

Then they started driving and twins' car followed them not knowing they are going to witness a horrible incident of their life.

CLEARING OUR HEARTS

AUTHOR'S POV

Alesia held Elijah's hand sensing a sudden uneasiness. "Are you okay, sweetheart?", Elijah asked immediately holding her protectively as he placed his hand on her tiny bump.

"Yes, I am fine but I don't feel good", alesia tells frowning.

Elijah smiles as he press a kiss on her lips then tucks her hair behind and tells, "Better now?"

Alesia chuckles shaking her head as she smacks him on his chest playfully.

However, their laughter didn't last when a truck from the left side suddenly hit their car where Elijah was sitting.

"Elijah!", Alesia screamed holding tight on her husband afraid, the driver gasped and Elijah's assistant screamed in pain as Elijah took impact not letting his wife get hurt a lot.

The car flew over the bridge and that felt like millions of hours to Alesia. At least they are dying together she thought as she teared up looking into her husband's eyes.

A sad smile painted on Elijah's lips as he held his world in his protective arms and a lone tear escaped his eyes looking into those teary eyes.

"I'm sorry, I failed you, sweetheart", Elijah whispered against her lips.

Alesia shook her head as she held her husband close to her and cried against his lips, "I love you". Elijah coughed blood and it

307

flood on his shirt making Alesia cry more, "Please don't leave me". She begged on last time closing her eyes.

"I love you too", she heard Elijah's voice in her head as she felt his wet lips on her forehead before the car flew down the bridge and the car blasted and Marco and Mario remained looking at their parents burning down the bridge as they were crying badly, too afraid for the consequences the driver who drew them there left the car at the spot and ran away for his life leaving two innocent children crying for their dead parents.

~~~

"Madre, didn't die then", Marco said gulping hardly as Andre was done with his side of the story and there is no doubt because he was speaking truth.

"She was alive, she was out of the car when engine blasted and she took us with her to Italy, we were living there, I think it wasn't living - surviving there", Marco tells looking with his red sore eyes into Andre's and this time he felt him as his family because now he knows it wasn't him who killed their father nor his mother.

"I can't even imagine", Andre tells placing his hand on Marco's shoulder and this time Marco smiled at him genuinely.

"Let's get your hand treated", Andre said smiling at Marco but Marco shook his head and spoke.

"I also have something to tell", Marco said gulping hard looking into Andre's eyes before lowering them unable to tell his deeds looking straight into his eyes.

"I met Odette, actually Mario and I met Odette in Italy when we were thirteen, she remembered us, it was the same day as she said accident took place", Marco tells sighing heavily. "But trust me, I didn't know she was the same girl we met years ago who was kind to us, who held our hand when others disgusted away, she showed us how it feels to be loved but unknowingly..........", Marco stops then look into Andre's confused eyes as he spoke.

"Trust me we didn't knew she was the same girl before we hurt her", Marco said standing on his feet.

"What do you mean?", Andre asked and the anger was visible in his eyes which were showing kindness few minutes ago.

"We... actually, I married her to take revenge on you, it wasn't even a true marriage, I faked it", as soon as those words escaped from his lips Andre punched him hard against his jaw in anger.

"How dare you fucking hurt my daughter!?", Andre growled as a hungry animal holding Marco's collar and punched him hard again.

Marco kept his eyes down taking each punch not defending himself because he knows he deserves it and the pain they felt knowing it was their doll after that night he knows Andre might be feeling much more because after all she was his lovely daughter.

And he wronged her, wronged him, when they were innocent.

~~~

"I swear to God! I will kill you if you keep me locked in this fucking house", Odette yelled at Mario before twisting his hand behind and pressing him into the wall.

Mario let her manhandle him smirking as he enjoyed every second of it. Odette pushed her body weight by pressing herself into him as she warned placing a butter knife at his neck. "Now you want to kill me sweetheart?! After last night letting my tongue fuck your tight cunt", Mario commented making blood rush to Odette's face.

Mario turned around locking her both hands behind her back and pushed her chest against the wall as he chuckled deeply in her ear his warm breathe fanned her.

Odette's breathe hitched and she started thrashing around under his touch but that made Mario smirk.

"You shouldn't be playing with a FBI agent, doll", Mario said mockingly making Odette grit her teeth in anger.

"You are a fucking traitor, you dumbass", she snapped still trying hard to get out of his grasp.

"You are the only one who could speak to us like this, this shit fucking turns us on", Mario comments smirking against her cheek.

Odette threw her head into his face smacking his nose hard but not too hard to let it bleed, Mario groans at the pain holding his nose in his hand while she takes the chance and free herself from his grasp and try to kick in his balls but this time Mario held her knee and pull her leg up trying to make her fall but he wouldn't let her get hit.

Odette smirked lifting her leg as he was doing and snickered as she spat, "I'm flexible you fuckface".

Mario's surprise was a visibility but that soon turned into a smirk as he commented making Odette piss off more than she already was.

"Whoa, that's great, we can try many positions", he said raising his eyebrows as he shot her a wink.

Odette groaned and yanked her leg out of his free grip and walked towards the couch plopping herself on it she pouted and folded her hands on her chest.

"This would have been a lot easier if it was Marco, when he is coming back?", Odette groaned as Mario sat beside her smirking.

"Missing my brother already?", he asked making Odette roll her eyes.

"Yes I am, he is kindest one among you both", she stated giving a cute glare at Mario.

"Uhmm, trust me when I tell you this doll, he is - with only you", he tells laughing as he shakes his head.

"What do you mean only with me?", Odette asks and Mario smile at her softly before telling.

"He locked his emotions at the time of our mother's death, he was most expressive among us but he didn't cry that day, he cried for you, that day when you......", Odette cut him off and said, "When you found I was your doll?".

Mario smiled as he shook his head and said, "No when I fed you vanilla unaware of your allergy and trust me he punched me so hard and that was the first time he did hit me, that fucker even warned to kill me if something happen to you". Mario said chuckling.

"Really?", Odette gasped placing her hand on her heart.

"Yes", Mario confirmed smiling at her.

"Even before you knew I was your doll?", Odette asked and her eyes twinkled making Mario swoon at her doe dark brown eyes.

Not to mention that referring herself as their doll made his heart thunder in his chest. Unable to form words in his over joy of having a normal conversation with Odette he just nodded his head conforming her doubt.

"Then what about you?", Odette asked raising her eye brow at him.

Mario stole his eyes away from her not answering her the embarrassing moment of his life, how he begged her to stay with him as he cried caging her in his arms.

"You weren't worried for me?", Odette teased and Mario blushed as he pressed his lips together.

Mario shook his head as no, but that made Odette smirk and she walked towards him, sat on his lap straddled him with her legs as she looked into his blue eyes.

Pushing his dark brown hair back, she placed her hands on his cheeks as she brought her lips close to his. Mario immediately closed his eyes expecting a kiss but she spoke against his lips instead.

"I know you were worried too, I heard your voice, I heard you saying to not leave you", Odette said the words she heard Mario speak before she fell completely unconscious.

Without opening his eyes he asked, "Will you leave me, will you leave us?"

Odette shook her head as no even though Mario couldn't see and said, "Meeting you that day was fate, we cannot fight against our fate, Mario".

Mario opened his eyes slowly as he saw behind her lashes and said, "You are a fighter, Odette".

"Are you happy? By not fighting against your fate?", he questioned her looking into her eyes for answer.

Odette smiled softly before pressing her lips on his she said, "I don't want to fight with my happiness, mario, please keep me happy". Even if she didn't ask both Marco and Mario did intend to keep her happy and now they could do anything to make her the happiest girl alive on the whole fucking planet.

BLASTFUL OUTING

AUTHOR'S POV

"What the hell did you tell?", Andre growls angrily hearing forbidden words from Marco.

"What did you fucking tell!", he snapped and punched hard against his chin and Marco coughed blood.

Spitting the blood Marco glared back at Andre as he spoke.

"I said we love Odette, we want to marry her", Marco stated without stuttering and sending a dangerous glare at Andre telling he will go to any extent if he will come between them and their doll.

"Do you have any idea what you are speaking?", Andre snaps unfazed by the glare of Marco.

He is mad, maddest of the madness whipped his head hearing two men loves his daughter and wants to marry her. Not to mention that they are brothers for god's sake. What will people tell if they hear or see his daughter marrying two men?!

Of course, they will speak badly about his daughter. Marco, Mario will be clean, and Andre wouldn't let someone talk about his daughter as if she is a whore or slut, not until he is alive.

"I know what I am speaking…. I also know what I will do if you try to take Odette from us, Uncle Andy", Marco said through his gritted teeth and a devious smirk forming on his face.

"You bastard!", Andre spat as his hands found Marco's collar and he gripped his neck trying to choke.

Marco didn't flinch an inch and slapped Andre's hand away in one push. Gripping his neck Marco snapped, "the only reason I am taking your fists is that I promised no harm to you to *our* doll, or else I would have separated your limb to limb without mercy just for thinking to take her away from us, hearing those words from your mouth is far away from acceptable".

Andre's eyes widened as he clenched his jaw hard, "What does she think? Do you believe my daughter will love you? As well as love your brother?", he asked making Marco narrow his eyes on Andre.

Without thinking he answered, "She loves us".

Andre laughed aloud, as Marco left his hold on his neck. Marco bit his inner cheek in anger as Andre laughed on his face. Without speaking a word, he kept his glare on Andre as he had his laughing fit.

"My daughter would never love you both", Andre challenged making Marco smirk.

"Why don't you ask her yourself", Marco mocked and Andre smiled widely.

"Boss!". Someone yelled from the other side of the door snapping both Marco and Andre out of their glaring game.

Andre frowned immediately as he walked towards the door and opened it to see Draco, Marco's right hand.

"Boss we have information that someone set bomb in FBI head office, boss Mario is not answering his phone", Draco said making Marco's stomach churn in fear.

"We need to go!", Marco said walking outside of the office.

"I will come with you too", Andre said panicked for his daughter. "There must be more bombs if someone was able to put them in head office, I can't risk my daughter's life", Andre said looking seriously into Marco's blue eyes, which were filled with fear, fear for his brother and their doll.

Without speaking he simply nodded his head and Andre followed Marco and Draco out of his home.

~~~

Odette kept kissing Mario as she grinded herself on him. Moaning at the feeling of his thick member in between her legs, she threw her head behind giving access to Mario to mark her neck.

When he bit a particular spot, Odette moaned loud gripping tight on his shoulders. Mario teased that spot with his teeth then soothed the pain with his tongue and smirked against her skin stopping his sweet torture on her body when she was craving for more.

Pulling himself away from her he saw her cute yet sexy flushed face and pressed one last kiss on her lips as he said, "come on, let's go out".

Odette groaned sliding off his lap and glared at Mario as she snapped, "As I said before, it would have been much easier if it was Marco".

However, this time she didn't intended those words for taking her out and both of them knows it. Mario just chuckles from behind as she angrily walks towards her room to get changed into clothes fit for going out.

"Ughhh! I will take revenge!!!", Odette tell herself punching her hand in air then shake her head crazily turning the tap on and wash her flushed face cooling it down and get dressed up in a pair of black leather short skirt and wear a knee length stockings, of course she had to get rid of previous panties because of Mario and she clench her jaw smirking as she find a black tongs and put it on with matching lace bra and white shirt.

She tied her hair up in a ponytail, put on Marco's leather jacket, and walked out of the room to see Mario changed in a pair of his blue jeans and white shirt.

A smirk plastered on his face as he saw her checking him out and he wolf whistled winking at her as he raked his hungry eyes from her head to toes biting his lip.

Odette licked her lower lip running her tongue on her lip piercing before she walked towards him and gestured to the door.

"That's marco's favourite jacket", Mario commented smirking as he shook his head trying to get rid of his thoughts about lifting her skirt and fuck her against the damn door.

"Oh! Well now it's mine", Odette commented smiling and she put her two fingers in her mouth and blew a whistle.

Nike and Gucci ran towards her woofing and wiggling their tails, Odette who kneed in front of them and cuddled for a few minutes before securing the leash around their necks and look up at Mario giving her best puppy eyes.

"Can I bring them with us please?", she asks and Mario chuckles softly as he nods his head making Odette grin widely.

"Thank you so much", she coos and hugs him innocently making his heart pound against his chest at her warmth.

"Come on babies, let's go", Odette tells running towards the car with leash in her hand following her hyperactive dogs.

Sitting in the car, she smiled at Mario before asking.

"So where are you taking us Mr de Luca?"

"To my head office first then to the carnival", Mario replied as he drove off to the destination.

~~~

As soon as both Mario and Odette got off the car, she excitedly held his arm without even realizing.

The bright smile on her face was beyond any starry night, which mario could gaze at without blinking.

"This is my second time to the police station, am excited", she coos smiling widely then it hit her that the first time she was here it wasn't a memorable thing to remember and her mood soured at the thought of that, night and unknowingly she tighten her hold on mario's arm.

Mario frowned as a sad expression painted his face he gently pressed his lips on her cheek gaining her attention.

"I am sorry to ruin your first memory of this place doll, I promise I will make it up to you by creating many good memories here", Mario said looking straight into her eyes as she smiled softly nodding her head.

"Let's go", Odette, said gaining a bright smile from Mario and he walked inside the office hand in hand with her.

Many heads snapped at their direction but one strong glare from Mario put the men in their place as they walked across the cabins to Mario's. Angela who was looking at them from the first time they stepped their foot out of the car gritted her teeth in anger as a tear escaped her eye. "So you stole Mario from me too", she gritted with disgust and hate in her voice as she looked at their joined hands enviously.

Odette explored the office as if it was a museum looking at every inch of the office and stopped at the name plate of Mario on the table.

She gazed at the marble plate where his name was engraved with golden letters and smiled as she turned towards him who was already looking at her intently.

"How you ended up being a cop when your brother is in mafia?", Odette asked him raising her eye brow.

"We both were good at studies, especially Marco, that's the reason why he could invent many things like nicotine free cigarettes". Mario said smiling at Odette.

"He is also good in marketing and investment, as I was good in computers – hacking and coding", Mario adds gesturing towards his certificates hanging on the wall.

Odette gawked at the medals and his achievements in awe with a complete impressed expression on her face but she shook her head in disbelief.

Mario walked slowly towards her and wrapped his strong muscular arms around her tiny waist as she leaned into his touch.

Bringing his lips close to her ear he whispered, "Becoming mafia or cop wasn't even in our wish list, doll, all we ever wished for was you in our arms and a stress-free and luxurious life we could give you".

"Now tell me how many should I check mark?" he asked pressing his lips on her ear making Goosebumps rise on her skin.

"Everything", Odette whispered bringing a smile on Mario's lips.

Just when they thought, they have everything in their life an ear bleeding blast echoed from the other side of the building and Odette screamed clinging on to Mario as he held her protectively.

"What the fuck?!", Mario growled as Odette held on him for her dear life, the door of Mario's office opened and Marco ran inside his office hurriedly and wrapped his arms around them as another blast echoed making her flinch in his arms.

"Hurry up we have to get the hell out from the office, now! There are eight bombs inside this office", Marco yelled over the screams and cries of the people inside and around the office who were startled by the blast and pulled them away from the office.

FIGHTING WITH FEELINGS

ODETTE'S POV

Marco and Mario covered me from both sides protectively and rushed me out of the office in hurry; I can see fear in Marco's eyes. I was happy that he was here but now am afraid, afraid of the danger lurking over us. Who would have done this? Who would have thought to blast the whole FBI office with these many bombs?

I see people running around for their lives, pushing each other to get out from here first. I see some are in uniforms and some are wearing plain white clothes that means they freed criminals and taking them out from here.

"Make sure, get all the criminals out and get them flocked at a place, don't take your eyes off them", Mario yells making it clear to his team who are helping with people to get out as soon as possible.

One side of the building is ruined, it fell to the ground as the fire was raging over every corner, some people are burnt and some are alive with their limbs detached, which made bile rise in my throat.

"Keep your eyes down, doll", Marco said covering the blood churning view in front of me and hurried me out of the office.

In no time we made it out safely and just when I took a breathe which I don't know I kept it locked inside my chest, another bomb blew behind us and we flew and fell below the steps with a gasp and I felt air get knocked out of my lungs due to the heavy impact then I realized Marco was the one who was under me and I collided into his chest while Mario covered my back as the blast happened.

Mario grunted as Marco took my face in his palms and wiped my tears, which I didn't felt flowing down my cheeks.

Sighing in relief Marco pulled me on my feet still holding me in his arms fearing my fall.

"Are you okay doll?", they both asked in unison and the worry dripping in their voice warms my heart.

I smile softly though my eyes are tearing up, nod my head and feel something dripping from my lip.

"It's bleeding", Marco, tells running his thumb on my lower lip and I wince. I feel Marco hiss as he touched my lip and take out a handkerchief from his trousers pocket and press it on my lip and I shut my eyes then my eyes widened at realization as I snapped them open and turned to see the office which was burning from different sides and specially where we tied Nike and Gucci.

"Nike and Gucci!", I gasp and Mario's eyes widened at the mention of our dogs.

"They are here?", I hear Marco ask his voice thick but all I could hear was the screams around me.

"They are inside", I cry aloud and try to run into the office but Mario wraps his hand around me tightly not letting me free myself from his iron grip.

"Mario, they are inside", I cry trashing around and a loud blast echoed from the building making me scream.

"No, no, Nike, Gucci", I sob tearing up as my body goes numb and I fall on my knees.

Through my blurry eyes, I see Marco running at the office and my eyes widened as Mario yelled, "Marco!".

"Marco! No! Don't go!", I cry and get on my feet though I feel weak in my knees and take my chance on Mario's shock and successfully pull myself from Mario and run behind Marco.

Marco's speed was definitely unmatched by me and I see with horror Marco running in between fire and disappeared into the smoke.

"Marco! Don't go, you promised you won't run away from me", I cry and I feel my heart thundering so loud in my chest that all I could hear is just my heart pounding.

"Doll!" Mario said as he caught me from behind and held me tight in his arms as I kept crying.

"Please, stop him, bring him back", I cry holding onto him but Mario shook his head as he pressed his lips on my head telling, "He will bring Nike and Gucci safely back to you".

"I don't want anyone to be hurt, please stop this Mario", I cry and another blast echoed making me sob.

I waited for longest minutes outside crying in Mario's arms and saw Marco coming out from the building, he broke the glass of the window and jumped out of it holding Nike and Gucci safely in his arms.

Draco and few men ran towards him and he handed Nike and Gucci to them as Mario rushed towards his brother and took off his jacket, which caught fire and crushed it on the ground with his shoes.

Without being able to stop myself I ran towards Marco and hugged him so hard that I felt his heartbeat against my ear and sighed heavily, breaking the hug I pressed my lips to his and relief washed all over my body as I felt him reply to my kiss.

He held me up in his arms as I cried and hugged him tightly and saw him smiling through my teary lashes.

"Don't ever break your promises you idiot, I was so afraid", I tell smacking his chest and a chuckle vibrated through his chest warming up my heart.

"Fire engine is coming", Mario said as he walked towards us with a relieved smile on his face and I wrapped my arms around Mario and kissed him on his lips too before getting back into Marco's arms.

"Don't ever leave me, don't run away from me", I tell crying in Marco's chest as Mario wrapped his arms around me.

"Sir, we were able to detect other bombs and it were all packed in pizza boxes, we diffused the remaining bombs and called ambulance as you ordered", a man in cop uniform came and said to Mario as he simply nodded his head.

"Are you okay, doll, are you hurt somewhere?", they said in unison and a smile formed on my face but it soon widened as I saw my father standing away from us with tears in his eyes, breaking the hug I ran towards him in his protective embrace and couldn't help myself from crying in his arms.

"I missed you dad", I cry in his chest and he simply rocks me in his arms as he ran his hand over my head lovingly.

"I'm sorry my little wolf, I missed you too, sweetheart but not anymore", he said and my whole body froze and my heart clenched in my chest thinking why he would say that and when I turned back I saw Marco and Mario who held their heads low not meeting my gaze as if they are guilty of something.

"What do you mean dad?", I ask him without looking at him. "We are going back to home, to France", he said making my heart feel a throbbing pain in my chest.

My throat felt dry as I tried to gulp the irritation crawling in my neck but it burned and I felt my vision blur with fresh tears as I look at them without blinking.

"Home?", I asked him and the word felt foreign on my tongue.

Home? What some other place could be home for me when my heart chooses them to be my home? Through everything they have put me through its easy for me to walk away from them but why my heart is not able to agree for the pain it's going to feel for walking away from these two person who aren't even looking at me after everything.

I stood there, lifeless without any moment as all I could feel is my heart beating at insane pace in my chest.

"You love them...?", my father asks as he placed his hand on my shoulder and I found myself nodding my head.

I didn't turn back to see him, I couldn't see him. I know how fucked up it might be to hear one loves two men and specially his own daughter.

What would I be if I want to love two of them? Hoe, slut, whore? These titles should make me feel disgusted but no. I don't think I am any of those for giving my heart for two men.

I love them and love doesn't have boundaries, I feel it in my bones that everything I want from them is my right, I deserve it, I deserve to have those two men in my life and I can't imagine my life without them. Just now, I saw Marco running into flames and the fear that rose in my chest is unexplainable, or I think I do not want to explain it because it is painful.

The same pain one would feel when dying brutally. As if someone ripped my heart out of chest and squeezed the life out of it and this felt weird because I feel same for Mario too.

Isn't it weird to have a single heart but enough place for two of them? May be I am being selfish? But I can't let them go away even though it hurts to keep them together in my heart. I like it, I love it, I love them both along with the pain I would feel if they broke my heart – I accept them, as my love, my life, my soul and my fate.

I don't want to fight against them, fight against my fate even though in end…it is going to leave me with nothing but I accept them and accept it as my destiny.

"I don't want to leave them dad", I tell him and this time I look into his eyes.

"I don't want to leave my home", I tell without blinking.

A wide smile plastered on my father's face as he spoke.

"Well…. Then I guess I had to drag you away, it's not our culture to see grooms before engagement".

My eyes widened as my jaw hit the floor and I looked at him as if I saw aliens flying in UFO waving their shirts in their hands as if they are some kind of rowdies of bollywood movies.

But the next words from my mouth made my father throw his head back as he laughed so hard that I never heard him laughing like that in my whole life.

"Dad!!! But those Assholes didn't propose me!!!!".

MESSAGE FROM UNKNOWN

AUTHOR'S POV

Andre took Odette with him to France to their home thinking it will be safe because Marco and Mario had to look into the roots to find who was behind the bomb blast and that too in the head office of FBI.

With their doll away from them it was already hard for them to remain sane but she went showing them middle finger and rolling her eyes for not proposing her for wedding and asked her dad about it as if it's a arranged marriage thing and her sour mood driven them insane that they were getting pissed off at anyone and everyone.

"Sir, we found this CD in one of the pizza boxes we were able to retrieve, it seems as a message because there wasn't any bomb in this", one of the team member of Mario said handing the CD to him.

"I will look into this, did you make sure everyone are treated and in good condition because I think I would like to have a word with everyone because no one can come inside the building and place bombs everywhere to blast". Mario stated coldly and the man gulped.

"Yes, sir, I made sure everyone is doing good now and I also brought the CCTV footage as you requested", he said and Mario nodded his head.

"Here is the Pen drive", he handed and Mario dismissed him immediately. "Any lead?", Marco who was taking out his frustration on boxing came into Mario's home office in his black gym shorts and matching wife beater.

"Yes, this is the CD I think the person who was behind the blast left it", Mario stated with a scowl as he put his spectate gaze on the CD flipping it in his hand front and back.

"Then what are you waiting for, play it", Marco said restlessly as he gulped down the water and sat beside Mario on the couch and the laptop was placed right in front on the table as he was working on it earlier.

Nodding his head, he put the CD in the laptop and let the video play.

For few minutes, there wasn't any moment or message, it was just dark making both Marco and Mario frown.

When they were, about to take out a creepy whistle echoed then the red bulb was turned on just enough for them to see someone sitting on the black leather couch.

"The de Luca brothers", the man pronounced every word with so much of hatred that they could feel it in them.

So similar, so familiar the man sounded but they couldn't put finger who it was. Their frown deepened as the man spoke again pouring himself a glass of bourbon and came forward to the camera but his face was covered in a mask so that it's just his eyes and lips on display keeping himself un revealed for their eyes but it seemed his eyes were on them as if he was seeing right through their blue irises challenging. "What a nice way to meet two great sons of Elijah", he said their father's name as if it was disgusting thing he would have ever pronounced on his tongue.

Twins clenched their fists and their teeth were gritting and they glared at the screen.

"If you found this CD then am really sorry, the pizzas didn't blast well as they were supposed to", he said and chuckled darkly.

"It was just a trailer boys, the real mafia king is back for his throne", he snickered and held his glass in a toast manner but the door of the Mario's office snapped open with a loud thud and he paused the video immediately seeing Bianca standing there in her worst form.

"What the hell did you two do!" she snapped angrily marching towards them but Marco was the first one to put her in her place.

330

He held his hand and stopped her with a deadly glare, which he gives to his only special exclusive enemies just before few minutes before their death.

"Have you both lost your mind? You both asked to marry that bitch! Your enemy's daughter, who killed your parents!?", Bianca snapped playing those same trip she used every time to bring out the monsters she wanted and used them against Andre for her own purpose.

"He is not our enemy, he wasn't our enemy", Mario said deadly, his voice so cold that gave chills to her spine.

"Even if he was our enemy, we are going to forgive him because he is father of our doll", Marco added making Bianca frown. "Doll!?", Bianca mumbled as a deep frown plastered on her face.

"Don't tell me that's the nickname you are calling that slut!", Bianca laughed throwing her head back and she didn't even came down from her laughing fit Marco walked straight towards her and snaked his palm on her neck and choked her so hard that she started struggling to breathe and her face turned red due to lack of oxygen.

"I dare you to call her names again", Marco growled as a possessed demon who was poked with a cold rod.

"I... I... Pl... please..." Bianca stuttered making Mario chuckle wickedly behind her which made her eyes widened because she didn't even saw him coming.

He placed a sharp knife against her throat as Marco slowly detached his hand giving him space.

"Because once you do, we will slit your throat without remorse that one day you saved our lives", Mario finished making her gulp hard as her eyes expressed fear.

Coughing loudly she took deep breathes as she nodded her head frantically making them smirk.

"Bianca, I think you should come back to us when you find the real person behind our parents' death if you want to stay alive or else…. It doesn't take much of the time to think it was you", Marco added making her eyes widen in horror as she shook her head as no.

"No, I didn't kill your parents, I swear, I didn't", she gasped shaking pathetically in front of them knowing what they would do if they think it's her.

"Well just hope for good", Mario snickered as Marco added.

"And… Next time when you take our soon to be wife's name from your mouth make sure you address her as Mrs De Luca, with your head down, never look into her eyes, never talk back to her or disrespect her, you know very well what is the place and respect Italian mafia family give to our woman as you pretended to be one….. You should know", Marco, said looking into her green eyes.

Bianca clenched her jaw and glared at them before turning her heels but her eyes fell on the laptop screen on which the video was paused and it didn't take long to recognize who it was.

Her eyes widened as her jaw almost dropped on the floor seeing the same hand once she was familiar with. The thick fingers with a crown tattoo on his middle finger and very visible sixth finger, which he was born with it beside his thumb, was too obvious to know who was behind the facemask.

She gulped hard and prayed internally before turning her back to twin making sure they didn't notice her looking at the screen and stormed out of the room slamming the door shut, ran towards her car before she dialled a number.

"He is alive, I saw him, this can't be true, we will all be dead", Bianca cried holding the phone with shivering hands making the person on the other side drop the phone in shock.

~~~

"We need to find who this man is", Marco said looking at Mario who was sitting with his laptop on as he was looking through the CCTV footages.

"Here", he said bringing Marco's attention towards the screen.

"The pizza boy?", Marco frowned as he said looking into the scene.

A white bike was stopped in front of the head office, which was pizza home delivery and a man took total of nine boxes with him inside which was obvious that someone have ordered it because no one would have let him in without a bill.

"What's the shop name? Zoom it?", Marco said and Mario compiled.

"The great pizza shop", Mario read and the pizza boy who went inside came out and then their eyes widened as they saw a woman.

A woman who was very familiar to them was walking out hurriedly with shivering hands.

"What the fuck Anna Donovan is doing there!", they both tell in unison and glare at the screen.

WE ALL ARE VILLAINS

AUTHOR'S POV

"She should be here, she has nowhere to go", Marco said getting out of the car with Mario.

"Let's see", Mario mumbled following him.

They entered in the Donovan mansion, which was locked from outside and without any guards and lights were completely off as if there wasn't a trace of life.

"Break the lock", Marco said as Mario smirked at him shaking his head.

He took a key from his pocket and put that in opening the door wide-open making Marco chuckle huffing in disbelief. They both walked silently without even making a slight noise into the building and checked every room of the down floor then the other.

A single room has light turned on and they know very well that if Anna is here she should be there.

Nodding their heads towards the door they sneaked inside finding Anna in the corner of the room with her head on her knees as she embraced herself and was crying miserably making them frown.

The curtains were dragged so that the light couldn't make in and one bulb of the bedside table was on illuminating the room with dim light but good enough to see each other.

"You should have been hiding somewhere else if you wanted to stay alive", Marco said in his hoarse voice and anger growing in his veins that it could blast any second.

"I know you will come for me – anywhere", Anna said raising her head from her knees and looked at the twins who was standing right in front of her.

"Of course I would, you put my family in danger, they could have died", Marco snaps clenching his hand and he was just a moment away talking his gun out and shoot her head.

"I know and am sorry", Anna said looking at their angry faces. Gulping hard she brushed her hair off her face and spoke.

"Elijah, my brother is in danger and I had to do that if not, that man have killed him", she said chocking on her breathe.

"Which man?", Marco demanded keeping his voice dark as she trembled in their presence.

"I don't know Marco, I just spoke to my brother, he said he was coming back to solve the matters with you", Anna said looking towards Mario as he asked him to come back and they could clear things.

Mario frowned but nodded anyways and Anna continued, "Then I got a call from a number telling that he will be dead if I don't do as said".

"Though I am not his own blood, I am adopted but he is your own blood Marco, Mario, his mother is your father's own sister who named her son's name after her brother's", she added as multiple tears rolled down her eyes.

"Come to the point", Mario stated not wanting to hear the emotional shit she was playing, telling how they are relatives and all when in fact they didn't even bother to be nice to them or help their mother out when their father died. When in reality Alesia did not want their existence to be known to her husband's sister.

"A man came to give me few boxes of pizzas and bike along with their uniform and said to drop it in your building but I didn't knew there were bombs in it", Anna cries hard as she clenched her dress tightly.

"Have you seen his face?", Mario asks sceptically looking her body language understanding if she is speaking truth or false and as much as he could tell, she was telling truth and was afraid – but not afraid of them but afraid of that man for her brother.

"No, I couldn't see his face because he was wearing a mask and glasses which covered his face but he was bald", she tells sniffing as she wipes her tears off her cheek.

Looking into their eyes she tells with a sad smile, "I killed so many people, I never wanted to hurt anyone and I know I couldn't even save my brother but am trusting him with you".

Her confession made them frown as they looked at each other then Anna who was smiling as she saw the family picture she has beside her. It was Elijah with his parents and Anna. That was the first day when they brought her home from orphanage and spoiled her with everything since they didn't have a daughter.

"I was a bitch for you both when we were kids", she said with a humourless chuckle and shook her head as more tears fell.

"I am so sorry for that, hope you forgive me", Anna said pressing her quivering lips together.

"But whatever you did, I deserved it", she said as she bit her lip stopping herself from crying more in front of them.

"Please save my brother Marco, Mario and if you couldn't then I will welcome him to me with open arms", with that she took gun which she hid behind her back and in a second she blew her brain with it that Marco and Mario couldn't react so fast and she fell dead with hopeful teary eyes with a welcoming smile.

"Shit!", Marco grumbled turning his back and punched the wall angrily.

"I just can't believe", Mario spat with his hands in his dark brown hair with a frown on his face and sour mood after seeing Anna die on them.

"We need to find that fucker", Marco growled walking out of Anna's room.

Mario who was standing inside, bent on his knees and wiped tears of Anna from her cheek then he said, "We all are villain in someone's life Anna, but you was just a kid and we should have forgiven you – not revenged, we are sorry and I promise we will save your brother", with that Mario closed her eyes letting heavens take over them.

~~~

"Check security cameras in front of Donovan villa and every road that goes through it, find a man who is bald and in pizza boy uniform with the same bike that stopped in front of our office", Mario ordered in his office to his team.

"Copied, sir", the man said working on the computer.

"Did you get details who ordered the pizzas", Mario asked another person who nodded his head.

"Angela, Angela was the one who ordered pizzas", the man replied making Mario clench his jaw.

Mario took his phone out and sent a quick text to Marco telling it was Angela who ordered pizzas and the reason behind shouldn't be that hard for them to crack because she was literally begging Mario to fuck her as she kept tabs on odette.

"Where is she?", Mario asked then his team member replied.

"She is missing".

As soon as Mario heard, his jaw clenched in anger and called Marco.

"That bitch is missing brother, let our men find her alive or dead, I don't give a fuck", he said making Marco nod his head though he couldn't see, "Will be on it".

"Mario, I got a text from our doll", Mario said and now his voice surprisingly joyful.

Mario's mood changed immediately and he checked his phone for any message from odette and his smile widened as he read, "Happy birthday asshole".

A heartfelt chuckle escaped his mouth at her snarky birthday wish to them and Mario's eyes fell on the clock on the table.

It's indeed their birthday; Mario didn't realize time that it was already past 12am and the next day have already begun which was their birthday and it's been twelve years since someone wished them on their birthday.

"I miss her", Mario said to Marco with a stupid smile on his face.

"I miss her too", Marco said sighing loudly.

"How about we go to France and get our birthday gift from her?", they both suggested at a same time and chuckled throwing their heads back.

"Let's go to our doll", they said before hanging up the call.

ICE CREAM TEASING

AUTHOR'S POV

"Odette you are mentally fucked up", Odette scolded herself as her eyes were fixed on Marco and Mario's pictures, which were on

Google where they both were posing for media on special events. Their images were from eighteenth birthday of them as Bianca introduced them to the families that they are de Luca brothers.

It's been just few hours since her father told that it's their birthday tomorrow and she was all gooey and mushy like if it's their first birthday.

Of course it is, their first birthday with her. But sadly they were in Rome and she is in France and according to her father she can't meet them before engagement and that's how their culture is.

She mentally rolled her eyes but was thankful that her father actually remember their birthday and shared it with her and she was able to text them exactly at 12.

Odette drifted off in sleep with her laptop still on, displaying twins pictures as Nike and Gucci were sleeping on the cosy bed she ordered for them. Thankfully, they weren't hurt because they hid in a corner where there wasn't fire and Marco rescued them in time but they were startled with everything so she had to bring them to the veterinarian.

It's been few hours Odette is past asleep but she heard some muffled noises as she groaned and stretched with a yawn she asked, "Nike, Gucci, my babies are awake?".

Marco and Mario who was inside her room and shushing Nike and Gucci to keep quiet but they were so excited to see their daddies.

Hearing Odette's question Nike and Gucci howled happily and she smiled opening her eyes but the sight in front of her made her eyes widen in utter surprise and her jaw almost hit the floor.

"What the hell you both are doing here?!", Odette whisper yelled making them grin guilty and get themselves in a proper position as they were kneed in front of Nike and Gucci with their finger on their lips gesturing those two cute dogs to keep quiet.

"Well we came to tell thank you for wishing us", Mario said shrugging his shoulders slightly with a sheepish smile on his face and Marco's expression matched his brother's.

"Also to take our birthday present", Marco said grinning widely.

Odette sighed rolling her eyes but a genuine smile painted on her lips but soon turned into smirk when she looked at them and around her room.

"You know, if dad finds out you are here he will surely, definitely kick your asses", she said making them smirk.

"Oh doll... He doesn't have to know, does he?", Marco said then turned to Mario who gave him subtle nod with smirk on his face which was mirroring his brother's.

"But how the hell do you came into my room?", Odette asked changing the subject eying them suspicious totally forgetting that the laptop is still turned on and the pictures of them are visible bright and clear for their blue eyes to catch easily but it seemed they didn't find them yet. "Oh, just when you drifted off to sleep watching our pictures, we entered from the window", they admitted making her eyes widen and a dark blush formed on her cheeks as she hurried towards the laptop and shut it off.

They both walked towards her who was sitting on her knees in the bed, Marco smiled pressing his lips on her forehead and Mario mirrored him by placing a kiss on the back of her head.

342

Goosebumps pricked her delicate pale skin at the contact of two sexiest men alive on earth and she released a satisfied hum making their smiles wide.

"Wait a second", Odette said before getting up from the bed in her black tank top and booty shorts, wrapped a robe and hurried outside of her room making them smile feverishly.

A few minutes passed before the bedroom door opened as they were sitting on her bed petting Nike and Gucci their eyes widened because of the thing she carried with her.

"Happy birthday day to you".

"Happy birthday day to you….."

"Happy birthday to my dear Marco and Mario, happy birthday day to you", Odette sang and her smile was brighter than before with the candles light on in her bedroom bright enough with two Bed lamps beside her bed.

Her eyes were bright and smiling as twins eyes held emotions, which they felt after a long time. For a second they saw their mother in her and that made their hearts soon for her more than it already is.

"Come on cut this ice cream", Odette said placing the plate on which she emptied a whole box of strawberry ice cream which was in the shape of the box but slightly melting due to the candles on it.

Shoving the knife in their hands she looked at them with a huge smile but seeing their sad features her smile fell immediately.

Biting her lip as she chewed her lip piercing and said softly, "I don't know how to bake or cook so this is all we have to celebrate, am sorry".

Her guilty voice made their heart feel a pang and they both shook thoughts of those bitter time, breathing deeply they exhaled and smiled at her.

"This is the first time we are going to eat ice cream, so thank you", Mario said making her frown.

"You both never ate ice cream before?", she asked in complete shock.

They both shook their head as Marco replied this time, "Never but not anymore".

Smiling at their doll, they both nodded their heads to each other and cut the ice cream and fed a chunk to Odette and she tried to feed them but they tsked shaking their heads with a smirk on their face.

"Where is our gift doll", Marco asked looking at her with his eyebrows raised and there was mischief in his eyes which made Odette gulp nervously as she shifted her eyes from Marco to Mario and they obviously proved they are brothers with same expression on their faces.

"Don't you see? It's right in front of us", Mario said as he devoured her lips slowly and sensually and Odette closed her eyes immediately holding his white shirt in her palm as Marco kissed her neck peppering butterfly kisses all the way as he slowly tugged her robe off her body and Odette let them do as they desired with a smile on her lips in between kissing Mario.

Savouring the strawberry ice cream flavour from her lips Mario pushed his tongue deeper when Odette moaned as Marco bit on a particular spot on her neck.

Mario groaned at the sweet flavour and fisted her hair gently deepening the kiss and Odette kissed him back moaning into his mouth as his tongue devoured her mouth.

With a smooch Mario broke the kiss, ran his tongue on his lips and smiled at Marco as he said, "I don't think it will taste better from plate brother".

"Uhmhm", Marco hummed and gently laid Odette on bed and asked her permission before taking off her clothes with his eyes to which she blushed and nodded her head looking between both Marco and Mario.

Lifting her up Marco took off her clothes in swift motion and Odette's cheeks turned red because she wasn't wearing anything under them and was naked in front of two pair of hungry blue eyes, which were devouring her with their looks.

Marco cut a chunk of the ice cream, holding it between his fingers he slid that from her lips to her neck from the valley of her breasts and they puckered at the coldness and the nipple piercings she had were looking more attractive on her perky pink pebbles.

He carried the ice cream spreading a line of it from her stomach to her pussy making sure it doesn't contact with her inner lips to avoid any infection and she flinched due to the sudden coldness at her sensitive area.

Mario leaned over and started kissing her lips as he smeared ice cream on her appetising tits and she moaned in delight feeling completely sensitive and her core clenched in need.

When Mario was feasting on her mouth and tits, fondling them in his large palms and tugging them, up to leave them back and licking them off made her wetter than before.

Marco slowly parted her legs, settled between them and kissed from her belly to her dripping core, which was almost covered in strawberry ice cream.

How badly Marco and Mario wished, that place was covered in their come but it wasn't the day for it, Odette isn't ready for that – not yet but she will be soon.

"Fuck!", Marco growled as he licked ice cream off her body as a hungry beast he attacked her cunt eating it out which tasted like strawberry ice cream along her sweet juice which he couldn't get tired off.

A breathy moan escaped her mouth as she fisted Marco's hair in her tiny palm and other hand was on Mario's hair as he was pleasuring her tits.

"Shh doll, we don't want your father to find out we sneaked into your room", Mario hummed as he kissed her lips taking every moan and gasp she released while Marco feasted on her cunt.

"Fuck! Doll, I can eat you out like this every fucking day, every minute of my fucking life", Marco growled against her lower lips sending vibrations to her core making her clench.

"Tell me, you want that?", Marco asked and Mario let her breathe and freed her lips from his assault on them to answer Marco.

"Yes, I want that", Odette gasped pushing Marco's face back where she wants him.

A throaty chuckle escaped Marco and Mario's lips making her whine as she was getting irritated because of delay of her building orgasm, which was ready to blast at any fucking second.

"You need to ask as a good girl, doll, what do you want Marco to do?", Mario asked his voice thick in lust as he gazed in her doe eyes.

"I.... I...." Odette stuttered flushing badly to speak what she wanted which made them smirk.

"Tell me and I will give it to you, doll", Marco groaned against her cunt, which she was trying to get friction on it by pushing her hips up so that it meets Marco's plump lips.

"I want you to fuck me with your tongue...please daddy", Odette begged which made Marco and Mario's cock twitch in their pants.

Rolling his sleeves of black shirt Marco hummed in satisfaction hearing her and kissed all the way her thighs and slowly teasingly let his lips kiss her cunt then licked her clit with his tongue While he assaulted her with his fingers through her canal and she moaned loudly and gasped. Mario held her as he sucked her right tit while fondling other making her roll her eyes back.

"Ahhh", she gasped while Marco started thrusting his two fingers inside her tight cunt making her gasp and groan as he hit her g spot repeatedly.

"Fuck! Just like that doll", Marco growled feeling her clench around his fingers as he assaulted her clit with his tongue bringing her on edge of orgasm.

Mario blew his breathe on her tits before leaving them in his palms and played with them as he created multiple hickeys on her neck and boobs making them dark red and purple and enjoying the view of them on her pale skin.

"Fucking hell! Her moans are fucking music to ears brother, do it again, she likes it", Mario growled as Odette drew a long breathy moan when Marco slightly gazed his teeth on her clit.

Pumping his fingers inside her, Marco repeated as he did before and Odette felt similar weight in her lower stomach but with a huge intensity.

She screamed and Mario kissed her lips swallowing it as a good amount of liquid gushed out of her cunt almost pushing Marco's fingers out and spammed all over his mouth and Marco took everything greedily drinking up all her squirt juices and retraced himself off her pink, swollen cunt and Odette sighed as Mario let Marco kiss her lips making her taste herself on his lips and she moaned and thrust her tongue in his mouth devouring her own sweetness mixed with ice cream when she broke the kiss Mario tasted her on her mouth and groaned in delight.

With painful hard ons both Marco and Mario laid beside her each side and Odette asked her voice ragged because of the pleasurable assault they put her through.

"How can you both share me and not be jealous?".

They both turned their heads seeing her flushed face and smiled at each other before telling in unison.

"Because if my brother is my life, you are love of our life, doll and without love, without you, there is no life, no us".

A LEAD

AUTHOR'S POV

"I have something to give you two, real gift", Odette said hearing birds chirping across her window as the sun started rising beautifully.

Marco who was playing with her hair while Mario who was massaging her feet stopped their moments and gazed at the ethereal beauty in front of them.

"What is it doll?", Mario asked his voice came out gruffly and hoarse because of lack of sleep, they came into her room when she was asleep at 2 am and watched her sleep till four am and then she was woken up by Nike and Gucci or else they wouldn't have disturbed her sleep.

"I... I will get it", Odette said getting up on her feet in her night suit and stumbled in her walk in closet. With a bright smile, Marco and Mario kept waiting and saw her coming out with a guitar, album and locket.

"What is this doll?", Mario asked as she settled on the bed in between them sitting on her heels while pressing her knees on bed she looked at them biting her lip nervously thinking it would be a good or bad idea to give them something related to their past.

"This guitar...Thi... this... this guitar", Odette stuttered badly and winced at her own behaviour.

"First promise me you won't be mad", she asked looking at them who frowned then nodded with a smile and marco said, "We can never be mad at you doll".

"Okay", Odette mumbled as she slowly slid the album towards them.

Mario took it in his hands and opened it, as soon as his eyes fell on the first picture he drew a sharp breathe, his fists clenched hard gripping the album.

Marco took it from his hand and didn't show his emotions as Mario but his gaze fell on their doll who kept her eyes closed with her fingers crossed.

He simply glared at Mario for not controlling his emotions and let her see his mad side just because of this.

Mario cleared his throat before pushing a strand of hair behind her ear and said, "We really didn't had a single picture of our mother with us, seeing her after so long I was angry that we couldn't find her killer and punished him for his crime of stealing our mother from us".

Odette's heart clenched and she opened her eyes looking between both Marco and Mario and said, "I'm sorry, we can leave this behind if you want but I thought you would be happy to see your family album".

Marco immediately replied her, "We are happy, it was just shocking but we are happy to find our memories which were almost fading after these many years".

Marco might be the cruellest among the twins but when it comes to Odette he turns understanding, calm and protective and consider her feelings before expressing his own but Mario is without a filter he is frank and clear but that doesn't means he loves her any less.

"I'm sorry", Mario mumbled and embraced her in a hug, which she gladly accepted and sighed in his chest.

"This guitar was your mom's.... as well as this pendant", Odette said handing them the guitar and the chain with a tiny gold heart pendant.

"Mario knows how to play guitar". Marco said smiling at her.

"Just as I inherited the art of painting from her, Mario inherited her love for music", he added making Odette smile widely finding something new about Mario.

"This pendant... It will look better on you doll", Mario said clutching it in his hand. Pushing her hair aside he gently put that chain around her delicate neck and secured it making her smile widely and her eyes glistened with tears because it was something of their mother's which their father gave to her and they thought she deserves to have it. But she soon pushed those tears away not wanting to spoil their mood and whispered a thank you pressing her lips to Mario then Marco.

Marco and Mario was flipping the album and watching their childhood unfold in front of their eyes making their heart clench in thought of them missing these all.

From their birthdays to picnic, where both their parents were smiling and holding them in their arms was something they forgot they ever had.

"You both look so cute", Odette giggled looking at the picture where Marco and Mario were playing with bubbles in a bathtub.

"I wish our kids looks like you both", those words slipped out of her mouth making Mario and Mario freeze and her eyes widened realizing what she just spoke and blushed brightly shoving her face in the pillow which was resting on her lap.

"You want to have kids?", Marco asked gulping and she didn't responded to his question and groaned in the pillow.

"You want to have our kids?", Mario asked and their voices was enough to send a pool of wetness in between her legs.

Thinking how she would escape this embarrassing talk, she simply got up from the pillow and glared at them.

"Last time I checked I wasn't even proposed to the engagement we are having tomorrow night and the wedding following morning", Odette said folding her hands on her chest and their smiles widened at cute pouty angry face.

"Princess!", Andre's voice snapped them out of their bubble and Odette's eyes widened hearing her father calling for her following a small knock on her door.

"Get up, we have to go for shopping", he called out still knocking on the door knowing how sleepy head she is and don't wake up easily.

"You need to go", Odette whisper gasped at Marco and Mario who was smirking at her.

"Nah, not unless you give us a kiss", Mario drawled making her clench her jaw in anger.

Narrowing her eyes at them she studied if they were serious and knowing very well the expression on their face she understood that they both aren't going to give up easily, instead of wasting the time quarrelling with them she gave a peck to each of them and tried to push them away out of the window but they didn't flinch.

"This is not what we call as a kiss", Marco said and grabbed her thick dark black hair and smashed his lips on her and kissed her passionately making her gasp in the kiss as he bit on her lower lip making it bleed. Pushing his tongue inside her mouth he devoured her thoroughly as if it's the last meal of his life and flipped her into Mario's chest gently making her whimper as her bosoms came in contact with his hard chest.

"Fucking beautiful", Mario said running his tongue on her throbbing lip where Marco bit and licked it gently totally opposite to Marco and kissed her delicately as if she was a flower.

Satisfied with kissing her as they desired both brothers jumped out of the window with the album and guitar with them along with the memories they made together. Leaving her completely shocked and wet not to mention she was frustrated and sleepy.

Huffing loudly she snuck her head out of her room greeting her father a good morning and shutting the door right on his face just before telling good bye leaving him in disbelief outside her room.

~~~

"Draco, is everything going as we asked?", Marco asked his right hand catching up with the task he ordered him before coming to France.

"Yes boss, we are trying our best, our men are all around trying to find Angela and Elijah, knowing they both aren't found in the warehouses we broke we think they are at some home and I started working on it", Draco said in single breathe.

"Tell me when you get a lead", Marco said then hung the call not listening to his reply. "Mario", Marco called making Mario snap his eyes from his phone to him.

"Is the surprise we planned for doll is ready?", Marco asked leaning forward to look at the laptop screen in front of them.

"Almost there", Mario said smiling widely. Marco hummed smiling at his brother then turned back to his work.

Keeping the album they brought beside on the table, he started working on the videos the man who blasted bombs in FBI office.

He could not tell if the man was bald or anything but what his attention caught was his finger.

Marco frowned thinking who this man could be and Mario who was sitting beside him put his legs on the table stretching and the album fell on the ground.

"Shit", Marco said bending down and as he was about to lift the album his eyes fell on the same finger and tattoo of the man who was right beside their father in the picture and he frowned, lifting it up he showed it to Mario who was sitting right beside him.

"Is there any way this man could be him", Marco said and this caught Mario's attention.

Their jaw clenched at the exact same tattoo and they gritted their teeth as Mario said; "Only Bianca could answer".

FREEDOM

AUTHOR'S POV

"Every thing we planned will be turned down to dust", Bianca said pacing around the room.

"You made sure he was dead?", Victoria Grayson asked her looking just as terrified as Bianca.

Their faces paled and tense as they sat in Victoria's home making sure they locked all the doors.

"I killed him myself with my own fucking hands Vicky; he can't be alive but…. But…. It was him in the video", Bianca stuttered as a bead of sweat fell from her eyebrow.

"You are going hard on yourself sweetheart, I suggest you to take a seat", Victoria said gently rubbing the back of Bianca's neck. Bianca relaxed herself in her hold and leaned forward brushing her lips on Victoria's and she quickly deepened the kiss trying to calm themselves from the storm they are expecting in their lives.

"They backed away from our plan Vicky, now we both are alone, we are alone to take our revenge from Andre", Bianca choked out holding Victoria tight in her arms and sobbed on her shoulder.

"When we are both, we aren't alone Bianca", Victoria said rubbing Bianca's back soothingly.

"I should have thought you are still licking dripping cunts instead of choking on hard cocks", a man's voice startled them both and their eyes widened as they heard the voice. It was same as it used to be but now it sounded a little thick because of his age yet it didn't stop Bianca from flinching.

"B… b…br…" Bianca stuttered badly as the man walked towards her.

Victoria who was holding on to her protectively shivered in fear seeing his face.

A long deep gash was on his face which Bianca remember inflicting on him for the first time when he found out she was a lesbian and what he did next was so inhuman act that she couldn't help but tried to kill him and run away but hitting his face with flower jaw wasn't enough for this monster to die not even two bullets in his chest.

Gulping hard she took a step back with Victoria tagging her protectively, with each step they took back Bianca couldn't help but tremble and the man who was looking at her wickedly as if she was his prey after a long time of fast.

The next second he took his gun out from the back of his pocket and shot a bullet straight through Victoria making Bianca scream.

"Vicky!", Bianca screamed at top of her lungs falling on her knees she embraced her dead lover in her arms and sobbed hard as if her heart was torn apart from chest.

"Vicky! Oh god!!!!", Bianca choked her face completely messed up with tears and mascara making her look as if she was homeless and laying on dirt on the streets.

"You whore!", the man spit yanking Bianca's hair in his strong grip making her yelp at the burning pain of her skull.

"Brother....." she cried placing her hand where his hands were pulling her hair.

"We might share same blood but a cunt slut like you will never be my sister you whore", he screamed throwing her harshly on the floor close to Victoria.

[Violence Ahead]

"Ahh", Bianca screamed when her head hit the while marble floor holding herself to get away from the monster in front of her.

"You fucking made those bastards kings of Italian mafia!", he snarled taking off his belt off his trousers.

"Please leave me", Bianca cried but a sharp pain erupted on her thigh making her whole body flinch and she screamed in pain.

"Why? To take fucking revenge of your dead lover?", he asked knowing and hit her again on her back and her voice broke with the agonizing scream she cried out.

"You tried to kill your own family for whores like you", he drawled hitting her again.

Yanking her hair with one hand, he smashed her head on the white marble floor drawing a lot of blood from her forehead which dripped on the white marble floor.

Wrapping the belt on her neck he pushed her on the floor with his feet on her face and warned her in a deadly tone, "You will behave well and stay by my side in this war or else I will fucking kill you".

Bianca cried out with her wide eyes nodding her head as yes afraid of her cousin's wrath.

When he left her free, she gasped and crawled back leaning on the wall with her knees close to her chest, she cried sobbing hard as her eyes fell on her dead lover.

"I can't believe... you are still alive", Bianca cried looking at her cousin with hateful eyes.

"Tsk, tsk, tsk, Bianca... the little girl who loved weak women than powerful men.... You thought two bullets could kill me. That you can buy all my people with money?" he snickered loudly.

"That day when you tried to kill me.....", Gabriel's voice muffled as if it's from under water as she started seeing black dots in her vision.

~THAT DAY~

"Are you sure you can handle your brother?" Victoria and Arianna asked Bianca who brought some money and plane tickets to get away from Italy.

"I'm sure, we just have to hurry before he comes searching for me, once we are out of this country we are safe", she retorted pacing back and forth grabbing necessary things they would need them.

"Okay, I am ready", Victoria said getting up from the couch. "I will just call at my home to inform my daughter and will be back", with that she went out of the apartment.

"Why are you standing as a statue? Hurry up we don't have much time", Bianca said looking at still Arianna.

"I... I don't want to come with you Bianca", she said looking at the floor.

"I.... I don't... lov..." she was cut off when Bianca strolled towards her angrily.

"What? You don't what?", Bianca asked with her voice dark and trembling.

"I don't love you", she said looking straight into Bianca's glossy teary eyes.

"Is... Is this because of those kids?", Bianca asked her voice coming out thick and gravely making Arianna gulp.

"No.... It's not because of those girls, it's because I don't love you anymore, I can't do this, I don't love you and Victoria in that way anymore am sorry", Arianna said holding Bianca's palms in her own as a lone tear escaped her eye.

Bianca took a shaky breathe and asked, "Do you love any man?".

There was hope in her voice when she asked that Arianna would tell yes, she knows that what they three have been doing is not going to be acceptable by the society and it's not going to be forever. If she wanted Arianna to have something forever as a normal people Bianca would let her have it with a man but her jealousy riled up when Arianna confessed her true feelings.

"N... no, I don't love a man but I....I love Julia".

Bianca's heart shattered at the mention of Julia's name. Since Arianna was pregnant with her twins Julia was tagging her as if she is her Shadow and Bianca felt uncomfortable leaving Arianna in Julia's presence because she read Arianna that she was falling for her and she couldn't let any other women have her except Victoria and her.

They were meant to be together and Julia's involvement in their life brought them here, where Arianna is rejecting to go away from this country and live a happily ever after life with Bianca and Victoria.

"But she doesn't love you as we do", Bianca reasoned hoping Arianna will understand her and change her mind.

"She have three children and a caring husband, she have a happy family", Bianca said gulping hard as her hands formed fist trying to maintain her composure.

"I know, it's not necessary that she reciprocate my feelings for her but I will always love her, away from her but will always and I can't be same with you or Victoria", Arianna said and a lone tear escaped their eyes.

"I'm sorry Bianca am not coming", with that Victoria walked out of the house.

As soon as she walked away from Bianca, she got mad, she lost her mind and started trashing everything around her and cried in frustration falling on her knees.

Burying her in her palms she cried without realizing someone has entered the apartment. Slowly taking her hands away from her tear-stained face her eyes immediately fell on those pair of well-polished shoes, which she clearly knows whom they belong to.

Her throat turned dry as she slowly lift her head to see Gabriel, her cousin. Her eyes were wide in shock as she couldn't speak or react looking at him.

"Brother", Bianca gasped looking at him as a wicked grin was decorated on his face.

"Let's go home little sister you can't run away from me unless one of us are dead", he said chuckling darkly as he yanked her with her hair and dragged her out of the apartment as if she was a sack of potatoes.

~~~

"Please let me go", Bianca cried trying to free her hair but Gabriel's hold on her was as iron burning her scalp so painfully that she thought the patch of hair would be in his hand any second.

"One thing.... Just one thing…I asked you to do, marry Elijah so that you will become queen of Italian mafia but you have to fuck around with whores like you!" he snarled pushing her on her bed.

"I don't want to be queen, I don't want to marry your boss", Bianca screamed at him without thinking about the consequences.

"If you talk back to me like this again you know very well that I won't think to throw you for my dogs to have you as they wish on their dicks………", he said giving a dramatic effect and grinned widely as he finished his sentence, "…… again".

Bianca's whole body trembled in fear remembering the days she was thrown on the men who work for her cousin and bile rose on her throat, which she pushed inside forcefully.

"I won't let you control my life! I have my own rights on my life! I can be with anyone I want", she yelled at her cousin getting off the bed.

"You wouldn't listen don't you, what a cunt slut, stay here so that I can call someone to punish you as you deserve", Gabriel said digging his fingers in her cheek.

Pushing her away harshly, he turned his back and Bianca took it as her first and last chance. Taking the flower vase, she smashed it across his face and yanked his gun from back of his pocket and shoot through his chest. Gabriel fell down with his eyes wide and clutching his gunshot wound wincing with pain.

A genuinely yet sadistic smile formed on her lips as she said, "You said unless one of us are dead I can't be free... Well now am free brother, see you in hell", with that she shot once again and dropped the gun on the floor and walked away desiring her freedom which she won – At least she thought she won.

~**NOW**~

"You thought you can kill me with two bullets! Capo of the great Italian mafia would die with fucking two bullets?!", he snickered wickedly then kicked right in her stomach making her cry harder as she wasn't able to breathe.

"Please kill me, just kill me", she cried in pain and agony.

"Not this soon little sister, not this soon", he said chuckling darkly and Bianca looked into his eyes.

"I will let you live, will give you freedom", he said shoving his hands in his pockets.

"What do you want in return?", she asked looking at him with narrowed eyes as blood dripped from her eyelashes to on her cheek. Coughing badly she put his amused look on her as he asked.

"My little cousin grew brain in her skull?", he gasped placing his hand on his chest and Bianca smirked.

"You think I just took two boys from the streets just one night and made them kings of Italian mafia?", she scoffed spitting the blood beside her.

"Right!", he said nodding his head.

"The boys you took....I thought they didn't have weakness", Gabriel said chuckling.

"But the way they acted outside of the office.... I found one, who is she?", he asked narrowing his eyes on Bianca.

"Odette Francois....". Bianca said through her gritted teeth.

"I made Marco marry her to hurt Andre but they both fell in love". She said clenching her jaw.

"Tsk tsk, enemy to lover trope?", he chuckled making her sigh.

"Not just enemy to lover...Its enemies to lovers", Bianca said looking into his eyes.

"Both I meant, both Marco and Mario with her and she fell for them too and marrying them tomorrow", she said clenching her jaw with her fists tightly clenched.

"Their doll, she is their weakness", she said and a wide grin formed on his lips as he said, "Why don't you bring that little doll for me... To play", he finished making her eyes widen in surprise then her smirk turned into a huge grin.

"For my freedom?", she asked and Gabriel nodded his head pushing his hand forward, Bianca looked between his face and hand and smiling in victory she let their hands meet fixing the deal of Odette's devastating future which she wasn't prepared for.

OH MY GOD

AUTHOR'S POV

Odette was watching the vampire diaries sulking that both Marco and Mario haven't called her since they ran off from her window leaving her all frustrated. The door of her room opened by excited Paul and Peter who literally jumped on her screaming happily.

Odette gasped and got on her feet and embraced two typhoons in her arms and they knocked her down on her ass making her laugh.

"Aunt Oddy!!!! We missed you!", they both said in unison giving her kiss each side of her cheek.

"Aww my babies, I missed you too", she said cooing as she kissed her heads and ruffled their hair making them whine.

"Didn't miss me?", aurora said leaning on the door with a bright smile on her face, which Odette returned immediately.

Rolling her eyes, she walked towards her sister and Aurora embraced her immediately.

"I always thought you would look good with twins but I never expected this scenario, two handsome Italian men, huh?", Aurora teased winking at her sister and Odette blushed hard.

Biting her lip she turned around to see Paul, Peter already made Nike and Gucci friends and a gentle smile formed on her lips as she suggested, "Why don't you go and play with them in the garden? They like to play fetch a lot".

"Really?" they both asked with bright eyes and Odette nodded her head and smiled, "really now go!"

They both ran holding Nike and Gucci in their arms safely in extreme excitement and aurora smiled widely looking at disappearing figure of her kids.

"So... you don't think it's weird?", Odette asked breaking the silence with an uneasy smile painted on her lips.

Aurora shook her head, smiled brightly at her sister and dragged her to her bed. Sitting on the bed, she held her sister's hand as she announced.

"Do you know? Marco and Mario made peace with Russian mafia, they allowed free roaming in the country and import, export too, they also said I could come anytime to meet you and said will bring you to Russia", hearing those words Odette gasped placing her palms over her mouth as her eyes welled. Once in a million years she never thought that Russian and Italian enmity will end and that too because of her. Because those two people are so in love, with her that they would do anything to please her and this feeling they gave was overwhelming to Odette and she could not control but tear up hugging her sister tightly.

"You are so lucky Odette and I would tell they are lucky too, to have a woman like you by their side", aurora said rubbing her sister's back and pressed her lips on her head motherly.

"Now..." she drawled breaking the hug and a smile on her lips is showing something secret, an unspoken hint of a promise. "Let's get you dressed for your engagement and this time you are wearing whatever I choose and you can't even deny".

~~~

ODETTE'S POV

"You really think this is okay?" I asked my sister twirling around holding my golden dress in my fingers.

"Yes! Why do you think something is not okay with the dress?", Aurora exclaims looking at the golden shimmer dress with a mid knee slit and off shoulder design. It's perfect and elegant, Aurora couldn't choose a better dress than this, neither I and I know my guys will love it with the way it's hugging on my curves but I still think something is missing.

Frowning I walk towards my closet and my hands automatically drift towards the stockings and I take a fish net stocking and grin at Aurora.

Ignoring her teasing smirk, I put them on and sit on the chair to let her continue doing my hair and makeup. My hair is tied up in a ponytail, the makeup is nude because of the bright colour of my dress and this looks perfect. Slipping on gold heels, I turned around to see myself in the mirror and my smile widened at how beautiful I look.

"Can anyone believe that you were sulking to get engaged to a single person few months ago and now you are ready to fuck both?!", my sister taunted. Faking a glare at her I giggled and hugged her murmuring a thank you and she handed me a envelope which made me frown.

"What is this?", I ask already on my way to open it.

A note inside it made me smile as I read it.

In dirt and dust we were,

But you held our hands that day.

Mended our shattered hearts,

Wiping our tears with your little hands.

Unknowingly planting the seed of love in our hearts.

Tying the soul roots together so hard,

You Killed our demons with your love.

We were mad – we thought for desiring an angel like you but you said we weren't any villains with your doe eyes.

A single prince for a princess like you would be too mundane,

So the two princes our mother raised are waiting for you under the stars,

Follow your heart to the sky, be our ~~doll~~ queen.

Where you belong above every life in our lives.

-your insanely fucked up lovers;

M&M ;)

"What the hell is this?!", I smile widely looking at Aurora who simply shrugged her shoulders zipping her mouth animatedly making me roll my eyes.

"Oh please tell me, where are they?!", I ask giving my shot to take anything out from her but she only shook her head.

"Ah ah, do as they said in the note...," she sang leaving me alone and I pout and stomp my feet reading it again.

I couldn't help but chuckle at how they have written doll then cut it off to write queen to make is rhyme but still they have to work on their poetic skills but am not going to tell them. But honestly I like anything they tell and everything they speak.

"Under the stars....." I think loud looking at the dark sky.

"Oh!", I squeal as it clicks that they could be in the garden and I hold the length of the dress and run outside into the backyard of the mansion.

Maids were giggling and smiling giving me warm looks as I passed through them and I returned their smiles with the same warmth.

But when I reached the garden, I frowned looking at the darkness. There were no one and out of nowhere, Paul and Peter popped from behind the bush and screamed, "Wrong place!"

I chuckled at how cute they looked and smiled knowing that they thought my dumb ass would run straight into the garden and did this a step ahead.

"Then tell me... The right place... Please", I cooed giving my best puppy eyes to my nephews and they both shared a look and bit their lip.

"It... we can't tell", they said crossing their fingers.

"But we can show you aunt oddy", they whispered looking around and that made me smile widely.

"Oh my god! You both are best boys of the world!", I cooed ruffling their hair with my both hands and they grinned widely shoving my hands away from their heads.

I pouted as they set their hair back as if I have ruined their hair – which I did and pointed towards the terrace and I smiled widely smacking my forehead. "Thank you so much!!!!", I whisper yelled and kissed their heads and ran inside the mansion towards the stairs passing through the maids.

My heart was thundering in my chest so hard that I was thinking that it might come right out from my mouth with the excitement am feeling.

Pushing all the giddy feeling down knowing I can squeak and squeal later in peace when am alone and get to the place where I was needed as fast as possible.

Huffing and breathing heavily I reached the terrace and placed my palms on my knees catching my breathe with a wide smile on my face that now my cheeks started to hurt like a bitch.

Standing straight, I fixed my dress and looked around to see only darkness.

"Mario... Marco....", I called walking further on the terrace and suddenly the whole place brightened up making me shut my eyes and immediately put my hand in front of them. Slowly peaking I see the whole building was decorated with flowers and fairy lights along with scented candles and two spotlights in front of me and there stood my men looking all dangerously handsome in black suits.

Their smiles were so bright that it reached their blue eyes which made my heart swell in joy.

I walked forward in the trace of enchanted azure eyes as if I was bewitched into the un escaping spell of bound called love. As I walked, further I noticed that a spot light was on me too and smiled shaking my head in disbelief.

Their eyes eying my every move and my every step as if they are trying their best to not take me off my feet right now. Their single look was seduction, voice was sin and today I swear I wouldn't mind being the sinner by accepting anything these two are having for me in store for our life time.

The whole floor was cushioned with rose petals and their musky citrus and pine wood essence filled my lungs even in the floral fragrance around me, that's how addicted I have became to them.

Their eyes darkened and jaws clenched as if hungry monsters ready to pound on their prey but I stood straight in their presence. They took a good few minutes before any of us have spoken.

"You look beautiful doll", Mario said devouring me with his eyes. Taking my left hand and pressed a kiss on back of my hand.

"As always", Marco added with same intensity and my stomach did nth number of somersaults making me feel giddy as he did kissed my right hand.

"I knew you would cheat, I said that poetry wasn't good for understanding but he said it's romantic", macro said breaking the ice and I chuckled shaking my head.

"Hey! I worked hard on that thinking for days!", Mario exclaimed punching macro on his chest and macro simply rolled his eyes giving me side grin.

"That was cute, I loved it", I admitted smiling at Mario taking his side.

"See!", Mario said throwing his hands around me engulfing me in a bear hug. Laughter erupted from me then my eyes drifted to macro who was pouting as a child whose candy was stolen.

Breaking the hug with Mario I walked towards macro and his lips stretched into smile immediately and he hugged me tight making me chuckle.

"So... Mario wrote beautiful poetry for me, what did you do?", I asked him raising my eyebrows and he shoved his hands in his pockets and smirked nodding his head upwards and as soon as my eyes saw what was in the sky, my breathe hitched and my hand flew to my mouth as I gasped.

"Oh my god!".

HAPPINESS

AUTHOR'S POV

As soon as Odette's eyes diverted to the sky she couldn't speak. She just kept looking at the beautiful view with glistening eyes.

The whole sky was lit up with drones, which were emitting bright light as stars. It was a hell of a show that how they were moving in sync and forming a three hearts, three hands holding together, a huge heart with we love you written inside it.

But what caught her utmost attention was they started moving and her gaze widened as it started to form words.

Doll

Please

Marry

Us

It happened so soon that she doubted if she read it in real, they didn't ask her, they pleaded.

They didn't demand, they begged and tears were threatening to fall from her doe eyes. Her breathe hitched when a ring was formed in the sky and she blinked her eyes for the first time since the show started and slowly lowered her gaze to see macro and mario both on their knees.

There was a ring in their hands – single ring in their hands and they were looking at her almost terrified like if they are thinking she would say no. They were nervous and gulped hard and their Adams apple bobbed making Odette gulp. Their hands are joined together as if trying to calm their nerves and other is in front of her holding a side of ring, which had three hearts and not to mention huge. That it would be definitely a statement jewellery with what ever she will wear rather than look like wedding ring but that wasn't her concern.

The girl who thought she wouldn't marry a man like her dad, have a simple life, be the feminist and fight for women's rights. She was going to run away from the marriage or worse hurt her husband who was marrying her under the contract to make alley with their family business.

Not even in her dream she thought she would fall in love and not one but two men. Marriage was far away.

Now looking into their blue eyes, she sees their love for her. She can see the truth of their feelings, which they have only for her.

The depths of their love for her, which they will drown in to raise her high, giving her wings.

She thought marriage would only crumble her independence but they gave her choice to choose and leave and she thought only a fool would leave them and she wasn't a fool.

With teary eyes, she nodded her head giving her hand forward, a huge smile spread on their faces immediately and they put the ring on her finger, got up on their legs and hugged her together. Holding her tight in their arms they breathed sigh of relief as they said, "I love you".

"I love you", repeatedly and Odette let her tears flow happily as she whispered back, "I love you too".

A beautiful blast echoed in the sky as she flinched slightly but her eyes soon travelled to the dark sky where in place of drones are firecracker and she haven't seen such beauty. Giggling she kissed their cheeks and they returned the gesture by giving her kiss on her lips which she gladly accepted.

The rest of the night went drinking, dancing and a romantic dinner under the starry night, which would be the memory Odette promised to take with her to her grave.

Where as twins thought that they were luckiest men in the world to get a princess as their mother used to read but in real life and they would do anything to keep her like this, filling her life with happiness and eyes with memories, which they would all cherish their lifetime.

~~~~

"I can't believe am going to marry them", Odette blabbered pacing around her room in her wedding gown.

"Aunt Oddy, come on, don't stress out, you will get wrinkles and you will look older than now", Paul commented rolling his eyes.

Odette narrowed her eyes on the little boy who stood across the room in his black suit, stopped on her tracks and folded her hands on her chest as she snapped.

"What do you mean older?! I look old?!", she asked feeling offended and glared at the little boy.

"Isn't eighteen means older?! You said you wanted to be older last year because the wedding was paused since you were seventeen", Peter retorted frowning and Odette exhaled heavily before correcting.

"It's not paused, it's delayed and yes, I guess you were right I said that", she admitted sitting on the couch.

"But you look beautiful, fine as wine, the older the tastier", Peter said and Odette smirked at them before telling.

"Did you hear your dad tell this to your mom?".

"No we heard grandpa telling grandma", they both said frowning making Odette laugh throwing her head back.

Her nose turned red as she came back from her laughing fit, her mood soured once again and twins rushed to her hugging her from both sides.

"Don't you think it's weird, you have only one aunt but two uncles?", Odette asked taking a huge breathe and twins smiled at her widely.

"You are stressed because you are having two grooms? But isn't it a good thing aunt oddy?!" Paul exclaimed excited.

"Why is it a good thing? When people will talk about it making me hurt?", she asked looking into their eyes.

"It's good thing because you got buy one get one free offer and mom is always happy when she get something in sale like this and people will talk bad because they missed the offer so we shouldn't let them make us feel hurt but enjoy the sale by ourselves and can tell them to fuck off bitches", Peter said making Odette chuckle and hug them tightly.

"I won't be telling to your mom you just used bad language", Odette said patting Peter's back and this made Paul smirk.

"Well if you tell, we will tell that you are our teacher", he said back making her eyes wide and the door opened revealing a stressed Aurora.

"What are you doing here boys; you are supposed to stay with macro and Mario! You are their best men!", Aurora said and their eyes widened in realization.

"Oh! We are leaving", they said as they ran outside making Odette chuckle.

"Oddy....." Aurora walked towards her sister and Odette's smile vanished immediately looking at her sister's stressed face.

"What's wrong rora?", she asked getting up on her feet and Aurora sighed heavily and hugged Odette.

"Mrs Grayson couldn't make it, it's okay, you can meet her tomorrow", Aurora lied knowing very well what happened to her.

Instead of telling that the woman whom Odette consider as Godmother was found dead in her apartment in Rome, her death was not natural but a murder and Aurora found this when she heard macro and mario speaking.

Frowning Odette broke the hug looking into Aurora's eyes.

"You are lying?", she asked sensing the turmoil in her sister's heart.

"Why would I?!", Aurora fought back staying on her words.

"I just got a call from her that her daughter's health is not fine and she is in emergency unit", Aurora said without stuttering.

Nodding her head Odette sighed then smiled sadly.

"It's okay, I guess I will meet her later when we reach Rome", Odette said making Aurora release a sigh internally.

"Now, let's go, your impatient groom are waiting for you", Aurora squealed making Odette smile widely.

Taking a deep breathe she nodded her head with confidence shaking her thoughts about what people will tell and walked out of the dressing room with a huge genuine smile on her lips.

Towards her destiny.

HER PUPPETS

AUTHOR'S POV

With every step, Odette felt blood rushing to her heart pumping so loudly that she could hear her heartbeat over the slow hum of the music, which was playing.

People were smiling, some were giving her looks, which she didn't want to describe. Holding herself gracefully, she made it inside the same church where she got married to macro.

If that day was most beautiful the church looked then today can't be described. It was ethereal as if she was walking towards the doors of heaven. Holding onto her dad's hand tightly she stopped right in front of two men who is now owning her heart and soul.

"Take care of my daughter", Andre said his voice fatherly towards the twins and they both smiled nodding their head.

"With our everything", they replied and forwarded their hands together and Odette held on their hands as she did when she stopped them in front of the park when they were kids and walked up on the stage.

"Do you remember the day I said how heaven would be?" Mario whispered in her ear bending to her height. Odette blushed and asked him teasingly, "twice but which one you want me to refer?". Mario smirked at her winking as he reminded, "When you kissed my shadow eagerly".

Odette rolled her eyes playfully and retorted, "Yes, with rainbow slides, flying unicorns and chocolate fountains".

"I was wrong, doll, so fucking wrong", he whispered in his husky voice. His breathe fanning on her earlobe making her body tingle with familiar sensation. Without letting her speak he added, "Because heaven is seeing you walk towards us in wedding gown and if this isn't heaven I fucking don't want it", he growled making her gulp hard and a beautiful smile painted on her lips and she blushed at his words.

Marco smiled and nudged her towards him and whispered, "last time I noticed you were wearing sneakers, why heels now huh?".

Odette smiled widely knowing he noticed the little details in past too.

"Yes, because last time I didn't want to miss my chance to run away as far as possible from you", she joked smirking at him.

"Uh-hmm, then now?", macro asked raising his eyebrow amusingly.

"Now... I don't want to run...... even if I run, I know I will trip and you would be there for me catching me in your arms before I fall", Odette said looking at him without blinking.

A beautiful smile formed on his lips hearing her reply. Looking into his eyes and their joined hands she said, "That's how much your feelings for me and mine for you have changed and first time in my life I like this change – because it was my choice".

Those words held her emotions. Odette wasn't the one who got much of choices without her rebelling but this time it's all real, she indeed was given choice and macro and mario gave her that.

"You will always have your say, doll, not only in your life but also in our business", macro's words made her eyes widen in shock but she couldn't ask anything what does that mean because they were already standing in front of the marriage officiant.

The marriage officiant started doing the ritual and she took their forms which was beyond beautiful than any Greek gods. Both in white button up and black trouser pants with matching s suit, which was settled on their muscular bodies, made her gulp and she thought how she was this lucky to have them both in her life.

Their blue eyes shining as they smiled at her without blinking as if she would vanish away if they do.

Following the vows Macro and Mario said, "I do", and Odette followed then when it was her time by saying, "I do".

This time the vows were real as much as the love they are carrying in their hearts, which was clearly visible to everyone witnessing their wedding.

"You may kiss your bride", the marriage officiant announced as Odette's heart was beating so loud in her chest. She couldn't hear anything specially the gasps escaped from guests and Andre smiled widely looking at the scene unfolding in front of everyone.

Two dangerous men who are well known for their unbelievable dominant nature and ruthless behaviour are kneeing in front of their bride.

Two mafia kings by blood who were a royalty in mafia families are on their knees for a woman – in front of a woman. A lone tear escaped Andre's eyes picturing his best friend, twin's father in them.

He was exactly like them and the kindness, which they are showing to his daughter was Alesia's. He couldn't be more thankful to them for giving these two men a life, which made his daughter the luckiest woman of the world.

Today he couldn't be more proud of them. He straightened his shoulder his chest swelling with pride as macro and mario took each hand of Odette in their own and pressed their lips on the back of her hand.

Odette's breathe hitched at the contact of their soft lips on her knuckles, which lingered on her soul.

Bianca who was sitting at the back clenched her jaw while her hands held the armrest of the bench so hard that her knuckles turned white and the inner part of her hand was imprinted with a dirty red mark of wood.

How badly she wanted to use them against Andre for her revenge but they fell for her head over heels as some sheep following each other, she thought Marco would go in vain in his love interest but she didn't expect same from Mario whom she was manipulating to bring chaos in between Marco and Odette.

However, today she realized witnessing everything that they may call Odette their doll but they were Odette's puppets. To bring them away she would have to use the strings, which Odette was using to play with those puppets in her hands, and they are love and feelings.

A cunning smirk made its way on her face as she planned her next move on her and she got up from the seat and walked out from there to put her plan in motion.

~~~

"That was some romantic shit, I can't get over how they kissed you", Aurora squealed as a teenager holding Odette's hands in her own.

Odette blushed brightly and her cheeks were hurting by the way, she was smiling since the time she stepped in the church.

"I can't believe I have two husbands now", Odette said looking at both Marco and Mario who was talking some business with Andre and his friends.

Odette saw her father smiling widely patting Marco and Mario's shoulders standing in between them. Aurora followed her sister's gaze and smiled as she spotted her husband Dimitri laughing along with Marco and Mario.

His silver blonde hair was shining brightly under the bright lights. He sensed his wife's gaze on her and smiled brightly and excused himself.

"Are you okay, sweetheart?", Dimitri asked wrapping his arms around Aurora protectively looking into her doe eyes.

"I am fine", Aurora replied blushing.

"Eww, don't blush rora, you are making me sick", Odette commented rolling her eyes as she folded her hands on her chest.

Aurora glared at her and Dimitri chuckled winking at Odette and said, "She can't help it".

Odette shook her head laughing as she looked at red face of Aurora and asked, "So you guys planning to give me a niece? We want more number of girls as men outnumbered us already".

Aurora smirked looking between Dimitri and her sister and said, "Don't you think we should be the one to ask, Dimitri?!". Hearing her sister Odette blushed brightly.

"There is nothing to ask sweetheart, we all know how Italian men are! If we have to ask something from them that would be begging to give a break to Odette from giving birth", Dimitri commented smirking as he teased his favourite sister.

Odette gasped placing her hand on her mouth and punched Dimitri's arm, he just chuckled shaking his head and Aurora laughed holding her stomach.

"I will kill you!", Odette snapped faking offended but her stomach tingled imagining having a family with Marco and Mario.

"It wasn't even few hours since you was declared Italian mafia queen and you want to murder our greatest alley?!", Marco teased standing behind her as his breathe fanned her neck. Odette jumped startled and Mario quickly wrapped his arms around her standing in front of her.

"You could have asked for a hug, doll", Mario teased smirking at her and Odette blushed looking into his mischievous eyes and gulped.

"Well I don't know about her but am definitely going to puke, it's so sweet to see you both like this with her but my tomboy sister and her blushing like a tomato is making me sick", Aurora joked smirking at Odette making her pout.

Marco and Mario chuckled along Dimitri and Marco said, "Well as much as I like your sister in stocking and leather jackets, I like her blushing like a freak".

"Knowing we are the reason behind her red cheeks makes our cocks so fucking..." Mario was cut off with Odette's palm on his mouth with her wide eyes and she glared at him making him smirk.

"Ahem, am taking my wife for a dance", Dimitri excused Aurora and himself chuckling, leaving the trio alone. "You can't tell things like that in front of anyone", Odette warned with her hand still on his mouth.

Mario licked her palm making her yelp and she scowled retracing her hand and wiped it on her gown.

"Eww, this is disgusting", Odette whined going back in Marco's arms glaring at Mario and the brothers' chuckled.

"You won't be saying that tonight when my tongue will be deep inside your pussy eating you good and clean", Mario said smirking and Odette blushed hiding her face in Marco's chest.

"Trust me doll, you will fucking love it", this time Marco whispered in her ear huskily making her breathe hitch.

PAINFULLY PLEASURABLE

ODETTE'S POV

With every step, my heart was thundering in my chest. I noticed how we were going back to the same hotel and soon I was standing right in front of the same pent house I stayed first night after my wedding with Marco. But today I was standing in the same room but with my two husbands who are looking at me with so much intensity that I want to crumble down and hide somewhere. But the looks they are giving me made me so wet that I need their help and I wasn't shy about asking what I need. I can't imagine if am this wet with just two of them looking at me like this then I can't fucking imagine what I will be when they touch me.

Diverting my gaze from my two men standing across me I gulped and a smile formed on my lips as I saw the candle light in the room along with rose petals decorated the room giving the musky and romantic touch wasn't something one can get used to and not get butterflies in their stomach.

With my peripheral vision I saw them looking at me with clenched jaws and licking their lips. When their hands slowly went to their suits, I sucked huge amount of air filling my lungs thinking I would be able to push my nervousness about having two of them at same time tonight.

Marco and Mario took their suits and shirts off letting their perfectly carved body in front of me and I didn't hesitate to admire the ethereal beauty of my husbands.

Husbands how weird it sounds but for me it sounds as sin, an unexplainable sin that I am not ashamed of committing again and again. The sin, which I would worship and let it consume me until I am not left with soul in my body.

There wasn't much difference between how muscular and well built they are, their hard chest and those abs, which one would gladly lick and suck on them. The only difference is Marco has tattoos on his both hands and chest and I immediately gulped hard looking at how different the tattoos are but how good they look together engraved on his body.

"Today...", Marco said looking at me in his thick voice as if he has difficulty in speaking.

"Only today.....", Mario added smirking at me with the fire in his eyes which I would let him burn me with it.

My heart raced in my chest as my pussy pulsed and clenched over nothing. The excitement running in my blood is getting so demanding that all I want to do is beg them to devour me but I am not going to miss the chance to play with my men.

"Today?!", I questioned walking towards them and traced my fingers on their chest to their abs towards the waistband of their trousers which were secured with belt.

Shamelessly gawking at their ripped bodies, I smirked looking into their blue eyes, which are darkened in the deepest shades of darkness I want to drown in.

"You will take lead", they both said in unison and my smirk soon turned into a wide grin as I let their words sink.

"And this is one day offer?", I teased raising my eyebrows to which they both smirked and Marco pulled me into him as he gripped my hair, pulled it back making me arch into him as I looked into his eyes with my parted lips.

"All I want to do is throw you on bed and watch when my brother fucks your pussy all good then fuck you myself", he growled and my smirk widened at his dominant voice which sent shivers to my spine.

Suddenly I was spinned and threw in Mario's arms. He caught me, and a low gasp escaped my mouth when I came in contact with him and he smirked.

"But we want to take things slow with you, only one if us will fuck you and it's your choice", he said and my heart swelled with an emotion I couldn't describe.

Looking into his eyes, I smiled.

A genuine smile.

Then took my steps back from him and nodded my head before asking, "I am in control?"

They both smiled and nodded their head answering "Yes".

"But only tonight", they both added afraid that I might get that wrong.

This time I smirked, a dirty and flirty smirk, which made their eyes darker then before.

"We will see", I challenged winking at them and slipped my wedding gown down revealing my naked self in front of them just in my sexy black lace set and their eyes immediately ate up my body and Marco fisted his hands tight and I heard Mario release a shaky breathe.

Swaying my hips I walked towards the bar and poured myself a glass of red wine and the next word, which left my mouth startled me.

"Strip", I ordered and my voice felt foreign to me as the demand left through the space between us and my eyes widened at how it felt.

Sucking up the shock, I sipped the wine and turned towards them looking into their eyes I ordered again, "Strip for your wife".

But as if sensing my turmoil they both smirked giving each other knowing looks and gracefully took off their belts and threw it somewhere as they kept their hunter like eyes on me, without breaking the eye contact then slowly slipped their trousers and boxers and kicked them off their feet.

Everything happened in teasing slow motion, which made me gulp and for a reason I was afraid to look down what they have for me.

Trying to loosen myself up for the whole night I planned to give my husbands, which they have earned and deserved with everything they did for me and promised their lives and soul to me making me queen I sat down on the bedroom bench.

Taking another sip, I felt confident when the alcohol calmed my pounding nerves and I leaned back placing my elbow back, twirled the wine glass, and let my eyes drink up the sinful view in front of my eyes.

My husbands' cocks were standing all tall and proud, thicker and veiny with those red mushroom heads, which I am afraid would even fit inside of me but the fear I felt was pushed away when their cocks twitched in my hungry sight.

I smirked licking my lips tasting the sweet flavour of fine wine on my lips with my eyes still on their cocks I ordered, "Knee".

Moreover, without a word I saw them oblige me.

These two men who were dominant their whole life are kneeing in front of me. Letting me control them, handing me the power, giving me the freedom to choose my first time to be comfortable is making me come almost at the thoughts without even touching myself.

My pussy was throbbing so painfully, clenching and unclenching around nothing but my own slick juices is making me crazy that I want my husbands to fuck me as if we are animals in heat.

Diverting my eyes from their monstrous cocks, I locked my eyes with their hungry ones waiting for my command but I know I could get much from them right before I woke up beasts in them.

Playing my last straw, I ordered.

"Crawl to me".

I thought my voice would stutter or shake but it came demanding as if it's not me who is speaking, as if I was possessed by a devil and I couldn't be more thankful for it.

Their faces darkened sending chills to my spine. I know I played my last chance and it was what I wanted to get from them before giving myself to them. I wanted to see if I could bring them to my feet as no woman would have done to powerful men like them and I realized now there is no backing away from the hungry lions in front of me.

"You are playing with fire, doll", Marco's voice was think and dark which made my pussy throb.

Without blinking, I kept my stoic face as I spread my legs wide for them to see. Mario growled as Marco sucked in a breathe.

Chugging the glass up drinking up the remaining content I threw the glass far away letting it shatter and the sound echoed in the dead silence of the room.

Marco and Mario's chest were rising and falling with the same rhythm as mine and this time my voice came out as a needy order as if I would die if they wouldn't listen.

"Crawl to your doll".

They did without wasting a second they crawled to me swallowing their pride, crumbling it for me they crawled towards me and I can only imagine how strongly they pushed themselves to do. This act might look weak to anyone but for me they looked powerful as if two hungry panthers walking towards their prey they held their heads up with their darkened eyes on me and soon they were in front of my feet and my heart swelled with the amount of love and pride that I might have grown few more heads and hearts to lock the feelings inside me greedily.

I released a shaky breathe and looked in their eyes before I spoke, "I married you both".

"I married two powerful men", I emphasised on the word *two* by pressing on it.

"I want you two be my firsts", my voice coming out strained yet strong.

"Tonight, I want you both to own me as no one could imagine, I want you both to take me today", I pleaded.

I pleaded though I had the power to order because I know they wouldn't think about hurting me and I couldn't think about my pain in front of the pleasure I could give to my men, my husbands. So I pleaded with my words and begged with my eyes.

"Please daddy.....", I wined which made them suck in a huge amount of breathe and their chest heaved still without touching me they both asked.

"You want to play with fire, doll?".

Biting my lip holding my lip ring in between my teeth before I left it free I answered, "And your doll is not afraid to burn".

That's what it took for Marco to lose his control on himself and in a second his hand was wrapped on my neck and mario tore off my panties in one go and I was thrown on the bed behind me and a gasp left my body along a squeal as I bounced on the soft mattress.

Mario crawled in between my legs and attacked my throbbing pussy with his tongue and Marco was kissing my lips as if he was sucking my soul through them.

A loud moan escaped my lips as I felt Mario's tongue thrust into my core and Marco took advantage of it, slipped his tongue in my mouth and explored every inch of my mouth as Mario lapped on my juices below driving me crazy.

Greedy for more I raised my hips pushing myself more into his mouth and he chuckled against my core, held me down with his tight hold on my things and ate me out making me scream.

His hold will definitely leave bruise on my skin but I would cherish it. When I thought it was too much Marco broke the kiss, tore my bra off, freeing my bosoms covered them with his huge palms and massaged them teasing me and my back arched reaching my high.

I was almost there but everything stopped.

"Noooo", I whined and Mario's fingers traced my inner thighs with a cocky smirk on his face with my juices covered on them he raised his eyebrow asking me what he wanted to hear.

What they wanted to hear. Assholes! But I wouldn't dare to tell that on their face when am underneath them seeking pleasure.

I gulped looking in between Marco and Mario and Marco was the one to command, his voice stern and demanding making my heart thump against my chest as he ordered.

"Beg for what you want Mario to do to you doll".

I exhaled heavily, diverted my eyes from the blue ones to another pair of same eyes and licked my lips as I pleaded, "Doll wants daddy to make her come".

"Good girl", Marco praised and my heart beat halted eating up the praise I felt good, it felt good. I want to be a good girl for the first time in my life.

"Do you think she deserves to come?", Marco asked Mario and my eyes found his immediately waiting for his answer.

"Fuck yes!", Mario growled and his mouth back on where I want him, where I need him.

He feasted on me as a hungry animal lapping all my juices while groaning making me clench around his tongue.

Marco attacked my bosoms, blowing air on my erect pink studs, which were begging for their attention and swirled his tongue around the areola and a shaky moan escaped my lips when he finally sucked the bubble making me roll my eyes back.

Pinching and pulling my other nipple with his hand he massaged it sending me to edge and my hands found his and Mario's hair and I dug my fingers in luscious silky brown curls and their pleasurable torture on me turned more intense. While Marco played with the other bosom, giving it same attention as he did to the first one and Mario rubbed his tongue on the bundle of nerves on my clit my breathing turned ragged and my eyes rolled back as I screamed.

A bloody scream when I came all over Mario's mouth and he hummed over my sensitive nub and ate up everything I offered.

"Good girl", Mario praised running his tongue on his lips and I sighed in content.

"Are you sure doll, you want to take both of us?", Mario asked and his voice gravely making my heart race.

Looking at his hard cock, which has pre come dripping made me lick my lips. Nodding my head I looked into his eyes before answering, "I'm sure".

"Fuck!", he muttered under his breathe and got up from the bed coming behind me and Marco came in between my legs this time and I saw him walking with his hard cock standing straight for attention.

"We don't have lube with us doll, you need to give me one more before we take you", Marco said making me gulp.

"Can you give one more for daddy?", he asked and I nodded my head.

"Words", Mario growled and I stuttered as I said, "Y... yes, daddy".

"Good girl, our doll is such a good girl", Marco hummed before playing with my clit with his thumb and my eyes rolled back as he pushed his two fingers inside my swollen drenching core.

"Ahhhh", I moaned and Mario kissed my lips immediately and I hummed, as I tasted myself on him.

"So fucking sexy", Marco growled as he pumped his fingers inside me with his thumb still working on my clit sending me to clouds.

He took his fingers out and sucked on them while Mario was leaving hickeys on my neck while my chest was all covered in the hickeys Marco gave.

Marco hummed with his two fingers in his mouth, took them out with a pop and spit on my clit while he rubbed it pushing his fingers back in my greedy core.

I arched my back as he increased the speed and with a breathy moan I gasped and came squirting all over his fingers that made him smile proudly.

"Fuck! That was so fucking hot!", he growled lifting me on my knees after giving me two minutes to come down from my high.

We were breathing heavily as Marco kissed my lips before Mario latched his mouth on my lips and my hands already found their hard members and they hissed as I pressed my thumb on the slits of their angry red head mushrooms.

"Though I want to fuck your cunt, I know Marco won't be able to control himself when he get inside your tight little ass, doll", Mario hummed against my lips pulling my hair back making me arch my neck and I looked into his eyes with my hooded ones.

Marco's eyes widened for a second, he immediately nodded his head to Mario and he smiled and I felt left out between these two as if they are communicating with each other in some mind chain as vampires.

Mario gestured Marco towards the bed, he laid with his back down and gave few quick pumps to his huge cock and I gulped nervously biting my lip.

"So wet", Mario commented with his hand between my legs and collected my wetness in his palm before he coated his cock with it as he kissed my lips one last time and I moaned begging for more.

Bringing the remaining wetness to my backside, he nudged me towards Marco and I gulped straddling him with my knees each side of his thighs.

"You need to relax doll, take deep breathes", Marco said noticing my nervousness as I nodded my head then replied, "Okay".

Inclining his cock to my opening, he teased me before looking into my eyes with his jaw clenched.

"Take slowly when you are ready", he said and I found myself nodding.

Mario's hands found my nipples from behind, he played with them flickering and twisting in between his skilled fingers and I laid my palms on Marco's tattooed chest.

His heart was thumping against my palm and I realized it's not only me who is nervous. My husbands are nervous too and it's not for them but for me. Circling his thumb on my clit Marco looked into my eyes and I nodded while slowly lowering myself down on his thick hard length.

My eyebrows furrowed in the discomfort and I stopped with my lips parted breathing as much as air possible.

"Good girl, keep going, take it slow", Mario whispered against my ear encouraging me as he kissed his way on my neck, shoulders and my back.

Nodding my head, I bit my lip as I slowly took Marco half the way inside me and I hissed in pain.

Marco increased his pace on my clit easing me and his hand on my ass gripping it hard it might bruise but it felt good. The pain was pleasurable.

"Almost there, doll, am so proud of you", Marco choked out breathing heavily as his forehead was glistened in sweat even in the blast of the ac.

"Ahhhhh!", I yelped and screamed when I felt myself taking him completely and it hurt, hurt like a bitch as if someone shoved a hot burning knife inside me and I couldn't help and fall limp on Marco's chest and a line tear escaped from my eyes.

"Do you want me to take it out, we can always take things slow, doll", I hear Marco's concerned voice in my ear as he caressed my hair pressing his lips on my head.

His heart in rhythm with my own and I found myself smiling before shaking my head.

"No, don't take it out, just give me some time", I requested and he nodded his head pressing kisses on my head.

"Good girl, am so proud of you doll, you did so well", Mario praised with his hand messaging my spine and I signed I content.

After a few minutes, I felt comfortable with Marco inside me and stirred a little and Marco grunted as if he was in pain and Mario chuckled.

"Mario... I want you too", I said and I heard Mario growl before he came behind me placing kisses all over my shoulder.

"Are you sure doll, we don't want to hurt you", he said and I nodded my head vigorously.

"Please", I begged and I felt Mario exhale a breathe as Marco brought my lips to his and started kissing them hungrily.

"Relax yourself", Mario said as his thumb circled over my puckered hole and I took a shaky breathe.

"Take a deep breathe and relax, doll", Marco whispered against my lips and I whimpered as I felt Mario's girth pressing against my opening.

"Tell me if it hurts, doll", Mario said pushing himself in and I gasped and cried out in pain when I felt his length inside me.

"Almost there doll, relax and breathe, take it in, you are doing great – fucking amazing", Mario growled against my ear and I nodded my head following his instructions.

"Ahhh", I gasped as I felt him fill me completely and my eyes rolled back in both pain and pleasure.

Now this is what I could get used to. Giving me few minutes to adjust they peppered my skin with kisses and teased my nipples as they kept whispering sweet things in my ear telling how I made them proud and such a good girl I am.

Getting used to the feeling of being completely filled I moved and Mario gripped my ass grunting.

"Do you want us to move?", Marco asked and his voice coming out strained.

"Yes please", I pleaded and they slowly started thrusting into me bringing out erotic and sinful noises from me. I moaned, mewled, gasped and begged for more and they increased the pace granting my wish.

"Fuck! Baby! You are so fucking tight!" Marco growled taking my lips in his mouth and kissed me ruthlessly as I moaned in his mouth taking his tongue and sucked on it.

"Fuck! Do you know how sexy you look with our cocks inside you?!", Mario grunted increasing his speed making me scream.

Yanking my hair, he brought me up as now I am seated on Marco's cock with Mario's still inside and this position was more intense than the previous one.

I clenched hard and Marco hissed groping my breasts as I clawed his chest, digging my nails Mario swallowed my moans kissing my lips impatiently.

I immediately screamed in his mouth as I came and this felt like as if am in a Milky Way galaxy. All I could see is stars, fucking stars with two cocks inside me and I enjoyed every second of it.

"Ahhhh, daddy", I moaned bringing my hand back and clenching my fist in Mario's hair and Marco increased his pace so hard that I thought I wouldn't have been still on him if I wasn't clenching on him tightly and Mario's hold on my ass.

"Fuck! You are amazing!" Mario praised and Marco soon found my clit and started rubbing his thumb while they both pounded in me.

I felt them twitch in me and they turned thicker and I rolled my eyes back moaning. Our bodies were sweaty and the room felt steamy and the only sounds we could hear was our skin slapping and their grunts along my moans and screams.

"Do you want us to come inside you?", marco growled thrusting animalistically and I nodded my head as I cried out.

"Will you take our come in your tight little holes?", mario asked and I whined biting my lip as I nodded my head without being able to form words.

"Words doll, what do you want from us?", marco growled and a slap landed on my left bosom and that made me clench around them.

"Fuck!", they hissed as I cried out.

"Please….. I want you both to come inside me, please daddy", I cried as I reached my high and came with a gush around marco's cock squeezing his orgasm along me. With a sexy grunt both marco and mario came inside me and my thighs shivered in the intensity of my mind blocking orgasm and I felt my insides warm with their hot thick liquid and fell limp on marco's chest.

"Ahhh", I hissed as I felt them pull out from me and pressed their lips on my head and I saw them smile warmly before whispering, "We love you, doll". I whispered "I love you both", before drifting into the darkness with a painfully pleasurable experience with a tired smile on my own face.

JUST A BEGINNING

AUTHOR'S POV

"Is everything ready?", marco asked draco on the phone.

"Everything is ready boss, I made sure it's safe and the guards and new caretakers are already moved in, the mansion will be ready when you get back", draco said confidently.

"Good, also put the Gardner on duty to plant flowers specifically all colours of roses as possible", marco said looking at sleeping figure of Odette.

A smile made it's way on his face as he saw her burying her face in mario's chest and clinging onto him in her sleep. Last night meant so much for them. She strained her body for them even though they wanted to take it slow, she wanted to please them and they weren't going to forget that night in their lifetime.

No matter how much marco wanted to crawl back into the duvet and sleep beside her he couldn't, he have to take care of their return as mario have done so much already and was stressed about finding the man behind the blast and he wanted to give some time for his brother to rest so marco didn't wake him up.

"Have you found angela?", marco asked frowning as he didn't hear anything about her.

"No boss, we have searched whole Rome but we couldn't find her", draco said sighing heavily.

"I think we should stop looking for her and find the person behind the blast he will spill where she is, I doubt she have seen him because as anna said he was wearing a mask, that man might have used angela's jealousy for his own benefit", draco explained to marco.

Marco thought about it for a second and then spoke, "Have you seen Bianca? I suggest you to keep an eye on her, I think she knows the man who planned the blast".

"I have seen her at your wedding boss but she left in between", draco answered and Marco nodded even he couldn't see.

"Bring me details of every person she meets, keep it low and only our trust worthy men to work against her", Marco ordered gaining a "Yes boss", from draco.

"The chopper will be up, you can leave whenever you want", draco said before Marco hung up the phone.

Putting his phone on the table Marco slowly walked towards the bed and slipped inside the duvet and snaked his tattooed arm around odette's waist.

Moaning she turned around now facing Marco and opened her eyes. The view in front of her can take her breathe away.

Those blue shining eyes and the dark brown hair messily resting on his forehead along with his ripped body which was decorated with tattoos. But what caught her attention was the bright smile on his lips.

"Good morning Mrs de Luca", Marco hummed huskily and Odette came down from her thoughts and smiled at her husband and blushed brightly remembering last night.

"Good morning, Mr de Luca", she said snuggling her face into his chest to hide the blush forming on her face.

"I love how you blush even after the way you took two of us last night", Marco teased smirking at her and received a smack on his chest.

He chuckled his body shaking with the laughter sending vibrations to Odette and she immediately covered his mouth with her palm.

Glaring at him she whisper yelled, "Shh, mario is still sleeping". Her worry towards his brother only made him more harder than before and Odette's eyes widened when she felt something poking her stomach.

"Oh god! Don't tell me!", she whispered shaking her head with her widened eyes making Marco smirk.

"What do you mean by don't tell me?! You don't want to know what happens to me when you are naked under the duvet covered in our marks and come?", Marco said making Odette turn redder than before.

Without being able to control himself Marco pressed his lips to hers and kissed her softly, passionately bringing out a soft moan from her lips.

"Having fun without me?", mario commented from behind, his breathe fanning her shoulder and she flinched in marco's arms making mario chuckle.

"How are you feeling doll?", mario asked her and she groaned placing her palms on her face, rubbed her tired eyes before muttering, "tired as fuck am unable to feel my legs and my thighs are stinging along with you know.....", she drawled off making Marco chuckle.

"A warm bath will fix this", marco said getting up from bed before pressing his lips on Odette's head and walked stark naked to the bathroom and soon the sound of water filling the bathtub echoed.

"I can get used to this", mario said pulling Odette in his arms making her giggle.

"Uh hmm....", Odette hummed and pressed her lips on mario's giving a quick peck making him smirk.

"Now no eww?", he teased making Odette roll her eyes.

Mario smacked her ass and she yelped glaring at him and he laughed as he got up on his feet and carried Odette in his arms inside the washroom.

~~~

ODETTE'S POV

"This is beautiful", I cooed as soon as my gaze found the Jacuzzi with scented candles around it with rose petals swimming in the warm water.

"Not more beautiful than you, doll", mario commented and I rolled my eyes instantly but the smile on my lips widened as I commented, "cheesy".

"Come on", Marco said and I stood on my feet and walked in the Jacuzzi and sat comfortably with help of Mario and Marco who held me possessively so I don't slip.

I moaned with my eyes closed and leaned back into marco's chest and mario joined us.

Taking a loofa mario scrubbed my feet massaging them with his fingers and I curled my toes pulling them away from him with a breathless laugh.

"Don't!", I warned but mario's lips curled up in a wide grin as he stated, "You are ticklish".

"Ugh!", I groaned and tilted my head towards Marco and saw his smile which was looking at us with adoration.

"Why he is such a tease?!", I whined earning a chuckle from him.

"What can I say you bring best out of him, doll", he smirked making me roll my eyes and I smacked his chest with my palm and he chuckled.

"If this is the best I bring out of him, I don't even know what worst can be", I exclaimed shaking my head.

"Oh trust me you wouldn't want to know, especially the worst you bring out from Marco", mario said his eyes sparkling with mischief and I was curious to know about it more as Marco shifted uncomfortably behind me looking anywhere but not me.

"What he is talking about Marco?", I asked smirking at him, if it's some blackmail material mario is using against Marco then hell! I am interested to know it.

Clearing his throat Marco shook his head cutely and I awed at him ruffling his hair.

"He won't tell you doll, that he almost fucked my ass in his sleep dreaming about you and that was the worst thing I woke up with him rubbing his dick on my ass", mario stated wincing at the memory making a disgusted face and my hand flew to my mouth and I laughed before turning to Marco.

I don't even need to confirm what mario said because Marco was red due to embarrassment and he wasn't looking at me but cutely glaring at his brother.

"Aww, you look so cute", I teased pushing his hair back and his attention diverted to me smiling he looked into my eyes then slowly down looking at my exposed chest which was covered in red to purple hickeys and rose petals were clinging on my skin because of the wetness.

He gulped visibly and his eyes darkened and a arm was snaked around my waist and I don't even need to turn to look who's hand it is. It's mario's.

"You need to take rest doll, relax, let me take care of you", he said and started rubbing my body with body wash and it felt so good, better than any massage I have taken in my whole life.

Still looking at Marco with my hooded eyes I saw hunger in his eyes and I don't even need to ask mario about his hard girth poking my ass cheek from behind.

Though how badly I am craving them my hollow cavities are sore and I couldn't take their enormous skilled cocks again, not just now but tonight?! Maybe! So biting my lip forbidding myself from telling them to fuck my brains out, I enjoyed the attention mario was giving.

Slowly marco grabbed my legs and stated massaging my calf and I smiled widely closing my eyes. I don't know what time it was and where I was when my eyes snapped open.

I was wearing nothing but a black lace set and was feeling fresh, that means I might have fallen asleep in Jacuzzi and they have taken care of me. Smiling widely I got up from the bed and saw the time. It was nine am and we woke up at seven so roughly I have taken one and hour of nap.

I heard sounds from out of the bedroom and the smell of freshly cooked bacon hit my nostrils and I almost drooled. I was hungry and the greasy savoury food after a tired night is better than anything else. Finding a note on bed along with neatly folded clothes I read it with a smile on my face.

"Wear my shirt, black looks good on you", it's definitely Marco.

Chuckling softly I put on jeans and marco's shirt which was indeed looking cool. Tying a knot down to make it look less large to my size but perfect I left top two buttons free and pulled the collar down making it look off shoulder. I don't want to hide their marks and I know they won't like if I did. So brushing my hair I put some lip balm on and walked outside if the room wearing my knee length boots.

"Whatcha doing....?", I sang as I spotted marco on the dining table with his laptop and mario in the kitchen cooking.

Marco smiled widely taking me in his shirt and nodded his head gesturing me to come towards him and I did without any hesitation.

"That smells good", I called out as marco made me sit on his lap while his one hand was resting on the keyboard lazily and his other hand was on my thigh drawing circles on it as he kissed my neck.

"Few more minutes, then you can eat", mario replied smiling at us still working in the kitchen with a apron on his blue jeans and white shirt.

"You look damn sexy in black", he commented and I smiled, "You look good in blue too, keep wearing blue for a change", I said knowing well that he wears black almost everyday.

"Busy?", I asked nodding my head towards the laptop.

"Nothing much, just business", he said closing the laptop but my eyes widened as I saw what he was doing.

"Don't!", I warned and took laptop in my hands and read, with each line on the documents my eyes kept widening a inch if that's possible.

Shaking my head in disbelief I peered at him. "You signed all your property on my name?! The weapon factory too! You know that factory was yours! It was your dad's for gods sake!", I glared my nostrils flaring in anger.

"Listen…..", marco said but I cut him off by standing on my feet.

"I don't want anything which I didn't earn!", I said my voice thick with anger. How could they think of signing everything their

410

parents left for them and the fruit of their hard work on my name just because am their wife?!

"Doll.....", mario chimed in between bringing the tray of food and I frowned looking at him.

"Don't tell me you are with him in this matter! You both know I wanted to do something by my own and this isn't happening, am not taking a single euro from you, which you have earned with utmost hard work", I declared with my chin held high.

They smiled lazily and gave each other looks which made me piss off more than I was.

"Why don't you want to take this? Because it's not yours?", Marco asked looking into my eyes with a smile on his lips.

I rolled my eyes and folded my hands on my chest and saw his eyes darkened but I didn't let that affect me.

"Yes, it's not mine", I quipped without stuttering.

"We are yours, Right?", mario demanded and I nodded my head vigorously.

"So that's final, doll, what is ours is yours and what's yours will be always yours", marco declared and his voice stern with dominance that left no gap for more conversation.

"We have signed our soul and life for you doll, this money and property is just few things among many others which were yours even before you came in our lives, we didn't had our queen before and now when we have we are handing the power in your hands", mario said and I sighed shaking my head.

"Why?", I asked looking into Marco's eyes.

His eyes spoke louder than his words and I know even before those words escaped from his mouth.

"Because you hold the power, power to bring two fucking kings on their knees, bring two fucked up monsters to their sense, bring two insanely wild flames to calmness because you are not afraid to try, lose and burn, doll".

"And we will burn the whole fucking world even before a spark of fire fell in your way", and this time mario finished the words marco started.

"Because you are our doll, ours to play, ours to cherish, ours to adore, ours to spoil and ours to worship and this is just a beginning, beginning of us".

PERIODS AND MOOD SWINGS

AUTHOR'S POV

It's been two days Odette came to Italy with her husbands, first she thought it was their honeymoon but they said its where they are going to live now, a new life, leaving all the past behind.

The mansion was enormous than the previous one. Indoor pool, a art space for marco and a music place for mario along with well equipped gym not to mention a red room which they haven't shown to Odette yet and many bedrooms but their rooms were special. Odette even had her own room and this time she had a walk in closet with so many clothes new and crisp with all the available sexy inners one could never think about affording in their whole life. Odette was so happy that she snapped few pictures of her closet and sent them to her sister to brag about but ended up blushing when Aurora commented, "I have only one man to rip mine, you have two, you obviously need many".

Marco's room was on her right side and mario's was on left but they go there just to get their clothes from the closet. Odette's bed was huge like it could easily fit five to six people and she thanked heavens when she didn't see any shade of pink in her room this

413

time. It's simple, black and grey room with golden decor which she thought was classic.

Odette's favourite part of her room was Jacuzzi in her bedroom and her favourite part of the mansion was theatre room and garden where she spent much time since she came to Italy watching her favourite vampire series.

The first day in Italy she spent in theatre room after exploring the mansion and a brisk walk in garden and second day she dragged marco and mario to have a picnic with her under the Eiffel tower.

Right now Odette, marco and mario were seated on the dining table having their breakfast and suddenly Odette groaned holding her stomach.

"I don't feel good", Odette said rubbing her stomach while mario was feeding her breakfast.

Both marco and mario's face married a worried expression as marco examined her pushing her hair away, rubbing his palm gently on her back.

"What's wrong doll? Should we call a doctor?", he asked. Odette shook her head before she spoke.

"No, it's not needed, I know this", she said getting up and rushed towards the washroom. Opening the toilet seat she lowered her pants and underwear and peed then wiped with the tissue and it came with a hint of blood.

"Bitch is back", Odette groaned at the sight of her period blood.

"Doll?", marco knocked the door and Odette's eyes widened.

"Are you okay?", he asked and she quickly got up from the seat and flushed.

"I'm fine, nothing I can't handle", she said huffing and winced at the pain. she strolled towards the cabinet and took a pad and put that on a neat underwear after wearing them she pulled her pants up and washed her hands before opening the door.

"You look pale", marco commented frowning. "You didn't like the food?", mario asked walking towards her and hugged her from behind.

"I can make some other food", he said smiling at her but Odette sighed heavily and walked away from him swatting his hands off.

Twins frowned and shook their head at each other silently asking what was wrong with her. Odette plopped herself on the bed, her stomach first and groaned immediately holding her stomach as he folded herself in a fetal position.

"Doll!", they both freaked and ran towards her. They were almost on bed but Odette glared at them before ordering.

"Don't you dare come near me if you want to live, am murderous right now", Odette warned with her stern voice.

"Are you upset with us? We didn't do anything wrong, did we do anything wrong?", they spoke to Odette then asked each other making Odette roll her eyes.

"You didn't do anything wrong, am just bleeding", she huffed putting the pillow on her face.

"Bleeding!!!!", they both exclaimed bewildered in fear and yanked the pillow away from her face.

Mario immediately pulled her up on her knees and started checking her head and marco was looking for any injuries on her body.

"Why didn't you tell us you are hurt?!", marco growled.

"Where are you hurt?", mario demanded.

"You dumbass idiots!", Odette snapped slapping their hands away with a glare.

"My fucking vagina is bleeding and it's normal because am on my period and it's also normal to have immense urge to murder someone during this time so better you get the hell out of my room and leave me alone for fucking three days!", she yelled and smacked marco with the pillow and kicked mario's ass with her left leg and they groaned, sighed heavily releasing a relived breathe.

"You almost gave us.....", they were immediately cut off with a loud yell from Odette.

"GET THE FUCK OUT!".

~~~

"It's been one hour, you should go and check her", marco suggested nodding his head trying to be intimidating on his brother but mario just rolled his eyes unaffected by his seriousness.

"You should go inside, not me, she listens to you better, if she saw me she will chop my head off first then ask it – why the fuck did you come", mario said raising his hands up in defence.

"It's not fair, I brought her chocolates and ice cream from the store, now it's your turn, you should do something good for her", marco said sternly folding his hands on his chest.

"Oh! Fuck! Yes! I am doing something good for her by staying away", mario argued back and Odette sighed heavily.

"You guys do know that I can hear you!", she called out from her room closing her laptop, she saw marco and mario peeping inside her room through the small gap of the door with wide grins on their faces vanishing all the crankiness from her.

"Come inside, am feeling better now", Odette said smiling softly to them who were looking as cute teddy bears.

Smiling brightly mario entered into the room first pushing marco off the way.

"Aha, I said when she lay her eyes on my handsome face, she can't resist but call me in", he gloated making Marco roll his eyes at his so called two minutes elder brother.

Odette raised her eyebrow amused at his comment but her lips curled up into a bright smile when she found ice cream and chocolates in Marco's hands.

"Those are my favourite", Odette said taking them from his hands excitedly and they both chuckled at her cuteness.

Munching on the Kit Kat as she scooped up a spoonful of ice cream macro cleared his throat as if he wanted to gain her attention.

"You need some?", Odette asked then without giving him a second to answer she shooed with her hand and spoke with mouth full of

417

chocolate, "Go get some for yourself am not going to share mine with you".

Marco chuckled rubbing his neck as he shook it vigorously. "No, I don't want your snacks but we need to discuss something", he announced making Odette frown.

"Is it something important?", Odette asked gulping the chocolate. Mario softly wiped the ice cream on her lips with his thumb and put that in his mouth and sucked looking into her eyes seductively making her gulp.

Smacking his shoulder macro brought their attention back to the important discussion he wanted to have.

"Yes, I mean, it's your choice, doll, we are just asking.....on wedding night we didn't use any protection in the heat of the moment and you are just eighteen and you have your studies to concentrate so... you want to use protection? Or not, It's completely your choice!", macro explained softly and Odette's heart swooned hearing him.

"Yes, though how much we would like you swell with our baby, we want it when it's safe for you, we think you are too young for this", Mario said smiling at her and she blushed and hid her face with her dark black hair trying to hide the redness crawling on her cheeks.

Clearing her throat Odette spoke, "I... I was on pills since my eighteenth birthday", Odette admitted blushing brightly then looked at macro whose eyes were darkened at the disclosure.

"I... I was expecting something will happen between us but you never came home after...", macro didn't let her finish her words and kissed her lips hungrily with his hand buried in her hair.

Odette gasped but smiled in between the kiss and kissed him back with same passion. Breathing heavily she broke the kiss and soon Mario brought her lips to her and kissed her and she moaned when he bit her lip little harsh.

Shoving his tongue inside her mouth he devoured the chocolate flavour of the ice cream and hummed when she started rubbing herself on him while her other hand was running inside Marco's shirt and he clenched his jaw roughly grabbing her ass.

"We should stop", Mario said breaking the kiss slowly and Odette bit her lip nodding her head with her flushed face.

"How about we see your favourite vampire drama, what is it called?", macro asked diverting the topic and she giggled.

"Its vampire diaries", she said and Mario rolled his eyes.

"I want you to close your eyes whenever that vampire of yours Damon comes on the screen, then only you are going to see the damn show", Mario growled making Odette smirk.

"No one is coming in between me and my vampire boys", she said giggling before ruffling Mario's hair making him groan and ran as fast as she could towards the theatre and Mario chased her to revenge.

Marco chuckled shaking his head, picking up her snacks he walked behind two freaky kids knowing very well that they will start pillow fight in between any show and won't even watch what's running on the screen.

FOUND HER

AUTHOR'S POV

"Marco, what do you think about this one?", Odette asked lifting the hoodie from the rack.

Marco who was seeing her smiled at her then nodded his head before telling, "It will look good on you".

Odette smiled brightly and happily put that in her cart, which Mario was carrying.

"You know, you should buy stockings, these will look good underneath that hoodie", Mario commented making Odette raise her eyebrows.

"I have hundreds of stockings! I don't need more", Odette said shaking her head with a small laugh making Mario smirk.

"That's what am telling doll, you may have but you won't be having them for long because from tonight I will rip your stockings off before fucking you or else I could fuck you on them", he said making Odette blush.

"Ugh! Don't talk about these things when we are out!". Odette whisper yelled, Marco and Mario chuckled at her bright red face.

They couldn't believe that she was the same girl who ordered them to knee and crawl towards her and took both of them at same time at her first and now she is blushing at the name of sex in public.

"I can never get tired of it", Mario whispered to his brother and Marco grinned. "Me too", he replied and his phone rang bringing Odette's attention on him.

It's been four days Marco was busy and Mario was tagging behind Odette and she was throwing a fit at Marco for leaving her alone with Mario specially on her shark days and she said she was a inch away stabbing a knife in his heart but Mario retorted that she couldn't because no matter how much he annoys her she loves his ass as much as he loves fucking hers. That made her blush again and stumble to the ground when she tried to run away to hide her face but Marco saved in time.

As a reward for going through the torture, she demanded to go on shopping then have some ice cream outside and the twins agreed.

Marco cleared his throat before giving an assuring smile to Odette he picked the call because she saw him stressed whole time and asking what was wrong.

"Its fine doll, he is just busy", Mario, said rubbing Odette's arm.

"Hello, Draco", macro answered the phone and what he heard next made him smirk widely.

"Okay, I will be there", macro replied making Odette frown.

Hanging up the call he smiled at her pressing a kiss on her head he nodded his head at Mario.

"Draco found Angela, said she was found badly beaten up and was thrown on the street from a running car", macro stated and Odette gasped.

"I will be coming with you, I have to ask some question to her myself", Mario said his smirk was deadly.

"Who is Angela?", Odette asked worried and they both sighed and shook their head.

"She is just one of the officers who helped the man to put bombs in the office", Mario stated snaking his hand around her waist.

"Let's get you home, we will continue this when we return", macro said making Odette frown.

Scowling at him she faced Mario and asked, "The same lady officer whom I saw in your office?".

"Yes, doll", Mario, confirmed making Odette half smile.

"Then I want to come with you both, I don't want to go home this soon, I will get something for Angela – you know some girl stuffs she might need? We are in mall anyways", Odette said giving Mario her best puppy eyes.

"That is not going to work on me", Mario said shaking his head and Odette glared at him before turning her head towards macro.

"Marco... it will take few minutes right? I don't want you to go for longer time and if I am there to remind you I think it's best, I don't want to stay alone at home", Odette whined with a pout of her plump lips and gave her best puppy eyes to macro and he gulped.

Seeing his throat bob Mario sighed heavily and Odette smiled clapping her hands.

"I know it will be easy with you, let's go", she said pulling their hands and walked towards the shops from where she wanted to buy few necessities for Angela.

~~~

"Don't leave our side, doll", macro said for the nth time as if she was a kid and will go missing if she walks away from them, making her roll her eyes internally.

"Okay daddy!", she groaned sarcastically and Mario smirked when macro smacked her ass hard in between the hallway towards Angela's room where she was kept in the hospital.

"Ouch!", Odette cried out rubbing her ass and looked around to sigh in relief for not finding anyone who might have witnessed the embarrassing situation.

Choosing to stay silent, she didn't speak anything and bit her cheek thinking the ways she will avenge it later.

"Do you think she will like these?", Odette asked as the trio stood in front of the door which was guarded by two guards.

"Doll, she is not our guest but she is our expected enemy, you don't have to buy anything for her", macro replied making Odette sigh.

423

"But I liked her, like she was the best looking officer – lady officer in the FBI and I support women like her!", Odette exclaimed dramatically making the twins chuckle.

"I think she will love these", Mario replied ruffling her hair and she smiled brightly before macro and mario opened the door for her.

Entering the room with her head held high with the bright smile on her face made her look powerful besides the two ethereal Greek gods. Which made Angela bite her tongue in jealousy. It was what she always wanted and seeing some other woman get them made her blood boil in ways she couldn't help but scowl at Odette.

"I think you are feeling well now to answer the questions we ask?", Mario asked and Odette elbowed him in the gut.

"What!", he asked in disbelief as she glared at him and macro was smiling at them where they three stayed oblivious to the jealous looks Angela was throwing at Odette.

"You guys need to chill", she whisper scolded Mario and diverted her eyes on Angela and sighed when she saw her in badly ripped jeans and shirt.

At least her face was cleaned and fixed with bandage just as her right hand's three fingers, which was plastered. Her bruises were visible and medicated. Overall, she looked beaten up.

"I brought something for you", Odette broke the awkward silence with her wide smile.

Angela raised her eyebrows amused when Odette dropped a bag beside her bed smiling softly. Angela was burning with anger when macro who used to show zero to none softness is now smiling at Odette as a crazy lover boy. Mario was of no use and she knows they both have already married Odette from Bianca.

"What are these?", Angela asked examining the things Odette brought for her in the bag. There were two t-shirts one white and another black with a grey hoodie with some free size pants.

"I think she should get changed into some comfortable clothes before you guys talk with her", Odette said looking at her husbands.

Marco and Mario gave each other some looks frowning then nodded just because to keep Odette happy.

"Okay, let's go outside I will call a nurse", Mario said holding Odette's hand.

"Actually....." Angela drawled smiling awkwardly.

"Actually, I would feel comfortable if Mrs. de Luca will help me", she requested making Mario glare at her.

Narrowing his eyes on her he threatened silently to which Angela gulped but passed her fear as the only thing she could feel was her burning jealousy.

"Its....it's okay I guess", Odette spoke making Marco tightens his hold on her waist.

Odette winced and frowned at him asking silently what his problem was.

"Our wife isn't your maid", Marco growled making Angela smile.

"You are getting me wrong Mr de Luca, I just thought Mrs de Luca will be happy to help me wear the dress she bought for me with so much love", Angela countered making Odette smile.

Odette could easily grasp negative energy from a person but the woman Angela is, she know well to hide emotions and act making fool of others and that's what she was doing.

"Of course I will be", Odette spoke excitedly and pouted at Marco and Mario.

"Please", she requested and twins sighed knowing she is not going to back off and they agreed going out of the room and stood right at the door before telling if something is wrong, she should scream.

"Come on", Odette said helping Angela to get up on her feel and gave her the trouser pants she brought which Angela wore after stripping her shredded jeans.

"Which t shirt you want to wear? White or black?", Odette asked and Angela made a disgusted face before looking at her.

"Don't you think these two colours are boring?", she mocked rolling her eyes.

Odette's smile immediately dropped as she saw a sudden change in Angela, which made her frown.

"What?", Angela asked in a whisper, yanking a black t-shirt from her hand and took her top off and got inside it before smirking at her.

"How does it feel living my dream Mrs de Luca?", Angela asked and Odette's frown turned into a scowl clearly understanding where she is coming from.

"Tell me, do they still fuck hard and rough as they love, tell me does Marco use whips on you before taking you roughly from behind? Tell me Mrs de Luca do they take turn after turn making you come on their cocks without giving you break until you pass out?", she asked smiling enviously making Odette's eyes widen in realization.

"You slept with them?", Odette gasped her voice low as a whisper but Angela heard her very well.

"Slept...... Hmmm? If you call fucking your husbands for twenty four hours as sleeping then yes! I have slept with them", Angela tells folding her hands on her chest and Odette fisted her palms so tight that her knuckles turned white.

They were talking in low voice that Marco and Mario were not able to hear them and smirking Angela fuelled Odette's anger more.

Seeing that dirty smirk on her few minutes back innocent face Odette smiled wickedly then rubbed her palms together before telling.

"It's been long I have put my hands to good use", with that she yanked Angela's hair making her yelp and the door burst open immediately revealing worried faces of Marco and Mario. Soon seeing the scene in front of their eyes and the mischievous smirk on Odette's face their cocks twitched in their pants.

They have heard Odette beaten up Bianca badly when she came to them demanding to get signed the factory papers as soon as possible and treat Odette as a slut but they did what she least expected.

"Doll", Marco called and Odette's eyes snapped back to her husbands but she didn't loosen her hold on Angela's hair.

Angela was a trained FBI agent who had so much practice and it was so hot looking her as a helpless ragdoll in their wife's hands.

"Oh! Husbands I was just making this bitch a bit comfortable before you interrogate her", Odette said before she twisted Angela's left hand and snapped her fingers back making Angela scream.

With the tears flowing from her eyes and the tut sound of the fingers following the scream was enough to understand that Odette broke her left hand fingers too.

Angela cried and trashed around in Odette's hold but Odette pushed her on the wall and smacked her head and Angela immediately whispered shaking her head.

"Please Odette", she begged and both Marco and Mario's chest swelled looking at how strong their doll was.

"Those fingers were the price for fucking my husbands", Odette said then kneed in Angela's stomach and she coughed blood making Mario laugh at how pathetic Angela was looking and Marco simply smiled widely.

"Pathetic bloody bitch", Odette spat and threw Angela, dusting her palms she walked towards Mario and Marco and said, "I'm going home with Draco, will be waiting for you both tonight".

With that, she swayed her hips and walked past her drooling husbands leaving them with a fucking hard ons.

JEALOUSY AND ANGER

AUTHOR'S POV

"You better start spilling everything Angela or else you know what we could do to make you", Mario said coldly his warning tone was vibrating in the hospital room.

"I ordered pizzas who knows there will be fucking bombs in it!", Angela hissed glaring at Mario.

Marco's jaw twitched in anger and looked around the room to find a small knife placed on the tray, which is used for operations.

His feet strolled there and in one second that was placed against Angela's neck pressing it so lightly that a single light cut was made but enough to draw some blood but not much that she could be dead.

"One last time, who was the person kidnapped you or should I say helped you to get away with the aftermath of the blast so that you can run to us later faking to be victim or else I swear to God, our doll broke your fucking fingers I won't mind to chop them off completely", Marco's deadly serious voice boomed in her ear making her heart pound against her chest so hard that she wanted to puke already.

"Please, I swear to God macro, I don't know who was that they just took me off suddenly when I was out for a evening walk to clear my head about the blast and then I found myself in fucking Paris today when I was thrown on the street", she cried making Mario scoff.

Marco simply retraced his hands off her and wiped the blood on the knife on her hoodie before smirking. "Get well soon", saying that he nodded his head towards Mario and he frowned but didn't question.

~~~

"If we kill her now we will have no lead, go to Bianca and try to make her speak anything about her brother who was supposed to be dead and let our little bird Angela fly thinking we trust her so that she could take us to that fuckers nest", Marco said making Mario smirk.

"You are really a mastermind", Mario complimented making Marco chuckle.

"We both are brother but you tend to think less when your blood is in your dick", Marco said and Mario chuckled throwing his head back.

"That was hot! Don't speak as if your dick wasn't active the second you saw our doll throwing fist on that bitch", Mario retorted making Marco smirk.

"I can't wait to get my hands on her", Marco stated looking at his lock screen picture, which he took on their birthday when she was asleep.

"Then hurry up, you know first come first serve", Mario said before he rushed through the hallway of the hospital laughing and Marco immediately followed him to the lift letting the laughter echo in the hallway making other patients and staff's bewildered because of their jolly mood, in fact this would be the first time they heard the twins laugh genuinely.

~~~

ODETTE'S POV

I was angry, I was mad but I didn't show it on my husbands as any other woman would when some bitch told her that she fucked her husband. In my case, the anger was double because obviously I have two husbands and bet I will play them nice when they bring their ass home but right now, I need a bath.

It's almost eight, the sun is down, the darkness was temptingly warm yet cold and I liked the weather.

So instead going to bed after eating something, I grabbed strawberries and Nutella. Walking into my room, I stripped my clothes before turning the tap on letting the warm water fill the Jacuzzi, dropped a lavender bath bomb and placed the tray of the snack I choose.

Roughly washing myself in shower before I got into Jacuzzi I sighed in content I moaned. "Ahhh", as I sink into the warm water and then threw my head back pushing my wet hair off my face.

Popping a strawberry in my mouth, I hummed and chewed the juicy sweet and sour fruit thinking anything but about the things Angela crippled bitch said.

They are my husbands and no one are allowed to see what's mine, far away experience the pleasure, which was my right. But they had her. She had them. The blood rushed to my head and my head pounded in anger. I was so angry that I didn't want to stay anymore in the bubbling warm water enjoying my alone time when they are torturing her.

Hell! That bitch might be enjoying it as well and getting off in her fucked up brain and that stirred the last blow of my anger.

Getting up from the Jacuzzi I put on a robe and hurried on the bed. I am frustrated and I thought only one way to release the tension building in me.

I dropped on the bed and spread my legs wide, pushing the robe off my thighs I gulped before slowly slid my fingers between my lower lips and caressed it with my two fingers, bringing the two fingers back to my mouth I sucked them wetting them with my saliva and let my fingers dance on my clit and rubbed it in circles as Marco did when I took him the first time.

That thought made me quiver and I mewled closing my eyes as I let my fingers do their job playing with my pussy and slowly thinking about Marco and Mario doing this to me I felt more wetness running out of my slick moulds and I moaned.

Arching my back on the headrest of the bed I slowly brought my other hand to my nipple tugged it and flicked it biting my lip as sinful sounds escaped through them.

When I felt myself more wet I shoved two fingers inside me and my breath hitched when I felt a tight slap on my pussy and my eyes snapped open with a gasp and there stood angry Mario but his lips were wickedly curled up.

My pussy clenched and unclenched around nothing as I quickly took my hand off myself and the shade of red am turned right now would be the darkest red colour one would have turned and I could get myself a Guinness record.

"I thought you said you will wait? But seems like you have already started", Marco chuckled coming into the room oblivious about the thing happened just few minutes before his arrival.

My one boob was out from the robe, my wet hair sprawled wildly and my barely covered naked thighs might look as if I was just out if the shower and Mario carried me to the bed.

Ha! Least did he know!

Gulping my fear, I looked right into Mario's eyes before raising my eyebrow questioning silently, 'why the fuck did you interrupt my pleasure?'

As if hearing my glare he smirked and tusked before looking back at Marco who was looking at us with confusion sensing the tension in the air.

"I didn't start without you brother, our little wife, now not so innocent doll was playing with what is ours and I caught her red-handed or should I say wet handed as she was dipping her fingers in her needy little cunt which is ours", Mario's voice sent shivers to my spine and my pussy clenched again and this time I almost came with the dominant look of Mario's face as if he would literally swallow me whole.

Marco's jaw clenched before he smirked taking predator like steps towards me I bit my lips awaiting what's written for me.

Definitely it was my bad luck that I couldn't come and release my stress but when I have my two husbands who would gladly get their faces between my legs I don't consider this as a bad luck at all.

"It's my fucking body, you Assholes, so nice of you – you couldn't tell me when I was confused to pick a dress for your whore, you were more than familiar with her size or should I mention sizes", I countered gritting my teeth.

Their eyes shone with amusement and their smirks turned wicked and they both stepped back and Marco locked the door as if someone dare to interrupt us when we three are alone in my damn room and Mario sat on the couch with his legs wide spread and visible bulge under their pants made me smirk internally.

"What is your name doll?", Marco asked looking straight into my eyes as he slowly took off his shirt's button one by one and I licked my lips ready to devour his those ripped delicious abs.

"I see you have forgotten", I commented smirking.

"Tortured her or fucked her, that you moaned her name, now you don't remember mine?", I asked daring him to tell it to my face.

"You are jealous because we fucked her?", Mario asked his voice so husky that I almost drooled and so did my pussy.

"No", I declared but my voice trembled with need as Mario chuckled mocking me further.

"Of course you are not doll, you are just angry", Mario stated making me clench my jaw.

"Because you both fucked her? Yes, in fact am furious", I said looking into his blue eyes.

"It's true doll, you are not jealous because we fucked her, you are not angry because we fucked her", Marco said taking me by surprise and now he stood in front of me with his pants on, the shirt is long gone letting my eyes eat up all the beautiful tattoos on his tight muscles of his chest and arms and I whimpered tightly closing my legs immediately trying to get some friction between them.

But his next words drained the blood from my face and I looked at him with parted lips because he was right. Fucking right.

"You are jealous because we fucked her as a whore, you are angry because you don't know about what she knew, about what we really do to the woman we sleep with", Marco said and a huge wicked grin decorating his handsome face and I immediately mewled and my eyes widened more than before.

"Exactly", Mario said making me gulp.

Yes, I am jealous because she took them both, as I didn't, angry because I don't know what they could do to women – no! Me, now it's me, only me.

I raised my head looking into their eyes daringly without blinking. Though my neck bobbed in excitement and nervousness but their smiles are unfazed as Marco said, "Just a little thing doll, you could have asked us…"

"And we would have treated you as our whore, just as the way you wanted to be treated", Mario's words made me moan and I should have felt embarrassed but I am so aroused that I have left all the shyness in a box and there it in a fucking ocean of thirst – thirst for my husbands.

"Now as our good little whore, take the fucking robe off and crawl to Mario and suck his dick off, he was waiting to get your dripping cunt for it but…….", Marco stopped with a smirk looking at Mario.

Mario's expression mirrored his as he completed his brother's sentence, "Because the stunt you pulled in our absence, you don't deserve to be pleasured but punished doll, now hurry your ass up, it's going to be a long night", Mario said and I gulped hard with my wide eyes and I felt myself obey as he ordered but with the excitement that I know I will come just by sucking his magnificent cock.

JUST GETTING STARTED

MARIO'S POV

I was so fucking happy that I found her in a position I could punish her. Hell my hand was itching to spank that little ass of hers and take her roughly but macro being always sweet and soft to only her said we should be giving her time.

Though I know she doesn't need time, she wants to get fucked as a slut, treated like our whore and likes to hear good girl in her ear while she come on our cocks and I did warned macro that this will be the day we had to see if he didn't take her as I said.

Well now, I think it's all crystal clear because his smirk is telling me he is happy to be proved wrong for the first time in his life.

Man spreading on the grey couch I looked at our little wife who was fully naked exposing her perky pink pebbles begging for attention, to be sucked and bitten, pinch and flickered. Her body was still little wet from her bath and her hair were dripping wet, she will catch cold if she stands like this with blasting air conditioner so I simply grabbed the remote and turned the ac off and taking my clue Marco turned the fan on and I saw Odette smile biting her lip.

My cock jumped at her sight and it was getting painfully hard and too hard to control my animalistic desire to fuck her tight cunt right now but not yet, she doesn't deserve to come because of the little stunt she pulled.

I know Marco is going to edge her and push her to her limit before giving her actual punishment.

I smirked wickedly at that thought, our little doll is thinking this would be her punishment but I can't wait when Marco tell her how he actually punishes.

Blushing brightly she came down on her knees and I licked my lips as she slowly crawled towards me as a little kitten, vulnerable and with slight fear which was obviously pumping adrenaline in her body because of the way chest is heaving profusely.

Marco made himself comfortable on bed, his eyes on her ass and those dark eyes made it clear that the bastard is fucking enjoying the beautiful view of her dripping cunt.

"You know what to do doll", I said my voice huskier than I intended and Odette looked up at me as she was kneeing, with her doe eyes, which were sparkling with excitement.

Gulping down she nodded her head and took her lower lip in between her teeth and her fingers indulged with my belt and took it off and opened my jeans.

Once again looking into my eyes she gulped before freeing my throbbing cock from my boxers and palmed it still gazing into my lustful eyes with her own and I grunted when she pressed her thumb on the slit of my red angry head of the cock and my head flew back in pleasure. Slowly pumping it with her both hands she held my thigh with one and other on the base of my cock and slowly licked the slit making me see fucking stars.

"Fuck! Doll…" I grunted as she slowly swirled her tongue around the head, took my cock in her warm mouth, closed her plump pink lips around my cock and started sucking it as if her life depends on it.

"Good girl, just like that doll, suck it as a fucking candy and take my cock deep in your throat", I said my voice coming out strained and Odette hummed around my cock and I felt my spine shiver as

jaw hard. Unable to hold back I fisted her hair and started thrusting enough to make her gag but not hard it would be painful for her and the room was filled with wet sounds, my grunts and heavy breathing while Odette was groaning and gagging.

I felt my cock twitch in her mouth, wiped tears flowing from my little doll's eyes and parted my lips sucking in air while I was reaching my high.

"Do you want me to come in your mouth, doll?", I asked her and she hummed rubbing her thighs together.

"Ah, fuck! Take it, doll, take everything as a good little girl", I groaned releasing my load down her throat with last lazy pumps. Odette took everything and swallowed down humming as some of my come dripped down her chin, with her still flushed face she wiped her tongue on her lip and took as much as she can and pushed the remaining in her mouth using her thumb making my cock twitch again.

Breathing heavily I yanked her off the floor and made her sit on my thighs before kissing her lips, devouring her mouth hungrily and passionately making her moan in my mouth.

Wrapping my tongue with her own, I squeezed her perfect round boobs, which are neither big nor too small just enough to fit in my palms.

Odette moaned arching her back and worked on my shirt buttons and pealed it off from me letting her naked body rub against my own hard toned body and when she started rocking her dripping cunt on my already hard cock I smacked her ass so loud that she

As I was rubbing the stinging area as she was breathing heavily Marco let his fingers trace her spine and Odette brought her mouth slowly around his cock and I let him enjoy a little before I smacked her ass again and this time her yelp was muffled with his cock and her breathing turned heavy, her thighs tightened and she turned feverish struggling to hold her orgasm in but I know with another hit she will fucking squirt it all over the place.

Smirking at Marco, I smacked her ass one last time and she moaned her legs shook as she squirted leaving Marco's cock and fell her face on the couch with her boobs on his thighs and Marco chuckled wickedly before whispering in her ear loud enough for me to hear.

"The real game is just started doll and I swear to fucking god, you won't be thinking about fucking yourself because from now on we will make sure we leave you all sore before we go to work".

"Do you want that? Huh?", he rasped and she nodded her head before crying out, "Yes, please". Smiling with satisfaction we both looked at each other nodding our heads.

"let's start it with Mario eating your cunt so that I could take you roughly on this couch", he said and Odette peaked biting her lip and her legs started shivering making me smirk and I dug my tongue deep in her cunt holding her ass up, ate her delicious cunt as if it was last meal of my life.

SAFE WORD

443

MARCO'S POV

Getting up from the couch I gave space for Mario and Odette so that he could eat her all really good, I would be damned if I said I wasn't dying to have a taste.

Ordering her to hold the armrest of the couch Mario looked at me with a knowing look, hell I know, what I was going to do with her right now.

I pumped my cock twice before bringing it to Odette's plump lips and tapped it on them, she opened her mouth with a breathy needy moan and mario spread her red cheeks before diving his tongue inside her cunt.

"Uh- hmm", Odette moaned around my cock and I grunted as she started sucking it before leaving the length to lick from base to the tip and I jerked my hips making her gag.

Her doe eyes up on mine as she whined and moaned when Mario lapped on her dripping juices. lucky bastard.

"Fuck! Take it all in my little whore", I said thrusting in her warm mouth as tears rolled down her eyes and whimpered her whole body formed Goosebumps and by the way Mario chuckled it's obvious that she clenched around his tongue.

"She is close", he said increasing his pace and I took my time while fucking her mouth because I wanted to come in her cunt not in her mouth.

"Ahhhh", Odette moaned as she came on Mario mouth and he slurped all her juices and wiped his mouth with back of his hand smirking and in one go I flipped her on the couch and took Mario's

444

place and settled between her legs with my hard throbbing length on her opening and locked my eyes with hers.

"What is your safe word doll?", I asked making sure she will be able to use it when she needs.

Surprising me she said, "I don't need any".

Mario smirked at her blunt confidence but I smiled at her softly tracing my fingers on her perky nipples, "You have to choose one", I said looking into her eyes.

Her lips parted breathing heavily and she bit her lip before speaking, "Are you going to whip me? Handcuff or blindfold me?". she asked and my cock jumped in excitement and Mario cursed under his breath.

"You want to get whipped? Handcuffed and blindfolded, doll?", I asked my voice breathless with animalistic desire to do those things to her but somewhere I know she is not yet ready for those things which would rush adrenaline into your blood and when things stop she would be crying without a reason and as much as I know her, she won't be liking the aftermath of the rough bdsm sex.

We need to take small step and should consider her comfort zones and right now, it's clear that she is into hard sex and threesome and that's fucking enough to turn any insane men like us on.

"Yes", she admitted biting her lip nervously and I kissed her lips before speaking against them.

"How tempting that sounds but no, not yet but I plan to do more than those things to you doll, fuck! You would beg for more too but right now we are going to fuck you senselessly until the only thing you remember is you belong to us", I stated biting her lip roughly.

"This body belongs to us", I said tracing her curves with my hands.

"This pussy….." I rasped cupping her dripping cunt and she moaned looking at me with those fuck me eyes, "…… belongs to us", I finished.

"By end of tonight, you would need one doll, so choose", Mario said his voice strained and hunger emitting around him just as me and she gulped nervous yet excited.

"What is your safe word doll?", I asked her again and this time she gulped looking between me and Mario before she smiled softly and replied, "Blue".

I grinned at her before thrusting my whole length inside her tight cunt and without giving her time to adjust I took her roughly.

"Oh my god! Marco", she cried biting on my shoulder and I grunted while thrusting into her pressing my lips on her sweet spot making her moan and scream in my fucking ear.

"Ahhh! It feels so fucking good", she moaned breathlessly and I smirked looking at her with my forehead resting on hers while she scratched my back with her nails wrapping her legs around me taking me more deeper as if there is any gap between us.

"Fuck, I can't stop thinking about how tight you feel around my cock", I rasped before pressing my lips on hers and ate all her moans and screams kissing her hard.

"Oh god! Am coming!", she cried and mario chuckled sitting on the bed with his cock in his hand pumping it lazily. "Yes, baby, you are going to come whole damn night, just like that give it to me, cream my cock with your come", I grunted with my parted lips increasing my pace bringing her to the edge. Her screams and moans along with wet noises of our sex and skin slapping was enough for my climax but then she clenched so hard on my cock drawing my own orgasm along her.

Grunting as an animal, I emptied myself inside her and kissed her lips one last time before getting up from her. Breathing heavily she supported herself on her elbows as I saw in between her legs and my cock already started twitching seeing my come dripping from her cunt. Pushing my come inside her I said, "We are going to fill you up so well that our come will be dripping from you tomorrow".

"Ahhh", she moaned pushing her hips and I raised my eyebrows amused.

"You want more doll?", I asked and she nodded her head before moaning "Yes please".

"Good because Mario is waiting for his turn", I said glancing at my brother who has a wicked grin on his face which made Odette gulp.

Slowly getting on her feet, she took a step towards him and I immediately stopped her.

"Uhm, no walking doll, only crawling, you were bad girl and bad girls don't get to walk with their cunt dripping with come", I said and she gulped blushing brightly with her skin already glowing with post orgasm glow.

Kneeing down she crawled towards Mario and climbed on him as he asked and he made her sit on his cock before kissing her lips passionately making her moan.

"No matter how much I would love you under me doll, I want you to ride me", and that's all it took for Odette to take all his cock inside her cunt and gasp holding herself by clinging on him.

Mario held her ass in his palms and slowly started rocking her back and forth and slowly Odette adjusted herself to the position where she could feel his cock deeper and she arched her back immediately pushing her luscious tits on his chest.

"Just like that doll, ride my fucking cock until you see nothing but stars", he rasped and Odette moaned riding him placing her hands on his shoulders.

"Oh my god! Marioooo", she cried throwing her head back and I fisted her hair and brought her lips to mine and kissed her swallowing her each and every gasp and moan escaping through her lips and pinched her perky nipples as they bounced in my palms with Mario's hard thrusts.

"You like that, doll, you like to ride my cock?", Mario grunted and Odette nodded her head before screaming "Yes".

Looking into my eyes she stated, "I love to feel you both inside me, please", she begged and I smirked.

"We aren't going to fuck your ass tonight doll, but I swear to God, you won't be forgetting tonight in your whole life", I promised and she came around Mario's cock screaming his name.

Grunting he released himself inside her and closed his eyes and Odette fell on his shoulder shuddering with her own release.

"Tired already?", I taunted and she smirked looking into my eyes and said, "You?, it's so sad! I was ready for another round..." she started getting up from Mario's cock and hissed at the empty feeling and Mario smacked her ass before warning.

"Don't tease Marco sweetheart, unless you want to be fucked on every wall of your room".

I looked at her wide eyes her smirk turning more mischievous and amusement washed on me as she said, "How about I want to get fucked on every damn wall of our home?".

Her words came out raspy yet fearless and confident sending blood straight to my cock and it twitched making me groan.

Wrapping my fingers around her neck I choked her little not hard to be painful but enough to warn her but she didn't even blink in fear.

"Trying to be feisty little thing doll, it won't take long until you realize you are thoroughly fucked as a whore and I just hope you don't regret it", I warned her and her eyes twinkled before she said.

"Few months ago I would have hated that word for me but now, I want to be your whore, treated like your slut because I know when I will fall in your arms limp, you both will take care of me as your queen", with her those words she tugged my dark brown hair with her palm and brought my lips to hers and kissed the hell out of them before kissing Mario's.

And we all know that the night is still young and we are in for a hell of a ride.

DREAMLAND

ODETTE'S POV

"Fuck! Am coming", I scream as Marco thrust into me roughly and my thighs tighten before my core shook sending shivers to every single bone inside me.

Just as my husbands promised, they did fuck me on every wall of my room and this one is the last but I don't think they want to stop yet and I don't want them to stop too.

"Come doll, come on my cock as a good girl", Marco said increasing his pace and I pushed my head back on the wall and arching myself into him as he was grabbing my ass in his palms he kissed my neck leaving a nth hickey and my eyes rolled back and pleasure I felt made my insides clench and I came all around his cock screaming his name as I scratched my nails on his shoulders.

He didn't stop yet just giving me some time to recover from the powerful orgasm he started thrusting again dragging moans and screams from my mouth and my eyes rolled back again with another powerful orgasm.

I felt warmness inside my sore core and I hissed in satisfaction with a smile on my face knowing he came too.

Kissing my forehead one last time he asked, "Tired?".

His lips were close to mine and I smiled against his lips and shook my head.

"I think I can take two more rounds", I said glancing over Marco's shoulder winking at Mario who was waiting with his hard cock.

God! Does that thing even rest?

"That's my girl", Mario said and Marco chuckled in the crook of my neck pressing his lips on the freshly made hickey.

Marco helped me on my feet, Mario strolled towards me smiling widely and I couldn't help but smile looking at his bright blue eyes, which are darkened and his beautiful smile.

"Do you have any idea how beautiful you look like this?", he rasped snaking his arm around my waist and pulled me close and our bodies collided.

I kissed his lips standing on my tiptoes, he hummed against my lips and kissed me back hungrily igniting the fire inside me, and I felt my core clench.

I was closing my eyes tightly feeling our tongues move together wrapping and fighting with lust for dominance and I gasped when my ass landed on something and opened my eyes finding myself on my dresser.

With a smirk on his face Mario pushed all the products placed on the vanity and few bottles which were of glass broke as soon as they came in contact with the floor and my breathe hitched when he flipped me as my knees and hands were on the table and I could see myself in the mirror when I turn my head to my right side.

451

Gulping down I met Marco's eyes through the mirror while Mario aligned his hard cock against my core and teased my opening making me grit my teeth in protest, a needy whine escaped my lips and they chuckled.

"Please", I begged pushing myself back on his cock and this time Mario held my hips tightly in his palms and thrust his whole length inside me and I groaned in satisfaction.

Without giving me another second, he started thrusting inside me and my eyes rolled back at the intensity of my orgasm forming.

Suddenly Mario cupped my neck and brought me back with his cock still inside me which was pounding it's way making me gasp, scream and moan and all I could hear is my own breathe and my voice echoing in the room along with Mario's pleasure filled groans.

"Look in the mirror doll", Mario said his voice strained in my ear and I did as he asked.

"Look at yourself how you look, those marks on your body, those wrecked hair and how your face turns in pleasure whenever we take you", he said gripping my neck just enough to drive me crazy.

"Ahhh, oh god! Please", I cried as I felt close to my orgasm.

"Fuck! You are clenching so hard doll, you like to watch yourself when we fuck you? Huh?", he rasped in my ear and bit it playfully making me moan.

"Ahh, yes, yes, Mario", I cried once again nodding my head frantically.

"Fuck! Look at that doll, how good your pussy is taking my cock", he said and I glanced at the mirror meeting his gaze first before looking at where we are connected and how his huge cock is going in and out of my dripping pussy.

My thighs are covered in mine and my husbands' come and my whole body is sweaty with purple and dark red hickeys and my boobs were springing up with force of his powerful thrusts and I found myself coming once again screaming his name.

"Such a good girl", he praised and I gasped a huge amount of air and met with Marco's hungry eyes.

"Marco… I want to take you too, please", I begged and I heard faint chuckle of Mario's near my ear but my eyes were on Marco's begging him to take me.

I want them both, I want them to take me and assure me that they couldn't think about doing this with someone else.

If they want me to be their whore, slut or anything I will be and they will be the same to me when I need them.

My husbands when it came to title, my slaves when I need them to pleasure me, my lovers when I want them to take care of me and I swear to God, I don't even need to ask them to be any of these because they fucking love and does everything with their own will and that drives me fucking crazy.

"Are you sure doll?", Marco asked his jaw clenched and face looked as if he was in pain and in fact he was but with his hard cock without any help and now I want to.

Nodding my head as yes, I smiled biting my lip. Mario smacked my ass and I clenched around him as a breathy moan escaped from me but my eyes were on Marco who was seeing us from behind.

"Please", I cried and I saw Mario and Marco exchange a look with each other and Mario took his cock out from me and flipped me and put it back inside and cradled me in his arms and Marco came from behind and I shivered when his tattooed arms cupped my breast and arched myself in Mario's chest.

"You are going to look in the mirror while we take you in this position", Marco whispered in my ear and I gulped and my pussy pulsed with Mario's cock inside and he grunted digging his fingers in my hips.

I looked at my left side as both my husbands sandwiched me between them. They both were standing ethereally and held me in their arms as if I weight nothing.

Marco looking into my eyes through the mirror nodded his head asking me one last time and I smiled nodding my head.

Pumping his cock twice he put that on my puckered hole and gently entered the tip inside me and I didn't push it out or fought it. Simply relaxed taking a deep breath time to time.

"Good girl", Marco praised and pushed his whole length inside and I gasped and dug my nails in Mario's shoulders.

"Good girl, are you ready?", he asked and I nodded my head after a minute adjusting to his length in my back hole.

"Yes", I rasped hiding my face in Mario's shoulder for support.

They both slowly started moving inside me and in this position, I can feel the skin between their two cocks and the way they are in sync drawing moans and screams from me.

When they slowed down their pace I clenched around their cocks in protest, looked in the mirror and saw how our bodies are joined together.

"Don't slow down, please fuck me harder", I ordered and my head fell back when they increased their pace and I rested my head on Marco's chest and Mario lapped on my perky nipple while Marco pinched the other.

I took my hand behind and fisted Marco's hair and other hand found its way in Mario's and my whole body was left on their mercy without me holding on them for support but in this posting I felt lighter and their speed increased and I came hard on their cock and Mario's lips found mine and he kissed me madly swallowing my moans and screams and Marco kissed my neck their breathing turned heavy as their muscles flexed under my touch and I felt their cocks swell inside me and I came again but this time they came along me too, filling me with their come as it dripped down from me till my knees I was so exhausted and tired and on verge of passing out.

Slowly dropping me on my legs but holding me safely in their arms, they kissed my forehead one last time and I hear Marco say, "Let's get you cleaned up".

"No, I want to sleep", I said back in protest hugging Mario in front of me and I felt his chest rumble with laughter and someone picked me up in their arms and laid me on the bed and they both joined each side of me and covered ourselves with duvet and the

455

lights were turned off as they both whispered before kissing my cheek.

"Sleep tight doll, we will be dreaming about you".

Smiling with my closed eyes, I snuggled in my blanket and drifted to the dreamland to meet my husbands in their dreams as they wished.

KIDNAPPED

AUTHOR'S POV

"I think your two husbands are remembering you that's why you are having hiccups", Alice said with a teasing smile making Odette blush.

"Oh, what's the connection between hiccups and missing someone, did your soon to be hubby Lorenzo taught you?", Odette teased her friend back smirking as Alice turned multiple shades of red at the mention of Lorenzo.

Alice and Odette became best friends from the day Odette joined the university and this time people are not so afraid of her as they know Odette is just as a normal girl who is cool to hang out with and nothing like a bitchy spoiled brat.

They just fear Marco and Mario specially the glare they send to the guys who talks to their wife and Odette calms them down with her magical puppy eyes, which they couldn't fight against.

Laughing by themselves Odette and Alice stood out of the gates of the college waiting for their own men to come and pick them up and Odette frowned looking at the time in her phone.

"They are late, they never come late", Odette sighed folding her hands on her chest with her phone in her left hand.

"They might be struck in traffic or something", Alice assured smiling softly at her.

But in next second a car stopped right in front of them and Bianca stepped out from it in her knee length skirt and white shirt.

Odette kept playing with the locket of her chain, which was twins' mother's and rolled her eyes looking at Bianca.

"Long time no see", Bianca smirked looking at odette with her evil intentions.

"I could poke my eyes to not see your face", Odette retorted holding Alice's hand and walking away from Bianca not wanting to hear anything.

"I bet you wouldn't want to if you want to see the man who killed your mother and your twin sister, what was her name again... Hmm Ivette", Bianca said examining her nails and odette halted her steps hearing her words.

Turning her head slowly she looked at Bianca with her glossy eyes but fire in them as she snapped, "the woman who killed them is dead, my dad killed her years ago".

"You think? She was alone who killed a French mafia boss's wife and heiress?", Bianca said looking past odette and smiled at Alice.

"I want to talk to your friend for few minutes, can you give that?" Bianca said and Alice shook her head looking at odette.

"Oddy, we should call Marco and Mario, we can't trust her", Alice whispered to odette and odette frowned biting her lip thinking what she should do.

Thinking Alice was right without speaking a word with Bianca she simply sighed and smiled at Alice and walked other side of the college and texted Marco and Mario telling she will be standing at this gate instead of usual one.

As she locked, her phone a speeding van came in front of them almost hitting them. Odette and Alice gasped taking a step back but the door opened and the person who was inside grabbed Odette with his one hand and the phone in her hand dropped down. Pulling odette inside the van, they speeded the van and disappeared from Alice's sight leaving her in shock and tears for her friend.

"Odette!", Alice cried running behind the van but Lorenzo's car stopped right beside her and he ran towards his fiance worried.

"Baby, what's wrong?", Lorenzo asked hugging Alice who was crying her eyes out.

"Oddy, someone… Someone…" she choked and a bone shrilling voice asked from behind.

"Where is my wife?".

"Marco?", Lorenzo said scowling at the way he spoke to his fiance.

Marco's heart was pounding hard against his chest and he was going crazy with every second thinking where Odette was and though he figured out something was wrong he was praying inside his head that he should be wrong and odette indeed should be somewhere around the college building.

"Someone took Oddy, it was a van", Alice cried and Lorenzo hugged her trying to calm her down.

Who could be fool enough to kidnap the Italian mafia queen, he thought internally while he pressed a kiss on Alice's forehead.

Without looking back at them or showing any emotions marco took his phone out and walked away from them towards his car.

"Mario, someone dare to kidnap our doll, hurry up find their location before they lay their finger on what's ours", Marco said burning in rage and Mario's eyes widened hearing it.

"I swear to God! I will fucking tear them limb to limb", Mario snarled taking his laptop out and tracing Odette's phone.

It didn't take two minutes and Mario informed, "Marco, her phone is showing the location, which is her college".

"She might have dropped it", Marco said frowning, looked around and found odette's phone on the ground and his heart felt a pang when he turned it on to look at her screensaver. There was a selfie she took in which Odette was laying in between them under the duvet they all naked and Marco and Mario asleep and she was grinning widely.

Clenching his hand around the phone he said, "I am going to burn everything around me brother along with myself find her, please", he begged and Mario's heart felt the pain in Marco's.

"Come back to home, I am calling Draco", Mario said before hanging up the call.

Marco sat inside his car and drove to their home hoping Mario would figure out how to find their doll without her phone to track her location.

~~~

"All the CCTV cameras are waste of use! The van didn't have any number plate and we couldn't find it just on the basics of its colour which is black!", Andre snarled throwing the phone in his hand.

"Bosses are trying their best to find where is their wife, we didn't receive any call from the kidnapper yet", Draco explained Andre who pinched his temple as a lone tear escaped from his eyes.

"*My little bad wolf, stay wild and fight*", he mumbled under his breath sitting on the couch of Odette's home.

"Mario", Marco called looking at the screen.

"That bitch!", Mario gritted out looking at Bianca who was talking with odette few minutes before her kidnapping happened.

"I am sure it has to be something with her", Marco added his voice dripping venom.

"Call Alice and ask what that bitch spoke about", Mario stated and Marco nodded his head picking up his phone.

"Hello", Lorenzo answered the phone, Marco put the phone on speaker . Mario, Draco and Andre listened attentively as he spoke.

"Lorenzo, I wanted to talk to Alice, before getting kidnapped Bianca spoke with Odette, anything she heard would help us get a step closer", Marco asked his voice came out broken making Lorenzo sigh.

"Bro she is traumatised, you know how she is close with your wife, she can't answer your questions right now but she mentioned that the woman was trying to convince your wife to speak with her alone about the person who killed her mother and twin sister but Odette didn't spoke with her and they both walked towards other gate", Lorenzo said making Andre's eyes wide.

"Thank you, please let us know if she have seen anything else", Marco said unable to ask anything and hung up the call.

"Why did she mention Odette's mother was killed? She is alive", Andre said frowning shaking his head.

"This is getting complicated, it's been two hours and we don't have any lead towards our doll", Mario snarled frustrated and Marco looked as if he was at the verge of tears.

"I think it's Bianca who is behind Mrs de Luca's kidnapping because it was her who saw her going towards other gate and she have every reason to hurt her and not to mention, the man who have two thumbs is her brother, who knows they both are together in this", Draco reasoned worried.

"Bianca's brother?", Andre snapped getting up from the couch.

The three men looked at Andre's pale face and Marco asked with his heart in his mouth.

"Do you know him?".

"That man was dead and it was Bianca who killed him", Andre said in disbelief.

"Are you sure that man has extra finger?", he asked and twins nodded their heads conforming Andre's fear.

461

"We need to find my daughter as soon as possible, if Gabriel is behind this, she is in horrible hands, please hurry up, do something, find my daughter", Andre cried out without shying or hiding his emotions in front of them and his words only made Marco and Mario's heart break in fear and pain which was like someone killing them poking needles in their heart.

"We can't track Bianca's phone, how are we supposed to find her", Mario asked in fear.

Andre's heart dropped in his stomach in defeat but his eyes snapped back at Mario and this time it was hope in his eyes.

"Locket, the locket she was wearing, it was your mother's and your father put a tracker in it, you can find location through it", Andre said hopefully but his excitement faded and his smile dropped as he realized.

"We can't track it, because the only system it can be traced was your dad's computer and we don't have it anymore", he said breaking down in front of his daughter's husbands.

"No, Mario, Mario can hack into the system... Right?", Marco asked Mario and he nodded his head a bit energetic than before and said, "I can try brother", he assured and sat in front of his computer set up and started working on finding the location of their doll.

REVELATION

AUTHOR'S POV

"Bitch! My husbands will kill you", Odette rasped glaring at Bianca who was sitting in front of her.

The room was bright and not as any dungeon but in fact a huge mansion, which was decorated minimal. It was guarded with many guards just as Odette's home and every guard have guns with them.

The men who dragged Odette didn't blindfold her so she was able to see all the way; from where she came to the room, she was tied to a chair.

Her hands and legs tied tightly so she couldn't escape and the struggle she put to free herself got her some serious bruises but that was her least concern.

"If and only if I keep them alive", Bianca snickered smirking.

"Fucking pussy you are, can't fight with me oldie, free me and watch how I break every bone of your loose body", Odette gritted out throwing draggers at her with her hateful glare.

Bianca's jaw clenched as she heard Odette's warning and she walked towards her and punched on her jaw. Odette couched blood and spit it on Bianca's face smirking which pushed her past her limits and she yanked Odette's hair behind painfully but Odette groaned in protest and fought her way against ropes.

Odette's black jeans was tore at her knee and it was bleeding badly but that went numb after sometime, her black shirt's first few buttons were broken free revealing her enough cleavage and Bianca smirked looking at the hickeys covered all over her neck and chest area.

"Hmmm, so I guess you aren't virgin anymore", Bianca chuckled tracing her finger on Odette's collarbone and she clenched her teeth hardly.

"That's none of your business bitch, take your filthy hands off me", Odette snapped angrily.

"So you started playing with little doll?", a hoarse manly voice snapped both of them and Odette turned her head towards the door and saw the bald man who was standing with his fingers tucked in the pockets of his black trousers and she noticed his one hand has two thumbs and a deep gash on his face.

His eyes were just as Bianca's, green and cold if anything else, that's dangerous. Odette gulped visibly in fear but didn't let her guard down.

"I do like girls but not when they are covered in marks given by someone else brother", Bianca chuckled and Odette's eyes widened as she let her words sink in her head.

"So this is French mafia princess, I don't see a reason they shouldn't be jealous to share this beauty", Gabriel said holding Odette's chin between his finger and thumb.

Gritting her teeth she restrained herself to say something when Bianca answered, "it's because I have taught them to share women, those two in a team were strength and those brothers couldn't live without each other when I found them beside their mother's dead body and I never wanted a woman ruin what I was building by coming between them".

"I see you have gone wrong there, after all a woman ruined what you built", Gabriel said nodding his head.

Sighing heavily Bianca turned towards her cousin and asked, "When are the lover boys coming to save their damsel in distress?".

Smirking wickedly Gabriel traced his finger on Odette's jaw towards her neck. "Let us torment them for few more hours, when I will drop them message of address where their little pretty wife is…. They will come running without thinking about the dangers lurking in the darkness around this mansion", Gabriel said making Odette's eyes wide.

"Until then take care of her", Gabriel said his voice now suddenly turned cold showing seriousness of his words. Leaving an afraid Odette for her husbands safety and a smirking Bianca, Gabriel walked out of the bedroom leaving them without another glance.

"So we have got some good long hours before your and your husbands life end so why don't we talk about something, how about I reveal how I chopped your sister limb by limb and found your mom?".

"Oh do you want details how I killed her?", Bianca snickered wickedly and Odette felt bile rising in her throat.

Tears rolled down her eyes as she asked, "You killed my sister?".

Bianca threw her head back and laughed humourlessly and Odette felt Goosebumps forming on her skin.

"Of course I did, the woman whom your father killed thinking she was the killer was my lover, my everything, so I took my revenge by killing your mother – your dad's everything, knowing the dangers of mafia family, she left you and your father unable to cope up with Ivette's death and surprisingly your father thinks she is still alive somewhere living her life". Bianca's laughter filled in the room and it rang in Odette's ears making her soul numb.

Her mother was alive all the way at some point but this woman hunt her down and killed her as well as she was the one who mercilessly killed her sister. Odette's stomach churned and she gasped for air with her bewildered eyes.

Her doe eyes and nose turned red with her tears staining her cheeks. "Why?", she asked her voice came out broken.

"Why? What was their fault? What was my sister's fault you killed her?". Odette screamed crying loud and fought against the ropes again tiredly.

"Hmm, you want to know why I did?", she asked and her voice turned cold and deadly as she answered, "Because my lover fell in love with your mother and grown love for you and your sister telling it was all new and she feel connected to you both in some way as she never felt with her previous surrogate babies", Bianca seethed her nostrils flaring in anger.

"I did everything for her but your mother had to ruin it by coming into our lives that she rejected me!". Bianca yelled yanking Odette's hair hardly and she yelped with tears streaming down her eyes.

"You were an obsessed sick bitch!", Odette said venomously looking into Bianca's eyes.

"If you have truly loved someone you wouldn't hurt a innocent kid nor stole the life of a mother away from her child, you are fucking Psychopath and no wonder why everyone hate you", Odette gritted out slapping the reality on Bianca's face.

Bianca smirked before dusting her hands and said, "Love... Such an amazing word, right? You were wrong someone really loved me, you know who?". Bianca asked her face turned down with a devastating smile and she dreamily announced.

"Your favourite nanny, your godmother, Mrs Grayson, remember her?". she asked puckering her lips.

"She loved me as much as I loved her, she never left my side as your surrogate mother did, she was loyal to me, so loyal that she helped me kill your sister telling where you were and also giving information about your mom after she left you". Bianca revealed and odette felt as if she couldn't breathe.

Gasping for air she shook her head denying the truth but Bianca added further, "Sadly the man you met few minutes ago killed her and I am going to kill him after he kills your dad and those love sick husbands of yours after that I will enjoy my time before killing you just as I killed your sister".

"No!". Odette choked out and her whole body shivered remembering the horrific memory of body parts of her sister falling on the ground and she felt as her screams were echoing in her ears. Her vision turned blurry and she welcomed darkness hoping to wake up and see her husbands. Little did she know they were already on their way to save their life, which lives in her.

NOT A GOOD BYE

AUTHOR'S POV

"We are almost there, the satellite image is showing large number of men and we did good bringing a team with us", Mario said looking in his laptop as Marco was playing with the guns ready to use them on the people who dare to kidnap their wife.

His muscles were strained just as Mario's and Andre was worried knowing Gabriel was the one behind all these.

"Draco stop the car, we should stop here and go by foot to not alert them", Marco said adrenaline pumping in his blood as a hungry lion read for hunt.

"Ok boss", Draco said stopping the car in the woods deep inside so that if someone passed by doesn't alert Gabriel.

"Here put this vest on, you shouldn't be coming with us in the first place", Marco said giving Andre a bulletproof jacket and he smiled sadly remembering how Elijah used to give him whenever they went on mission.

"Are you ready?". Mario asked fixing his vest and Marco did same and nodded his head determined to save their doll.

"Come on let's go", Mario cheered and ten men along with Andre, Marco and Draco followed him towards the mansion which showed Odette's location.

Twins heart was beating so hard with fear thinking about the worst scenarios they might find their doll in God knows which condition and the only thought of seeing her hurt drove them crazy with anger and they swore they would kill everyone to anyone who was behind this.

Reaching the mansion Draco and Marco knocked up the security guards near the back gate twisting their heads, they fell limp on the ground and Mario got inside the security room and took off any locks and alarms that were installed in the mansion with his technical skills.

"Drag these bodies in the bushes", Andre said and both Marco and Draco did and entered into the gate sneakily hiding in the dark.

"The door is open but we have five guards in the room, we can't use guns to kill them from afar they may alert others", Mario said looking at the wristwatch he have which was showing the satellite image.

"Draco and I will go through the window and knock them off while you send some guards to do the same with remaining three, find Odette at any cost", Marco stated and nodded at the window gesturing Draco to follow him and he did gladly.

Doing as they planned everyone examined the surrounding looking for any cameras but didn't find any.

"All clear", Draco said through Bluetooth searching a room as others spread out looking for Odette in every room they came across and shot some guards with their guns, which had silencer.

Leaving everyone in the pool of blood twins walked as ghosts without making a noise of their moments not even their footsteps and so did their team whom they trained to be flawless killers.

"Wasn't as hard as I expected", Mario said and Marco replied, "We still have another floor, doll should be here".

"Let's go", Mario said and pushed the door open to find it dark and it smelled shit and fear crawled on his neck thinking the chances of odette being here.

"Marco", Mario whispered and he turned on the torch light of his phone and found their badly beaten cousin Elijah.

Mario released a relived sigh though he felt bad for Elijah but he was glad that it wasn't odette.

"Take him out", Marco said to Andre and he simply nodded his head knowing very well that he couldn't fight his own way with marco and Mario telling he will come with them when they were on enemy's territory.

Sending six guards with Andre and their unconscious cousin for their safety they moved out of the room with Draco and four guards. Taking off their bulletproof vests, they examined the surroundings.

They didn't see any other guard in front of them as far as they could but a single thermometric image showing a person was inside the room and they hoped it to be Odette and snapped the door open but to their surprise, they saw a Gabriel.

"Gabriel", twins growled and he smirked looking at twins in pure amusement.

"Finally…..", Gabriel said keeping himself comfortable on the chair and suddenly five gun shots were heard making Marco and Mario alert but it was too late.

Their four guards and Draco were lying on the floor in the pool of blood and they could swear they were dead.

Surprisingly five men walked inside the room behind them with their guns pointing at twins and their eyes glared at the woman who walked her way through the guards straight to Gabriel and sat on his lap.

"Fucking bitch", Mario gritted looking at Angela who shamelessly puffed her boobs and gabriel groped her one boob massaging it as she moaned throwing her head back on his shoulder.

"The other room had a magical room, you know those gadgets won't work there", Gabriel explained why they weren't able to see people in the mansion.

"Now drop your guns if you want your little wife alive", Gabriel commanded and twins growled.

"Where is she?", Marco demanded losing his patience and took a step forward but the guards shoved the gun around them making him halt his steps.

"Resting, I guess – after what I did to her", he said winking and faking that he might have touched her inappropriate way and both Marco and Mario went ballistic hearing his dubious answer.

They knocked the guards off making Angela gasp and Marco raised his gun and shot straight at Gabriel but he used Angela as shield and she dropped dead on the ground with a bullet in her chest.

"Stop or I will shoot her brain off", Bianca announced coming into the room with odette at gunpoint.

Marco and Mario's hearts shattered looking at their doll, injured and covered in blood. Marco's black shirt she was wearing was opened revealing few inches of her bralette and a lone tear escaped from their eyes thinking what Gabriel have said might be true.

Their gazes were filled with shame that they couldn't save her but Gabriel chuckled and said, "Don't worry, I don't do teenagers, am not a pervert".

Marco and Mario's heart felt a bit ease and they silently asked if Odette was alright with their glossy blue eyes which were filled with weakness, because of her and her heart clenched at the sight.

"I'm fine", Odette answered giving them assuring smile but winced as her dried lips stretched and the wound opened and fresh blood started flowing through it and her husbands felt like their souls were pulled out from their bodies.

Bianca yanked Odette's hair back and she hissed. She kept her hold tight on Odette's hair and pressed the gun on her shoulder warning twins.

They lowered their guns and dropped them down fearing Bianca wouldn't think twice before shooting Odette.

"Good boys, now drop on your knees in front of new Italian mafia king", Bianca chuckled and odette clenched her jaw hard.

Slowly with the knife she had in a holster under her jeans, which she sneaked out when she got the chance, she worked it on the rope secretly.

"I thought the great mafia king's sons doesn't cry but look at you, indeed your mother made not only your father a pathetic weakling but also you both", Gabriel mocked smirking.

Both twins clenched their jaw in anger and glared at the man who was smiling evilly with satisfaction.

"I guess I did right killing her", he revealed their steps immediately hollered towards Gabriel but Odette's wince made them stop in their place.

"You bastard, I will fucking kill you", Mario seethed in anger as Marco's heart was literally bleeding seeing odette in that condition.

"You wish? But right now I wish you both knee in front of me if you don't want my cousin to kill your little doll", Gabriel chuckled and they both gulped considering it.

Odette who was able to successfully cut the rope around her wrist, which was tying her hands back fell down, she shoved her elbow in Bianca's ribs and the gun fell from her hold.

Immediately Marco rushed towards Odette wanting to protect her but a gunshot rang in the room taking away Odette's and Marco's breathe.

Gabriel who pulled his gun out to shoot Marco but Mario took the bullet in his shoulder and another bullet in his chest groaned in the pain and fell to the ground.

"MARIO!". Odette screamed and Marco rolled on the floor and took the gun and shot straight into Gabriel's head and with another one he shot Bianca.

"Mario! Oh god!". Odette cried cradling her husband's head on her lap with tears rolling down her eyes.

Mario smiled weakly wiping her tear away and Marco dropped on his knees in front of his brother his hands shivering in fear of losing him. Noticing it, Mario took his hands in his own and gasped for air as Marco asked.

"Idiot, why did you step in between when you know you would get hurt?". Marco choked out lifting his brother in his arms with his week knees and he didn't stop his tears falling down this time.

Odette covered her mouth as she sobbed looking at Mario's condition as he replied the same words Marco said to Mario in the park when they met their doll for the first time.

"Nothing hurts me more than seeing you get hurt brother".

"Take care of our doll", with that Mario closed his eyes in his brother's arms.

EPILOGUE

~THREE YEARS LATER~

ODETTE'S POV

I can't believe three years of my life passed in a blink of an eye. Tears streamed down my eyes as I looked at pregnancy test, which was showing positive. Today is graduation day and I know Marco has planned a surprise for me, which I heard over him ordering around maids to make it perfect.

Three years since that incident happened. Three years since I know, I have lost someone. Three years since I said good-bye to everything related to them and moved on in my life for good.

Wiping my tears, I smiled in the mirror placing my palm on my stomach where I have my little bean.

Someone knocked on the door and I signed turning around to find our maid Sophie.

"Mrs de Luca, Master Marco is waiting for you", she said smiling and I nodded my head before fixing my white knee length dress, which Mario likes. Draping the graduation coat over my dress I walked downstairs keeping my excitement and nervousness closed in my heart. As soon as my husband found me walking towards him he gently wrapped his hands around me and pressed a kiss on my forehead.

"You are looking breath-taking, doll", he complimented and I blushed looking down. No matter how many years it's been, he could always make me blush.

"Come on let's go or else you will be late for your own graduation ceremony", Marco said and guided me in his car.

Huffing and folding my hands on my chest I groaned, "I wish Mario was here".

Chuckling to my complain Marco spoke, "You do know how jealous he was when he left, that he wouldn't be able to spend time with you as me, he can't do anything doll, as founder of de Luca academy he should be there before anyone else".

Right! How can I forget, Mario and Marco didn't wanted to be in the mafia anymore or should I say they didn't want the dangers it would bring to me if they were mafia kings and mario bought a university and it's de Luca academy now, I had to graduate in that college since Mario thought I should and after graduation I will be joining in Marco's company - De Luca corporations. Whereas their cousin Elijah is handling the Italian mafia.

Not to mention my husbands worked day and night to raise their name in educational and business field, my batch will be the first to graduate from the university and all the merit students got internship in our company.

"Nervous?". Marco asked holding my hand and I smiled rolling my eyes.

"Who wouldn't be when you are going to take memoranda from your husband", I said and the car halted making my heart pound in my chest.

Draco opened the door smiling at us and I smiled back at him. Past three years it was a miracle both Mario and Draco survived. I couldn't be happier. Marco and Mario appointed Draco as my bodyguard, we grew a sibling bond and it feels good to have a brother.

"Mario is going crazy", Draco mumbled shaking his head making Marco and me chuckle.

"Oddy!", my sister Aurora yelled from the front row seats as soon as she spotted me in the hall and I mentally smacked myself. Can anyone believe she is Russian mafia queen?

"Ugh mom, please don't scream as a teenage girl", both Paul and Peter covered their faces embarrassed.

Aurora sent a death glare to her sons and my eyes restlessly found Mario who was seating on the stage along with some other chief guests but no one could come to comparison to my man, correction – men.

His blue eyes already on mine and he was looking delicious in his blue suit jacket and trousers and a white shirt.

His eyes devoured my body in his favourite dress of mine, the way he licked his lips got me clenching my thighs and Marco's grip on my ass tightened bringing me back from my naughty thoughts.

"Doll, behave well if you don't want to get punished", Marco warned and I smirked winking at Mario and met Marco's gaze after seeing Mario smirk.

"Having you both inside me till I pass out? It's a pleasurable punishment I wouldn't complain", I whispered back smirking earning a smack from Marco.

~~~

The ceremony passed on and my dad took multiple images of me with my husbands, Alice, Aurora, Dimitri, Paul and Peter. I didn't let Draco out of the picture since he is more of my brother than my bodyguard. When I was receiving memorandum I couldn't digest the fact that my family howled and clapped as if I didn't graduate but found a cheap way to travel to moon in a car.

Mario was so proud giving me the memorandum and the way he bragged Marco didn't have a picture with me made us roll our eyes.

"I can't believe your husbands postponed graduation ceremony for two weeks, along that my wedding was postponed too", Alice complained huffing.

Chuckling I wrapped my arms around her giggling and said, "I can't wait to see you in a wedding gown".

"Fuck yeah! And I can't wait to see you as my maid", Alice joked but my two possessive alpha men growled from behind making me sigh.

"I was joking, I meant brides maid, maid of honour", she corrected herself stuttering looking at Marco and Mario.

"Come on", I signed walking towards my husbands and hugged them before pressing a kiss on their cheeks standing on my tiptoes.

"I have heard about the surprise you planned for me, can't we see it now instead of waiting till tonight?", I asked them seductively.

"Doll... I swear to god!" Marco warned and Mario smacked my ass and I smiled wickedly.

"What? Planning to punish me?". I asked raising my eye brows with a teasing smile.

"Fuck yeah!", Mario and Marco said in unison and I smirked.

"Then I won't be giving you the surprise I planned, in fact I wanted to give it right now but...." I said folding my hands on my chest and their eyes widened and lightened up thinking what I have in my bag.

"Tell us, it's not fair you know what we planned and we don't know about it", Marco whined as a kid making me chuckle.

"Uhmm?", I said poking my tongue in my cheek.

"Please", they both gave me puppy eyes which I couldn't resist.

"Okay fine", I said gesturing them to bend down so I could whisper it in their ear and they did as I asked making me smile.

"I am… Pregnant", I said and they froze in their places with wide eyes, slowly a smile stretching on their faces taking my breath away and they hugged me in their arms and I heard them sniffle and their tears fell on my shoulders.

"We love you so much doll, we love you so much, thank you", they said their voice ragged and heavy.

My own tears fell from my eyes and I replied, "We love you two too".

~9 Months Later~

"Oh my fucking god!" I screamed standing in the leaving room as my water broke.

Hearing me both Marco and Mario rushed towards me panicked, throwing anything in their way to reach me as fast as possible.

"Doll are you okay?", Marco asked and I cried out holding my stomach.

"Do I look like am okay, you dumbass my water just broke and it's hurting as hell", I seethed breathing heavily.

"Oh my god! Babies are coming", Mario smiled excitedly and I glared at him.

"I… I will bring the bag", he said running to get the necessities we packed to welcome our twins.

"Doll, please don't cry, everything will be okay", Marco assured kissing my head as he wiped my tears.

480

As soon as Mario ran out from our bedroom with the bag Marco ordered Draco to start the car panicked and the three men shivered as if they are under labour making me mad.

"Fucking stop shaking and drive to the hospital fast or else I will be giving birth in your fucking car", I scolded tears streaming down my cheeks and Marco carried me into the car with his wobbling legs.

"Doctor! Doctor!", my husbands yelled in the hallway of the hospital grabbing attention of everyone making me turn red in embarrassment.

"Please save our wife", Marco said and I smacked his head hard and Mario had guts to laugh his ass off.

"Oh god! It's okay, you will be fine Mrs de Luca", my gynaecologist assured rushing me into the delivery room.

Within few seconds I was laid on the bed, many machine attached to my pulse and fingertips with my legs spread open in front of an old doctor and my husbands standing each side of me holding my hands.

As pain hit me, I screamed top of my lungs breathing heavily. "I will fucking shoot all the bullets inside your skull if you don't stop my wife's suffering", Marco threatened the doctor and I glared at him in disbelief.

"I will fucking kill you if you dare threaten the doctor... Ahhhhh", I gasped, Marco pouted and I saw my doctor fight to control her smile.

"I swear to God! We are not having sex again!", I groaned and Marco and Mario's eyes widened in fear.

"Doll, please we can use protection, we can have anal sex", Mario begged and both Marco and I sent a deadly glare at him and he immediately shut his mouth placing his finger on his lips.

This time my doctor chuckled.

"You are dilated Mrs de Luca, try to take deep breathes and push", she advised and I nodded my head.

"Ahhh", I screamed and dug my nails in Marco and Mario's hands and they kissed my head and pushed my hair away from my sweaty forehead.

"Almost there I could see the head", doctor said and I took a deep breath before pushing again.

Soon I felt something huge dropping out from me and my baby's cries filled in the room and doctor placed him on my chest.

"One more time, the other baby is almost out too", doctor said and in two minutes my other boy was out too and was placed on my chest.

"Oh my god", I cried happily when I saw two pair of blue eyes looking at me stopping their cries.

My little son's eyes were exactly like their dads. Bright, deep and I cannot be happier to have four pair of blue eyes seeing me with love.

Marco and Mario wiped my tears and kissed my lips one at a time as they cried happily.

"We are so proud of you doll, thank you so much", they said and I signed smiling widely.

~~~

When I woke up I have been changed and the room was different. Marco and Mario were walking in the room with wide smiles on their faces looking at the bundle of joy in their arms.

My sons were cooing and talking with their dads as they were telling them something, which I couldn't understand clearly.

"How long I was passed out", I asked my voice ragged and I felt my throat dry.

"Almost an hour doll", Marco said rushing towards me and I tried to sit up but Mario ended up helping me holding baby in his one large arm.

"You were having fun with your dads?", I cooed at my sons as they placed them in my arms.

They happily smiled and blabbed something making me chuckle and I took that as yes.

"What are we going to call them doll?", my husbands asked and I smiled dreamily before looking at two little babies, which we made.

"Darius de Luca and Davina de Luca", I announced and kissed my sons on their foreheads.

"Beautiful names", my husbands praised kissing my cheeks and I smiled widely.

I can't believe. It was like yesterday I met Marco and Mario in the park and one single kindness I showed them made them fill my world with the happiness one would kill to have. Who would have thought the little girl I was who told them to read a fairy tale that they would make her life one. Actually better than any fairy tale one would have read.

And I hope my sons turn into the beautiful men like their dads are one day. As I found my love in their fathers, someone could find their love in my sons too. I hope I could raise them into good men for their own dolls but little did I know the saying as father so sons would be this real.

That they will fall for a same girl as their fathers for *their baby doll*.

THE END

THEIR BABYDOLL

AUTHOR'S POV

Happy birthday to you!

Happy birthday to you!

Happy birthday to our dear hazel...

Happy birthday to you!

A huge group of audience sang along with Mario, Marco, Odette and Hazel's parents.

Hazel is a cute little seven years old girl with hazel eyes. She is Marco and Mario's one of a close associate's daughter. Henry is her elder brother who is three years elder than her.

"Hey, pumpkin! Don't forget to make a wish", Henry reminded his little sister who is wearing pink fluffy frock and a tiara as a princess she is.

Grinning the little girl's eyes roamed all over the hall looking for those blue pairs of eyes.

When she found them a far smiling at her softly she blushed and turned her head towards her parents.

"Does this wish turn true?". she asked innocently making her parents heart swoon.

"Sure it does, baby", her parents Mr and Mrs Lopez answered smiling at their daughter.

In excitement, she closed her eyes and folded her hands on her chest as she prayed.

Grinning she opened her eyes and blew the candles and cut the cake happily hoping her wish comes true.

"My little princess, what did you wish for?", Odette asked kneeling in front of the little girl smiling widely.

Hazel's excitement perked hearing the question from her favourite aunt.

"I wished to marry Darius and Davian, Mrs De Luca", hazel beamed telling her secret wish to odette.

Odette's eyes widened hearing Hazel's wish of marrying her twins. They were Harry's best friends and study in the same school as hers. Odette was so shocked that her jaw literally hit the floor.

Seeing Odette's shocked face Hazel frowned puckering her lower lip as her eyes glistened with tears.

"I know it is wrong, mama said we have only one heart and we are supposed to marry only one prince", Hazel sniffed making Odette's heart swoon.

"Aww, no princess, we can love both prince it's not wrong", Odette said wiping a lone tear which escaped Hazel's eyes.

"It's okay to love them both, I did", Odette spoke again and this time looking at both Marco and Mario who was standing beside their ten years old sons ruffling their hair and pulling their leg as Davian and Darius were whining but their secret half smiles gave away that they love their dads company more than anything.

"BUT THERE IS SOMETHING... THEY DON'T LIKE TO SHARE".

COMING SOON

ABOUT AUTHOR

https://www.amazon.com/author/skilledsmile

INSTAGRAM

@author.skilledsmile

@byskilledsmile

MY OTHER WORKS

FORBIDDEN SERIES (STANDALONE)

BOOK 1: HIS FORBIDDEN OBSESSION (COMPLETED)

BOOK 2: HIS FORBIDDEN LOVE (COMING SOON)

BOOK 3: HIS FORBIDDEN DESIRE (COMING SOON)

BOOK 4: HIS FORBIDDEN PASSION (COMING SOON)

Printed in Great Britain
by Amazon

22493270R00274